the
fairest
of
dreams

A Novel
by Michael Mitton

Part 2 of the Dorchadas Trilogy

An Amazon self-published book
© Michael Mitton 2020

ISBN: 9798656714341

Imprint: Independently published

First published 2020

The author asserts the moral right to be identified as the author of this work

I found this novel had the unusual combination of zipping along at pace and opening up deep themes. Michael is wise in the ways of the soul and that richness of experience shines through the pages. The novel's central character is someone at crisis point in terms of loss in his own life which has led to letting go of the certainties of his faith. We follow his external adventure but it is this deeper adventure of seeking to find himself again in a more expansive faith landscape that ends up lingering longer in the mind. If there is a venn diagram with spiritual direction in one circle and a good story in another, this novel is the intersection!

Jonny Baker
Friend, Pioneer, Missioner, Imagineer

In this way,
He disarmed the spiritual rulers and authorities.
He shamed them publicly
by His victory over them
on the cross.

St.Paul
Letter to the Colossians

PREFACE

For close on thirty years, I have been writing non-fiction books, so embarking on writing fiction felt like a risk. In fact, it took me five years to pluck up the courage to publish my first novel. I imagine that the transition from writing non-fiction to fiction is probably a similar kind of experience to that of a violinist taking up the oboe, or a painter taking up sculpture. Some of the skills and disciplines still hold good, but so many new ones have to be learned. So, I went back to school under the tuition of webinars and books on novel writing.

The more I learned about the world of fiction-writing, the more the task seemed daunting. And yet during this time, the characters of Douglas and Dorchadas would not leave me alone and, in their own way, told me not to get too hung up on whether or not I had all the necessary skills. They kept pestering me to get their story down in words. So finally, I gave in and got to work on a novel that I called *The Face of the Deep* and self-published it just before Christmas 2019.

Some writers of fiction have the whole plot mapped out in their minds before they begin and being fairly orderly by nature, I had always imagined I would be that kind of writer. However, I discovered I am of a different type. I did have a map, but as soon as I headed along a particular path, the characters themselves decided they preferred a different direction of travel. This, I believe is a very common experience of fiction writers, but it was a new and somewhat disconcerting experience for me. For example, when Douglas goes to meet Dorchadas in a local coffee shop, he is served by Kath who decides to tell a major piece of early-life trauma, that completely knocked me off the course I was expecting to follow. Readers of my first book will know that Kath plays a significant role in that story, and I think all of us now agree that we are delighted she elbowed herself into the story in the way that she did.

Early on in the writing of that book, I developed a conviction that it was to be the first of a trilogy of books. This was all very well until I arrived at Glasshampton Monastery in early January with precious little clue as to how the story would develop in the second volume. People were writing to me saying how much they enjoyed the first book, and how they were looking forward to the next one. But when I first arrived at the monastery, I sat in my room in the fading January light with a very blank page in front of me. Rather than embarking on the second part of the trilogy, I imagined myself writing apologetic emails to those hopeful readers. However, once I settled down in that beautiful Worcestershire monastic home, a new story started to catch light. My good friends, Douglas, Dorchadas, Kath and others sprang to life again. A couple of minor characters took a few steps towards centre stage, and some who were off stage in *The Face of the Deep* made their way on to the stage for this novel, and I am pretty sure that they have every intention of having their say in the final volume of this trilogy.

One of the rewards of writing a book is the receiving of correspondence from readers. I have been very moved by the messages I have received, which has made me realise that many people are asking similar questions about life and faith that are raised in the pages of these novels. Some of my correspondents who are not familiar with Irish names have asked me about the correct pronunciation of a couple of them. Dorchadas, of course, is not a regular name but is the Gaelic word for darkness. So, if the helpful audio prompt on my Gaelic language website is correct, the *ch* in his name is as in the word *loch*. His name is often shortened to Dorch. The Irish manage to keep that soft *ch*, though the English are more likely to pronounce it *Dork*, the humour of which is not lost on Dorchadas himself (see *Face of the Deep* p.29). As regards Saoirse, well, it seems there are a variety of ways of pronouncing this name. I was on the island of Inis Oírr, off the West Coast of Ireland recently, and was delighted to find a shop by the harbour using that name. I called in and the local owner of the shop said he had named the shop after his daughter. I asked him for the correct pronunciation of her name, and he assured me that it was *Seersha*. The other word that crops up in these books is *sláinte*, the equivalent of the English *cheers,* and I have usually heard this pronounced *slancha*.

I worry greatly about how the wonderful people of Ireland feel I am portraying their countryfolk, and I hope so much they will forgive me for any unintended misrepresentations. I have regularly visited Ireland for both work and holidays for the last twenty-five years and my experience of the people and the land is always one of healing and renewal. Much of the action of this trilogy takes place in the town of Dingle, which I know well. However, for the sake of the story, I have had to take some liberties with the geography and plan of this town and its surroundings, for which I hope the people of Dingle will forgive me. Similarly, I have taken great liberties in my imagining of the Sheffield Diocese as it appears in these novels and all references to churches and personnel are entirely fictional.

Various friends kindly looked at an early script of this novel, and several remarked, not surprisingly, that they were struggling to remember people and plot lines from the first novel. *The Fairest of Dreams* will only really make sense if you have read *The Face of the Deep*. To save you trawling back through the first novel, I have provided a summary of the plot as an appendix at the end of this book.

Finally, a note about when the story takes place. I embarked on the first novel, assuming that the events in the story would be happening in 2019 and 2020. By the time I was well on the way of writing the second story, it was clear that the world would be changed dramatically during 2020. And as I write, there is no clarity about when we will be able to return to that blessed world of freedom, where we could enjoy simple things like a pint of Guinness with friends in a crowded Irish bar, without worrying about social distancing. The reader will have to imagine therefore that the events of these stories took place in the pre-COVID days.

As I study the comments sent to me by readers of *The Face of the Deep* I feel a sense of renewed hope that, whatever earthen vessel we may craft, when we put it into the hands of God, there is always the surprising possibility that somewhere within it, there can be found a treasure for others. This is my hope for all readers of *The Fairest of Dreams*.

Lo! I will tell the fairest of dreams,
that came to me at midnight
when mortal men abode in sleep.
It seemed to me that I beheld
a beauteous tree uplifted in the air,
enwreathed with light, brightest of beams.
All that beacon was enwrought with gold.

The Dream of the Rood

Jesus' opponents believed
that power was strengthened
by hanging on to it with all your might;
Jesus revealed that true power
was to be found in letting it go.

Paula Gooder
Journey to the Empty Tomb

CHAPTER 1

She was bored as she stood by the kitchen sink and stared at the world that lay beyond the latticed window. It was a world that looked dreary and cold. Far too cold for her liking. This was the grand and spacious garden for which she had yearned for many a long year. She turned up the corner of her mouth in a half-smile as she enjoyed the imperious magnificence of the size of it. And yet... Strange how she was now rather missing the adventures that had gained them this highly expensive house. Something to do with the thrill of the chase, she supposed. The locals referred to it as 'the mansion', which was exactly how she viewed it. And it was exactly how she wanted them to view it. But now she was actually in her dream house, she felt an unwelcome sense of disappointment. She had never sighed so much in a house. Somehow, nothing she could do managed to make it feel like home. Come to think of it, she had felt a long way from home for a long time now. Somewhere within her there was a disturbing longing. But to pursue that longing felt too disturbing, so she shut down all thought of it before it caused any trouble.

There was another little home to which she was now devoted. It was the tall, state of the art fridge, and it was to this home that she now made a rather unsteady passage. She paused as she grasped the handle. She noticed her hand. Not for the first time had it caught her attention recently. She didn't like the way it looked. It was a hand that belonged to an old person. She didn't like the way it trembled and fumbled with the handle. But once it had done its job of opening the door, she quickly forgot the hand and rested her eyes instead on the brightly-lit scene that greeted her. Three bottles of welcoming Chardonnay lay ready and waiting along the middle shelf. She reached the one she had opened not so long ago and was pleased to discover there was still just enough with which to refill her glass.

She had developed a little ritual: The bottle to be carried from the fridge to the table. The neck of the bottle to be stroked in devotion for a few moments. That curious mix of delight and guilt. Then the pouring. The trick at this stage was to pour without spilling, to reveal no sign of over-indulgence. Easy for the first bottle, but harder for the second and near impossible for the third. But this time, no spillage. She congratulated herself and sat down in her usual chair at the end of the large pine kitchen table. She sipped from the refilled glass and then for some reason today, for a few very unnerving moments, she thought of Christ handing the cup of wine around at the Last Supper. Why should she think of such a thing? She never had been one for religion. That was her husband's world, and just at the moment, she preferred as much distance as possible from that world. What strange tricks the mind could play.

She was spared more thoughts of religion by the intruding sound of the ring tone of the mobile phone. That shattering single tone, so sharp on the ear. She smiled a mischievous smile. It was his phone, and she liked answering his phone because it always annoyed him. Further, she also suspected there were some calls he never told her about. She thrilled at the thought of catching him out. She stretched her arm across the table and grabbed hold of it. She smiled a thin smile as she heard him emerging from his study calling out, 'I'll get it. Don't answer it.' Too late! She pressed the green button and heard a voice she thought she recognized but, having not heard it for some time, could not quite place.

'I said, "I'll get it",' he snapped as he entered the kitchen and grabbed the phone from her.

'Yes, sorry. Who is it?' he said in a more composed voice as he walked to the window and stared out at the large expanse of wintered lawn. 'What?' he said. She was intrigued by the alarm she saw in his face, and she sat up straight. He covered the phone with his hand and frowning at her, said, 'Go and make yourself busy. Go and do your hair or something.' He was making a swatting gesture with his hand. She smiled, pulled out a stool, and placed her once very eye-catching long leg on it. She put her hand behind her ear, raised her eyebrows, and looked at the phone with an enquiring look.

He sighed hard. 'Just a minute,' he said to the caller and marched into the sitting room. 'Go on'. She got up and stood in the doorway, careful not to let him see her. She listened hard, clutching her cool glass with both hands.

She was intrigued by the unusual anxiety in his voice. 'What? Why are you using this number?... Say again.... How can that possibly...? You assured me... Well, sort it, for God's sake. Get them to take him out... What?... Yes, of course, I'll get across to you what you need. Just let me... What?... Oh, for f... How the hell did *he* find out?... They've been over to see him?... Christ!... Of course, I'll be bloody careful. I always have been and always... What..? Well, when? Look.... Hello? Hello? For Christ's sake.'

She quickly returned to her chair as he walked slowly back into the kitchen. 'Someone nice?' she said, enjoying his evident discomfort. But as he walked to the window, she saw something she very rarely saw in him: vulnerability. 'What is it?' she asked, feeling almost a touch of compassion.

He stood looking out at the garden, turning his phone over and over again in his hand. 'You can tell me,' she said, eager to discover the cause of his discomfort. He turned to her. 'There's a problem. That job - that one two years ago. You remember - Cairo. Well, the operative, who, I was assured, was thoroughly reliable, is now in custody in Nairobi, would you believe?'

'Oh, God,' she said, and the compassion was quickly replaced with annoyance.

'And what's more,' he said, moving slowly back to the table. 'He's bloody confessed, can you believe.'

'Oh, God,' she said again, draining her glass and rising from the table. Annoyance was becoming fear. 'Has he mentioned your name?'

'He never knew it and I want it kept that way. He did mention Sheffield apparently, but nothing more than that.'

'Oh, God,' she exclaimed yet again.

'That's not all.' He paused. He was reluctant to tell her, but he knew she would get it out of him sooner or later. 'Intelligence is on to it and they have been over to Ireland and told *him*.'

'Oh, for God's sake! This is getting worse and worse,' she said, grasping the back of the chair to steady herself.

'It will be all right,' he said in the controlling manner that so often convinced others, but seldom convinced her.

'It better had be, or you're sunk, matey.'

'Or *we* are sunk, matey,' he said, and not for the first time she saw a frightening coldness in his eyes. 'And always remember, will you, that it was you who put me up to this.'

'Oh, yes, here we go... Always my fault isn't it?' She started to think about the next bottle - it looked like she would need it.

He turned around and started to leave the room, but then looked back at her and said, 'For Christ's sake. Look at you. And it's not even lunchtime! Get yourself a coffee - a strong one.'

She smiled and moved unsteadily over to him and placed an arm around his shoulder. 'Better we don't fight, darling. If things get bad we are going to need to stick together.' She flicked his ear and he flinched. She stepped back, and leaned her weight on the kitchen table and said, 'We did the right thing. *You* did the right thing. Always remember that. That little minx deceived lots of people, but she didn't deceive you or me, did she? She got what she deserved. Now your man in Nairobi.' She pointed vaguely out of the window attempting to indicate a faraway city. 'He's secure. I'm sure of it. You always do your homework well. Nothing if not thorough is you. Now off you go - you've got that meeting to get to, haven't you? And yes, I'll have a coffee, don't worry.' She made her way over to the sideboard.

He was about to leave but then noticed her fumbling attempts to operate the coffee machine. He came over and said, 'Here, let me,' and prepared her an extra-strong coffee. He waited by the coffee maker while it gurgled away and produced the necessary sobering drink. He said nothing. His thoughts were too loud. He then placed the steaming mug in front of her as she sat at the table. She had placed her elbows on the table and was resting her head in her hands. He reached out his hand and stroked her auburn hair. Not for the first time did he marvel that one person could be both his greatest strength and his greatest weakness. In the days that followed, he would reluctantly come to the conclusion that, as far as he was concerned, the weakness would have by far the greater influence. What would have astonished her, would have been the knowledge that this one phone call had set in motion a chain of events that would lead her to discover not only her strength but her freedom and her way home. But not today. As he left the room, she pushed the mug away from her in disdain. She rose from the table and returned to the fridge.

CHAPTER 2

The St.Raphael Guest House was beginning to feel like home to Douglas. Elsie O'Connell had moved him into the largest of the guest rooms which included a large bed, a couple of comfortable armchairs, an antiquated wooden desk directly in front of the window that overlooked the street below, and an upright chair that creaked in protest at the slightest movement of its occupant. On the walls hung a random selection of pictures including a classic seascape, a much-faded painting of a geranium plant, a photo of Dingle in 1938, and a Victorian crucifix whose Christ was lacking one arm. Even though the furniture and decor were not exactly to Douglas' taste, nonetheless he found the room ideal. He was currently the only guest in the house, and Elsie had told him that it would likely stay that way for a few weeks at this time of year. He welcomed the peace and quiet this brought to the house, though Elsie was not short of friends dropping round and partaking of considerable quantities of tea and cake.

On this, the first Sunday of the year, Douglas was awoken by the sound of church bells summoning the faithful to early mass. As he got up, he was aware that for the first time in a long while he felt almost content. It was a feeling he savoured as he parted the curtain a little and looked out on the town of Dingle that was still waiting for the sun to haul itself up from the January night. Douglas had not written in his journal for a couple of weeks, and he decided it was time to try and gather his thoughts together and take stock of where he was. So much had happened in recent months, it would be impossible to summarise it all, but writing in his journal was for him a way of trying to clarify and order his thoughts. So, he settled himself at the desk, with his chair complaining at his every move, and began to write.

<u>Journal 5 January</u>

I'm back in Dingle after a difficult Christmas with the parents. Did some sorting in the Vicarage and had a nice day out with Mavis and Alice. But I'm back now, and its good to be back. Since the storm, I've felt very different. It's not got rid of the grief. Still miss my Saoirse terribly, but somehow, I no longer feel emotionally paralysed. I'm moving again, though only slowly - just taking a few faltering steps and still stumbling occasionally. Every day I think back to my mysterious visit to the night-time Garden of Gethsemane - the curious mix of extraordinary peace yet terrible foreboding. I remember Mary and her gentle voice. And I remember poor old Dorch looking so frightened and dejected. Where exactly were we? 'Deep memory', Mary said. And she assured me that Dorch would be OK. But just where is he? So glad he survived the storm.

It's a wonder either of us made it out of that wild sea. The truth is I tried to drown myself, but Dorch stopped me. Then we were transported to the peaceful Garden. And there, from a distance, I watched in sorrow and amazement at the sight of dear old Dorch lying down next to Christ, both of them sobbing like little kids. Something about that scene did a wonder in me, a wonder I really can't explain. But I guess in that moment I knew that God <u>understood</u>.

It's by no means answered all my questions, but a new kind of faith was planted in my soul that day. It's nowhere near robust enough to carry out a priestly ministry. The bishop has given me a three-month sabbatical and I've got until the end of this month to decide about this. But I doubt if I shall be returning to the parish. God knows what I'll do with myself. - Perhaps I mean that? *God* knows. Does he?

Then there was this mysterious meeting with the man from British Intelligence. In his cold, clinical way, he reported that my Saoirse was killed not by a terrorist but by a hired assassin who was especially targeting her. I find it so hard to write that. Anyone who met Saoirse could see she was the gentlest, kindest person. But she was passionate, and she hated acts of violence, and in particular, she hated the arms trade. I remember going on her laptop many months after she died, and found a lengthy file of material on both the illegal arms trade and the institutional stuff. She hated both. According to this Intelligence man, she was on to someone - probably in Sheffield - and she was threatening to expose them. The guy said he would contact me, but I've heard nothing since that first meeting.

So I find myself in a new story now. A mystery: Who was responsible for arranging her death? What dreadful darkness was unleashed to embitter the heart of someone so severely that they would seek to kill such a kind and innocent life? What powers of darkness and evil stalk this world to cause people to do such terrible things? After this Intelligence guy spoke to me, I felt a surge of energy - a determination to see light overpower such darkness. It was like the passion that was in Saoirse took hold of me. The man swore me to secrecy - well, actually he said, 'tell no mortal soul'. I shall honour that, but as it happens I do know someone who claims not to be a mortal soul! The only thing is, that particular someone - or ex-angel as he claims to be - has gone AWOL. I am so longing to see him again, as I really need to talk to someone about this.

And how is Dorch? He was so broken that night in the garden. What happened to him? Must have been awful for him to be taken back to the very scene of his demise. But that's where I last saw him. Did Jesus forgive him? Restore him? I suppose he could be back as an angel again, winging his way… Oh no, he told me he didn't do flying. I do hope he's not gone back to being a proper angel. I liked him so much as a human.

Look at me, I'm writing now as if I really believe he is an angel. But then, 'There are more things in heaven and earth, Horatio, than are dreamt of in your philosophy.' Maybe my philosophy is starting to have better dreams. And why shouldn't it?

Elsie is calling me to breakfast. I really can't go on eating these huge breakfasts.

*

Douglas entered the cosy dining room and gathered his usual bowl of fruit from the dresser and, as he settled himself at his table, Elsie came in sporting a very different hairstyle. The beehive of previous weeks, that had never quite recovered from the storm, had been replaced by something as remarkable. Douglas tried not to show any consternation as she entered the room, but his first thought was that Elsie had replaced her hair with a crow's nest. There was no clear or obvious style to it, and it was now coloured jet black with streaks of vivid green. This, resting above her vintage cat eye glasses with their brightly coloured rims, and her heavy eye makeup, made for quite a sight.

'Here's your coffee, Douglas. I hope you slept well,' she said, and as she poured the coffee. Douglas was almost overwhelmed by the fumes of hair spray. 'Well, what do you think of it?' she asked as she stepped back, and patted her hand to the back of her head.

She looked somewhat vulnerable as she stared at Douglas waiting for his answer, so he replied, 'I like it, Elsie. It's very... very contemporary.'

'Well, now, that it is, son. That it is.' She smiled, sensing that she had received a compliment, and then said in a rather confidential voice, 'The truth is Douglas, I've been... you know... on my own now for too long. I've been watching Kathleen getting to know that Peter, and it's made me feel a bit... you know... on my own. So, I'm thinking of taking up that onshore dating that the girls in town tell me about. It's not just for the youngsters. They do them for people of my age, that they do, Douglas. You know - mid-sixties. Or, maybe late sixties. Anyhow, you have to put up a photo of yourself, of course. Well, I says all this to Connie, my hairdresser, and she said I needed to do something with my appearance. She said, just what you said, that I needed something more complimentary. More up-to-date, if you get my meaning. More with it. So, this is the result. And, what's more, Connie knows how to do the internet and promised to help me, sure she did.'

She continued to look at Douglas for reassurance, standing near him with the steaming coffee pot in one hand, the other tapping the firm, heavily-sprayed head of hair. 'Well done, Elsie,' he said, trying to by-pass references to hair. 'Any man would be very lucky to find you. I'm sure the on*line* dating would be well worth exploring.'

'Och, now you're just trying to charm me! I'll be fetching your eggs and bacon.' She started to make her way to the kitchen and just as she was about to go out of the door, she turned and said, 'Oh, by the way, Kathleen told me that Dorch has been seen in town again.' She then bustled out into the kitchen.

'Oh excellent,' said Douglas and he put down his spoon in his bowl and closed his eyes. This was the news he had been waiting for. The last time he had seen Dorchadas was only a few weeks back, but it felt like months. Memories returned of the seashore - a scene, frankly, he was trying to forget. The two of them there in the fury of the gale, the shouting, the anger, Dorch swaying in the wind with wet hair blowing wildly around his anguished face, the fighting him off in the surf, and the sense of the ending of it all. For several moments, Douglas felt the darkness of it again.

'Is the fruit no good today?' Elsie's voice startled him, for he was so deeply in his thoughts. 'Oh, no, it's excellent as usual, Elsie. Thanks so much.'

'Well, here's your cooked.' She looked at him as she placed the food in front of him. 'You were worried about Dorch, weren't you? Did you think he'd died under those waves?'

Douglas knew there was no way he could explain to Elsie about what happened in the waves that mysteriously opened to that extraordinary experience in the Garden of Gethsemane, so it was simpler to answer, 'Yes, I did.'

Elsie paused and added, 'Son, it's no business of mine, but I did hear a bit from Ciaran.' She looked awkward and played with the several rings that adorned her hands. 'I mean, as I say, it's not my place, but he did see you throw yourself into that raging sea. Well, two and two together and that... I just want to say, I understand. I nearly tried the same thing after my loss. Not in the sea, but... Well... I just want to say, I'm mighty pleased you are still with us, son.' She grasped his arm and her eyes started to well up, and not wanting to display any emotion, she quickly changed the subject saying, 'Now, get to work on that breakfast, Douglas, will you? It will do you a power of good, it surely will. The hens must have been in a grand mood when they laid them eggs. The yokes are something lovely, they are.'

As Douglas worked his way through his breakfast he felt a mix of anxiety and comfort. How many others had guessed that Douglas was trying to end it all under those raging waves? What would they think of him now? And yet he was comforted by Elsie's kind understanding. As he ate his eggs his thoughts returned to Dorchadas. It was likely he would meet up with him soon. How would he be? What had happened in that night-time garden as he lay there in the cold grass? He was longing to find out.

CHAPTER 3

Happily for Douglas, Elsie had a nephew called Johnny who was, as she called it, 'in cars'. When Douglas returned to Ireland after Christmas, a young man with a bright smile had welcomed him at the airport, introduced himself as the said nephew, Johnny, and ushered him to a somewhat elderly Ford Fiesta which, though it showed clear evidence of several close encounters with a variety of obstacles, nonetheless, assured Johnny, it was in perfectly good condition. The young man told Douglas that he owed much to his Aunty, so Douglas could have it free of charge for as long as he wished. Douglas tried to argue with him about payment, but Johnny would have none of it. As Douglas drove away from Cork towards Dingle, he marvelled yet again at the depth of hospitality he had experienced in Saoirse's homeland.

So, after his breakfast of delicious eggs on this particular Sunday, Douglas decided to drive out around the Dingle peninsula, and though the rain swept in from time to time, he enjoyed the experience of touring a coastland that he had grown to love. Always on days like this, he felt the uncomfortable mix of delight and sorrow. He delighted in the sheer beauty of the surging sea, the beckoning Blasket Islands, the ever-changing sky filled with swooping gulls, and the sturdy, mist-draped hills. Yet every wave of delight was accompanied by one of sorrow. He grieved that he could no longer share all this with the wife he had loved so deeply. This was her land, and she would have loved to have shown it off to Douglas. But her estrangement from her parents prevented her from returning to her homeland during the two short years of their marriage.

He enjoyed exploring the little single-track lanes and after a while, he found himself by the beautiful ruin of Kilmalkedar church. As the rain had stopped, he decided to explore this church. After parking his car, he made his way up the uneven pathway past ancient Celtic crosses into this unroofed, hallowed place of worship. Although it was a January day, the church somehow felt warm. He walked thoughtfully up the eight hundred-year-old nave and found a ledge on which to sit. He gazed west out through the remains of the elegant doorway to the sea in the distance. The low sun emerged from behind the wispy clouds and he delighted in the way the winter sunlight played on the hills and sea. It reminded him of the time he and Saoirse had visited the East coast for a brief holiday, in their first winter, in conditions similar to this. They had huddled together on a hilltop near Robin Hood's Bay. 'Don't you love the sea, Dougie,' she said, rubbing his arm with her gloved hand.

'I do,' said Douglas, as they gazed out at the restless waters, both their souls animated by the sight of the ocean. For a time, they watched in silence, and then Douglas remembered some lines from Walt Whitman and recited them:

Sail forth - steer for the deep waters only,
Reckless, O soul, exploring, I with thee, and thou with
    me,
For we are bound where mariner has not yet dared to
go,
And we will risk the ship, ourselves and all.
O my brave soul!
O farther farther sail!

O daring joy, but safe! Are they not all the seas of God?
O farther, farther, farther sail!

He felt the thrill of the ocean as he recalled the lines he had learned as a teenager. He turned to look at Saoirse and found her eyes filled with tears. 'I'm sorry,' he said, 'I didn't want to upset you.'

She turned to him, wiping her eyes quickly, 'No Douglas. No, my darling. The words are so beautiful. Why have I never heard them before? But I was thinking, my Dougie, you have such deep waters in you, and mine feel so shallow by comparison. Your faith is so strong and goes a mighty long way down in that soul of yours. I am so sorry I can't share it with you. Does it make me feel a long way off, Dougie, when you are up there in church preaching from that dear heart of yours while I'm at home, sat in front of the fire in my long socks, and reading my novels?'

Douglas looked at her beseeching eyes. He always found it curious that their not having a shared faith was more of a burden to her than to him.

'But I preach from my heart because of you,' he said, stroking some windswept hair from her face. 'And in that way, you are up there with me in the pulpit.'

Saoirse laughed - 'Saoirse Romer in the pulpit preaching! Can you imagine what they'd make of that! That would empty your church, Vicar!'

They both laughed, and then Saoirse looked serious again and said, 'I think one day, I will find this God you love so much, my Dougie. In my own way and my own time. Can you wait for me?'

'I'd wait for you for a lifetime, my darling,' said Douglas holding her even tighter. 'And as I often tell you, I see more of God's life in you than I do in any of my congregation.'

She smiled. 'Well, you are a bit biased, you know.' She leaned her head on to Douglas' shoulder and looked back out at the sea, her eyes glistening in the cold breeze. 'And Dougie,' she said. 'If anyone can help me discover that all the seas are the seas of God, as your wee poem says, then it is you. Just look at this heaving world before us, so full of energy and life! It would be somewhere like here, Doug, that I would meet with your God. It would be somewhere like here, under a wild, wide-open sky, gazing at the rolling waves, with the salty wind smarting my face, cold yet fiery. Not inside the walls of a church. Much as you love them, Dougie, I find it hard to breathe in those places.' They were quiet for a moment. Douglas thought of his rather tight, indoors faith that all of a sudden felt rather musty. He felt in all honesty that it had never ventured far from a church porch.

Saoirse then tapped him on his knee in her mock schoolmistress way and said, 'But doesn't your bible say that darkness was over the face of the deep? Shouldn't we be afraid of that dark, Doug? Perhaps we should keep clear of the deep waters?'

She looked quizzical, waiting for Douglas' response. 'Yes, it does say that. Right at the beginning. But it also says that the Spirit of God moved on the face of those waters. And it says that God called out, "Let there be light!"' Just as Douglas quoted this, sure enough, right on cue, the sun slipped out from behind a cloud and the sea sprang to life in a glory of shimmering life.

Saoirse laughed her infectious laugh and asked, 'Did you arrange that, Reverend Romer? I am most impressed!' They squeezed each other tight in the beam of winter sunlight and continued to gaze at the sea until the cold breeze caused them to flee to the warmth of a nearby teashop.

Douglas recalled all this as he sat in the remains of this roofless, hospitable church. Perhaps Saoirse had good reason to be anxious about the dark, for it was a darkness of evil that had robbed her of her precious life. In the last two years, this kind of thinking is where Douglas' spirit would have slumped and the hideous despair would wrap its icy cloak around him and his soul would shrink under its weight. But something had shifted in him since the time in Gethsemane. Some new energy was making his soul more resilient to such cold. He did not know how, but somehow, he wanted to not just surrender to the dark, but to challenge it, and to witness the power of light taking it down. But what exactly was the power of light?

As he was dwelling on these thoughts, a beam of pale winter sun broke through the clouds and shone on the little church. Douglas smiled as he wondered if Saoirse had arranged it. But he was abruptly shaken out of his thoughts by a voice from the chancel behind him that called out, 'Ah, well now. There you are, Douglas. I finally caught up with you, I have.'

It was a familiar voice - wonderfully familiar. He turned around and there, clambering over a broken wall of the ruined church, was a very familiar tall figure dressed in duffle coat and jeans. 'Dorchadas, you old…' cried Douglas as he jumped up and raced over to his friend and hugged him. Both men laughed with delight at seeing each other. Stepping back, Douglas looked up at the rugged and kind face that had become so familiar in those days in the autumn. 'Well, just where did you spring from?' he asked, still beaming with joy. 'And where have you been these last few months? And how did you know I was here? And how did you get here? And…'

'Now, do you mind if I just have one of your questions at a time please,' said Dorchadas, taking Douglas' arm and leading him through the timeworn nave to the ornate west door of the church. 'Well now, it's a beautiful day, don't you think, Doug?' he asked as they stood in the doorway for a few moments.

'Well, it's a little calmer than when we last met, Dorch,' said Douglas smiling.

'Oh, yes, I think I remember,' said Dorchadas, scratching his thick head of dark hair. He laughed and added, 'My, that was a storm, wasn't it? Well now, Doug, we've got much to talk about. What say you we head down to a little café I know that's not far from here, and get ourselves a nice hot cup of tea.'

'That would be good, Dorch,' said Douglas. 'That would be really good.'

'I hear you have a new wagon,' said Dorchadas as they made their way down the path.

'I do. And, generally speaking, it works.' When they reached the car, Dorchadas struggled to open the passenger door, which finally gave way when Douglas kicked it hard from the inside.

'Less likely to be broken into, I suppose,' said Dorchadas, doing his best to wedge his lanky frame into the rather cramped seating.

On the short journey, Dorchadas explained how that morning he came to St.Raphael's just after Douglas had left. Elsie had told him that Douglas was driving around the peninsula, so he went in search of him. Through a mixture of hitch-hiking and walking, and using some guesswork about the sites he thought Douglas might visit, he had eventually caught up with him at Kilmalkedar church.

As they rounded a bend of the coastal road, Dorchadas called out, 'There it is.' He attempted to lean forward in his seat and pointed to a little cottage that was part way up the hillside. Dorchadas directed Douglas to a little track that wound its way up to the house. At the start of the track was a hand-painted sign saying, 'Tourist Tea and Coffee. Parking. Dogs welcome.' The rain returned as they bumped their way up to the property. As they got out of the car, Douglas was far from certain that anyone was in, let alone open for custom. However, as they opened the latch of the front door, a welcome warmth greeted them. An elderly lady got up from a seat by the turf fire and said, 'Oh my, Dorchadas. You are back in these parts, now are you? It's grand to see you again.'

'Aye, that I am, Brenda. Been away for too long, I have. Now, I have my friend Douglas with me, and we are just aching for a cup of tea in this cold weather. Have you got a brew for us today?'

'That I have, Dorchadas. And welcome, Douglas. Put your coats over there and then sit yourself by the fire will you, and I'll see what I can get for you. My, it gets dark early nowadays, sure it does. And look at that rain, would you? Don't you think we have had enough by now? Now, kindly turn that lamp on will you, Douglas?'

She disappeared for a time into a back room but soon returned with a tray containing a large pot of tea, mugs, milk, sugar, and two generous slices of rhubarb tart. 'Thought you'd like a piece of the tart to keep you going. I made it this morning. You'll love it, you will. I put a touch of ginger in it, which is just what you need in this weather.' She placed the tray down on a table by the fireside and continued, 'Now if it is all right with you, gentlemen, I will leave you to it, as I've got to go and do some baking for tomorrow's visitors. Got a large group of walkers arriving for coffee, would you believe.' Given the weather, Douglas found it hard to believe, but did not question it, and thanked her. She made her way out to the kitchen, calling out, 'And just put some turf on the fire when it needs it, won't you?'

'That we will, Bren,' called Dorchadas. Then, turning to Douglas he said, 'Well, now, Doug, shall I pour?' Dorchadas carefully filled the mugs and then leaned back in his chair warming his hands around the hot mug. The amber light from the freshly stoked fire flickered across his face. 'So now, my old friend, how have you been these last weeks?'

Douglas found it hard to know where to start, but because he always found Dorchadas to be such a good listener, he managed to fill him in on just about all that had happened to him in recent weeks, though he did not include the meeting with the Intelligence officer in Killarney. He wanted a bit more time before he raised this subject. 'But what about you, Dorch? What happened to you in the Garden? Were you OK?' he asked, for he was very eager to hear.

Dorchadas drained his mug and placed it carefully on the tray. He inhaled a long breath and looked over to Douglas, who noticed the vulnerability in his face.

'Well now, Doug...'

A voice from the kitchen called out, 'Will you be wanting more of the rhubarb?'

'No, we're just grand thanks, Bren,' called back Dorchadas, and picked up his uneaten tart and set to work on it.'

'I'd forgotten to go at this, as I was so interested in hearing your story,' he said with his mouth full. 'Not bad, is it?' The room was quiet for a while as he continued to shovel the rest into his mouth.' Douglas was aching to hear Dorchadas' story and waited patiently. 'Hm. More than a little ginger, I'd say. But it's all helped to warm me up! Right, where was I Doug?' Dorchadas put down his empty plate and wiped his mouth and beard with a serviette.

'You hadn't started, Dorch,' said Douglas, now showing a little impatience. But he was beginning to realise that this was far from easy for Dorchadas, so he added, 'Only if you want to though, Dorch.'

'Thanks, Douglas. I do and I don't if you get my meaning. I'm not going to be able to say too much, because there are just some things that can't be gathered into words.' He paused, sighed, brushed off some crumbs from his thick, bottle green pullover, and continued. He was now recalling vividly that extraordinary visit both of them made to the Garden. 'We were there for a long time. Was it minutes? Hours? Or days maybe? I don't know. It was the one place in time and space that I did *not* wish to visit: the Garden of Gethsemane, on the eve of His death. You know my shameful story, Doug. You are one of the few who know. I'm truly sorry you have had to know all this - you had enough on your own plate. But it was part of His plan, so there it is. Anyway, there I was - taken back to the very place of my downfall. The place where I was sent to help Him in his hour of need, and I failed. The place from which I ran as a dismal coward. As Mary told us, this place wasn't the actual thing - it was what she called "deep memory". I get that, but I can tell you, Douglas, it was mighty real enough for me.'

Dorchadas was frowning and shuffled in his chair. He pulled out a cushion from behind his back and placed it on the floor beside him. He leaned forward and threw a piece of black turf on to the fire, which welcomed the new fuel with a spray of sparks. Still leaning forward with his hands clasped and his elbows resting on his knees, he looked at Douglas and said, 'Now, Doug, I can't say too much about this because of the emotion - you know how it is. But, one way or another, I found myself lying down in that Garden beside Him. He and I both lay there for a time, our faces buried in the cold grass. He was in… well, a wretched state, sure he was. I didn't think He'd noticed me, and all I could feel was this helpless sense of shame, and wishing I was anywhere else but in that place. But then, he lifted his poor face, with them dear veins bursting something awful with grief and sorrow and…'

Douglas noticed quiet tears emerge in the corner of his friend's eyes. Dorchadas looked into the fireplace as the tears became rivulets that followed the deep contours of his face. He made no attempt to brush away the watery evidence of his emotion and, he continued his story, staring at the glowing turf in the fireplace. 'You know, Doug, love is truly wonderful and yet it can burn holes in you, don't you think? Not holes that destroy - quite the opposite. Do you know what I mean?' He turned his face towards Douglas.

'Yes,' said Douglas. He had known such burning.

Dorchadas breathed in a long breath and looked up at the ceiling. 'I was loved… I was forgiven… I was healed. And that's all I can say about it.' He turned and smiled at Douglas, and in the glow of the flickering fire, this face seemed to Douglas to be as holy a face as he had ever seen. It was a generous face, the creases bearing testimony to the range of emotions displayed through it. It was one that looked like it might be just about to burst into laughter. Or tears. It was a face that Douglas had got to know so well in the autumn, and in such a short space of time, it had become the face of one of his closest friends. And yet, in these moments, it was more than that. It was a face that had something about it that seemed to be from beyond time. Something of the feeling of that sacred time that they experienced in the Garden returned to him. Now here, in this little, hillside cottage in the fading light, the veil between this world and the next had thinned to such a degree that Douglas felt unsure about which world he was inhabiting. And in those hallowed moments, Douglas had an almost overwhelming conviction that the tear-stained face that was smiling at him through the silky smoke of the glowing peat, truly was the face of an angel.

In that little hillside cottage, with the taste of rhubarb still sharp on his tongue, and the fire warm on his cheek, Douglas knew, without any of the doubts that had so assailed his soul in recent months, that he had become a believer. However weird it would sound to his rational self and to others, Douglas felt certain that this friend in a bottle green jumper and faded jeans truly was one of God's angels. And yet, at the same time, this angel was also as human a soul as he was ever likely to meet. It was as if he had moved to a different seat in the theatre of his life, and his view of the things of heaven and earth now looked quite different.

Douglas reached out a hand to Dorchadas and said almost in a whisper, as if he were in some great cathedral, 'Thank you so much, Dorchadas.'

Dorchadas took the hand gratefully and held it firmly. Then, releasing it, he eased back in his chair and said, 'Now, you've not told me everything, Doug, have you?'

Douglas did not feel ready for the attention to shift now to him but replied, 'No I haven't, Dorch. You are quite right, there is more. And, as it happens, you are the only person I can tell. And I am very much hoping you will be able to help me. So, when do you want to hear about it? Now or sometime later?'

'Ah, that makes sense, Doug,' said Dorchadas thoughtfully, ignoring Douglas' question. He sighed for a moment and looked back to the fire. He added, 'I didn't know if I'd be called back, you see. I was beginning to think that my service as a human in this world had come to an end. But then I got the call to come back here to Dingle, and I... well, I was surprised to hear that I was going to be working with you again.' He frowned and looked down. 'I mean, to be honest with you, Douglas, I feel I failed you the last time, and...'

'Stop right there, Dorch. Please, never, ever suggest that again. You saved me. Right?'

'Hm... We were both saved, Doug,' said Dorchadas nodding his head, still looking at the floor. 'We were both saved.' He raised his head and looked at Douglas. 'But I guess I have to accept that I may have done you a bit of good. And maybe I can do a bit more good. I really pray so, Doug.'

'So here you are, Dorchadas,' said Douglas with a frown, yet a twinkle of humour in his eye. 'You could have been released back to a nice bright heaven. But you were sent back to a dark and drizzling January day in the far South West of Ireland. And sent back to sort out this problematic English Anglican priest. Good luck to you, Dorch!'

Dorchadas sighed and smiled. 'Aye, Douglas.' And with a mischievous look on his face added, 'And He said He loved me!'

Both men laughed, and as they did so, Brenda breezed back into the room wearing an apron, the state of which was a sure testimony to her labours in the kitchen. 'Will you be wanting any more of the tea or the rhubarb, gentlemen?' she asked, trying to find a clean part of the apron on which to dry her hands.

'No, no, love' said Dorchadas standing up with care to avoid the low beam. We must be going. Let's pay up and be on our way.'

'Och, get away,' said Brenda waving her hand. 'I don't want any money off you. It's the sabbath today, it surely is. The tea's a gift. Take it as a blessing from the Almighty if you will.'

'Well, that we will, Bren. We are truly blessed. Thank you, love,' said Dorchadas, and gave Brenda a hug.

And so the two friends drove down the track to join the road taking them back to Dingle. They agreed to meet that evening so that Douglas could fill in Dorchadas on the rest of his story. It was a story that was growing increasingly heavy in Douglas' soul, and he was longing for the chance to share it with this friend

CHAPTER 4

It was almost like old times when Dorchadas and Douglas met up at *The Angels Rest* that evening. They settled themselves at a table away from the singing group, as they knew they needed a significant conversation, and for that, they would need to hear one another clearly. As usual, they were each clutching a cool glass of Guinness. They were both quiet for a moment, and then Douglas looked at Dorchadas and said, 'Dorch, I want to confess something.'

'Oh, aye?' said Dorchadas with one eyebrow raised. 'You do know, Doug, that I am an angel and not a priest?'

'It's not quite that kind of confession,' continued Douglas. 'I think it will surprise you, actually Dorch. It's a confession of belief. I just want to confess that… I believe you.'

'You believe me? Well, that's nice to know. But you believe me about what exactly?'

With great conviction, Douglas answered, 'Dorchadas, I believe you are who you say you are. I believe you are an angel. Disguised as a human, but an angel nonetheless. I understand now. I see - you know, with the eyes of my heart.'

Dorchadas put down his glass and with his elbows on the table, he brought his hands up to his mouth. He was frowning and for a few moments he seemed to be studying hard the surface of the table, and Douglas wondered if he was praying. He then said, still looking at the table, 'Actually, I lied to you, Doug.'

'What?' said Douglas, leaning back in his chair.

'When we talked before - you know, about my being an angel and that, and you said you didn't believe it, and I said that it made no odds to me. Well, that part was not the truth.' He turned and looked at Douglas. 'I was wrong to say, "it made no odds to me." It actually makes all the odds to me.' Douglas felt both relieved and curious. Dorchadas explained further, 'At that time, here in this very pub, when I first told you, I could see your poor soul was in a pretty busted state, and I wanted to make clear that our friendship would not depend on your believing me to be an angel. I suppose I was just trying to make it all more comfortable for you, and I didn't want us to waste time arguing about whether or not I was an angel. It was really not the most important thing.'

Dorchadas looked back at his glass and thumbed away some of the condensation from the side. He continued, 'When I first visited Earth as a human, I didn't know what to say or how to explain who I was. I was given no instruction about this. Them senior angels just left me to it and here I was - on planet Earth. Well, I'd visited Earth plenty of times, but not as a human. This felt totally different.' He looked up at Douglas and went on, 'I mean you got bladders for one thing. That took some getting used to. And you get cold, which is no fun. And you get tired and have to sleep. And you get to feel sick if you spin yourself around too much!' Both of them chuckled.

'I thought at first that people would notice that I was a former angel, but, of course, I soon discovered that no-one suspected a thing. I was a bit taller than most, but that's hardly enough to signal angelic ancestry. Well, I didn't like to keep it all a secret, so I thought I best tell people what I was.' He took a sip from his glass and then looked at an old picture hanging on the wall next to them. Douglas noticed the uncertainty, even hurt in his expression. 'Generally,' he continued, 'the response was not a favourable one. In my first several visits, I would tell people and, of course, I got the response you'd probably expect. There were some nice exceptions, though. I had one piece of work to do on a slave plantation in the Caribbean. About twenty years before emancipation, I think it was. Them dear people - they accepted me - the slaves, that is. They had no trouble believing me. The owners didn't believe me, of course. They hated me. Tried to kill me, actually.' He took a sip of his Guinness.

'So, how many different times and places have you been to in your human form, Dorch?' asked Douglas, now intrigued by the range of possibilities.

Dorchadas breathed in and answered, 'Too many, I think. I feel a bit tired of it, if I'm honest, Doug. That's the human bit of me, I suppose. Or do you think it is the angel bit?' His cocoa brown eyes looked away with a quizzical look, but then turned back to Douglas and said, 'But the point I'm making, Doug, is this: when someone actually accepts that I am who I say I am, I can't tell you what it means to me.' He reached out a hand and placed it on Douglas' shoulder and said, 'So thank you, Doug. I'm truly grateful. It means the world to me. Sláinte.' Both of them lifted their glasses and clinked them together and swallowed a draft.

'So, moving on,' said Dorchadas. 'Was that what you wanted to tell me, or was there something else?'

Douglas felt a little apprehensive about disclosing something so significant, but he was eager to share the information he had been given. But before he could get one word out, there was a cry from near the doorway, 'Oh, the saints be blessed, you're back Douglas!'

Douglas turned around, and there was the ample figure of Kath. Douglas stood up and waved as she ploughed her way through the growing crowd. She came up to Douglas and kissed him, smack on the lips. 'There!' she said, 'I love giving them something to gossip about!' and wheezed her infectious laugh which turned into a brief coughing fit.

Dorchadas was also laughing and came round the table to greet her and said, 'It's no use, Kath. The whole town now knows about you and your Quaker man, Peter.'

'Oh, stop that Dorch!' she said, still red-eyed from her coughing, and looking a little embarrassed. 'Don't believe a word of it, Douglas. Now there's nothing improper happening, you understand,' she said as she placed her hands on her hips. 'Well, seriously, it's great to have you back, Doug. And Dorch, I know I said it yesterday when I saw you, but lovely to see you. But listen, I'm not stopping as it happens. I just told Ted I'd pay my bill from last night, and then I have to be off. But Doug, pop in for a coffee tomorrow morning, won't you? I'd love to catch up with you. I've got loads to tell you. And you'll meet Peter as he's staying with a friend nearby and helping me in the café this week.' She turned to the bar, but then came quickly back and added, 'And oh, you heard the big news? I've given up them ciggies, and now I puff away at those electronic gadgets. "Vapes" I believe you call them. Peter persuaded me, and, do you know, I'm quite taking to them. One they call "Ruthless Raspberry" is my favourite at the moment - I'll show you tomorrow. You'll be right impressed Douglas, you surely will. Now, can I order you another Guinness before I leave?'

Douglas was about to decline, but before he could, Dorchadas said, 'That would be grand, Kath. Most generous of you, now.'

'Och, not at all, Dorch. I'll ask Ted to send them over when they're done. You enjoy yourselves now.' And with that, she pushed her way through to the front of the bar, paid her dues, and ordered the pints for her two friends.

'Dear God, that woman's changed,' said Dorchadas draining his glass. 'Isn't it a wonder to behold, Doug?'

'Yes, yes. It really is. I've become very fond of her and Kevin.'

'And you've had a big part to play in their lives in recent weeks. Life-changing for both of them, I'd say.'

'Oh, I hardly...'

'Now stop it, Douglas,' said Dorchadas with a surprising note of severity. 'You take it from me, son - you weren't sent here just to receive. You are here because you have much to give. Both of us have been mangled wrecks in our time. But this is the measure of grace, Doug. Despite all of our many failings and frailties, any one of us can be carriers of the light, even the most busted of us. What is it your man Leonard Cohen said? "There's a crack in everything and that's how the light gets in." Something like that, I think. Well, the light has been breaking out through the cracks in you, Doug. Kath and Kevin would be the first to give testimony to that, they sure would. So, don't go despising those cracks if you don't mind. But now, before we get interrupted again, tell me what it is you wanted to talk to me about.'

Douglas had prepared an ordered way of telling Dorch, but that was now lost to him due to the various interruptions. There was a burst of applause as one of the singers came to the end of her song, and when it settled, Douglas made an attempt to share with Dorchadas this important piece of information he received before Christmas. 'As I was saying,' he started, 'I now recognise you are not mortal. At least you are mortal, only you are also an angel. So I can tell something to you - you as an angel. If you see what I mean...'

'Douglas - what is it you are trying to tell me?' asked Dorchadas with a furrowed brow.

Douglas sighed. 'Well I have received some information and I was told to tell no mortal soul.' He lowered his voice, looking around to check no-one nearby could hear. Another song had started at the far end of the pub. He moved closer to Dorchadas and, in a voice Dorchadas could only just hear, he said, 'I had a meeting from someone from British Intelligence. It was about my Saoirse.' Dorchadas looked hard down at the table, frowning, straining both to hear and comprehend. 'He came to Killarney and we met in the hotel. I told you the terrible story of how Saoirse was killed by a terrorist in Cairo. Well, this guy told me that Saoirse was not killed in a terrorist act, but by a hired assassin that was specifically targeting her.' To hear himself say these words was starting to cause Douglas distress, and he drained his glass to steady himself.

'Go on, Doug. If you can,' said Dorchadas focussing on Douglas and holding his empty glass tightly.

'Apparently, Saoirse had discovered that someone she knew was dealing in arms - illegally. I've told you how much she hated the arms trade. Well, it seems she was on to this person - goodness knows how, but she was. And had confronted them, which of course was not the best idea. Well, they were a good deal more cold and violent than she presumed because they decided to… you know… deal with her.'

'And here's your Guinness, gentlemen,' said a voice that shocked both of them as they were so deeply engrossed in the conversation. Ted placed the two glasses on the table and removed the empties. 'By the kindness of Kathleen, gentlemen. And good to see you both back, if I may say so. Sláinte.'

'Yes… thank you,' said Dorchadas not wanting for a moment to leave this important conversation.

'Doug, have you told anyone about this?'

'No, Dorch, you are the first. "No mortal soul", remember?'

'And when was it that you were told this?'

'End of November.'

'And have they been in contact since?'

'No. I've heard nothing and I have no number to contact. The person who came didn't even give me his name. He showed me a card that had no name, only his picture, and I remember seeing the initials NBIS. I looked that up later and I think it is National Ballistics Intelligence.'

All through this conversation, Dorchadas was staring down at the table, his eyes darting from side to side. But now he looked up and said, 'Oh, Doug, I am so sorry. That's not easy news for you to hear, is it, son?' His luxuriant eyebrows nearly met through the force of his frown as he added, 'You could be in danger, Doug. I guess you know that.'

Douglas felt a twitch of anxiety. He had been trying to put to one side any thought of threat to his own life. He decided to move on and apprise Dorchadas of another part of the story. 'And there's another thing I need to tell you about. Back in that Garden, after Mary took you over to Him, she came back and spoke with me.'

'Oh, you had a wee chat with her, did you? Dear Mary of Magdala. Do you know, she gave me such strength. I was so grateful to her.' He looked away thoughtfully for a moment, then taking a sip from his glass he looked back to Douglas and asked, 'So did she help you too, Doug?'

'Well, yes, in several ways…' For a few moments, Douglas remembered very clearly his conversation with Mary in the Garden, and he quickly put most of it to one side, for such remembrance brought with it strong feelings, and he wanted a clear head for this conversation. So he focussed on the important piece. 'She said, and I remember her very words, "In the days to come there will be another darkness you will have to face, which you must face with great courage." And she added, "Dorchadas will be with you to help."'

'Did she, now?' said Dorchadas with the hint of a smile. But the smile disappeared as he said, 'Douglas all this feels serious to me. The darkness of grief that you experienced all but killed you, yet you survived. And you survived, Doug because you have an open heart. All right, a wounded heart. Yes, terribly wounded. But it is an open heart, and because of that, you have been able to see things. But Mary has warned you of another darkness. Not grief this time.' Here it was Dorchadas' turn to lower his voice. 'I fear, Douglas we are talking about the darkness of evil. There's no pretty way of putting it. And if there is one thing evil loves Doug, it is violence, especially the terrible violence humans do to one another through them dreadful weapons.'

Douglas recoiled at this talk of evil. He had never felt comfortable with the subject, nor with the way Christians managed the subject. He had generally kept clear of any reference to evil in the days of his ministry. But he had grown to trust Dorchadas, and so he knew he had to consider what he was saying.

'Well, Dorch,' he said, reaching out for his new glass of Guinness, 'I hardly think I'm up to a kind of Superman contest with the powers of evil. But I have to agree with you. Saoirse did chat to me about the arms trade, and from what she told me, even the so-called 'legal' trade sounds hellish - literally. Of course, I'm opposed to it, but I really can't see myself rising up as a campaigner against it.'

'No, son. I don't think that's what's being required of you. Let's just see what unfolds. We won't need to go looking for this - it will come to us. I don't fear evil, Doug, but I recognise its power, and I've seen what terrible things that power has done to this world. Thanks for telling me, Doug. I'm only too glad to help.' Dorchadas was about to say something else but then paused. He seemed to be listening to something in the distance. He remained alert for a few moments, and then looked at Douglas with animated eyes and said, 'Doug, I think we are being given some help. Are you ready?'

'Ready for what, Dorch?' said Douglas.

There was another round of applause as another singer had finished their song. When it settled, Dorchadas reached out and clasped Douglas' hand. 'Are you ready for a meeting, Doug?'

Douglas turned his head to one side and said, 'I think I know what you mean by "meeting", Dorch. Just who had you in mind?'

'I think I know just the person who might be able to help us,' said Dorchadas. 'Are you up for it, Doug?'

Douglas took a long and steady draught from his glass and then placing it carefully on the table in front of him, looked up at his friend and said, 'As ready as I'll ever be, Dorch.' And he closed his eyes in readiness.

CHAPTER 5

By now Douglas knew what Dorchadas meant when he said 'a meeting', so he simply closed his eyes and waited, and sure enough, the sounds of the pub faded. In fact, it became so quiet that all he could hear was the sound of his and Dorchadas' breathing. He opened his eyes and found that he and Dorchadas were sitting on a rock in what appeared to be a desert. It was evening, just after sunset. There was still heat radiating from the rocks and stones around them, but the air felt cool.

'Look. Over there,' said Dorchadas, pointing ahead of them. Douglas peered into the ever-darkening landscape but there was just enough light to see a cave at the entrance of which someone was gathering some wood into a bundle. 'There's our man, Doug.'

'Which man - please tell me, Dorch. I don't want to make an idiot of myself.'

'It's your man, John. You know, the Baptist. He's the one to help us this evening. In the dwindling light, the two walked towards the cave and, sure enough, there in the mouth of the cave was John. He looked much as Douglas expected him to look - dressed in his camel hair tunic held in place by a cord around his waist. He was crouched on the ground and had just succeeded in igniting a bundle of dry shrub through the use of his wooden hand drill. A flame flared up to greet the neat pile of wood placed above it.

'How are you doing, John?' said Dorchadas as they approached.

John was startled and sprang up from the ground and peered at his visitors. 'Is it...? Why, yes, it is! It's you, Dorchadas!' and with that, he threw down his fire-lighter sticks and came over and gave Dorchadas a warm embrace.

'Does everyone in the bible know you, Dorch?' asked Douglas quietly. Dorchadas pretended not to hear and said, 'John, this is my friend, Douglas. As you can see, he's coming in from another time.'

'Greetings Douglas,' said John and came over and surprised Douglas by hugging him as well. 'Yes, this thing about time is wonderful, isn't it? In God, all history is happening at the same time. It's so beautiful! Come, I'd like some company - it's been quite a day.'

There were several large stones just inside the cave which served well as stools, and the men settled themselves as the fire started to take hold. John seated himself and brushed his dark, unkempt hair from his face. 'It's been a hot day,' he said, 'but it gets cool so quickly. You'll be glad of this fire soon. I wish I had some food to offer you, my friends, but I'm afraid my larder is quite empty. There's a bees' nest just around that corner which gives excellent honey, but there has been no time today to fetch any. The bees are most generous and always allow me to take a little of their bounty. Never been stung once, you know.'

Douglas was gradually getting used to these meetings, but he felt a bit unsure of being introduced to this zealous prophet, who might easily catch sight of some hidden sin in his soul and then start screaming about the vengeance of God at him. But he was soon to discover that John was not quite the man he imagined him to be.

'You say it's been quite a day, John?' said Dorchadas reaching out his hands and warming them by the fire that had caught nicely.

'When did we last meet, Dorch? It wasn't so long ago was it?'

'No, only a few weeks ago in your time.'

'Ah yes, well then, well then. Let me think.' He got up and using a stick, raked some ash that was falling from a burning branch. Douglas was surprised by how quickly night had fallen, and now, as he looked out through the cave's wide entrance, he saw that the sky was starting to become flecked with shimmering stars. He felt he was in a most delightful place.

'Well, Dorchadas, you saw the big crowds when you last came,' said John, smacking Dorchadas on the knee. 'There's more coming now. They're even coming out from the city - so many of them. I'm at the river every day. You see, Douglas, God has told me to go down to the river every day and baptise people - you know, slosh water all over them and tell them that He is much more interested in forgiving them than punishing them. Some people find it very hard to believe that God is on their side, you know.' A piece of wood fell out of the fire and John jumped up and kicked it back where it belonged. 'The dear people, Douglas,' he continued. 'You should see them. I mean, life is tough enough as it is, without the leaders of our religion making it so much tougher for them. Which they do, I'm sorry to say. Most of them at any rate.'

'So, what happened today then, John?' asked Dorchadas.

'So yes, Dorchadas. It certainly has been quite a day, I'll say so,' said John, with his face lighting up in excitement. 'You see *He* came today - my cousin Jesus.' He poked the fire again with his stick. Douglas looked at this New Testament prophet carefully. John was a sight to behold. He was so animated, so full of life. His head moved to and fro rapidly as he spoke so that his long hair

47

flew and flapped around him, often hiding his face completely.

He brushed his tangled hair out of his face as he looked at Douglas and said, 'He took me completely by surprise actually, Douglas. I was at the river. You should see them coming up out of the water. The look on their dear, wet, beaming faces. Men, women, even children. The sun sparkling on them; their laughter as they climb back on to the river bank; the sense of real freedom; the wind of heaven gusting about; the glory of God rampant in the desert! I am the most privileged of men to be a bearer of this light.' He was up again adjusting a piece of wood, and then back in his seat in moments.

'But today, He came, Douglas. My relative, Jesus, came!' said the prophet as he smacked his knees in delight. 'He is the Messiah, I know it. Not many others knew it - not until today at any rate. It didn't surprise me that He came, but it did surprise me that He came right into the river. He joined the queue, and I watched Him coming along the line. I smiled knowingly at Him as he got closer and He smiled back. I assumed that when He got to me, He would baptise me. I was looking forward to it. But no! When He got to me, He said, "I am one of them, so you baptise me." Well, can you imagine it, Dorch?' John asked with his bright eyes looking at Dorchadas. He glanced at the fire and said, 'Oh, Dorch, would you throw that bit of wood on the fire, please. It will be chilly soon.'

Douglas was mesmerised by this animated prophet and appealed to him to continue. "Yes, yes,' John said, 'Well, I know it's hard to believe, but I actually *did* baptise Him. I mean, He had no sins to confess which was what this baptism was really about. Anyone looking at Him would just know - there is no sin in Him. At least no sin of *His*.' Here John slowed down and looked hard into the fire.

'When I lowered Him down into the water, I did feel sin. Not *His* sin, you understand, but the sin of the world. It sounds ridiculous, doesn't it?' he said, looking at Dorchadas, who was sorting some bits of wood for the fire. 'But I saw Him as a lamb. A sacrificial lamb, taking on Himself the sins of the whole world so that everyone could be free of the things that bind them. I mean - think about it. God Almighty coming to this world, not as a great and mighty conquering hero, but as a lamb! Not even a full-grown ram! His power is so different. I felt it, Dorch,' he said, patting his heart, 'I felt it here.' Douglas noticed a look of anxiety on the face of the prophet.

Dorchadas had settled back on his stone and looking at John said, 'I know, lad. I know you feel things. It's the cost of being a prophet. You have to feel so much, and I know the weight is unbearable at times.'

'Thanks, Dorch,' said John, and a broad smile dispersed the look of anxiety. 'Oh, I wish you could visit me more often. Apart from Him, I think you are the only person to have understood this.' John then looked wistful for a few moments, and in those moments, Douglas saw a little of the burden this prophet had to carry.

'But don't stop,' pleaded Dorchadas, keen to get to the heart of the story.

John continued, 'Well, I did baptise Jesus. Down He went, and I held Him steady in the strong current of the water. He was down a long time and I started to get worried. But then up He came out of the water with such a force that the waves from Him nearly knocked me over. And then...' and here John's mouth started to tremble. He looked at Douglas and continued, 'Sorry, but it was extraordinary. Well, ordinary at first actually, because a dove flew by - just a regular dove. We get lots of them in the wilderness around here, and they naturally fly down to the river. But I suddenly realised this was no ordinary dove. I knew without any doubt that this was Holy Spirit coming, and coming so that we could see her with our own eyes. I know, Douglas, I said "her" - it was a female dove, you see. I know my desert birds. That's how Holy Spirit wanted to be seen - tells us something, don't you think? I mean Holy Spirit choosing to manifest herself as a 'she' and as a very earthly dove. Well, apart from anything else, it tells you she's at home in this world, doesn't it?'

'Yes,' said Douglas, marvelling that he was hearing this famous story from the lips of the prophet himself.

'Yes,' said John. He stood up in the mouth of the cave and cut a dramatic figure, lit by the flickering fire and with the deep, starry sky serving as a magnificent backdrop. 'Then, there was a voice - a real voice that came out of heaven.' John now spoke in a more hushed voice as he continued. 'Not up there,' he said, pointing up at the sky, 'because of course, heaven is not *up*. But in those moments when the voice spoke, all of us who were there became aware of a quite different dimension. I really can't explain it to you, gentlemen, but we knew that we were standing with one foot in this world and one foot in the other. The voice could be heard in both worlds. It... Well, it brought those two worlds together, if you see what I mean.'

'What did the voice sound like?' asked Douglas, eager to hear what the voice of Almighty God sounded like.

John looked puzzled for a moment and blinked several times before saying, 'I don't know. I really don't know, and yet I know I heard it, and all the people there heard it. What did it sound like? That's a very good question, Douglas!'

'Maybe it's what it felt like that was important,' said Dorchadas, who was smiling at John.

'Yes. Yes, Dorchadas. It felt…' John paused and shook his head with his lips pursed. 'It felt like we had all come home, Dorchadas. It felt like we had all come home after being away a long, long time.' He sighed and then added. 'And the message of the voice was so simple and so strong. It told us what I knew, but no-one else there knew. It was speaking about the man in front of me soaked to the skin and swaying in the current of the river. It said, "This is my son. This is the son who I love so much. This is the son who delights me." Something like that, wasn't it Dorch? Sorry, I don't actually remember the precise words. They were clearly the words of God. I almost got the impression they were not intended for us. God just blurted them out, if you like, because he was so excited. Oh my, imagine if the Pharisees heard me say that!' He smiled an anxious smile, then looking at the fire, he said, 'Dorch the fire is going down.'

'Sorry, John, I'll see to it,' said Dorch, and dutifully got to work gathering some more wood from a nearby pile and throwing it on the fire.

John came and sat next to Douglas. 'Douglas, I'm sorry, you probably think I'm insane. Most people do, but I think I have witnessed one of the greatest moments in history today.' He sighed and then started to look downcast. 'After the voice, He hugged me tight, you know. He then clambered up the riverbank, and the little dove fluttered all around Him and led Him off away from the river into the desert. It's way over there.' John pointed out to the now completely dark world beyond the cave entrance. John gazed out into the dark night for a while, then said, 'He's out there somewhere, all alone. I don't think I'll get to hug Him again. It was perhaps a good-bye hug.' He sighed another long sigh.

Douglas observed that John had the type of face that could hold many different expressions in fast succession. His mouth and eyes seemed to be constantly on the move. Expressions of despair, hope, joy, sorrow, anxiety, peace - all these and many more came and went with exhausting speed. But for a few moments, John's face locked on to a frown as he looked at his two friends and he said, 'But not long after He left, a group of Pharisees came along. I mean, they had witnessed all that I've been telling you about. But, for some reason, it meant *nothing* to them! Can you imagine it? No, they are so set in their ways. A God who comes as a lamb and a dove does not suit them.' He shook his head. 'They called me out of the river, so I had to leave off baptising the people, and they told me how wrong I was, and that I was misleading the people, I was acting treasonably towards Herod and that I was a heretic. Well, when they get like that, I'm afraid it's like putting a spark to a pile of desert shrub and sure enough, my fire was lit. I felt the fire of fury in my guts, Douglas.' John now stared into the fire so that the flames were reflected in his eyes in a way that startled Douglas.

Both John's fists were clenched. 'It's not a fury of hatred, Douglas. It's a fury of extraordinary love.' He thumped his knees with his fists for a few moments while expressions of anger and delight took brief turns on his face. The frown returned as he said, 'There's wickedness in some of those men, Douglas. I mean, real wickedness. I see it in their eyes. They crave power. They want to control the people. And do you know what's the easiest way for religious men to control people?' Douglas shook his head. John continued, 'The easiest way to control people is to tell them that God is quickly offended by humans when they think or do wrong things. And then you tell them that when He is offended, He is angry and He will punish them. And so the people get frightened. You then tell them that only

52

you know what offends God and what doesn't offend Him, and only *you* know what they must do to appease His anger. You've then got them in your power. You are the one who tells them when they upset God and what they have got to do to appease His anger. The people, therefore, spend their lives fearing God and fearing you, and they are utterly dependent on you if they want to keep out of trouble. Well, Douglas, our God has not put us on earth to live these short lives in a state of fear. We were sent for love, not fear. We were sent to be free!' He brushed his tangled hair out of his face and smiled his broad smile again, revealing several gaps in his teeth.

He grasped hold of Douglas' arm and said, 'I see it, Douglas. There is a dark power behind them, driving them, desiring to destroy what is good in this world, keeping the people enslaved, causing them to live shadowy half-lives, undermining the plans of their Creator.' He scratched at his wild mop of hair and looked down at the dry earth of his cave. 'And that dark power will plan to destroy Him, I have no doubt. He's battling with it right now, out there somewhere, in the wilderness. Just Him and the Destroyer. But let me tell you this, Douglas.' He inched closer to Douglas, close enough for Douglas to smell the sweat from his day's work in the desert. He put a hand on Douglas' shoulder and looked him in the eye. 'It is the meek who will inherit the earth. He told me that. It is the poor who will overthrow the rich. The powers and principalities will fall, Douglas. It may kill some of...' He paused and took Douglas' hand and looked hard at it, with his head slightly bent. He stroked it for a moment and then brought it up to his cheek. He held the hand against his beard and said, 'Oh, dear brother, I am sorry. I have just felt it...' He started to weep. Douglas' hand was soon damp with the prophet's tears.

'Dear brother,' said John staring into the fire, and for several moments he continued to hold Douglas' hand firmly to his cheek. His face was contorted in grief as he eventually released the hand and turned to Douglas saying, 'It was a violent death. I am so sorry. But you must know that her death is not in vain. She was good and her goodness will triumph. Be patient, dear brother. Be patient. You will see.' He was nodding hard now at his visitor whose crumpled face betrayed his grief. John wiped Douglas' face with his rough hand and said, 'Do not be afraid, oh, man of God. The Lord is with thee. Evil is great, but you will prevail. She has given her life and oh, it is such a precious life. Love will prevail, dear brother. It surely will.'

Douglas was full of emotion and confusion and yet sensed within him an extraordinary reassurance and a strength. He looked back at John who now looked like a wreck of a man. He had let go of Douglas' hand and was swaying and weeping as he sat awkwardly on his stone seat. His hair had fallen over his face again, but he brushed it back and said, 'I know my fate, Douglas. It's all right, I know. He has shown me. I'm a bit afraid, but not too bad.' He smiled briefly and then sniffed hard and wiped his nose on his sleeve. 'It has to happen. They will think they have won. But they will be so wrong. You wait and see, Douglas.' He nodded at Douglas and then turned to Dorchadas, who had been sitting as still as one of the desert rocks. John said, 'Dorchadas, come.'

He reached out his hand to Dorchadas, who came over and knelt beside him and John laid his head on the former angel's shoulder. 'Your friends are here, Dorch,' said John, in an almost child-like voice. He started to stroke the front of Dorchadas' jumper. 'They visit me often. Many of them are smaller than I expected. They come there.' He waved his hand to the area outside the cave entrance. 'Some have wings, you know. What are those wings made of? Such fine material, it seems. Like bees' wings, and yet so strong. Such beautiful colours. Colours I've not seen in this world.' He paused for a few moments then added, 'You didn't get the wings, did you? Perhaps... You know, when you return. When the time is right.'

Dorchadas said nothing. His eyes were closed and he was gently stroking the hair of the prophet. He was rocking slightly and, to Douglas, it seemed that for a few moments John was like a babe in his arms.

John then pulled back and said, 'Some of them are with Him tonight. They are there to help Him.' He nodded as he looked out of the cave. And then he looked at Dorchadas and said, 'Dorchadas, they still love you, you know. You do know that Dorchadas, don't you?' His look of sharp anxiety returned to his face. 'Dorchadas, please tell me you do?'

'I didn't know that, John,' said Dorchadas in a slow and broken voice. 'I knew *He* welcomed me back, but I wasn't sure what they would think. I wasn't sure if they would ever welcome me back.'

'Well, take it from me, Dorchadas, they love you. And when your time comes, there will be a hero's welcome for you.'

'Oh, no..' cried Dorchadas, and it was his turn to sob into John's shoulder. He was now the babe. Douglas felt keenly for Dorchadas and moved close to him, and for a moment the three clasped each other in reassurance.

After a while, John freed himself from the little group and sat on his haunches and said with delight, 'Look at us! You know what this is, don't you, Douglas?'

Douglas looked at the red-faced prophet who was wiping his nose and grinning wildly, 'This - what we have just experienced - is the Kingdom of God! This is what wins out in the end. You'll see. This is what wins in the end.' He then got to his feet and moved to the far end of the cave saying, 'Now you'll need this.' He fetched a long stick which had some kind of flammable substance at its end, for when he plunged it in his fire, it burst into flame.

'Now take yourself for a little walk under the stars. It will do you both a power of good. It will help with your healing. Then, when you are ready, you can go home. Go on... I need to get my sleep, there will be thousands down at the river by dawn and I need to be with them.'

He passed the torch to Dorchadas who simply smiled and said, 'Thank you, John. Thank you.' Dorchadas beckoned Douglas forward and led the way, clutching the burning torch.

Neither said a word as they walked out into the wilderness. They neither knew nor cared where they were going. They walked for a while and then stopped. Dorchadas extinguished the torch, and in the thick darkness of that desert night, they lay down on the ground that still held some warmth, and stared up at the brilliant canopy above them - a multitude of glimmering lights.

'Not all of them are stars,' said Dorchadas, after they had been lying there for many minutes. 'Some of them are my friends, you know. They love it up there.'

'And now you know that they will be pleased to see you, Dorch,' said Douglas continuing to admire the heavenly spectacle above him.

'Aye, that I must believe, Doug. Hm... That I do believe,' said Dorchadas.

Douglas was never sure what happened next, but one way or another he must have made his way from the pub and back to his bed at St.Raphael's. He awoke in the early hours to attend to the demands of his bladder, still full of the memory of his meeting in the night-time cave with this desert prophet.

He was soon back in his bed and sound asleep. Not long before dawn, he dreamed that he was back in the desert again. It was daylight and John was with a group of men dressed in black and white robes. Douglas knew these to be the robes of the Pharisees, and John was pleading with them. They were angry and pointing accusingly at John. In the dream, Douglas walked closer to the group, and John turned and put his hand up to stop Douglas. 'Be careful, my brother' he said. 'Be aware of the viper in the flock. Do not be deceived. Be wise. Be strong. You will prevail.' Douglas was puzzled and was about to turn back, but before he did, he took a look at the group of angry Pharisees. Among them was one face he recognised. He was horrified to see it. Standing there in the centre of the group, red-faced with anger and holding in his hands a Kalashnikov automatic weapon that was pointing directly at Douglas, was none other than Gerald Bentley OBE - the very man who, a few weeks previously, had made it clear that Douglas was no longer wanted at his home church in Sheffield. The shock of the dream woke Douglas with a start. He turned on his bedside light and drank all the water from the glass on his bedside table. The dream felt so real, yet so shocking. He could not get Gerald's cold and vitriolic stare out of his mind. After a few moments, he turned the light back off and tried to return to sleep, but it was a dream that no amount of willpower could dislodge, and there was no further sleep for him that night.

Darkness had compassed about with clouds
the body of the wielding God,
that lustrous radiance.
Wan under heaven shadows went forth.
And all creation wept,
wailing the slaughter of its King.
Christ was on the cross.

The Dream of the Rood

The power Jesus represented was a power
unlike any experienced before or since.
It was not enacted with violence
or displays of military splendour,
but with love
and self-sacrifice.

Paula Gooder
Journey to the Empty Tomb

CHAPTER 6

She was slumped, as she usually was at this time of day, in the armchair by the fire. The glass on the table beside her contained a limp piece of lemon and the dying remains of an ice cube. A copy of *The Radio Times* lay at her feet. But she stirred when he came into the room, and for a change, he was smiling.

'What are you looking so pleased about?' she asked, pulling herself up in her seat and instinctively grasping the glass beside her.

'I think we have done it,' he said, as he came into the room holding a brandy glass in his hand, swirling the amber-coloured liquid within it.

'Done what? Sorted the problem in Nairobi?'

He sat down on the sofa, placed the glass on a side table. 'No, as far as I know, Nairobi is quiet.'

'I told you to get that assassin taken out before he talks.' She sipped the last dregs from her glass. 'How come this glass is always bloody empty? Would you be a darling?' She waved the glass in his direction.

He ignored the request. He put on his patronising look and said, 'It's not exactly easy taking someone out when they are under armed guard in jail, is it? Anyway, there's no sign of him talking.'

'Hm,' she murmured, still waving her glass.

He breathed in, betraying his impatience. He pulled at his trouser legs and leaned forward. 'Look, let me tell you the good news.' She noticed his smile of satisfaction as he said, 'You'll be pleased to know that our little chum, the Vicar, will soon be gone from the parish for good.' She recognised his smug look as he lifted his brandy glass and said, 'So here's to his staying in that soggy, rotten, rebel land of Ireland for a good many years to come.'

'I've got nothing to here's it with,' she said. She guessed there would be no response, so placing her glass back on the table, she said, 'So he's not coming back here? No more the vicar?'

'No! He's gone. And no coming back.' He sipped from the glass and looked triumphant.

'Go on - tell me how you did it,' she enquired.

'Well, now,' he said, rising from the sofa. 'You know I've become chummy with the bishop.'

'Which one? There are several in the diocese aren't there?'

'Yes, there are a few. Well, it's her ladyship, the bishop of Tankersley – the one responsible for money, clergy deployment. All that sort of thing,' he said, as he made his way to the dresser.

'Oh, yes, you've mentioned her before. The one who holds the power.'

'The very one. Well. Guess what?' he said, now rising from the sofa. 'It seems that she is a little susceptible to, shall we say, the blessings of mammon.'

'Your bribed her?' she said, narrowing her eyes.

'Oh, come, come, Angela, I don't think we should use that term in the church, do you?' he said as he carefully replenished his glass.

'Don't forget me,' she called, lifting her glass and waving it hopefully. Again, he ignored her request and walked back to the sofa. 'Oh, for Christ's sake,' she sighed, and hauled herself out of her seat and walked unsteadily to the dresser. She poured herself a generous gin and tonic. 'Can't be arsed to get the ice,' she said as she returned to her seat. 'Go on, tell me more. I'm intrigued. Is her ladyship just a teeny-weeny bit corrupt then?'

'Oh, far be it from me to suggest such a thing.' He looked to the ceiling and stroked his chin as he said, 'But following our initial discussions the other night, I had a little think and I called her just now and said I thought the Diocese might find that a hundred grand could come in handy.'

'A hundred grand?' she cried. 'Good God! Of our money?'

'Don't worry, I've just secured another job in Somalia which will bring in most of that - half of it's in already, the rest will be here next week. Anyway, our "nest egg", as you call it, is looking very healthy at the moment. And our dear vicar loved to talk about the blessings of giving, so I'm simply practising what he preached.' He smiled his thin smile and took another careful sip from his glass before placing it with great care on the table beside him. He enjoyed precision.

'So, you've given a hundred k, and in exchange, she gets rid of him.'

'Not in exchange. Oh, no. We're the Church of England, please. No, no. But I find with our dear old national church, that when you make a rather sizeable gift, they are more amenable to, shall we say, listening. So, when she'd got through her several hot flushes following my announcing the donation, I simply asked how things were with our roaming Reverend Romer. She said his sabbatical was going to end soon and she was expecting him back in February. Well, I then used, shall we say, my powers of persuasion.'

'Let's just say your power full stop.'

He smiled with his mouth but not his eyes and said, 'How sweet, dear. Anyway, I said the PCC was very concerned da di da. The congregation was declining da di da. Even when he was well, he wasn't performing da di da. You know, all that stuff.' His face turned stern as he thumped the arm of the chair and said, 'I made it bloody clear to her that his return would kill the church. No-one wants him back.'

'Somebody does - that old witch, Mavis,' she said, cradling the crystal glass in her hand.

He sniggered and said, 'She's as thick as two old Prayer Books, so she's hardly a threat to us.'

'Oh, I'm not so sure. Anyway, go on. Did you persuade her ladyship?'

'Well, after I had said my piece, she did let slip that, in her meeting with him last year, he offered his resignation.' He smiled and then took a delicate sip from his glass.

'Oh, did he now?' she said, pulling herself forward on her chair.

'He did. And though she didn't accept it then, she said she could see no reason why she shouldn't accept it now. She wasn't fully sure of her ground though and said he might contest it, in which case it may cost the diocese a pretty package to shift him. I said if that were the case we might be able to help.'

'Hm. Sounds like more money,' she said, frowning.

'Oh, it wouldn't be much,' he said. 'The point is she's convinced. She's going to get rid of him. She obviously has a bit of a soft spot for our cussed cleric and I could tell she was struggling. And so I revealed my cuddly and compassionate side. I told her how it was clear he was struggling greatly since his bereavement and for him to stay would only cause him more pain and frankly more humiliation. She really needed to take this action to protect him.'

'You clever sod.'

He took another tiny sip from his glass and smoothed back the last remaining hairs from his head. 'It's just as well that the diocese is in such a mess financially. She's under extreme pressure from all quarters to raise money.' He paused and then added with a frowning smile, 'What a very useful thing money is, dear.'

'Mm...' she said. 'It is not just useful. It's essential. And now we have it, we will make damn sure we don't lose it.' She put her glass down and was tapping her fingers on the side of the chair. He looked across to her and was annoyed that she was not looking more triumphant. He had, after all, succeeded in removing the problematic vicar from the parish. What more could she want?

'What is it?' he asked, frowning at her. 'Why aren't you more pleased?'

She then turned to him and said, 'Now listen. I'm not convinced this great plan of yours will work.' His brow furrowed further and he was about to protest, but she got in first. 'Just getting him out of this parish, does not mean he won't find out about the killing of the Irish hussy.'

'Well, it gets him out of our immediate way. While he's around here, he could start developing suspicions. He's pretty dense, but even he might smell a rat. So to be sure, I want him well away from here. She won't give him a parish in this diocese, so he'll be off my patch, probably down south somewhere, and he'll quickly forget about me. Besides, I'm far from convinced that he's got it in him to try and track down her killer. He'll leave it to Intelligence, and they are not going to do anything. They have far bigger fish to fry. Take it from me: we can relax.'

'I don't think we can,' she said, fixing her gaze on the fireplace.

He started to redden. 'For God's sake, woman, I've killed off the Irish tart, and I've got rid of him from the parish. Isn't that enough for you?'

She turned to him and gave him a fierce stare. 'I am not losing all we have fought for, I bloody well am not. I want to be sure, absolutely damn sure, that no-one will find out about this, because if they do, we will lose the whole sodding lot. I have fought tooth and nail to get us to where we are, don't you forget that. And don't forget my mother's estate. It's *my* money as well as yours we're talking about, and I am not losing a penny of it.' She grabbed hold of her glass, taking a gulp of the liquid.

He was gripping the arms of the chair. 'You can get nasty when your ambitions are threatened, can't you?'

'I certainly can. I am *not* giving any of this up,' she said as she banged her glass on the table, splashing the carpet as she did so. 'Now listen, I am not happy with this. I...' she breathed in hard through her nose, and then looked at her husband with a cold stare. 'Ok, you have got him out of the parish. Well done. Bloody expensive, but that's beside the point. The point is this: while he is alive, no matter where he is in the world, there is every risk he will discover you had her killed. I agree that British intelligence has far more important cases to be dealing with. They are not interested in some silly Irish girl. And we know full well they are not interested in illegal arms. They want to keep the arms business going, both illegal and legal - the whole bloody economy depends on it. So, I'm not worried about them. I'm sure that chase has run out of steam. But I am worried about *him*.'

'And so am I,' he said, almost shouting. 'That's why I've got him out of our lives. He's harmless over there in Ireland.'

Her face reddened. He knew well the hardness he now saw in her expression, and he knew he had to take note. She pulled herself forward in her chair and sat up very straight. He started to feel rather small as she continued. 'Yes, he's naive and stupid, but he loved that girl, that was plain to see. God knows what he saw in her, the meddling bitch. But love her, he did, and he now knows that she was targeted by an arms dealer. Just think about it. He's not just going to hang around wandering the blasted highways of Ireland waiting for the British Intelligence to do sod all about it. I have no doubts about this. He will be doing his own investigations. Probably hired a private investigator, I shouldn't wonder. You may find he is much closer than you think to nailing you. And once he knows it's you, he will be delighted to see you put behind bars. That's if he doesn't put a gun to your head first, and I wouldn't bet against that. Bitter anger can change a man.'

'Oh, come on…I know him. He's a broken wreck of a man. He's finished. He's not got it in him to do any of that.'

But her desperation was now driving her. 'I'm not convinced. I want this dealt with properly. He won't rest in his bed until he finds out who did it. All right, I didn't know the man like you did, but he now knows his wife was targeted by someone in Sheffield who arranged her murder. You mark my words, it won't be long before he tracks you down.

'But I've spent a hundred k,' he protested, thumping the arm of his chair.

'And what a bloody waste of money that was! Let me be perfectly clear about this.' She drained the last of her gin, stood up, and, though unsteady on her feet, she was steadfast in her conviction and her stare. She pointed at her husband and in an ominous tone of voice said, 'I want him dead, Gerald. Do you hear? Not just out of the parish. Not even out of the country. I want him eliminated. Wiped out. I want him dead!'

CHAPTER 7

It was eventually a headache rather than sleeplessness that got Douglas out of bed, and he fetched a paracetamol from his bathroom. For a while he looked out of his window and watched the strong breeze catch hold of a sheet of newspaper, causing it to dance erratically on the pavement. The carefree lightness of the paper was in contrast to the weight he felt in his soul following the dream, the memory of which had lodged firmly his waking mind. He decided to write in his journal.

Journal   6 January

Quite a day yesterday. Met up with old Dorch again. So good to see him. I was driving around the peninsula and stopped off at this ruined church and as I sat there enjoying the peace, he suddenly turned up! He feels like a friend I've known all my life. He took me to this little tea shop up a hill. Don't know how he finds these places but we had tea there and a really good catch up. We had a good chat about the time in Gethsemane. Very strange but wonderful experience over tea - I finally <u>saw</u> Dorch. I mean, I felt I saw him as an angel - no longer any doubts about it. Yes, a retired angel who now looks like a human. It no longer feels weird to believe it. He said it touched him very much that I now believed him. I suppose it would. I think I'm one of the few who does believe him. Anyway, we met up again at the Angels Rest last night and I told him about the Intelligence officer and the grim news he brought. It was <u>such</u> a relief to tell someone. And he's not a 'mortal soul'! It was a seriously helpful conversation, though I'm still not sure there's much I can do about it, though I do feel a growing determination to find out who was behind the murder. It's gone very quiet from Intelligence. Not sure how committed they are to finding this man.

Anyway, there was then another 'meeting', this time with John the Baptist (Yes!). We met him at night. He wasn't at all what I expected. Poor guy displayed real mental health issues. But I guess such cracks really do let a lot of light in, as Leonard Cohen would say, and my, he had light in bucketfuls. I was expecting a lot of ranting and raving from him, but instead, the three of us (Dorch was there) were huddled together in a cave in floods of tears! I think there was real healing for both Dorch and me actually. I guess Dorch introduced me to him, as he was someone who, like my Saoirse, challenged the powers because of the strength of his convictions. And like her, he paid the ultimate price.

Still don't know how I got back from the pub to my bed, but for most of the night, I slept well. But then when I woke up this morning I recalled a very vivid dream. I was back in the desert and John was there and a group of Pharisees. One of the Pharisees was none other than old Gerald Bentley and he was holding an automatic weapon aimed at me!! What the hell do I make of this? Is my paranoia getting the better of me? Or was the dreaming giving me a crucial insight? Could it be that Gerald is behind all this? Gerald - an arms-dealer?? He can be a bit nasty at times, but I can't honestly see him smuggling arms around the world. Besides he's very involved in the diocese and Bishop Pauline thinks the world of him. Unless it's Angela? No-one knows much about her, apart from the fact that she's inebriated half the time - can't see her organising that kind of thing. I'll have a chat with Dorch.

Something is definitely happening in my spirit. Faith is being rekindled, but it is different. It doesn't feel familiar, and yet it feels warm. I'm not working at it, just seeing what happens. But I'm praying again - just a little. Think I might pray for a few moments and then it's breakfast. I'm preferring, still, silent prayer at the moment. Words somehow get in the way.

*

When he arrived downstairs he was surprised, and pleased, to see Kevin sitting at his table sipping a coffee.

'The top of the morning to ye,' he called, as Douglas entered the room

'Don't give me that blarney!' said Douglas as greeted Kevin. This was the man whose story of forgiveness had tipped Douglas over the edge on that fateful day in October. But he was also the man who, during those days of recovery in the weeks following, had become the best of friends.

'So good to see you back in Dingle, Doug,' said Kevin, settling back into his chair. 'Thought I'd come and disturb your breakfast for a few minutes and find out how things are.'

'Will you both be wanting the cooked,' called Elsie from the kitchen.

'That we will, Aunty, please,' called back Kevin. 'That OK with you, Doug?'

'Yes, she knows what I like by now, Kev. She's become my Irish mother.'

'You'll find no better, that you won't.' He then leaned forward and asked in a confidential tone, 'So what do you think of the new haircut?'

'It might take me a little while to adjust... but it's very "her".'

'Now that it is, Doug. That it surely is!' He threw back his head and laughed, revealing several missing teeth.

'You two in there talking about my hair, are you?' came the voice from the kitchen.

'Now why would you be thinking that, Aunty, darling?'

'Because the whole sorry town's talking about it, that's why,' she replied as she re-entered the room with a steaming pot of coffee. 'Good morning to you, Douglas. I hope you slept well, son.'

'Yes thanks, Elsie.'

'Now about the hair, lads. Do you think I should keep it this way?'

'Tell me, Aunty Else - do *you* like it?' asked Kevin.

'Well, I think it's up with them fashions. The girl on the sports news has a hairdo just like this. Though I do understand she's about a hundred and forty years younger than me.'

'Aunty,' said Kevin, reaching out his hand and clutching hers, 'you are one of the most beloved people in Dingle. You just be yourself. I think the hair looks grand.'

Elsie started to fill up and said, 'You know Douglas, there was a time when young Kev here was so different. You had such a hard heart at one time, son,' she said, turning to Kevin. 'But now look at you. Pretty much every time I see you, you fetch the tears from out of my eyes!' They all laughed. Elsie sat down for a moment and continued, 'The thing is, I've been watching your mum, Kevin, getting friendly with that Peter. My God, years back that was such a dreadful story. You know all about it now, son,' she said, patting Douglas on the hand, 'and you have been such a help to Kath, sure to God you have.'

'And she to me, Elsie. You both have.'

'Aye, well. All that stuff's in the past now, thank God, and I'm happy for her that she is getting to know Peter. He seems a nice enough gent. Though I'm not sure about a ponytail for a man of his age. Kath says it gives the man dignity. That I'm not sure of, but all that's beside the point. Now, where was I?' Douglas was about to help her when she continued, 'Look, I'm not going to spoil your breakfast, but I just wanted to explain, you know, that seeing my sister stepping out, so to speak, well it's made me realise that I'm a wee bit lonely, that's all. My Daniel's been in his grave over five years now and, you know… Maybe I should make myself more presentable and… well, available. That's all I need to say.'

She got up, but Kevin took her hand and said, 'Aunty Else, you are a mighty special woman, and you are beautiful. Any man would thank the saints in heaven if he were lucky enough to go out with you. I'll say a wee prayer for you at the mass later.'

'Och, I'm sure the Almighty's got much more important things on his mind than that, Kevin, but bless you, son, for the thought. Now let me be getting your breakfast.'

'I doubt whether he has,' said Kevin as she made her way out of the dining room.

'So, is your mother really stepping out with Peter?' asked Douglas.

'I'm not sure she would go as far as that, Doug. But I think they are just getting to know each other again after all those years. You'll have to ask her yourself. You'll be looking in on her today I hope?'

'Yes, I'll pop up there for a cup of tea soon.'

'Good man yourself, Doug. She'll appreciate that.'

The two men chatted together over their breakfast and were just having their final sips of coffee when Elsie came into the room all of a fluster waving a piece of paper saying, 'Oh, God forgive me, Douglas. I was supposed to give you this. I got a phone message from your bishop's office early this morning. They tried your mobile, but it must have been switched off. I wrote down the message which is about you having a facelift or some such thing.'

'A facelift, Elsie?' asked Douglas as he reached for the note she was clutching. He read it quickly and smiled. 'Face*Time*, Elsie. Thank you.'

'Never heard of it, Doug, but I hope it'll do you good. Sorry about forgetting it,' she said and left the room.

'The news OK?' asked Kevin.

'Yes, just a note from my bishop saying she wants to FaceTime me at 10.05 this morning.'

'Is that usual - for your bishop to call you?'

'Actually, she hasn't spoken to me for quite a while. But I am due back in the parish early next month, so I suppose we have to start making plans.'

'Do you want to go back then, Douglas?'

'No, not at all. But what else can I do? I've got to earn a living somehow.'

'Och, we can find some work for you here in Dingle, I'm sure we can. Father Pat could probably employ you.'

'I'm just not sure about church work yet, Kev, but thanks all the same.'

'You could join me at the garage. Once the season starts we'll need more staff. Tourist cars are forever breaking down.'

'Thanks, Kevin. That could be good. But I don't know much about cars.'

'I'll soon teach you. There's nothing to it.'

Elsie returned with the breakfast, which both men soon consumed. Kevin wiped his mouth on his serviette and said, 'I'd better go and open up. Durlach's got a problem with his clutch - yet again, would you believe. So, have a good day Douglas,' he said rising from the table. 'Chat again soon.'

'Will do, Kev,' said Douglas, and returned to his bedroom where he prepared his laptop for the meeting with his bishop. Remembering how kind she was when they last spoke, he felt very relaxed about it.

*

'Hello, Douglas. Can you hear me? Are we connecting?' The face of the bishop's chaplain was frozen for a moment, giving him the appearance of a gargoyle.

Douglas tried to suppress his laughter as he replied, 'Yes, hello I'm here. Let me just get my laptop to a place where there is a better reception.'

The gargoyle returned to being the familiar bearded face of the thick-set chaplain again as he said, 'Oh, jolly good. I think we are getting somewhere. Righto, I'm in her study and she's coming through in one and a half minutes. Can you stay put there and wait by the screen until she comes? We seem to have a good connection now, thanks be. Hope you are doing well, old chap. Tata.' His face disappeared from the screen, and while Douglas waited for the arrival of the bishop, he looked at the extensive bookshelf on the far wall, trying to make out if he recognised any of the books, which he couldn't.

Sure enough, at 10.05 precisely, the smart figure of Bishop Pauline entered the room and settled herself at her desk and fiddled with the screen so that her image darted to and fro for a while making Douglas a little dizzy. 'Morning, Douglas,' she greeted, as the image finally settled. She was again in her smart suit top, though her bishop's shirt looked a very vivid pink, the colour no doubt distorted by the transmission process.

'Good morning Bishop, I hope you are well?' said Douglas.

'Quite well, thank you.' Douglas noted she was definitely in formal mode and no sign yet of the warmth that was so evident at their last meeting. 'Straight to the point if you don't mind, Douglas, as it's a busy day. It's about your situation, of course.'

'Yes,' said Douglas. He could sense she was nervous.

'I've been giving it a lot of thought and prayer.'

'Thank you, Bishop Pauline.'

'Not at all. I've also discussed it with colleagues, and you will appreciate that we are not only concerned for your well-being but also very much for the well-being of St.Philip's, which you have served so faithfully for just over 10 years now.'

'Yes...' said Douglas, now feeling some uncertainty.

'Has your sabbatical being going well, by the way?' she asked.

He was about to tell her a bit about his time in Dingle, but he noticed that she was now looking away from the camera and attending to something on her desk, so he simply replied. 'Yes. Going well, thank you.'

'Good, good…' she said, but her attention was elsewhere. 'Would you excuse me for a quick moment, Douglas.' She turned her head to one side and called out, 'Clive! Clive!' Douglas heard the door open to the study and guessed the dutiful chaplain had entered the room. 'Clive, I see Benedict is trying to get me. I do need to speak to him urgently, so could you tell him I'll call him in ten?' Douglas heard the door close and the bishop's face reappeared again. 'So sorry Douglas. You know how it is.' Douglas did know how it was, but he couldn't help feeling he was fairly low down on the pecking order of her priorities this morning.

'So, as I was saying, we've been considering the situation very carefully, and I would like to put a suggestion to you, which I hope you will think and pray about.'

'Yes,' said Douglas obediently.

'And it's this. We would like to suggest you now resign from St.Philip's. I think it would be hard for you to return now, and I think you and they need to move on. You did offer your resignation when we last met, and having considered this carefully, I would now like to accept it.'

'You refused it when we last met, Bishop.'

'I'm not sure, strictly speaking, I did refuse it, Douglas. More deferred it.' She looked uncertain.

Douglas felt anger in his stomach as the conversation developed. 'Well, have you spoken to the people at St.Philip's?'

'One or two, yes.'

'By one or two, do you mean Gerald Bentley, by any chance?'

Douglas saw the bishop flush and he knew he had touched a tender spot. She quickly gathered herself and said, 'Yes, of course, I meet Gerald at many meetings and he has expressed a lot of concern about St.Philip's. And about you, of course.'

'I'll bet,' retorted Douglas. 'You told me he was frightened of you. Are you sure it is not the other way around?' He astonished himself by his sudden boldness.

'Douglas, will you kindly remember you are talking to your bishop. I do expect some respect. Now, of course, I will be asking the Archdeacon to go and meet with your PCC and explain the situation. I am thinking of *you,* Douglas. You have been through a very tough time professionally, emotionally and spiritually, and in my view, a return to St.Philip's would be very detrimental to your well-being.'

'And to Gerald's,' responded Douglas in a low voice.

'Now Douglas,' she continued, pretending not to hear, 'I'm sorry, but I don't have very long and I am simply calling you to ask you to consider this. Once you have resigned, we can talk together about what you can do next. I have already got a couple of possibilities to put to you. The Bishop of Oxford was speaking to me yesterday about a very interesting post which I think could really excite you.'

The anger was still rumbling in Douglas, and the more the bishop spoke, the more he become certain he did not want to be back in a parish church, in her or anyone's Diocese. He felt very disappointed with the bishop who seemed to have lost the kindness he had seen in her at their last meeting.

'Let's put us both out of our misery then, Pauline,' said Douglas, butting in to the bishop who was starting to outline some legal business to do with resignation. 'I will resign from the parish. I'll write to you this week. But frankly, I am not convinced this is best for my well-being nor the church's well-being. Whatever you have been told by Gerald, there are plenty in the church who are hoping for my return. But I have every confidence that they will manage without my returning.'

'Thank you, Douglas,' said the bishop, somewhat taken aback by the sudden surrender. 'That's very... very gracious of you.'

Douglas could see how relieved she was, but he did not want to let her off the hook entirely. 'But may I just say one thing before we part. I am not sure I am the biggest problem here. You might have solved the Douglas Romer problem, but I am not at all convinced you have any idea just how big the Gerald Bentley problem is. God bless you in trying to solve that one, Bishop.'

Again, the bishop looked flustered, but quickly covered up by saying, 'Yes, well that won't be your problem now, will it? Now, if you will excuse me, I will have to go. We will be in touch, God's speed.' And before Douglas could offer his farewell, the line was cut and there was silence.

Douglas leaned back in his creaking chair and sighed. He felt in a state of shock. He could hardly believe he had just handed in his resignation. And why did he mention Gerald Bentley? It was clearly the result of the vivid dream which was affecting him like a hangover. The rudeness to the bishop was so unlike him. Yet something was stirring in him. Something wasn't right. He could see the bishop was under pressure from someone to get him to resign. Who was it? And was it really that important?

78

He needed some fresh air, so he decided to take a long walk by the coast. He sent a message to Kath to let her know he would be round in the afternoon, not the morning, and he set off at a brisk pace to the sea. Of all the words that rang around in his head from this last conversation, the ones that rang the loudest were those of the bishop: 'Yes, well that won't be your problem now, will it?' Douglas was developing a growing suspicion, if not fear, that Gerald Bentley could well be very much his problem.

CHAPTER 8

Douglas had not been down to the sea since the day of the great storm in November, but he decided he was strong enough to visit the very place where he and Dorch had met on that wild day and ended up wrestling one another in the raging, Atlantic surf. He walked up to the mouth of the estuary, and sure enough, there was the dinghy that a man called Ciaran had been securing on that fateful day when he saw two men floundering in the waves and dashed in to save them. This must have been the place where it all happened.

A pale January sun made a brief appearance before thinking better of it, and tucked itself behind the cloud and remained there for the time that Douglas sat on a stone overlooking the bay. The conversation with the bishop rumbled around in his mind. Was he right to push her about Gerald? She *did* look very uncomfortable when he mentioned his name. He knew Gerald well enough to know how skilful he was at manipulating people. Without a doubt, he had succeeded at manipulating Douglas on some occasions, especially during the last couple of years when Douglas had no energy to resist him. But was Gerald really the man behind Saoirse's murder? This felt fanciful. It's one thing to be a damn nuisance at a PCC meeting, but quite another to be booking a hired assassin to bump off a British tourist in Egypt.

But then there was the issue of Gerald's wealth. Where did it come from? He said he was in banking, but whenever Douglas asked him to say more about his work, he always clammed up. They had just bought that huge mansion with an enormous garden and electric gates. That would certainly have cost him well over a million. Where did he get that kind of money?

Douglas went over all this in his mind again and again. And then he thought about Saoirse. The Intelligence officer had said that it was likely she had suspected someone of arms dealing and had confronted them. Yes, that was like Saoirse. If she thought someone was into that, she would have spoken to them. She seemed to have no fear of people. But wouldn't she have said something to Douglas about it? What did she think of Gerald? She hardly ever met him, as she didn't come to church. But then she did say he had come into school on one or two occasions. He went as Chair of the Board of Finance, and she said he had to discuss some funding matters with her.

A few memories started to awaken in his mind now. He was gazing at the calm sea in the bay, but he saw none of that as he recalled her coming in from school late one afternoon - probably about six months before she died.

'Nice day?' he said as she threw her bags on the hall floor and went into the toilet.

'Not bad,' she shouted through the door

'Tea?'

'You bet - I'm gasping.'

He put on the kettle and waited for her in the kitchen. She came in and gave her usual kiss, but he could see she was a bit distracted.

'What's up?' he said as he poured the steaming water into the teapot.

'How well do you know that Gerald Whatsit from the Diocesan Finance Thinggy?' she asked. She always liked to make out she was totally ignorant of anything to do with church.

'Gerald Bentley?' said Douglas, stirring the teapot.

'That's your man,' she said as she kicked off her shoes and pulled up a chair at the table.

'Well, I don't really know him that well. I mean, he's been in the church donkey's years, and he seems to run the diocese as far as I can see. Has got the bishop round his little finger, so people say.'

'Has he got you round his little finger, Vicar?' she asked with a teasing smile, wiggling her little finger at him.

'When he tries to, I give him this finger.' Douglas put up his middle finger to her and they both chortled. 'But why are you asking?'

'Oh, it's just that he came in to school to see me today. There's some reorganising going on with the Board of Education funding and he had to fill me in. All seems fairly straight forward. But I have to say, Dougie, I didn't take to the man.'

'Why not?' He passed a mug of tea to Saoirse who took it gratefully and added a teaspoon of sugar.

'The man gives me the creeps, if I'm honest with you, Doug,' she said, stirring her mug.

'Oh, I don't think he's *that* bad, is he?'

'What's his business?' she asked, holding the mug to her lips and looking at Douglas with a frown.

'Banking, I believe,' said Douglas, settling himself at the table. He loved her frown and he wanted to kiss her, but he knew she was trying to say something important.

'I'm not sure it is, Doug,' she said, sipping slowly from her mug. 'There's something about that man, and I'm not sure what it is. He's making a lot of money. I know bankers do, but I just don't think that's where his money is coming from. He's got something else going on, I'd say.

Sorry, I know he's one of your flock and that, but I don't like him, Doug.'

'Irish instinct again?'

'Don't you go dissing it, Reverend!' she said and gave him her school teacher disapproving look.

'No, no, of course, Mrs. Romer,' said Douglas smiling. 'But seriously, I can't think Gerald is a crook if that's what you are suggesting. He's a menace at times, but I hardly think he's got criminal blood in him.'

He watched Saoirse sipping her tea and looking down at the table. She said nothing for a time, and then ventured, 'And what about his wife? Is he married?'

'Yes, married to Angela, though we hardly ever see her. Mostly, because she doesn't get up much before midday. A little bit fond of...' Douglas mimed drinking from a bottle.

'Mm, that would make sense.'

'Make sense of what?'

'What's driving her to the drink then? I mean she's got a palace of a house to live in, hasn't she? Don't they live in that massive place just up the road?'

'That's the one.'

'So - you've got all you ever dreamed of. Then, why do you drink? What's making you so unhappy? And I wonder who's driving who?' She paused and looked out of the window for a moment and then added, 'I mean, she might be the driver. You know, pushing him hard to rake in the cash she feels she deserves. But money's a drug, isn't it? The more you have, the more you want.' She held her mug to her lips, lifting a questioning eyebrow to Douglas. 'Just speculating, Dougie.'

'Well Chief Inspector Mrs. Romer, you are probably right.' Douglas could contain himself no longer, and he

83

came around, knelt beside her and squeezed her tight. 'It's what they will be saying about us soon,' he said. 'I'll be plotting a few hideous crimes, embezzling the church's funds and we shall escape to some exotic country and I will have driven you to drink.'

She giggled and nestled her head into his shoulder. 'You already have,' she said, and then leaned back saying, 'This tea's a bit tame, don't you think? I've had a hard day and I've got to spend a whole evening with the Minister of this parish.' She placed the back of her hand to her forehead and called out, 'Vicar, open the wine! This woman needs help urgently!'

A sudden and cold breeze brought Douglas' mind sharply back to the present. He had been laughing at the memory. He and Saoirse had laughed so much together. But as he recalled the conversation, he realised that Saoirse had sensed that there was something not right about Gerald. That conversation was about six months before she left for Egypt. He thought no more about it at the time, but now the conversation had gained new significance. He was intrigued to know what further contact Saoirse might have had with Gerald. Did she discover some shady arms dealing? Did she confront him one day? If so, where and when? She never mentioned any of this to Douglas. Why would she keep it from him?

But then maybe Gerald had nothing to do with it at all, and his dream was just his innate paranoia getting the better of him. In many ways, it would have been so much easier if Saoirse's death was caused by some random drive-by terrorist shooting. The idea of her being targeted was somehow even more disturbing than a terrorist atrocity. Douglas wondered whether he should try and contact British Intelligence. What were they doing? Or should he be taking some action? But he was no detective. Should he go back to England and have a frank conversation with Gerald? But the man was hardly going to admit it. He felt weary. Much as he wanted to bring the perpetrator of all of this to justice, he had no energy for embarking on his own investigations. Maybe this was something he just had to entrust to the God he was gradually rediscovering. He sighed a long sigh and threw a stone into the water.

'How, you doing now, Mister?' said a young voice behind him. He looked around and there was Grace, the teenager he had met a few weeks back in the playground.

'Hello there, Grace.'

'Oh, you remember me, then?'

'Yes, we chatted in the playground, didn't we?'

'We did, and we wondered if life was a dump,' she said. 'Mind if I join you?'

'No - take a seat,' said Douglas, offering her a nearby stone on the shore. She was only wearing a light jacket. 'You should be wearing a coat,' he said as she sat down.

'Oh, you're my da now, are you?'

'Sorry, Grace,' said Douglas smiling. 'No, I'll promise not to behave like a parent. I'll try and be a friend. You been at school today?'

'Aye,' she said, as she brushed her long brown hair from her face. 'Term just started.'

'How was it'

'Boring again.'

'You still think life's a dump then?' said Douglas, throwing another stone into the sea.

She looked puzzled and Douglas saw a brief smile cross her face, the kind of smile that changed her countenance completely. But as soon as it came, it was gone again.

'It's not a dump, I know that. It's just… I've seen things. I've seen better. That's all.'

She looked up at him with an enquiring look, wondering if he would catch her meaning. He didn't, and he wanted to, so he asked, 'Well, what sort of things?'

The girl was quiet for a few moments and kicked her foot at some stones. 'Just things,' she said and then added. 'I will tell you one day, Douglas. When the time is right. She looked at the bright face of her watch and said, 'Well, I have to go now. Nice seeing you.'

Douglas was a bit taken aback by her abrupt departure but he stood up and said, 'Who is your dad, by the way?'

She turned her head to one side and said, 'Jerry's his name. You know him.'

'I've not met anyone called Jerry,' said Douglas.

'No, you've not met him. But you know him. Anyway, have a good day,' she said and walked a few paces away before turning and saying, 'That Dorchadas friend of yours is back by the way.'

'Yes, thanks I've seen him,' said Douglas. She waved without looking back, and in a few moments, she was gone.

'Most curious,' said Douglas to himself as he strolled back along the beach to the town. What did she mean about "seeing things"? And just who was Jerry? He didn't know anyone called Jerry. She got that bit wrong. Nevertheless, the stroppy teenager he met in the autumn seemed to have quite a bit more about her than he realised. He glanced at his watch and remembered that he had told Kath he would be at her café in the afternoon, so he quickened his pace.

*

The sun made another unconvincing attempt to take a look at the wintry earth just as Douglas arrived at Kath's shop. There was no-one in the small café. He was somewhat taken aback to hear classical music coming from the kitchen, rather than the usual Country music so beloved by Kath. He called out, 'Are you in, Kathleen?'

A man emerged from the kitchen wearing an apron and polishing a cafetière with a tea towel. He was tall if slightly stooped. He had a neatly trimmed beard and his grey hair was brushed back and gathered in a neat ponytail. Behind his round-rimmed spectacles shone kindly blue-green eyes, bordered with blonde eyelashes. He stopped his polishing of the cafetière and in a quiet voice, he explained, 'Good afternoon to you. Kathleen's just out to fetch some flour, but I'll be happy to serve you if you'd like to sit at the table. Can I get you a cup of coffee, sir?'

Douglas paused for a moment, and then asked, 'Do you mind me asking, will it be you making the coffee?'

'Ah, I'm guessing you've visited this café before,' he said with a knowing smile. 'Yes, it will be myself making the coffee. And as it happens, I've just picked up a very nice supply of Tanzanian beans. Mix of Arabica and Robusta. Would that suit you, sir?'

'Thank you,' said Douglas, never imagining that he would experience such an exotic blend in this café. He sat down at the table, and as was now his custom, folded a paper serviette to steady the wobbly table.

The man disappeared back into the kitchen. Douglas guessed the man must have been Peter, but he thought he would let Kath introduce him. In a few moments, the door opened with a sudden crash, and in walked Kath with her arms full of several bags of flour.

'Would you believe it? They're out of self-raising flour, for God's sake. It makes you wonder, it surely does…' She then saw Douglas at the table. 'Oh, Doug. It's good to see you, son. Let me put these bags down. They're something awful heavy they are.' She pushed her way through the fly curtain into the kitchen and he heard Peter say, 'Oh, Kath for pity's sake, why didn't you let me get those for you? What with your bad chest and everything.' He then heard various snippets of conversation to do with self-raising flour and the weather before Kath re-emerged saying, 'Doug, did you meet Peter, just now?'

'Well, I did but we've not been introduced, Kath.'

'Oh, the saints in heaven have mercy on us. Peter, would you get yourself in here now, please.' she ordered.

Peter emerged clutching a large coffee pot, some milk and a mug and came over and placed them on Doug's table. Peter and Douglas were duly introduced and Kath said to Peter, 'Peter, would you be a darling and fetch us another couple of mugs so we can join Douglas. There's plenty in that pot. And bring in that jam sponge, if you would. I'll put the 'closed' sign up on the door and we can enjoy a wee chat for a while.'

She sat on one of the rickety chairs and pulled out an e-cigarette. 'So here we are, Doug. My new friend, Mr. E-ciggie. My vape. What do you think of him?' She held the e-cigarette up for inspection.

'He looks very fine, Kath.'

Kath's laugh brought on a fit of coughing, during which she fiddled with the device. Red-faced with exertion from the coughing, she lifted the device to her lips which started releasing profuse amounts of smoke. 'Blueberry with hints of rose and apple,' she said, and then wheezed her laugh again, almost choking herself in the process. 'Got this winter cough, would you believe, Doug. So Peter here persuaded me to switch from the tobacco to this thing. Says it will be better for my lungs, but so far you wouldn't think it, would you?' Peter returned and placed the coffee and cake with great care on the table. 'Now sit yourself down, love,' said Kath patting the seat beside her.

'It's good to meet you, Peter,' said Douglas, genuinely pleased to meet the man who had been such a significant figure in Kath's life.

'And it is very good to meet you, Douglas. I doubt very much if Kath and I would have met up again had it not been for you. We both owe you a lot, we certainly do that.' Douglas liked Peter's gentle manner, and he could imagine him being very much at home in a Quaker meeting.

'Kath tells me you're a Quaker,' said Douglas, plunging the cafetière and starting to pour out the coffee.

'Oh, God,' sighed Kath, and then took a long draw from her e-cigarette which only produced a brief bout of coughing this time. Peter looked slightly awkward and started to say something when Kath butted in. 'It's a slightly sore subject, Doug.' Kath and Peter looked at each other, Peter betraying a hint of a smile.

Kath took a sip of her coffee, winced at the unfamiliar flavour, then said, 'The thing is, you see, Doug, Peter invited me to one of his meetings in Adare. I thought it would be very nice. His religion is important to him and, as we are getting to know each other again, it seemed the right thing to do. And I was inquisitive, to tell the truth. He explained to me that in the meeting we'd all sit in a room together in silence. Well, when he said that, I thought "hold on a minute, Kathleen Griffin. Can you honestly see yourself sat in a room for a whole hour with no-one saying so much as a word to break the monotony?" But then himself assured me.' She nudged Peter who smiled at her. 'He said we wouldn't have to endure the full hour in silence because every now and then someone would chip in with a word from the Almighty to keep things ticking along.'

'I'm not sure that's quite how I put it, Kathleen, dear...' said Peter.

Kath took a fresh puff of her vape and continued without responding to Peter. 'So, I says to Peter, "Well that would be all right, sure it would. Because that will make it a bit exciting. I can sit there and wait for an interesting word from Himself up there."' She pointed to the ceiling and then sipped at her coffee. 'So, I goes up to Adare and meets Peter at the door, and I'm early, would you believe it, Douglas? Anyway, nice friendly welcome from the people at the door, and then in we go to the meeting room. Very nice room and that, perfectly warm and comfortable, and quite a little crowd there, even though it was ten minutes to go before kick-off. Well, I settle myself down next to Peter.' She took a long inhalation from her vape, then continued through the mist of blueberry. 'A man sits down next to him, and I get up and say, "How d'ye do? I'm Kathleen from Dingle. Pleased to meet you," and I reach out my hand to him. Oohhh, well, there I go breaking Rule number 1! I thought the silence started at 10.30, I did, but oh, no. He forgets to tell me this important piece of information, that as soon as the first person steps into the meeting room, everyone keeps their mouth firmly shut. That's when the big silence starts. Thanks very much, Peter for that one.'

Peter chuckled quietly. Kath sucked hard at her vape that appeared to be diminishing in vitality. 'God, you have to work hard at these things. I have to confess, I do miss the nicotine, Doug. I don't rightly know how long I'll last with this thing. Anyway, where was I, Peter?'

'You'd just greeted the gentlemen next to me...'

'Oh, aye. Well, that was soon sorted and we all settled back down again to a nice bit of peace and quiet. Well, I was waiting for the action, I was, Doug. I mean, I was thinking, any minute now the Almighty is going to speak to us through one of these ladies or gents, and I was getting a bit excited, to tell the truth. Yes, I know, I've changed a bit. I'm getting to quite like this God of yours, you know, Douglas. Anyhow, minute by long minute went by and not a word from any of them.' She sat back in her chair and briefly raised her eyes to the ceiling. She then looked back at Douglas and said, 'Well, I mean Doug, even the most saintliest of us would get a bit agitated, don't you think? You've been told that God's going to say a direct word to you, and you're on the edge of your seat waiting, you sure are. Well, I looked at each one, and no word of a lie, Doug, each one looked sound asleep. Dead to the world they were...'

'They were meditating, Kathleen,' said Peter in his quiet voice, still bearing his hint of a smile. 'And I'm not sure I ever said anything about a *direct* word...'

'Meditating, my...' interrupted Kathleen. 'Anyway, I was waiting for this word from God, but a whole wearisome half hour went by, and I was just fit to burst, I surely was. So finally, in desperation, I calls out, "Oh, for the love of God, won't one of you get up off your Quaker arses and give us a holy word from the Almighty! Or are we all going to sit here like stuffed peppers for the next half an hour without any word at all from heaven?"' At this point, Peter, who was carefully cutting the jam sponge, gave way to the laughter he had been trying to suppress.

91

'I'm so sorry, Peter, love, but I just couldn't contain it any longer.' Peter carried on handing out the cake and just shook his head and smiled. Douglas also joined in the laughter as all too clearly imagined the scene.

'God forgive me, I didn't mean to be quite so blunt' said Kath as she pulled her slice of cake towards her. 'But it did the trick though, Doug. It was like uncorking the bottle, it surely was. From then on wee words from God were flying out like greyhounds from their traps. It was a grand meeting. I thoroughly enjoyed myself, I surely did.'

'Aye, Kathleen. It was a grand meeting, that it was. It was certainly different,' said Peter and for a few moments placed his hand over hers.

'And Douglas, love, do you know what?' continued Kath after taking a large bite from her sponge cake. 'One elderly gent staggered to his feet and he quoted the most beautiful Scripture, sure he did, about God sorting out the high and mighty, and raising up the bruised reed, or some such...'

'I think it was a couple of scriptures...'

'Oh, I'm not fussed how many it was, Peter, love. But the thing is this,' and she turned and gripped Douglas' hand tight. 'He went on to say words to the effect, "God knows every bruise that our poor bodies and souls have suffered in this world, and he is reaching out right now." And then, Doug, he went on to say, and I remember this bit word for word, I surely do: "And I see His hand, wounded by the nail, reaching down and touching every sorry cut and bruise in this room."' Kath was now filling up and looked to Peter for reassurance, which he gave through a nod of his head. She looked back at Douglas and said, 'And Douglas, do you know, and honest to God I'm not making this up, but I saw that hand too. I saw it as clear as I'm seeing your hand now. And I saw it reach right down...' She struggled for words for a few moments and then pointed to her heart and squeezed out the word, 'Here.'

She then grasped her mug of coffee and drank most of its contents, screwed up her face, and said 'Dear God, what is this that you have been feeding us with, Peter? Tastes nothing like coffee to me, sure it doesn't. Where did you manage to find this stuff?' Peter said nothing but gave a knowing look to Douglas. 'Anyhow,' said Kath, patting Douglas on the arm, 'I've been telling my story, which you probably had no wish to hear. But what about you, Douglas. How was your Christmas?'

Douglas sipped his coffee, which to him tasted excellent, and paused for a few moments. He did not want to rush away from her story. But he could see she wanted to move away from the powerful emotion of it, so he said, 'To be honest, it wasn't good, Kath.' He had grown to trust Kath a lot and, even though he didn't know Peter at all, he instinctively felt he could trust him.

'I'm sorry, love,' said Kath, stuffing her tissue back into her sleeve. 'I've told Peter just a wee bit about your troubles.'

'Well, to be honest, Kath, since that... episode, shall we say, by the sea, I've actually been much stronger, and I even have my days when I think life's worth living again.' He looked at Peter and said, 'I'm off work at the moment, Peter. Sort of sick leave until... well, for a while.' Douglas remembered the morning's conversation with the bishop and, for the first time that day, realised that his future was now very uncertain. But he did not want to discuss that with Kath and Peter just now. 'Sorry, where was I?'

'You went home for the holiday, son,' said Kath, with her mouth full of the final portion of her cake.

93

'Ah yes. Well, I say "home", but where is home? I only briefly looked in at the Vicarage and had a cup of tea with Mavis and Alice. You met them when they came over in November, Kath.'

'Aye, that I did,' said Kath. 'Both lovely ladies they were.'

'Anyway,' continued Douglas, 'I didn't stay in Sheffield long as I didn't want to get involved in any church stuff, so I went to my parents who live near Oxford. I've had a tricky relationship with them really. Dad's an alcoholic, though he seems to be dry just at the moment. Mum, well, Mum's a bag of nerves really and nearly always manages to annoy me. She's a good person, but we are just so different.'

'Well, you can't choose your parents, Doug, that's for sure,' chimed in Kath. 'Just ask Kevin, poor sod!'

'If I got on with my Mum like Kevin gets on with you, Kath, I'd be a very happy man,' said Douglas smiling warmly at Kath. 'The problem is, frankly neither my Mum nor Dad managed Saoirse's death at all well. Dad hit the bottle big time, and Mum became a bag of nerves and always managed to say the wrong thing. And sure enough, this Christmas, at least seven times - I was counting - she asked if I had met anyone yet.' Douglas sighed. 'I'm not ready, Kath. I'm really not. I wish I was closer to her, but to be honest, I've told *you* far more about myself than I've ever told her.'

All the while Peter was listening intently to Douglas, so much so that Kath tapped him on the hand and said, 'Drink up your coffee Peter, darling. It's getting cold.' She was right, Peter had quite forgotten he was drinking coffee, and he immediately drained most of the mug. He attempted to say something, but nothing coherent came out, and all he was able to say was, 'I'm so sorry, Douglas. What a hard

94

road...' He took off his silver-rimmed spectacles and wiped them on a silk hanky he kept in his shirt pocket. As he did so, Douglas noticed moisture around his eyes.

'Don't fret yourself, Doug,' said Kath. 'Poor old Peter has become a terrible softy, that he has. He's been in the counselling trade for God knows how long now. You'd think he'd have become hardened to people's sufferings, wouldn't you? But no, quite the opposite.'

'Thanks, Kath...' said Peter, replacing his glasses. 'It's not just your very sad bereavement, Douglas that distresses me, but it is your parents. Does it really cost that much to listen to your child?'

'Oh, for God's sake!' exclaimed Kath, cutting across Peter. 'I'll be forgetting my own foolish name next!'

'What is it, Kath?' asked Peter, looking concerned.

'The mention of parents, of course. I've been meaning to tell you, Douglas. Now, I don't think you are going to like this, but I must tell you nonetheless. Saoirse's parents are likely coming to town next week. I don't suppose you've heard yet, have you?'

Douglas felt a stab of anxiety as he heard this report. 'No, why would they be coming here?'

'It's just over a year since Ruby Kennedy's funeral and there's going to be a memorial mass for the girl. The family have chosen next Thursday as that would have been her 70th birthday. I'm not into this kind of thing, Doug, but apparently they felt that her funeral got a bit lost behind Christmas last year, or something like that.'

'Oh my,' said Douglas. Kath was saying something, but Douglas' mind folded in on itself and he felt a surge of unwelcome fear. The two people who personally blamed him for their daughter's death were coming to Dingle. He did not feel ready to meet them at all, and certainly, they would not want to see him here.

He felt he needed some air, so he stood up and said, 'Thanks, Kath, for letting me know that. I.. er.. yes, thank you. And thanks for the coffee. And great to meet you, Peter. Forgive me.' He looked at his watch and said 'I'm sorry, but I need to be somewhere else.'

'That's fine, son,' said Kath. She reached out and grasped his hand and said, 'Don't you be worrying about them coming. We'll be here to help. We'll think of a plan, we surely will.' Kath was frowning as she watched Douglas speed out of the café.

'What is it, Kath?' asked Peter. 'Who's Ruby? And why such a reaction?' A great deal in Kath's world was a mystery to Peter. A delightful mystery, though he did not like to see such concern on her face.

'Douglas was married to Saoirse, and her parents live in Cork,' Kath explained. 'I've never met them, but Ruby, the one who died last Christmas, was Saoirse's aunt. Ruby was a quiet lass, and I knew she had lost a niece, but only recently did I twig that the niece was Douglas' wife, Saoirse, God rest her. I went to Ruby's funeral and I remember seeing a hard-looking man sat at the front of the church. Oh, he looked as cold as a witch's…' She looked at Peter and checked herself. 'Well, he looked a very cold man. Anyhow, I was chatting to Kerry in the fish and chip shop a couple of days back…'

'What was that about your new diet, Kath?' enquired Peter with his eyebrow raised.

'Oh, for God's sake, Peter, I need my days off. Now, where was I?'

'Something about witches and fish shops,' replied Peter.

Kath reignited her vape and continued, 'So I was. Well, Kerry knew the family a bit and I asked him about them, and he told me that the man I'd seen at the front of the church at the funeral was called Niall Flynn - that would be Saoirse's da. Married to Orla, who was Ruby's younger sister. Kerry said Orla was a perfectly nice, if very shy, lady. But, Niall, so he says, is a nasty piece of work. I also spoke to my Kevin about this Niall. He knows of him and is pretty certain he has links with the Real IRA.' She exhaled her vape which enfolded Peter in a purple mist. She tried to disperse the mist with an extravagant wave of her hand.

'And, what's more, Kerry told me this,' she continued, leaning towards Peter. 'At the graveside, just as they were piling the earth upon poor Ruby, Niall let rip at Father Pat. Can you believe it?'

'At that kindly priest I met yesterday?' asked Peter.

'Aye, that's the man. And yes, I'll admit, Peter he's both priest and kindly.' They both smiled for a moment before Kath continued, lowering her voice. 'Well, poor old Father Pat just happened to mention Saoirse to Niall, so said Kerry, who was standing right next to them at the time. 'And do you know what your man, Niall says to him?'

'Go on.'

'He looked at Father Pat with such a stone-cold stare and told him in no uncertain terms that his daughter was dead and in hell because she had committed the great sin of marrying a Protestant. He was effing and blinding enough to shame even me. And, what's more, he went on about the judgement of God and all that garbage. God save us! Kerry said it was awful, and Father Pat was right upset, poor love. I mean, at the graveside and all. You'd think the man would have some respect, wouldn't you? Kerry said

Orla pulled Niall away from that graveside leaving Pat and the other mourners in a terrible state. Well, I imagine they were.' She took another deep inhalation and added, 'Sounds familiar in a way Peter, love, doesn't it? All that judgement stuff. We've been there.'

Once again moisture had gathered in Peter's reddened eyes. He shook his head for a while and then looked up and said, 'Oh Kath, poor Douglas. Did he know that's what Niall believed - that horrible judgement stuff about Saoirse?'

'I don't know, Peter. I hope to God not. But I have a worrying feeling that he does.' She grasped Peter's hand firmly and said, 'We need to take care of that lad next week, Peter. It won't be easy for him. It truly won't.'

CHAPTER 9

The following morning Douglas decided to check his emails and he was pleased to see one from Mavis. As always when he got an email from her, he could see in his mind's eye her bent figure leaning over her laptop, her forefingers working away, her face pressed near to the monitor, her eyes straining to peer through the thick and unclean lenses of her spectacles, and he could hear her regular rebukes of herself for the many typing mistakes.

Hello there Douglas. It's me again, your old friend Mavis. Just checking you got back to Ireland all right and the weather's not too bad with you. We've had a bit of snow here but we're keeping warm, I'm pleased to say. It was so good to see you just after Christmas and you are looking better by the day. That Irish sea air is doing you a power of good.
I'm glad you felt I was keeping your house in good shape.
I thought you should know that Brian came round to chat with me. He says Gerald has been going on at him about the house. He thinks the Diocese should be letting it and is worried it will be getting damp and that, but I told him I'm keeping the heating on and everything's fine. Brian didn't seem too fussed, but you know what Gerald is like. Always with an eye for the money. He and his good lady seem to be well settled in that big house up the hill - massive place it is. Even got a swimming pool would you believe. I bumped into Mrs. Bentley yesterday. I think she'd had one or two sherries if you ask me. Sorry, I rattle on, even in my emails.

99

Will you be back at the end of this month? People in the church are asking and they always seem to think I will know the answer. So I don't want to bother you, Douglas, but if you do know anything it would be handy if you could let me know so I can stop their pestering. Personally, I'm not sure you are ready to come back yet. Perhaps the bishop will give you another few months' leave?

Me and Alice are getting on so well. I love having her in the house. She's off to the hospital today to get her eyes checked again. She has all but lost sight in one eye now, poor thing. She's had this trouble most of her life and she's so patient with it, but I do feel sorry for her. But it's wonderful how she manages on the busses and that. She's still lonely, poor soul, and so sore from that terrible marriage. She didn't deserve all that.

Both of us have fallen in love with Ireland since our visit to you. One day we'll both come and visit you again, if we may. It was wonderful to be in that pretty town and to enjoy the sea breeze. And I did like your friends there.

Well, this has taken me most of the morning to write and I need to get a little bit of lunch on the table. Isn't the national news terrible by the way? Too much violence in this world. I know, I can hear you saying that I need to pray more, so I will!

Take care, Douglas
much love
Mavis
xx

Douglas always enjoyed hearing from Mavis, and he liked the idea of her and Alice coming out for a visit again. It had worked so well in November when they came out. He had a suspicion that Mavis was trying to get him and

Alice together, but thankfully she was far subtler than his mother in the whole area of match-making. He still felt nowhere near ready to consider another relationship, but nonetheless, he had to admit that there was something very lovely in Alice. And he agreed with Mavis, that there was something inspirational about the way she managed both her broken marriage and her sight problems.

He was just about to leave his laptop when his FaceTime registered an incoming call. It was from his Californian friend, Frank, the priest who at one time had served in the next-door parish and had been such a strength to Douglas at the time of Saoirse's death. Douglas was more than happy to answer the call. A large black smiling face appeared on the screen. 'Hi, there!' it called, 'You wearing a leprechaun outfit? Looks like it!'

'Franklin, my friend. How's it going?' laughed Douglas.

'Just fine, Father Romer, just fine,' said Frank teasingly. 'Thought I hadn't parleyed with my English buddy for a while and it was long overdue. You got a few minutes?'

'I sure have,' responded Douglas.

'Oh, you speaking Californian now? I thought you were learning Irish!' He laughed his ebullient laugh again, rocking back from the screen. Even in his bleakest times, Douglas found the laughter from this joyful face was always infectious. 'You still in Ireland, aren't you?' he asked after he had gathered himself.

'Yes, still here, Frank. When you coming?'

Frank roared with laughter again, 'Booked on the plane tonight, buddy.'

'What?'

A huge laugh again, 'Only joking. Just wanted to see the shock on your face!'

Both men laughed. 'It would be great to see you here, Frank. Seriously you'd love it so much here. But I know you can't leave Daisy at the moment.'

'Well, Doug, that's one of the things I's going to tell you about, as it happens.'

Douglas pulled himself up to the screen and listened closely. He had felt such concern for this couple since Daisy got her diagnosis in the summer. 'As you know, Doug, the prognosis was poor. In fact, it got worse and worse during the fall. So, we got chatting together and we just said, "We don't like this cancer and we want rid of it." I mean, it just felt like a brutal enemy and we wanted to fight it.'

'Well, you've certainly tried lots of different therapies, Frank.'

'Of course, we have, but curiously enough, Doug, we didn't really get down to serious prayer about it. I mean, to be honest, we are so ticked off by the tele-evangelist stuff and the screwy promises of the God channels, we just stayed well clear of the whole darn business. But then I got to thinking that this Jesus I'm supposed to be serving, didn't do a bad job of healing in his time, did he, Doug?'

'No..', said Douglas, feeling he was moving on to rather more shaky ground. He still had not resolved the dilemma of God not saving his Saoirse. And the whole painful problem of God miraculously curing some people and apparently ignoring the plight of others was one Douglas was nowhere near resolving.

'Well...' continued Frank, 'there is this big high Anglican church just up the coast. Full of smells and bells. You'd love it, Doug!' He grinned, remembering how he used to tease Douglas about his low-church ways. Douglas smiled at the happy memory of their mutual bantering.

'Well, they don't just do the smells and the bells, they also do the healing. So Daisy and I decide to go and give the place a try. You can't lose anything, can you? I mean if they start getting all manipulative, I'd just pull back my shoulders and do my quarterback threatening stance - you know, the one I used at Synod a couple of times!' Douglas laughed. He loved Frank's humour. How he missed him after he returned to the States.

'So, we drove off to this church,' continued Frank, 'and we spent the weekend there because they had this conference happening with some big speaker guy from Oregon. We both thought he was pretty goofy, to be perfectly honest. Must have been to the same school of preaching as you, Doug!' More laughter.

'But when it came to the prayer time, we both went forward. And there was my lovely Daisy all coy and nervous, waiting her turn for prayer. And this pretty young girl comes up to her and asks to pray for her. Well, Daisy nods her head and the girl reaches up - she's quite a bit shorter than my Daisy - and puts her hand on Daisy's shoulder, and all the while I'm thinking, "Why couldn't they send over one of the experienced dudes? Or Mister Big Speaker himself? We want the top guys over here. My Daisy's terminal and we need the best team." So, I was just standing behind her, grumbling to myself, when all of a sudden, my Daisy's flat out on the floor. Well, can you believe it, Doug?'

'Did she faint or something?' asked Douglas.

'That's what I thought at first. But "Resting in the Holy Spirit" they call it, Doug. "Resting in the Spirit". Nice term isn't it? You kinda go down but not out, if you get my meaning.' Douglas didn't, but he let Frank continue. 'Well,

103

the girl knelt beside her and my, she started telling that cancer what she thought of it. She sure let rip! I can tell you, it was something to behold. I'm pretty sure she threw in the odd swear word too, Doug! I mean, I thought that in itself would put an end to all heaven's support there and then! But she just kept at it, binding this and loosing that. She was like a boxer in the ring and she gave that cancer every blow she could think of. If I had been that cancer, I'd have been knocked out by the third round. I have never seen anything like it, Doug! And incense and chanting going on all around us too. It was a riot. And one of those high church priests had hit the deck as well. He took some finding under that pile of gorgeous red chasuble!' He rocked back in his chair laughing again.

Douglas was finding it almost impossible to imagine the scene, but, feeling both intrigued and disturbed, said, 'Go on, Frank. What happened then?'

Frank moved closer to the screen and spoke in a quieter voice. 'The girl stopped her hollering as quickly as she started, and then she started to sing in tongues over my Daisy. You know what I mean by "tongues", Doug?' Douglas nodded with some uncertainty. He was always rather suspicious of anything too charismatic. 'Well, do you know what, Doug? It was the sweetest song I have ever heard in my entire life. I can't tell you...'

Frank brushed away the tears that were now forming in his eyes and threatening to run down his ample cheeks. 'I can't explain this to you, Doug, but I couldn't stay standing at the sound of that song. It wasn't a song from this world, Doug. It was truly awesome. I felt I was on holy ground. You know what I mean? I just slumped to my knees. And do you know what? I started to sing with her. Well, you know what my voice is like, Doug. It's enough to bring a sudden end to any glory meeting. But this time,

I started singing *in tune*. Only God knows how that happened, Doug. But I was singing in tongues - yes me of all people! I'm against that kind of thing. But I was doing it. And I was singing in harmony with this young girl. We were singing a song of paradise over my Daisy, and she just lay there like Sleeping Beauty. In fact, she looked so peaceful that I thought she had died. She looked like she was resting with the angels in heaven. But as our singing came to an end, she opened her sweet eyes and she looked at both of us and said, "I'm back". And then she said, "I've seen Him." And it was pretty clear to me that she had, Doug. You should have seen the look on her pretty face. And she said more. She said, "When I saw Him, I begged to go with Him, but He's sending me back. It's not my time." Then she looks at me, Doug...' Frank's animated face distorted into a grimace as the emotion got the better of him for a while. He then recovered himself and continued in a husky voice, 'Sorry, Douglas... So, she looks at me and says, "Honey, you got me around for quite a while longer."

Douglas was completely taken aback by this story. Frank had been such a good friend and colleague and both of them had always been wary of any kind of service like this and stood together in their opposition to all forms of ecclesiastical manipulation. All this was so unlike Frank, and Douglas felt somehow betrayed. Yet, there was no doubting the genuineness of the experience.

Frank continued, 'I know what you are thinking, Doug, but let me just tell you the rest. We drove home in - well, in a state of bliss to be honest. We knew she had been healed of her cancer. Of course, she went straight to the medics and asked for the tests, and neither of us was surprised when they said there was no sign whatsoever of the cancer. They said they would stop the chemo. They have cancelled the operation and she is going to go in for

105

three-monthly checks. Doug, I really don't know what to make of it all, but I can assure you we are living every day in thankfulness to God. Even if she is only in remission for a short time, it is still extra time together and it is a wonderful gift. But you know, there are plenty of folks out there who are far more deserving of the healing, and they have not had it. And there is you, my friend, over there in Ireland, and look what you've gone through. I don't know that I'll ever make sense of it, Doug.' The bright smile had been replaced by an expression of deep concern. 'None of this is fair, Doug,' he said shaking his head. 'But when you receive such grace, you just have to take hold of it.'

'Of course, you do, Frank,' said Douglas, keen to reassure his friend. 'And quite honestly, if I was God, I'd be rushing to cure Daisy. She's such a wonderful woman.'

'That she is, Doug. That she certainly is. You know, she can't tell me what she saw in those moments she was on the floor. Every time she tries to tell me, she just fills up and can't get a word of sense out. So I just told her to leave it alone as it's clearly not for sharing, but for living.'

'Good advice as always, Frank'

'And Doug, she heard my singing and she was very impressed!' The laughter came again and then stopped abruptly as he continued. 'Now, Douglas my friend, there's one more thing, and I've got to be going in a minute, cos I can hear Daisy calling up the stairs. So let me keep this brief.'

'You- brief, Frank?' More laughter.

'You know me well, dude! Listen, Daisy and I have been talking. You know that we came into this whole heap of dough from her family, and it's way more than we are ever going to need. We wanted to do something to thank God for his blessing. So - and don't you go arguing with me about this, Douglas - we want to send you enough money so you can live for a year without worrying about income. We were praying, Daisy and me, and Daisy had a strong sense that you were not ready to return to work yet. In fact, she senses it may be time for you to be leaving that parish in Sheffield. So, she said, we must give you enough for a year, to give you time for more mending and some space to think about what you do next. And if I were you, Doug, I would stay put there in Dingle, because it sounds a great place. And you never know, we really might come over and visit you. I'm sure we have ancestors there!'

Douglas laughed, but he also felt stunned by this offer. Everything in him wanted to refuse such generosity - how could anyone want to lavish such a gift on him? But he also could see that Frank and Daisy were determined. So he said, 'Frank, I honestly don't know what to say. I'm overwhelmed. The timing... It just couldn't be better. Only yesterday, Frank, I spoke to Bishop Pauline...'

'Uh, oh,' said Frank smiling broadly. 'Which Pauline did you get?'

'Not the best one, Frank.'

'Ok. She wants you out?'

'How did you know?'

'She doesn't like messiness, Doug. I remember that clearly. She'll want your church sorted soon. Is she giving you a pay-off?'

'No, I've resigned.'

'Far better that way, Doug,' said Frank nodding. 'You got no obligations. Well, there you are, Daisy was right. So, old friend, if you could let me have your bank details we'll send the dosh over. Hey, I'll be like that wealthy fella in your congregation - you know, the annoying guy who likes to have his finger in every darn pie. What was his name?'

'Gerald?'

'Gerald! That's it. Is he still Chair of the Board of Finance?'

'Yes, he is and you are not in the least bit like him, Frank!'

Frank laughed. 'Glad you said that, Doug. Don't know why I mentioned him really. Sorry to lower the tone. Now look, I have to dash, dude, so you take care now. Daisy sends lots of love, as do the kids. Don't forget to send me the bank details...' He looked over his shoulder and called, 'Yes, honey I'm just coming now. Hey, why don't you come and say "hi" to Doug?' He paused and then said, 'Douglas, she's just coming...'

Frank moved his large frame from his seat, and his face was soon replaced by Daisy's. She was still without her hair from the recent chemotherapy, but her face was beaming. 'Oh, Douglas, honey. How good it is to see you. How are you doing, darling?'

'How good to see you, Daisy. Frank has told me all about your story.'

'We are truly, truly grateful, Douglas. But what about you?' she asked, betraying her usual generous heart of always considering others before herself. Douglas filled her in on the headlines of his news and thanked her profusely for the gift. But it was clear that these American friends needed to be on their way to collect their teenage boys from somewhere, so they brought their conversation to a close. Daisy's brief appearance was enough to convince Douglas that she had indeed experienced an encounter with something wonderful and beautiful.

'I'll hand you back to Frank, sweetheart,' she said as she got up, and Douglas heard her saying, 'And Franklin, we need to be leaving *now.*'

Frank appeared briefly and said, 'She may have been to heaven and back, but she's still giving out the orders, Doug! Take care, now, my friend.'

'Take care, Frank. And thanks...'

The line went dead and Douglas was left sitting in his room stunned by both bits of news. A gift was coming his way, out of the blue, so there was no need to rush out and try and find a new job. Douglas felt a great sense of relief. And of gratitude to these wonderful friends. And Daisy? What was this miraculous healing business in a church of shouting healers and felled priests? He was so thrilled for her. He had assumed that both he and Frank were going to find themselves widowers together. And yet some great power beyond the world of medical science and skills had restored her to health. He shook his head. How could he make sense of that? This was all good news, but it also raised some difficult questions. 'This calls some time with Dorchadas' he said, and he leaned back in his creaking chair, so grateful that his angel friend had been given more time in the little town of Dingle in this winter season.

CHAPTER 10

Dorchadas was lodging at the Presbytery, so during the afternoon, Douglas walked down to the church in the pale January light. He arrived at the large, grey building and rang the doorbell which, as far as Douglas could tell, made no sound at all. However, in a few moments, the tall and burly figure of Father Pat came to the door. 'Good afternoon, Douglas,' he said in his usual welcoming manner. 'How good to see you. Won't you come in?'

Douglas had increasingly warmed to this kindly priest, whose church he had taken to visiting more regularly. Douglas judged him to be in his mid-sixties, but he still supported a thick crop of youthful-looking dark, curly hair. He wore heavy, black-framed glasses, behind which shone two bottle-green eyes. He had a deep, resonant voice. Douglas had often imagined that he would have made a great Shakespearian actor.

'Well, I've actually come to see Dorchadas,' said Douglas. 'I believe he is staying here.'

'You're not wrong there, Douglas. Dorchadas is indeed back in Dingle and he's here in the Presbytery in his usual room. But I'm sorry to say, he's out just at the minute and not likely to be back before dark. However, he did say if you were to call, he would very much welcome an evening meal with you.'

'Oh, that would be great. I can't contact the man as he doesn't carry a mobile. Did he say which restaurant?'

'Well, as you know, not so many are open at this time of year, but he suggested the one on the seafront with the excellent fish pie. I should know its name, but it has slipped my ageing mind. But Dorchadas said you have been there before and you'd know the one.'

'Ye...es,' said Douglas cautiously. 'We did have a rather... well... unsuccessful meal there in the autumn.'

'Ah, that would it explain it. Dorchadas did say something about there being a need for the healing of the memories.'

'Well, that would certainly be good,' said Douglas, who was just about to turn to leave when Father Pat said, 'Douglas if you have a few minutes, could I have a word with you about the memorial mass that's happening next week for Ruby Kennedy?'

'Yes, sure,' said Douglas, though unsure quite how he could be of help. Father Pat ushered him into the Presbytery, which felt distinctly cool and damp, and smelt of tobacco. Although the priest did have a housekeeper, there was little evidence of her work in the study. Scattered all over the priest's study were books, papers, half-drunk mugs of coffee, and un-emptied ashtrays. The priest had to work hard to clear a chair for Douglas and then seated himself at his desk on a very ancient and distinctly unsteady rotating chair, whose leather handles had worn off long ago. An outdated, electric bar fire threw some welcome warmth into the room.

'Please forgive the ashtrays,' said Father Pat. 'I'm trying to give the wretched things up. But you know what it's like. Now, let me see...' He was searching through what Douglas assumed to be the most recent avalanche of paperwork on his desk. 'Ah yes, here we are,' said the priest, drawing a sheet of paper carefully from the pile. 'These are the notes I took from the family about what they want from the service.' He lifted his glasses on to his forehead and then pulled the sheet up close to his face for a few moments, before returning it to the desk. 'I presume you know the family well, Douglas? Ruby's sister, Orla is handling the arrangements. I believe Niall and Orla Flynn are your parents-in-law?'

Pat threw a smile at Douglas as he asked the question but immediately replaced it with a look of concern as Douglas replied. 'I can't claim to know them well, Father,' said Douglas, frowning and looking firmly at the priest's desk.

'Oh, Douglas, you know me well enough now. Do call me Pat - the whole town does, for goodness sake.' He briefly furrowed his brow which served to lower his glasses from his forehead to his nose. They fell neatly to their correct location.

'Thanks... Pat,' said Douglas, shifting his position in the chair to avoid a particularly uncomfortable and threatening rogue spring. 'But yes, you are right. I was married to Saoirse, their daughter...'

'God rest her soul,' interrupted Pat and something about the way he said it endeared Douglas to him. He seemed to sincerely mean it.

'Thank you. Well, as you may know,' Douglas continued, drawing in a deep breath, 'Saoirse did not get on well with her parents. To be honest, she came to England to escape from them, and, if the truth be told, to escape some of their values and religious and political convictions.' Douglas felt he could be honest with this priest.

'Ah...' said Pat, knowingly. 'I did see something of those convictions at Ruby's funeral.' He was reluctant to share any of that terrible graveside scene with Douglas.

'They did come to our wedding, but hardly spoke to me, and that was the only time I saw them,' said Douglas.

'Quite, quite...' said Pat.

'I think they blamed me for her death.'

'How could they possibly do that?' asked Pat, leaning forward and frowning.

'She shouldn't have married an English Protestant. In their view, it was an offence to the Almighty. As Niall saw it, I was the one who seduced her; I was the one responsible for her corruption; she gave in and was therefore punished by God.'

'That is a terrible religion, terrible… But I'm sorry to say, not unknown.' Pat's dark eyebrows twitched for a moment and then he leaned forward, causing his ancient chair to creak alarmingly. 'I sometimes wonder why we bother with religion, Douglas. You're a priest as well, I believe, and I don't know about you, but I have my days of thinking that the way we do our religion has been more of a curse to this dear world than a blessing, I honestly do.' Douglas was amazed to see the priest remove his heavy glasses and wipe his eyes with his handkerchief. 'But there we are,' he continued as he sat upright, 'we can't do too much about it, and in the end, all we can do is be obedient. I'm a great believer in the power of love, Douglas and love always comes in humble packages. Love is not tribal. It doesn't take sides.' He looked out of the window for a few moments at the grey stone church across from the presbytery. 'I don't like institutions, because that's where these terrible beliefs are devised. Religious institutions are probably the worst. They have caused such grief in our world, don't you think? We are the people of the cross, are we not? It's that which gives us all hope, doesn't it?'

Douglas was a little taken aback, firstly by the display of emotion at the failures of the church, and secondly by this sudden philosophical exploration, and all he could say was a rather limp, 'Yes, indeed.'

Pat looked hard at him for a few moments and then continued, 'Well, anyway, we have this service for Ruby to sort out, and, oh my, Ruby was such a darling. You would have loved her, Douglas. A quiet, sweet-natured lady. Well-loved in the town. Never married, though did have a lady friend at one time, so I believe. But she had none of the prejudices of Orla and Niall. She was taken by the cancer sadly. For some reason, she did not want people knowing - didn't want them fussing over her, I suppose. She was already a bit fond of the bottle, so she decided to make out she had become a heavy drinker. So you'll find most folks here think it was the bottle that killed her.' He paused for a moment and looked out of the window as a seagull started to squawk from a nearby rooftop.

'Now the thing is, Douglas,' he said, grasping his notes again and placing his glasses to his forehead, 'you, Orla and Niall are the only relatives, believe it or not. Unusual for an Irish family, don't you think?' He chuckled, and the glasses fell heavily back to the nose. Douglas didn't smile as he felt decidedly awkward at being regarded as one of the family. He wanted no prominence at all at this event, so that when Pat said, 'Would you do a reading?' he very quickly declined.

'Ah. I understand,' said Pat, and Douglas sensed he genuinely did. 'To be honest, I thought that's what you would say, but I wanted to ask because I know how much Ruby would have loved you and, had she known you, she almost certainly would have wanted you to say something at the service.'

'Thank you so much for asking, Pat,' said Douglas.

'I don't know why they are having this service, to be honest with you,' said the priest putting down the papers and pulling the glasses off his nose for a moment. 'Ruby wouldn't have wanted the fuss. But it's Orla and Niall who pressed for it. I'm wondering if it's Ruby they're grieving for, or whether this grief is really about Saoirse?' He put his glasses back and looked at Douglas enquiringly.

'I think that without a doubt they would not have approved of the Protestant service we gave Saoirse in England,' said Douglas with half-raised eyebrows. 'There was no mass and no reference to Mary, the saints or the faithful departed, and no prayers regarding purgatory…'

'And that's what would have upset them, Douglas. I'm sorry to say they'll be convinced that the soul of their daughter is in the fires of purgatory and if only she had had a proper Catholic mass, she would be in Paradise. Don't get me wrong, Douglas, I will have nothing to do with that superstition, but it is strong in them.'

'What a terrible thought…' said Douglas, who was seized for a moment with anxiety at the thought of his beloved Saoirse being tormented by flames and demons. But then he remembered Mary in the garden and also Ben at the school, and he let out a sigh of relief. 'It's alright, he said, not specifically to Pat, but more to himself, 'I've been told that she is in a state of "sparkling peace".'

'A state of what?' asked the priest, leaning forward in his creaking chair.

'Sparkling peace,' said Douglas, who was now looking out of the window.

'My, my, what a beautiful thing, Douglas,' said Pat. 'Do you mind my asking who it was who told you that?'

Douglas did not have the energy to tell Father Pat the stories and experiences that had been so significant for him, even though he felt Pat would have been a sympathetic listener. So, he simply said, 'I would like to tell you one day, Pat. But I'll just need to be a bit stronger. But be assured, that those who told me are very reliable.'

'That's good to hear, Douglas. Good to hear.' Pat beamed his generous smile. 'Well now, Douglas, I'll try and do my best for the service. Ruby was a popular lady, so I expect there'll be quite a few there. I gather there's a do in the hotel afterwards. This means, Douglas, you'll almost certainly find yourself having to talk to Saoirse's parents. Will you be all right with that?'

'I guess I will have to be,' said Douglas. 'I'm not sure what we'll have to say to each other, but if Niall looks like he's coming over to thump the living daylights out of me, perhaps you could arrange for a group of blokes to rescue me!' Douglas laughed, not altogether convincingly.

'That I will, Douglas! That I will,' said Pat.

They got up and, dodging the various piles of papers and books, they made their way to the front door. Douglas paused as he was about to leave and said, 'Father Pat, I hope you don't mind me coming to Mass. I don't feel quite ready to go to an Anglican church just yet, and my friends here in Dingle come to your church.'

'You are most welcome, Douglas. And may I say "off the record", that if you should come forward for Communion and you happen to have your hands open at the altar rail, I must warn you, I take my spectacles off for the distribution and without them, my eyesight is none too good, so it may just be that I drop a wafer into your Protestant hand by mistake.' He winked, 'I do hope you don't mind.' And then added, 'I know He doesn't mind,' pointing up to the sky.

*

'So, back to the fish pie!' said Dorchadas, probing the steaming pot in front of him with his fork.

'Yes,' said Douglas, pausing a little, with his hands resting on his cutlery. Looking hard at the dish in front of him he continued, 'I surprised myself by ordering it if I'm honest, but the hideous events of my last meal here haven't put me off it, oddly enough.' He looked up at Dorchadas, smiling. 'I have been avoiding this place. I thought they might not allow me back in! However, I'm determined to behave myself this evening. I will have just the one pint of Guinness and I have every intention of keeping this pie in my stomach, not distributing it liberally around the streets of Dingle, as I did last time.'

Dorchadas laughed. 'I was none too clever that night either. What a lot has happened since then, Doug, eh?'

'Yes, a lot of healing for me, Dorch,' said Douglas blowing on a forkful of fish to cool it.

'And for me,' said Dorchadas with his mouth full. He chewed thoughtfully, took a sip of the Guinness, and then leaned back and said, 'Douglas, I am glad you were with me.'

'With you - where, Dorch?' asked Douglas.

'In that garden.'

'I wasn't much use to you, Dorch.'

'Och, you were, Douglas. I can assure you, you were. Funny, isn't it? You humans imagine it's one-way traffic - you humans needing us angels. But, you know, there are times when we need you. We need to be close to your flesh and blood humanity. We love to hear the beat of your heart. We need to feel your beautiful trust in the One you cannot see. There are times when I've seen one angel running up to another telling them of something one of you has done in this world of yours. An act of great love or

117

great faith. That always touches us.' He paused for a while and then added, 'And there are some times when we need humans because we are the ones feeling burdened. We're not all as strong as you think. It's not the survival of the fittest in the Kingdom, you know. I needed you in that garden, Doug. I knew you were there when I was soaking that grass with my tears. And I drew great strength from you, I surely did.'

Douglas found it hard to fathom how he, in his broken state, could possibly have been of help to Dorchadas. But before he could protest, Dorchadas continued, 'The main thing, Douglas, is that I was given another chance.' He played around with the pie for a while and then looked at Douglas and said, 'Even us angels don't understand everything, you know. That Garden - him all busted and broken there, literally sweating blood through the agony of it all. It's not what we were expecting. I did not expect to see Him so... so weak and powerless. I assumed the only way to conquer the dark forces that were gathering around him, was by power and might and legions of the mighty warrior angels, and a cracking great war to end all wars. I had a clear vision of it all in my mind, Doug.' He sipped his Guinness slowly and then looked to the ceiling for a few moments. 'I think most of us angels did, to be fair. A grand show-down.' He looked back at Douglas. 'We do rather like that kind of thing, you know. We love a bit of theatre. And we can be pretty impressive when we come as a gang. You should see us, Doug.' He smiled his endearing smile and carried on eating for a while, then added, 'Startled them shepherds on the hillside at his birth, they did.'

They both chuckled, and then Douglas paused his eating for a few moments and said, 'I am so pleased, Dorch. I'm so pleased you were given another chance.'

Dorchadas looked across to his friend and replied, 'Aye, son. Aye.'

Both men were silent for a time as they ate their meal. Then Douglas looked up and said, 'I had a phone call today from a good friend.'

'Oh aye, Doug? Go on, son. Who was this friend?'

Douglas told him all about his phone call with Frank and the story of Daisy's healing and the gift of a year's salary. Dorchadas listened so hard that Douglas had to keep reminding him to eat his food. He was determined that they should both finish their meal this time. Eventually, both story and meal were finished. Dorchadas sat back and drained the last of his Guinness which prompted an involuntary and loud burp.

'Oh, I do apologise,' he said as both men giggled like schoolboys. 'I'm still not used to these bodies and I've been in one long enough, Doug, I surely have!' He then became more serious. 'Doug, this is a truly beautiful story you've told me. Frank and Daisy sound wonderful - I want to meet them, I surely do. Tell them to come over and meet old Dorch before he's gone from this world.'

'Gone from this world, Dorch?' said Douglas looking concerned.

Dorchadas looked down at the table for a few moments and said, 'I can't say too much, Doug, but I think the time is not too far off when I will be, what you would call "reinstated". You see, this world is not my true home. To be fair, it's not your true home either. And any one of us may be called home at any time. But you are not to worry about this. You've got this angel eejit around for a fair bit yet.'

Douglas was partially reassured, and put his hand across the table on to Dorchadas' arm and said, 'Please be around just a bit longer Dorch. I don't think I'm ready to lose you yet.'

'No, son. I know. I don't think you are. And my work is not done, and my healing's not done. And besides, you've been given a year's salary and I'd like to get my fair share of Guinnesses out of that! So, don't start planning my farewell ceilidh just yet.'

'I won't, Dorch. I certainly won't,' said Douglas, squeezing his friend's arm.

'But Douglas, listen. We must think about Daisy's healing and the way that young girl prayed for her with all that yelling and screaming. It's very interesting and very telling.'

'Yes, Dorch, I did want to ask you about that. I mean, I'm truly pleased for Daisy and Frank. And, there's no doubting their sincerity. Clearly, something miraculous happened. A power was released into Daisy's body and the cancer was shifted. I'm delighted...'. He paused.

'But?' enquired Dorchadas.

'You are getting to know me well, Dorch,' said Douglas raising an eyebrow.

'But that power doesn't touch every life. Is that it, Doug?'

'Pretty much, Dorch. I know what you will say: "It's a mystery, Douglas, that you humans can't understand"' Douglas mimicked Dorchadas' accent and gestures.

Dorchadas smiled his broad smile, scratched his beard for a moment, then added, 'I'll qualify that a bit, Doug. It is a mystery that is not for understanding. There are some things in this Universe that are not meant to be understood.'

'But to understand - to know a reason - can ease the pain.'

Dorchadas looked down at his empty plate for a while and then, returning to look at his friend said, 'I know, Douglas. I know. But you have choice over what you do with your "not understanding". On the one hand, it can make you slump into despair where you cease believing that anything wonderful will ever happen to you again. On the other hand, it can make you wake up to excitement.'

'Excitement, Dorch?' asked Douglas, frowning.

'Yes, excitement. Because every now and again a shaft of heavenly light makes its way through the clouds of this world. And none of us can turn on that shaft of light. There's no method, no secret formula, no secret knowledge. All you can do is to wait for when it is given. So you never know when them dark clouds will part. It can happen at any moment. Daisy was resigned to managing her life under the dark cloud of the cancer. And by all accounts, she was making a cracking good job of it. But then, all of a sudden... the light!' Dorchadas clapped his hands loudly, much to the surprise of those sitting near him.

Douglas smiled as Dorchadas looked thoughtful for a moment and then said, 'Douglas, I tell you what. Would you be willing to meet a friend of mine tomorrow morning? He's someone who has an interesting angle on this.'

'What kind of meeting, Dorchadas?'

'What kind of meeting do you think, Douglas? said Dorchadas, with one of his bushy eyebrows raised.

'All right,' said Douglas with some hesitation. 'What time and where?'

'11 am in that wee bookshop with the café?'

'I'll be there Dorch,' said Douglas nodding. Then drawing his phone from his pocket he said, 'Now I'm

121

paying the bill. Apparently, I've come into some money today.'

'Well thank you, Doug. And may I say, this fish pie supper was much better than the last one.'

Both chortled for a few moments and were grateful for the considerable healing that each of them had received since their last meal in this place. Douglas pulled up the collar of his coat as he made his way back through a chill wind to St.Raphael's. He felt a mix of curiosity and anxiety about the meeting that was to come the next day. His curiosity was to do with the fact that all the characters from ancient history that he had encountered through these meetings were nothing like he imagined them to be. His anxiety was because the meetings also had a strange ability to both comfort and to disturb.

CHAPTER 11

Douglas woke early and decided to get straight to work on his letter of resignation to the bishop. The anger he had felt towards her the previous day had dissipated somewhat and the offer from Frank had removed all pressure from him. He was sure that his days at St.Philip's had come to an end, so he was comfortable with the decision, even if he did feel very uncomfortable with the process from the bishop's side. Having availed himself of a printer just before Christmas, he got to work on an old-fashioned style letter, putting St.Raphael's address at the top.

Dear Bishop Pauline

I am grateful to you for the time you gave me at our meeting at your house in the autumn, and our meeting yesterday via FaceTime. I am very grateful to you for the three months' leave that has been proving very therapeutic.

You made it clear in our discussion yesterday that you believe my time at St.Philip's has come to an end, and I have also come to the same conviction. I therefore formally offer you my resignation as Vicar of St.Philip's Church. It has been my privilege to serve in this wonderful church and parish these past ten years. I will gladly complete the various forms required if your secretary could send them to me at the address above.

I am planning to return to the UK this weekend where I will make some plans for vacating the Vicarage and putting my things into storage. I appreciate it is short notice, but if there was any time in your diary, I could come and see you on Friday afternoon.

You may be interested to know that yesterday a very generous friend offered to support me financially for the coming year. It is my intention to remain in Ireland for the foreseeable future. This land is proving to be a very renewing home for me.

It is my view that St.Philip's has a strong future, though whoever succeeds me will need to be made of robust material to manage some of the strong characters who, as you know, can be very challenging.

I shall use the coming year to review my vocation. If I do return to parish ministry, my expectation at this stage is that I will seek to work in a different part of the country, where I can make a fresh start.

I wish you well in your leadership of the diocese

yours sincerely

Revd Douglas Romer.

Douglas felt a sense of relief as he completed the letter. He thought long and hard about the reference to "strong characters" in his letter. But he was pretty sure that Gerald was the one pulling the bishop's strings, and he wanted to register acknowledgement of this ungodly power that was having far too much influence over the church, the diocese and, in his reckoning, the bishop. However, all powers notwithstanding, he felt a great sense of freedom at writing this resignation letter, and after breakfast, he printed it off, and within moments the letter was signed, enveloped, and in Douglas' hand on the way to the Post Office.

After posting it, he decided to check his bank balance and was astonished to see there had been a sum of £30,000 paid directly into his account from a bank in Los Angeles. Frank and Daisy had been true to their word and here was the clear evidence of their astonishing gift, shining up from the banking app on his phone. For a few moments he lent against a wall in the street and, weeping quietly, he whispered, 'You are kind, my Lord.' As he did so, he could swear he heard Saoirse's voice from somewhere just behind him saying, 'There you are, Dougie darling. You're going to be all right, my love. You are going to be all right. What did I say?' For a few moments, the veil had become so thin he could smell the sweet fragrance of her perfume, and feel the soft touch of her hand on his cheek, and with his eyes still closed he whispered, 'Thank you, my sweet. Thank you.'

Douglas was so taken aback by this experience that he needed to walk by the water's edge for a short time. Everything felt acutely alive to him. The seagulls swooped down on the bay and he saw them as child angels in a playground tumbling and laughing together. The clouds in the sky were catching the glint of the sun and under the force of the breeze, they became celestial shape-shifters, dancing with one another to a tune that only they knew. Even the boats on the bay, bobbing up and down on the incoming tide seemed to have personalities, and he could almost hear them chattering and laughing with one another. And during this time, while the veil was so thin, the voice of Saoirse remained. As he rested his eyes on the waters in front of him, he heard a verse of a much-loved poem in his mind. It was a poem by a Victorian mystic, Augusta Theodosia Drane, and it was taught him by his mother. But he heard it now, not in the voice of his mother, but in the voice of his beloved Saoirse. She might have been standing right beside him as he listened to her lilting voice reciting,

> Once, only once, there rose the heavy curtain,
> The clouds rolled back, and for too brief a space
> I drank in joy as from a living fountain,
> And seemed to gaze upon it, face to face:
> But of that day and hour who shall venture

125

With lips untouched by seraph's fire to tell?
I saw Thee, O my Life! I heard, I touched Thee,-
Then o'er my soul once more the darkness fell.

'I have seen and heard and touched, my Dougie,' he heard her say. And then he heard her infectious chuckle followed by, 'And She is my life, darling. My Life. Our Life.' Her chuckle faded into the sounds of the breeze on the water and Douglas laughed as well as wept. 'You always wanted Him to be a Her, my love!' he called out over the waters. 'And why not?' he thought. 'Why would a God of love not meet with her in the way that was easiest for her?'

For a time, Douglas sat on the shingle inhaling deeply both the sea air and the memory into his lungs and soul, until, after a time, he heard the church chiming 11 am and remembered he had an appointment with Dorchadas. He rose from his holy ground, warm and more whole than he had felt in a long while.

*

Douglas arrived a little late at the café bookshop. He passed by the tempting bookshelves and entered the small catering section of the shop, and sure enough, there was Dorchadas reading a book, and at his table stood a steaming latte. When he saw Douglas coming, he hailed him, and cried, 'Come and sit yourself here, Doug. Great timing. He'll be here in a minute. Now, what'll you be having?'

'The same as you, please Dorch,' said Douglas as he took off his coat and settled himself at the table. Dorchadas disappeared to the counter, just out of Douglas' sight. There were not many others in the café, and so far no sign of the person they were supposed to meet. But then Douglas heard the sound of the café door opening and Dorchadas' voice calling out, 'Och, there you are, *Capitano*! Come along in. Let me get you a cappuccino, which if I'm not mistaken, is to your liking.' From the sound of laughter and backslapping, Douglas assumed that whoever had come in was a good friend of Dorchadas. But then most people, living and dead, seemed to be a good friend of his. Dorchadas and his friend soon came to where Douglas was seated, with Dorchadas holding a tray of coffees which he placed carefully on the table.

Douglas rose to welcome the new guest who turned out to be a Mediterranean-looking man of medium height, with dark hair, tanned face, a neat moustache, and wearing camouflage jacket and trousers. He smiled warmly at Douglas, and as he reached out his hand, Dorchadas said, 'Douglas, meet my good friend, Captain Antonio De Luca.'

'Very pleased to meet you, sir,' said Douglas with instinctive respect. 'I'm Douglas Romer.'

'It is a great pleasure to meet you, Douglas Romer,' said Antonio in an unmistakable Italian accent. As they all sat down, Douglas was seriously perplexed as to the identity of this gentleman, but he was confident that it would soon become clear.

'So, Doug,' said Dorchadas, 'I've filled Antonio in on what you were telling me about yesterday when I met with him earlier for breakfast. But I'll let the man tell you a bit about himself.'

Antonio took a sip from his cappuccino and looked up at Douglas and, wiping his moustache with his serviette with meticulous care, he said, 'Well, I think you know I am, how do you say - *travelling* - is that what you say, Dorchadas?'

'Yes, that about does it, Tony,' said Dorchadas, sipping his latte.

'Well, Douglas, let me put you quickly out of your misery, as I know you will be wondering just who I am. This "travelling" - it is curious, no? In my original time, I am a Centurion. I'm in the great Army of Rome and I appear in your Bible stories as the man who has a very special meeting with Jesus of Nazareth. Let me tell you about this if you will, please?'

'Yes, of course,' said Douglas, intrigued.

'Well,' started the Italian, now sitting upright in his chair. 'I worked in both Judaea and Galilee. At first, I was posted to the town of Capernaum in Galilee - a very nice town, Douglas. You have been there, Dorchadas?'

'Aye, I have that, Tony,' replied Dorchadas.

'Well, I can tell you, Douglas, that it is hard work being a Roman Centurion,' continued Antonio. 'Oh yes, especially in Galilee. Whoa, it is.' Antonio leaned back in his chair as if to emphasise the challenge of working in Galilee as a Centurion. 'But the Roman army looks after its Centurions, and one of the ways it does that is to give us slaves.' He said the final word with emphasis.

Douglas was about to take a sip of coffee when Antonio reached out his hand and grabbed his wrist, 'I know, I know, Douglas, my friend. You don't agree with them. Dorch has warned me. But don't write me... out?' He looked at Dorchadas.

'Off,' instructed Dorchadas.

'Precisely,' said Antonio. 'Anyway, the thing is Douglas, in the time I come from, there are many different types of slaves, and many different ways of treating slaves. And some of us truly *love* our slaves - they are like one of the family. We treat them well; get them birthday presents; they play with our children and they wouldn't leave us if we paid them to. Other owners, however...' His brow furrowed. 'They are cruel - won't say more about that now.

'So my slave - he's called Leander. I gave him that name when I saw he had the courage of a lion. Well, one day, Leander get sick. Oh, awful sick.' Here Antonio mimed the illness, groaning, and swaying and clutching his stomach. Douglas leaned back in the face of the emerging theatricals. Antonio noticed the signs of British reserve and smiled, saying 'Forgive me. I forget that you people have no *vitalità*! So wooden!' He laughed and then continued with his story. 'Anyway, Douglas, my poor Leander, oh, he was so sick. And then he couldn't walk! Couldn't move a muscle! He just lay there.' He grabbed Douglas' arm and said, 'Oh Douglas it was breaking my poor heart to see him. We tried some medicines, but none of them worked. My Claudia kept saying, "You must do something, Antonio!" And I said, "I know, I know, but what *can* I do?" And then I remembered something.' He leaned towards Douglas so far, that Douglas had to push back in his chair again. 'I remembered Jesus of Nazareth.' He sat back up smartly and grinned at both men.

'Had you met Him before?' asked Douglas.

'Yes, I had met Him before and I was very impressed. You see I am a Centurion and I know the disciplines of Army life. We give orders and we obey orders. So, you see, if I say to one man here,' - he pointed to his right - '"Hey, get me another coffee", he would say, "*Si, Capitano*!" And he get off his backside straight away and off he'd go. And I saw Jesus of Nazareth do this not with people, but with demons and disease. He would say, "You go - shoo - away - clear off! He got very angry with those illnesses and with the demons. Not with the people - no, no, no, no. But He saw there was a very dark and bad power behind some things, and He did not like that power. No, He did not! And He made clear that He had a power that was far greater. I could see that. I recognised such authority. Nobody that I knew had power over those kinds of things. Not even the Emperor - oh, but don't tell him I said that, Douglas, please!' He laughed nervously.

'I think it is most unlikely that I will be seeing him,' said Douglas taking a sip of his coffee.

'Ah good! Well,' continued the Italian, 'by good chance, Jesus was coming into town, and as soon as I heard He was in town, I ran to Him and I fell on my knees.' Here Antonio clutched his hands together and leaned towards Douglas. 'And I say, "My Lord, my poor Leander, my lion-heart, he is sick, sick, sick. He no can walk! Please come and heal him." And I am crying.' Antonio frowned and ran his fingers down his cheeks to mark his flow of tears. 'So many tears from my eyes. And my nose is full of *moccio* - how you say?'

'I think we get the idea,' said Dorchadas, keen to prevent too much detail.

'Yes, well, I am feeling *so* upset, you see. I forget myself, and I know my men are embarrassed to see me like this. It is not like a Centurion should behave at all. No dignity you see, Douglas, but I was so desperate.' Antonio grasped Douglas' arm and said, 'And for a moment, I glanced around at all the people around me. Soldiers looking down at the ground, ashamed of their *Capitano*. Others frowning at me - disapproving of this Gentile soldier who was daring to talk to their holy man. I lost my

130

confidence and was about to go away. But then Jesus - He took hold of my hands, and He lifted me up from kneeling on the ground, and He look at me with such kindness. And He say, "Let me come and see him".

Antonio released Douglas' arm and sat back looking forlorn. 'Well, I then realised that He couldn't, could He? I was a Gentile, and He wasn't allowed in the home of a Gentile. I should have thought of this before.' As he said this, he hit his hand against his forehead. 'But then, Douglas, I thought, "Of course - He does not need to come to my house. His authority could reach anywhere." So, I look at Him and I say, "No need for you to come to my house - I am not worthy of that. But I know all you have to do is say the word, and my Leander will be healed. I know this, Lord." I *did* know it. It is how authority works.'

For a few moments, Antonio was still and gazed into his coffee. He then looked slowly up to Douglas with his eyes brimming with tears and said, 'He then... He say I have great faith. Great faith. I don't know about faith... I just know I love my Leander, and I know this Jesus can heal him. That's all I know. But Jesus took my hand and He look so... *compassionevole*. He too had tears in his eyes. He was like that, no Dorch?'

'Aye, that He was Tony,' said Dorchadas nodding. 'That He was.'

Antonio took a sip of his coffee and wiped his moustache before continuing. 'I did not want to leave Him, Douglas. I just wanted to stay with Him, but I was also eager to see my Leander. Then Jesus say to me, "It will be done, just as you believed it would." Well, Douglas, when I heard that, I knew He had given the command and that my Leander would be better. I was so happy and I rushed to hug Jesus. Yes, Douglas - me a Roman soldier embracing a rabbi! I could hear the gasps of the people!

131

And as I did, He whisper words in my ear.' Here Antonio's face puckered again and, lowering his head and his voice, he said, 'They were precious words. Beautiful words. And in that moment, I knew that not only my Leander had been healed, but something in me also had been healed. *Vita,* Douglas. I felt Him giving me life.'

Antonio paused for such a long time, that Dorchadas had to prompt him, saying, 'And Leander?'

'Oh *scusi*, Dorchadas. I ran back to my home, and who should be there at the front door standing on two strong legs, with his arms waving above his head, but my Leander! Oh my. He was saying *"miracolo!"* And my Claudia was there weeping. And my daughter was there weeping. And the other slaves came out and they were weeping! So much *emozione*! But not surprising because my Leander was healed!' Antonio leaned back in his chair and in a much louder voice said, 'Healed' and threw his head back and laughed in delight.

Dorchadas said, 'Tony, you are certainly a brilliant story-teller,'

'Oh, thank you,' said Antonio, smiling shyly.

'But tell me, Tony,' said Dorchadas. 'You were a Roman - what we would call "Pagan". You didn't believe the Jewish God, did you?'

'Well, Dorchadas, I very much respected the Jewish people and their religion. Yes, you are right. At that time I did worship the Roman or pagan gods, but I am the kind of person who doesn't just believe something because all my neighbours believe it. I will choose for myself, thank you very much. But more than anything I need to see it working. And when I saw my Leander up and running around, I knew for certain that this Jesus had authority over sickness. No question. So, in time I became a disciple - of course. He was the one I would follow.' He shrugged his

132

shoulders and held out his hands. He continued, 'Quite a few soldiers also became disciples. For the same reason as me - they saw His power.'

'But…' ventured Douglas, 'forgive me, but that power doesn't always work, does it? I mean, it worked for Leander, and I'm delighted it did. But sometimes you tell things to go, and they don't. People keep their disease - they die. The power doesn't save them.'

'Yes, yes,' said Antonio. '*Molto triste*. Very sad. But you see, Douglas, I do not think God is the soldier who runs here and there at our command. We don't say to God, "Hey, you run and heal my mother here! Hey, God, go and provide money for my friend now! Hey, bring the rain for my fields now!" No, no, Douglas. That's what we would like, no? We would like God to be our slave. But can you imagine what terrible owners we would be? So, my friend, I don't understand any more than you do. But what I know from my story, is that this Jesus of Nazareth has power and authority. That's all.'

'But…' said Douglas again, 'and I'm sorry to keep questioning, but in the end, the powers of this world defeated Jesus. The fact is - you Romans crucified Him. Roman authority and power killed Him in the end. It won and He lost. He didn't have the power to stop them.'

Antonio's face fell. He leaned forward and said in a quiet voice, 'They *thought* they had defeated Him. You know, Douglas, I am sorry to say I witnessed many crucifixions. As a young soldier, I had to carry them out myself. It was the most terrible, terrible thing. And as a Centurion, I would stand by and ensure my men did a proper job. It made me so sick.' He shook his head many times. 'Why are men so cruel, Douglas? Why? I just don't know. But I have seen many crucifixions, and I saw *His* crucifixion. I was there. I was posted to Jerusalem about six months before that terrible day. I could not believe our leaders would allow that - my soldiers *hated* doing it. They liked Jesus - He had done nothing to harm them. He used to chat with them. You know, ask about their mothers and fathers and children, have jokes with them. I would see them laughing with Him.'

Antonio smiled for a few moments before continuing. 'Actually, He healed several of them, as well. No, they did not want to hurt Him. But if those soldiers failed to do their duty, they would end up on the cross. So, they had to do what they were told. So, you can imagine how I felt, Douglas, seeing that wonderful man being cruelly nailed to the cross. Well, Douglas, as I say, I have seen many men on those crosses. But when *He* was on the cross, it was different. So different. I have never seen anything like it.' He grasped Douglas' arm again, 'I'm telling you, Douglas, that man was in control of things every step of the way. I was in no doubt that He could get free of us soldiers and that wooden cross at any time He wanted. But He *chose* to go through with it. I saw His limp body hanging there, Douglas. And I *still* saw the power in Him.

'I don't understand it, but as I looked up at that cross, I knew He was not the victim but the Victor. Yes, He suffered great pain and death, but some mighty power was released there. I know Douglas. I know power and authority when I see it, and I saw it there. Something happened and something changed. And do you know something, Douglas, there is only one word for it. *Amore* - love. Love was the victor that day, dear Douglas.' He let go of Douglas' arm and leaned back in his chair and sighed. 'And that is what I now have to do - tell people about His extraordinary love. I think that is why I am here today.'

134

All three sat in silence for some time, before Dorchadas leaned across and grasped Antonio's hand and said, 'Thank you, Tony. We're so grateful to you for coming.'

'No, no. Thank you for listening to my story,' replied Antonio. He glanced at his watch and said, 'It is time for me to leave now, I think.'

He rose from the table and stretched out his hand to Douglas. 'It has been good to meet you, my friend. I'm sorry, I have done all the talking. I should have asked you to tell me more about yourself. Forgive me.' He pressed both hands around Douglas' hand and was just about to part, when he paused and, looking searchingly at Douglas, he frowned and said, '*Amico mio*, I sense danger...' He hesitated for a few moments, and Douglas could tell that Antonio knew something, or could see something unseen to Douglas.

'Danger?' said Douglas, anxious to find out more from the Captain.

'Yes, danger,' replied Antonio. 'But it is not a danger to fear. The authority of light is strong. It is getting stronger in you. I can see this. And Douglas.... I think we may meet again. Now,' he said, releasing Douglas' hand, 'I really must leave. *Arrivederci* to both of you.' He bowed and, looking at Dorchadas said, 'Dorch, I'll probably see you again somewhere, sometime?'

'Quite likely, Tony,' said Dorchadas, standing up and embracing him. They watched Antonio march out of the café.

'Another?' asked Douglas lifting his cup and looking at Dorchadas.

'That would be grand, Douglas. Same again if you would,' answered Dorchadas.

Douglas soon returned with the drinks and, settling at his seat, said, 'He's not how I imagined him, Dorch.'

'Ah, Doug, but your imagination is expanding I think. His is quite a story, don't you think?'

'Yes. Puzzling though isn't it? You have Jesus one moment doing that incredible remote healing of Leander, and the next he's hanging from a cross. One moment, he's a powerful healer, and the next he's dying and is totally powerless.'

'Is that what you think, Doug?' asked Dorchadas. His long eyebrows twitched as he continued, 'Do you think he was without power on that cross? Did you not hear what the man said?'

Douglas sighed and looked down at the smooth dark surface of his Americano. He had read books and books on the cross of Christ. He had preached on it dozens of times. He had his theologies of atonement just about buttoned up and could give a tidy explanation of it to any enquirer. But this was different. He had just spoken to a man who claimed to have actually *been* at the cross. Someone who witnessed it. He lifted his spoon and disturbed the surface of the hot liquid then looked up at his friend. 'I don't honestly know what to think, Dorch. I used to have all this stuff sewn up. I could deliver a good sermon on the Cross. Even preached in the Cathedral on one Good Friday. The Dean told me he most impressed. But now, Dorch, I just don't know.' He lifted his cup to his lips and, breathing in, savoured the fragrance. 'I suppose the problem is, I've been trying to understand it. And maybe it is not for understanding?'

Dorchadas smiled. 'Well, Douglas, my friend. Maybe we are getting somewhere.'

Douglas chuckled. He felt a sense of relief at not having to understand everything anymore. A sense of contentment momentarily filled his soul, only to be dislodged by an uncomfortable thought. Returning his cup carefully to the saucer he looked at Dorchadas and said, 'Dorch, have you heard about Ruby Kennedy's memorial mass?'

'Oh, aye, Doug. That I have. Father Pat told me about it just this morning as it happens.'

'You know what that means, Dorch, don't you?'

'Well, it means the good lady will be honoured, which is fair enough.'

'Yes, but did Pat tell you that her sister Orla will be there along with Niall. And you know they are Saoirse's parents.'

'Pat told me that, son.'

'And you know what they think of me?'

'Aye, Doug. Pat told me that, too. But I don't think you should worry yourself too much about seeing them.'

'No?' said Douglas, far from certain that he should be free from such worry.

'Well, I know they were bitter about Saoirse marrying you and that. But water under the bridge, surely?'

'Let's hope so, Dorch. But,' said Douglas, not satisfied with Dorchadas' reassurance, 'what did Antonio mean about that danger he could see?'

'Ah, aye. He did say that. But didn't he say it was a danger that you need not fear?' said Dorchadas, attempting to rekindle the reassurance.

'Yes,' said Douglas in a way that revealed his uncertainty. He leaned back in his chair and sighed. This was one of the few occasions where he did not feel reassured by Dorchadas. Both men were quiet for a while. Dorchadas felt an inner conflict. He could not deny he also sensed danger. Real danger. But his friend had been

137

through so much and he was reluctant to entertain the thought that more troubles might be coming his way. He had been warned not to get too close to humans, else he might lose that vital ability to see clearly. As he looked across the table to Douglas, he realised that this was an instruction that he had failed to keep.

CHAPTER 12

Douglas decided to return to St.Raphael's and make plans for his brief return trip to Sheffield. As he reached the house that now felt very much like home to him, he noticed an ancient yet impressive Harley Davidson motorbike parked opposite the front door. On the saddle was chained a brightly-coloured helmet depicting several garish skulls. He entered the house and heard a conversation in the dining room. As one of the voices was Elsie, he popped his head round the door to greet her.

'Oh, Douglas, darling, there you are,' said Elsie, who was wearing a tight-fitting black dress to complement her jet-black hair. She added with some hesitation, 'I'd like you to meet my new friend, Bull.'

Douglas tried his best to disguise his surprise at the scene he beheld, for Elsie was sitting at one of the dining tables on the other side of which was a large gentleman with long grey hair that was tied up with a yellow bandana. He had a scraggly beard under which appeared signs of a fading tattoo. A grey T-shirt was attempting to cover a large stomach, and over the T-shirt hung a well-weathered, black leather waistcoat decorated with a variety of badges. He looked up at Douglas and grunted 'Hey', and then proceeded to excavate some tobacco ash from a pipe he clutched in his hand.

'Pleased to meet you,' said Douglas holding out his hand. Bull chose not to notice the hand and carried on working on his pipe. 'Is that your bike out there?' said Douglas.

'Yep,' said Bull.

'Have you been friends for long?' asked Douglas looking at Elsie, trying not to betray his surprise.

'No, no, Douglas. We only met today,' said Elsie. Douglas noticed her coyness. 'You had a good morning, Douglas?' She asked.

'Er, yes. Been with Dorch.'

'Oh, aye,' said Elsie and looked down as she straightened the table mat in front of her.

'Well,' said Douglas, 'I've got some things to do, so... Nice to meet you, Bull.'

'Hm,' said the biker as he vigorously stuffed some fresh tobacco into his pipe.

'I'll be in my room, Elsie,' said Douglas, starting to feel protective of his landlady.

'That's fine, Douglas. We're having a grand conversation here.'

'Great.'

Douglas made his way up to his room, somewhat puzzled by Elsie's new friend. He texted Kevin to see if he knew anything about Bull. Kevin texted straight back saying he didn't but thought he knew what might be going on and that he would call round soon.

Reassured that Kevin would now keep an eye on his aunt, Douglas settled into the surprisingly comfortable armchair that Elsie had recently placed in his room. He leaned back and dozed in a peaceful sleep for a time until he was awoken by the sound of the front doorbell. He could hear sounds of Kevin being greeted and he heard Elsie offer him a cup of tea.

For a time, Douglas just enjoyed the peace of the room as he sat back in his chair. He let his eyes wander around the room which now felt so familiar. He found himself glancing across at the 1938 black and white picture of

140

Dingle. He got up to inspect it more closely and recognised it as one of the main streets of the town - a road he now knew so well. It looked like it was a warm, summer day, for those in the picture were wearing light clothes and they cast dark and distinct shadows. He thought of all the people living their lives in that period of history - lives that were as real to them then, as his was to him now. He studied each figure, wondering how each had spent the life they had been given. He was drawn to one figure near the front of the photograph: a tall man, striding down the street on his own. He studied the figure carefully for a few moments, running his finger over the glass to clear any dust. He then stepped back and smiled. There was no question about it: the man walking down this Dingle Street on a summer's day in 1938 was none other than his friend, Dorchadas! 'Well, you do get around, Dorch. You really do!' he said out loud.

Still chuckling, he turned to the Victorian crucifix hanging near to it. It looked all wrong with one arm missing, and the other arm stretched out above him. Douglas wondered why Elsie kept it. And yet there was something intriguing about it. It reminded him of someone he had seen in a movie. He puzzled for a moment as to who that someone was, and then he remembered. 'Rocky!' he said out loud. It almost felt blasphemous to think such a thing, but he could not deny that the figure as it presented itself from this broken crucifix, looked like a picture he had on his wall at University of the boxing hero, Rocky, fist-pumping the air above him in triumph. 'Not quite your normal image,' said Douglas to himself. 'I hardly see Christ on the cross as a prizefighter. But maybe Antonio would see it that way?'

For the next half hour, he set about making plans for his brief visit back to the UK. He booked his flights for early Friday morning, to return Sunday afternoon. He also emailed Mavis to let her know he would be back over the weekend. He then thought about Bishop Pauline and realised if he was to see her on Friday, he could not wait for his snail-mail letter to get to her. So, he emailed a copy of his letter to her and enquired if she had a spare moment on Friday. Not likely, he supposed, knowing her diary, but it was worth a try. He ignored all the other emails and closed his laptop, and as he did so, he heard sounds of movement downstairs. Firstly, muffled conversation in the hall, followed by the familiar sound of the front door closing. He glanced out of his window and saw Bull don his helmet and start up his Harley Davidson, the noise of which must have been heard throughout the town, if not well beyond it. In a cloud of blue smoke, the bike roared away, taking this surprising new friend of Elsie's with it.

With curiosity getting the better of him, Douglas went straight downstairs to find out a bit more about this unexpected visitor. As he arrived at the foot of the staircase, Elsie said, 'Oh, Douglas that was a mistake, sure to God it was! Go, both of you, and settle yourselves in the parlour and I'll make us a fresh brew. Sort the fire would you, Kevin.'

Kevin and Douglas settled themselves in the small room at the front of the house. Kevin stoked an almost dead fire and brought it back to life. He turned on the table lamp. Douglas sat in a Windsor wheel-back chair near the fire and said, 'So just exactly who was he, Kev?'

'I think I'd best let Aunty Else explain,' said Kevin, returning to his duties at the fireplace.

Elsie came in with a steaming pot of tea and an assortment of mugs. As she placed them on a table by the window, she said, 'Well, that'll learn me, sure to God it will. Douglas, I was telling you just the other day that I was wanting to … you know, make myself a bit more available. Well, I did a little bit of research and found this netsite.'

'Might that be "website", Aunty?' ventured Kevin.

'That it might be, son. It was called *Silvermates*. So, I went down to Clare at the hairdresser's, and she helped me get all set up on her computer, she did. She took a picture of me to up...laid?' She looked at Kevin for help.

'Up*load*, Aunty Else. Upload,' said Kevin.

'Well that she did - my photo with my new hair, and this smart dress' said Elsie patting her hair as she said so. 'And she said she'd keep an eye on the website for me. Well, within minutes this man called Bull had contacted. She said he looked a nice gentleman from his photo. Well, all I can say now is that Clare cannot have had her eyes tested for some time. Anyway, I was hopeful, and before you could say how d'ye do, we set up a meeting at Kath's for 10 am today. But of course, when I get there this morning, that woeful sister of mine is nowhere to be seen. The door firmly shut and locked and the 'closed' sign in place. Off with that Peter somewhere I suppose. Never said a word to me about that.'

Elsie poured out the tea into the mugs from a pot that dribbled alarmingly. She took no notice of the mess she was creating and continued her tale. 'So I'm hanging around outside her caf, and this gentleman, Bull, turns up in that thundering machine of his, nearly frightening the living daylights out of me, so he did. He was nothing like the man Clare described to me, and I was a little taken aback, I don't mind saying so.' She handed the mugs out to Kevin and Douglas and sat down. 'Well with the caf closed, I didn't want to be seen in any other coffee shop in town with him, so I had to bring him back here, didn't I?'

'Not wise, Aunty...'

143

'Kevin, love,' she said with her reproving look, 'I can deal with all sorts, I can assure you. In this trade, you have to. But thanks, love, for your concern.' She leaned over and patted his knee. She then looked bashful and said, 'Well, you could both see the man was hardly suitable. I can't say I took to the gentleman at all. He was definitely not the full shilling apart from anything else. It was hard to get a word of sense out of the man. I suspect the drugs had got the best part of his brains a long time ago. And it was clear he was... well, disappointed when he saw me.' She looked downcast, but then added, 'However, Douglas, he was very complimentary about my hair, I'll have you know.'

Douglas smiled. Kevin reached out and clutched his aunt's hand. Elsie looked up and said, 'I'm all right, Kevin. While I was making the tea out there in the kitchen, I was saying to myself, "Elsie O'Connell, what in God's name has got into you? Look at what you've got - all your friends in Dingle, who you love to death, they do. You've got your sister, Kath, who's the best of sisters, she sure is, even though she drives you half-crazy most of the time." And then I says to myself, "And you've got your two boys - your Kevin who you've known since he was a wee babe in arms, and Douglas here, who you've only known a matter of weeks, yet he's become one of the family, so he has." So, I says, "Pull yourself together Elsie, and be thankful for what the good Lord has given you." That's what I said, Douglas. There are times you have to give yourself a good talking to, don't you think, son?' She gulped down her mug of tea, put it firmly on the tray beside her, then placing her hands on her knees she said, 'So there we are.'

'You are very wise, Elsie,' said Douglas, but there was so much more he wanted to say, yet could not find the words. He felt a powerful emotion but was not sure what the emotion was. To prevent it from overwhelming him, he steadied himself by saying, 'Elsie, I'm going back to England for the weekend. I've got a few things that need sorting out. I'll need to leave first thing Friday.'

'Of course, son. Of course. And who knows what hairstyle I'll have when you return!' They all laughed as Douglas made his way out of the parlour and went back to his room.

*

Journal   8 January 11 pm

Curious realisation earlier today. Elsie had her first rather disastrous attempt at online dating! Her gothy hairstyle caught the attention of a guy called Bull who turned out to be an old Hells Angel. Met him briefly. Definitely no future in this relationship! Kevin came around and he and I had a cup of tea with Elsie after Bull had left. Elsie really is a great woman. She was so honest with us. I did admire that. But she said something that nearly tipped me over the edge. She said she thanked God for her 'two boys' - Kevin and me! At one level she hardly knows me. But then I have shared more of my fears, longings, and hopes with her than I ever would with my own mother. We have often had long chats at breakfast. It's made me realise that I have spent so much time and energy lamenting what I have lost, that I have failed to see what I have been given. Here I am in a strange town in a strange land, and yet it feels like home. I have been given Dorchadas, Kath, Elsie, Kevin. And I'm getting to know people like Fr Pat who is very special. And Peter is someone I can instinctively trust. I've had other friends, but somehow all of these feel different. More real in a way. Of course, none of them make up for the loss of my Saoirse, but that's not the point. They are not here to replace her, or to fill the gap that she has left. But they are people who are helping me to manage the gap. They are the kind of friends that I have not had before. I'm living deeply and honestly with them. I have been so self-protecting in the past. It was Saoirse who was the first to draw me out of myself and she healed something in me. And now the healing continues with these new friends that I am making here in Ireland. I can be myself with them. These friends are healing something in me.

So, yes, I am feeling better. However, there is still that nagging worry about Saoirse's assassin and that disturbing meeting in the autumn in Killarney with the Intelligence officer. There is also this worrying thought that Gerald Bentley is somehow tied up with it all (that disturbing dream). Part of me just wants to forget about it - it's too painful. And yet, for Saoirse, I must find out who her killer was. And yet, to embark on that hunt just feels overwhelming. It still hurts me so much to imagine anyone on this earth would want to kill that beautiful life. Did I idolise her too much? Did I love her more than I love God? Yes, I am sure I did, if I'm honest. But it was because my image of God was not right. That image is changing. Could I love God again, as much as I loved my Saoirse? It's hard to imagine. I'm not pretending anymore. I'm feeling my way back into faith, and it's tentative. But something is going on. Maybe Mary Coleridge was right:

Sunshine, let it be or frost,
Storm or calm, as thou shalt choose;
Though thine every gift were lost,
Thee thyself we could not lose.

146

I must mention that I had an amazing FaceTime call with Frank, who told me all about a crazy healing service he and Daisy went to. Anyway, the upshot seems to be that Daisy is much better, if not completely healed. I am so pleased for them, but it also leaves me confused. One minute God zaps Daisy and she gets healed, but then there are loads of other people who are longing for healing and pray like mad and they don't get healed. And there are people who get shot and killed and don't get protected. I chatted about this to Dorchadas and he arranged another of his 'meetings'. Taking these in my stride now. This time the centurion whose slave was healed. Turned up as an Italian captain! I suppose he did help a bit. I loved hearing the story of the healing of his slave - called Leander apparently. The most interesting bit though was when he talked about the cross. Said he was there himself. Incredible! But he said the dying figure of Christ looked more like a victor than a victim. What an interesting comment. Dorch says such things are not for understanding, and I guess he's right. It's wonderful that there is such power for good and healing around. But there are also the powers of darkness. There's awful news that Saoirse's parents are coming to town next week for Ruby's memorial. If anyone hates me in this world it is Saoirse's dad. Now he really could want to kill me! Here I go again - my paranoia getting the better of me. Dorch has told me not to worry about it.

Two more important things. Dear Frank and Daisy have sent me some money - £30k!! So generous of them. I know Daisy got an inheritance, but surely, she should keep it all for the boys? But they insisted, and I must say it is so timely. I can now relax for at least a year, and I want to stay here. So, I have resigned. Back to the UK on Friday

147

and hoping to see the bishop. I think she's relieved I'm on my way.

So, all good news really. Just need to get my paranoia under control!

CHAPTER 13

The rain and wind woke Douglas early the next morning. Though he tried to muffle the sound by burying his head under the duvet, it was to no avail. So, he reluctantly hauled himself out of bed and made his way downstairs to the dining room. He gathered his plate of fruit and sat in his usual seat and spent some moments gazing through the window. He became fascinated by the playful way the swirling wind toyed with the sheets of rain, flinging them against the houses in the street that was still in semi-darkness.

'When it's in this mood, you can't argue with it,' said Elsie as she brought in Douglas' plate of bacon and eggs.' Quite often nowadays she would fetch a mug of coffee and join him at his table. 'So, what are your plans for today, Douglas?' she enquired as she settled herself at his table, warming her hands on her mug.

'I don't really know, Elsie. There's always the inevitable emails, I suppose.'

'God bless 'em', said Elsie, not knowing quite why she said it.

'Yes, Elsie. I hope He does,' said Douglas, as he pierced the yoke of his egg with his fork. 'I wonder what He thinks of all this emailing?'

'Och, I dare say He gets fed up with them like the rest of us do. Don't suppose He's quite so ill-tempered about it, though!' They both laughed.

While the rain hurled itself against the windowpane, the two of them talked for a while about the weather.

Then Douglas asked, 'Elsie, how well did you know Ruby?'

'Ruby Kennedy?' Elsie paused holding the mug to her lips for a moment. She then put down the mug and nodded, saying, 'Ruby was a fine lass. Quiet, you know. Kept herself to herself, she did. But she was a little too fond of the bottle, sad to say. Not that any of us would judge her for that. But it killed her in the end, it did.'

'Actually,' said Douglas, 'I've found out that it wasn't the wine that killed her. She had terminal cancer, but she didn't want people to know. I'm not sure why, but she preferred you all to think it was the bottle that took her.'

'Is that a fact?' said Elsie, raising her eyebrows to her jet-black hair. 'I never knew that, Douglas. Come to think of it, I never saw her rolling around in the streets if you get my meaning. She did have the marks of the wine around her mouth quite often. But no... I have to say, never got to see her pissed.' She paused briefly and then added, 'Oh, sorry, Douglas, son. I always forget you're a man of the cloth, sure I do. Forgive my language.'

'I'm a friend, Elsie, not a man of the cloth,' said Douglas.

'That you are, son,' said Elsie, and smiled. 'No, I liked Ruby, and I'm sorry she had the cancer, poor woman. Did she come over much to England to see you and your wife?'

'No. Sadly, I never met her.'

'Well, you will have met her sister, Orla, and her husband.' She pursed her lips. 'Strange couple I have to say. But, Douglas, forgive me. They're your family, and I don't want to speak ill of them.'

'No, no, Elsie.' Douglas reassured her. As he finished his breakfast, he told her of his experience with his parents-in-law.

'My God, Douglas. You poor soul. I am so sorry, son,' said Elsie, her intense frown revealing her sorrow. 'Feelings have run very high in our land, you know. There have been terrible things in our past and there are those like me, who have learned to forgive and move on. And then there are those like Niall that are determined to keep fighting an old war. God knows why they do. Where does it get them, Douglas? Just into more hatred and more fighting and more bloodshed. What in God's name is the point of it? And talking of God, wasn't it Himself who taught us to forgive? I mean, if Niall is the good Catholic he says he is, he should be doing a hell of a lot of forgiving, shouldn't he?'

'It's not easy for some, Elsie,' said Douglas, looking down at the table.

'Oh, God, Douglas,' said Elsie.

'It's all right, Elsie,' said Douglas turning his attention to the rain-splattered window.

'May I ask you, son...' said Elsie, lowering her voice. 'Have you been able to... You know, forgive?'

Douglas breathed in deeply and looked at Elsie's kindly and compassionate face. He smiled at her and said, 'I'm on the road, Elsie. I'm on the road.'

'That's good, son. That's good.' She got up and added, 'Well, have a grand day if you possibly can in this weather.'

Douglas made his way back up to his room. The conversation brought back vivid memories of his conversation with Kevin in the church on that fateful day of the great storm - the outer storm of the wind, rain, and raging sea, and the inner storm of his own sorry soul. It was the thought of God forgiving Saoirse's murderer that had caused him to snap that day. But that was some weeks ago, and he felt stronger now. Strong enough to revisit questions that had so often haunted him. As he settled himself at his desk and opened up his laptop, his thoughts became so loud that he started speaking to himself: 'Forgive? Yes, Kevin has been forgiven by God. I get that. But can I forgive Saoirse's murderer? Can I? How can I? It would be betraying her, surely? And what if I meet the very man who planned her death? Could I possibly forgive him? Or if I met the guy who pulled the trigger now in jail in Nairobi? I'm sorry, Elsie. I'm sorry, Dorchadas. I'm sorry, God, I just don't think I can do it. I'm not about pretending anymore.' For some time, he sat at his desk with the palms of his hands pressed against his eyes which started to feel very tired.

A sudden splatter of rain against the window disturbed him and he glanced down at the computer screen that shone brightly in his room on this gloomy winter morning. He looked at it and saw in his inbox that there were two unread emails. He recognised the first sender, for it was from Clive, the Bishop's Chaplain. The email was brief and read:

Dear Douglas
The Bishop will be pleased to see you on Friday afternoon at 16.40. Please be prompt.
best wishes
Clive

Douglas felt glad she had found a slot for him, for he wanted to properly sign off with her and to do it soon.

The second email looked like spam as it was from a number rather than a name. However, he opened it and it read:

Please destroy this as soon as you have read it.
We met last November in Killarney.
This is to reassure you we continue with our enquiries. We have made some progress but as yet have no further information to share with you.
Please be assured that every effort is being made to track down the culprit.
We do however encourage you to be on your guard.
If you have gained any information that would be useful to our enquiry, please contact the British police. They will know how to get a message to us.
Do not attempt to reply to this email. We will be in touch again in due course.
NABIS

Douglas stared hard at the screen. His first response was to laugh. Such a message like this felt like it belonged more in a James Bond movie rather than in the regular life of Douglas Romer. This whole British Intelligence thing felt so far removed from his normal life. But as he read it through again, other feelings emerged behind the initial laughter: disappointment that no progress had been made; horror, as he revisited the unwelcome thought of there being some evil man in the UK who was behind the plot to kill his wife; fear at the thought that this evil man might discover

Intelligence was on to him; and dread that this man might discover that Douglas had been told. What if they supposed Douglas knew who the killer was? Or were worried that he would soon find out? Would they not dispose of him, as they had of Saoirse? Would such a man not easily recruit one of his contract killers, sending him over to Ireland to hunt down his prey? It would be an easy enough task for a professional assassin.

Douglas was tapping his fingers on the desk as if playing an imaginary piano. Was paranoia starting to get the better of him? Or was he entering a time where the grim world of the illegal arms trade that was responsible for Saoirse's death, might now turn its ugly attention to him? He inhaled sharply and stopped his tapping. Such thoughts caused a sharp pang of fear to grip his soul. He immediately deleted the email and inhaled another deep breath, sucking the comforting air into the agitation that he felt in his chest.

He stood up from the desk and walked around his room, tapping his mouth with his finger. What a curious world he now inhabited. For two years the great force with which he had had to battle was that of grief - a force that demolished his faith in God and very nearly took his own life. And now, just as he was coming out the other side of that force, another one was showing sinister signs of emerging: it was the force of cold, raw fear. Specifically, it was a fear of people of violence. The one responsible for Saoirse's death could, feasibly, be lining up Douglas as the next victim. But it was not just this person of violence. There was Niall, Saoirse's hot-headed father. There was no question, Niall hated Douglas and held him responsible not only for Saoirse's death but, as he would see it, her incarceration in purgatory. Could he draw on some warped theology to justify slaying the perpetrator of his daughter's demise? Would he feel duty-bound to take justice into his own hands? There was a strong rumour that he was still connected with a terrorist group, so he would have no qualms about carrying out a murder if he believed execution was a justifiable punishment.

Douglas sat slowly down on his bed. All this was so far-fetched, and yet he could not deny it was also plausible. 'I need to see Dorchadas,' he said and pulled his coat and hat from the wardrobe. Elsie heard his rapid footsteps on the stairs, but by the time she looked out of her parlour, the front door had slammed shut and he was gone.

He called first at the Presbytery, but Father Pat's housekeeper reported that neither Pat nor Dorchadas were in, and she had no idea where either could be found. Douglas, therefore, decided to go for a drive somewhere to clear his head. His car was reluctant to start as it complained about the driving rain. Eventually, it conceded to Douglas' determination and rebukes and it coughed itself into life. Douglas decided to drive to the north of the peninsula, and as he reached the little town of Feohanagh, the rain ceased and a welcome sun broke through the heavy cloud. Thus, Douglas spent several hours clearing his head by striding around coastal paths and beaches before returning to Dingle. Calling in again at the Presbytery, he was pleased to discover that Dorchadas was at home this time. After a brief chat, they agreed to meet up again for an evening meal.

Before leaving for the meal, Douglas decided to take a photo of the 1938 picture of Dingle that hung on the wall of his room. When he arrived at the pub,

155

Dorchadas was already there and beckoned Douglas over to his table. They greeted each other and Douglas sat down and opened the photo on his phone and pushed it in front of Dorchadas. The tall man drew the picture up to his face for close inspection and then handed the phone back to Douglas. He chuckled and looking at Douglas he said, 'Not aged much have I?'

By now Douglas was familiar with the many peculiar facets of Dorchadas' life and personality, but he was still a little taken aback by this calm confession that he was the very man striding down this Dingle street on a summer's day in 1938. 'To be honest, Dorch,' he said, 'this takes a lot of believing. In my normal world, time travel is pure fantasy. I mean, I know - you are an angel and all that. But it's not easy for me to be having supper with a man, who also appears as large as life on a photo from the 1930s!'

'You see, Doug,' said Dorch who paused momentarily while the barman placed a couple of pints on the table. 'Thanks, Terry,' he said, acknowledging the barman. 'You see, none of this will make any sense to a rational mind.' He pulled one of the glasses towards him.

'Try me,' said Douglas, taking a sip from his glass and looking hard at his angel friend.

Dorchadas held his glass and looked into it as if trying to draw out some wisdom from it with which to explain the impossible to his friend. 'The thing is, Doug, all time is in Him. We dwell in Him, and therefore we can effectively travel in time, if that's what you want to call it.'

'We? Does that include me?' asked Douglas, frowning.

'Indeed, it does, son. You've been to Egypt to meet Jacob in his dying days, haven't you? You've been in a cave with the great Baptist, have you not?'

'Yes, but… imagination, Dorch.'

Dorchadas smiled and took a long draught of the dark liquid. 'Aye, imagination, Douglas.'

'Yes… Say more.'

Dorchadas put his glass carefully on the table, then looked at Douglas and said, 'Imagination, Doug. Not explanation. This is the journey you have been on. All this is much easier for us angels, of course. It all makes perfect sense to us and I'm truly sorry it's a puzzle to you. But, you see, when I…' For a moment Dorchadas paused and looked down at the table. 'When I was sent to Earth as one of you, I was sent to different times and places. But I have always appeared as I do now.' He leaned back and tapped his shoulders, then continued, smiling his endearing smile. 'So wherever and whenever I turn up, I'm always old Dorchadas with my Irish accent and my fine looks. Don't comment on that bit, Doug. Not even angels get to choose their looks. Anyway, most of my work has been in this beautiful land.'

'Why in Ireland, Dorch? Was it your choice to come here?' asked Douglas.

'Aye, it was, actually,' said Dorchadas picking up a beer mat and playing with it. 'You see, we angels love the stories of you humans. I mean, we just love humans because we love God. We work all over the world, of course, and we get to know human stories - the longings, the hurts, the hopes, the loves. We just love being there, unseen, but in the thick of it.'

157

'Must be a bit shocking at times - seeing all the violence and stuff,' said Douglas, drawing thoughtfully from his glass.

'Not shocking, Doug. But deeply sad,' replied Dorchadas, placing the beermat back on the table. 'And it was the sadness that made me choose this beautiful land. You see, I saw this land many, many years ago. When I was an angel, I was actually sent to meet the young Patrick when he was out in them cold, cold fields as a slave, poor boy.'

'You mean the great St.Patrick of Ireland?' said Douglas raising his eyebrows.

'Aye, the very one. But I have to say, Doug, he was nothing like he appears in most of them stories, paintings and stained-glass windows that you get all over this land. Oh, how he would laugh to see all those! No, no, no. He was as human as you are, Doug. Made of true flesh and blood, with bags of fears and hurts, poor son. A very insecure man in many ways. But, my, he had wonderful heart-sight, because he had such great faith. On that hillside, in the dreadful days of his slavery, soaked to the skin by winter rain and stinking of sheep, he would lift his soul in prayer and sing hymns of praise that would impress even the Cherubim and Seraphim. And that's how he got a glimpse of yours truly.' He lifted his glass and smiled.

'He saw you?'

'Oh, aye. There are quite a few humans who catch sight of us, Doug. We don't mind a bit - in fact, we rather like it. Well, cut a long story short, son, because you've got a plane to catch in the morning, so I hear.'

'How did you know that?'

'Oh, I came by earlier looking for you, and Elsie told me.'

'Right. I'll come on to that. But tell me more about Patrick and Ireland.'

'Och, well, as I say, Doug, I could keep you here for six weeks telling you about that lad. But just let me say, his was a beautiful soul. And he was originally what you would now call a Brit because that's where he came from. But he had such a big heart for this island. As I'm sure you know, he escaped being a slave, went back home, but he was called back here to tell the good news of Christ. And so, he did - spent the best part of his life here just telling people the stories of the gospel. Oh, you should have heard him, Doug!' Dorchadas turned his head to one side and looked somewhere over Douglas's shoulder as he reminisced. 'I mean, the man didn't have a lot of what you would call natural confidence. He was no great orator. But he would come to a little hamlet of people, and when he first arrived, they would all be suspicious and that. But he would come and sit down with them and start to chatter, or play with their kiddies, and make them all laugh. And before you knew it, he'd be telling them about Jesus, the man from a land down in the Mediterranean a long, long way from Eire, and yet who was also the Son of God, raised from the grave, and therefore was up and about among the people of all lands.'

Dorchadas sipped from his glass and continued, 'And I would watch Patrick sometimes take a couple of sticks and make them into the shape of the cross. With such tenderness, he would tell them the story of his Lord giving up his life for all folks. As he did so, his lip would quiver and tears would stream down his dear,

159

weathered face. He never minded shedding a tear or two, did Patrick.' Dorchadas looked at Douglas with both a smile and a frown. 'I think that's what touched the hearts of the people, Doug. They knew he was on their side, and he was talking about a God who was on their side. A God who was for them. And my, they were pleased, because up until then they all thought God was a terrifying power that you had to do your level best to keep on the right side of.'

Douglas listened hard as Dorchadas continued. 'And it was not just Patrick of course. There was the gorgeous Brigid - ooh, a fiery young lady if ever there was one!' He smiled as he reminisced. 'But, you know, we angels would queue up to go and visit her community. The worship, Doug... The people there would sing a singing that... Oh my... There was the breath of glory in it, Doug. It was a singing you'd want to inhale into the very core of your heart.' He took a slow sip from his drink. Douglas could feel the radiance of the memories as Dorchadas recalled them. He felt a nostalgia - had he not always harboured a yearning to know an expression of faith that was something like this?

'So, the years went by in beloved Eire,' continued Dorchadas. 'The fires of faith, hope, and love burned bright - so bright, they did. And they spread far and wide. And then the darkness, Doug. The darkness.' Dorchadas' expression changed so fast that it took Douglas aback. His white and ginger eyebrows twitched as he continued, 'The enemy planted terrible seeds of hatred. Year after year we watched those beautiful fires die down and we found ourselves working hard in a land that knew such suffering and violence and, at times, desperate poverty. Oh, how those dear people suffered, they surely did.'

Dorchadas paused for a few moments, lost in some sorrowful thought, before he said, 'And yes, in my human form I was allowed to return as an Irishman. I could hardly believe it, Doug.' His eyes glistened as he continued, 'I mean, I had lost my place in the company of heaven, but in His mercy, He allowed me to come to the very people of Earth that I loved so dearly. That's kindness, for you Doug. That's mercy, isn't it?' He brushed the leaking water from his cheek and looked at Doug with a quiver of a smile.

'Yes, Dorch,' said Douglas, 'I think that is. So here you are, in the land you love.'

'Aye, here I am.' He shifted in his seat and continued, 'And I've moved around the years. Here and there, as required. And, yes, one of those times was, as you have found out, in the late thirties. It was a lovely summer, it sure was. But a terrible one for a sweet girl who needed help. Dreadfully broken-hearted she was, but I'll say no more, Doug. These stories are private, as you know. I hope I did some good for her.'

'I'm sure you did, Dorch,' said Douglas looking across at his friend with warm appreciation. 'Dorch, I expect you have done far more good than you could ever possibly imagine.'

Dorchadas smiled and then chuckled. 'Back where we started, Doug. The imagination! Sláinte!' Both men laughed and raised their glasses.

They both enjoyed their meal as they continued their conversation and only at the end after a second glass of Guinness did Douglas talk to Dorchadas about his growing fears. He found Dorchadas understanding, and perhaps it was the beer or the comfort of a friend, but by the end of the meal, Douglas was feeling less anxious. As they were enjoying an after-dinner coffee,

161

Douglas said. 'By the way, Dorch, I notice that when you speak of God, you usually say 'Him'. My Saoirse always rather wished it was a 'Her'. What do the angels think about that?'

Dorchadas smiled. 'It's a pity your Saoirse never got to meet young Brigid of Kildare - they would have got on very well! No, Doug, language is very difficult, isn't it? I mean, we angels never use gender words for God. Granted, Jesus was a man, of course, but he's only one part of the Trinity. If you could see the blessed Trinity with the eyes of the angels, you would not be saying Him or Her as it happens. But don't you think it is sad, Doug, that there are some who regard 'Him' as a terrible threat, and there are others who see 'Her' as a terrible threat. That speaks of deep wounding in humanity, don't you think? And I think your Saoirse was very sensitive to people's wounds.'

'Yes, she certainly was, Dorch.' Terry, the barman, came over with the card machine, and the newly-wealthy Douglas waved his phone over the machine to cover the cost of the meal. As he tucked his phone in his pocket, he looked up at Dorchadas and asked. 'Dorch - did you… I mean, as either angel or human, did you ever see my Saoirse?'

Dorchadas, who was just about to stand up, settled back in his seat and leaning forward he said in a quiet voice, 'No, Doug. I never saw her. But I felt her presence once or twice, and I heard the language of her heart - just a little.'

Douglas looked uncertain, so Dorchadas continued. 'I'm not sure I'm going to be able to explain it, my friend. But it was when I was an angel. The intuition of an angel is a marvel, Doug. But, be sure of this, I only caught a glimpse of her spirit. I knew nothing of her story. Everything I know about her life is from what you have told me. When I first met you, all those weeks ago, my old intuition kicked in. I sensed your connection with Saoirse. No facts - just a feeling. So, at one level, I knew nothing, but at another level, I knew something. I think that 'something' has helped me on those occasions when you ran short of words.'

Douglas looked hard at him, and for a moment Dorchadas was very uncertain of what his friend was thinking. In fact, Douglas was more looking through him than at him for he was catching sight of something - a reality that for most of his life he dismissed as fantasy. In a quiet, almost distracted voice, he said, 'I understand, Dorch. I think I understand.' Then, in a more focussed way, he said, 'Dorch - do you mind telling me, what did you think? I mean what did you think about that heart, whose language you think you heard?'

Dorchadas closed his eyes for a moment and appeared to be drawing up a memory from his previous angelic life. He then opened his eyes and looked at his friend saying, 'I felt, Douglas, that hers was one of the most beautiful hearts I had ever encountered. I think you were privileged to be married to a young lady whose heart had a touch of Paradise about it. That I surely do.'

As Douglas walked back to St.Raphael's, it was that last comment that rang in his ears and in his soul. If initially there was some disturbance in him at the thought of Dorchadas somehow knowing Saoirse, it was soon replaced by a sense of comfort. It was a comfort that here in his new home of Dingle, there was a friend who knew his Saoirse, albeit in this curious angel kind of way. But as he reached the front door of

163

the guest house, the comfort he had enjoyed, was disturbed by an unwelcome thought that intruded on his contentment. It was the thought that next week, there would be two other people in Dingle who had known Saoirse very well indeed: namely her parents. He sensed that any conversation he might have with them about her would feel very different. It was that thought that gave him a troubled night's sleep.

CHAPTER 14

Douglas had to rise early in the morning to get the early flight from Cork. He crept out of the house and clambered into his Fiesta, which begrudgingly came to life and transported him to the Airport that was teeming with business people making their way off to meetings in other parts of the country and the world. There were also some excited holiday-makers eager to get free of the winter dark to escape to some sunlit land far away.

It wasn't long before he was making his way into the house that at one time had been such a happy home for him. Mavis had clearly been in, as the heating was on and the post had been placed in a neat pile on the hall table. A note on the kitchen table read:

Hello Douglas.
I hope you had a good flight. You'll find milk and bread in the fridge. Looks like you've got some food in the freezer, but let me know if you need anything. I've not told a soul you are back. I should close the curtains as soon as you put any lights on! Would it be OK if me and Alice came round tomorrow morning just for a catch up? I think you said you were staying til Sunday. Will be nice to see you again.
Take care.   Your friend Mavis.

'Thank you, Mavis,' said Douglas out loud. He was so grateful to have a friend that he could trust here in Sheffield. He then made himself a coffee and picked up a jotting pad from the sideboard and started making a list of things that needed doing. The main thing was to check out storage companies as he wanted to vacate this house as soon as he could. So the morning was spent in research and phone calls, all to do with plans for closing down the Vicarage.

Later in the afternoon, as darkness was falling, he drove off to the bishop's house. His car in England was a good deal more reliable than the Fiesta in Ireland. But already he loved the Fiesta more than his VW Polo - a car to which he was, at one time, extremely devoted. He drove down the drive to the bishop's house and he felt a sense of relief that this would be his last visit. A rather nervy Clive welcomed him at the door, explaining it had been a very busy day, and that the bishop had much to clear from her desk before a demanding meeting in the evening. After taking an order for tea, he steered Douglas into the room that served as a waiting room, and there he duly waited, listening to the unhurried sound of a ticking clock. True to form, the bishop entered the room at precisely 16.40 and came over and shook Douglas by the hand with a warmth that surprised him. She ushered him into her front room and sat Douglas by a welcome log fire. She gathered a couple of cups of tea that were waiting on a tray near the window and gave one to Douglas. As Douglas drew the cup to his lips, he smelt the distinctive fragrance of Earl Grey, the bishop's preferred brew, if not entirely his.

'Oh, I shall be glad when the lighter evenings return,' she said, as she settled her trim figure in the chair opposite Douglas. This time she was armed with no iPad and appeared altogether less formal. She took a sip from her cup. 'So, Douglas, you really do want to leave us, then?'

'Well…' said Douglas, a little taken aback at the fact that the bishop did seem genuinely sad that he was leaving. 'I felt it was necessary to come to a clear decision sooner or later. I think this is best for me and for St.Philip's.'

'Yes, Douglas I do understand and I support your decision. We can get on with the formalities in due course. But how are you, now?' she asked, sipping from her china cup.

'I'm actually feeling quite a bit stronger, thank you, Bishop.'

'You are looking better than when I last saw you.'

'Thank you.'

'And, if you don't mind me asking, where are you with your faith? We discussed that a little last time.'

Douglas looked at his bishop, with her hands cupped around her Earl Grey tea, and her head leaning towards the fireplace. He could not deny the genuine kindness he saw in her. 'It's early days, Pauline. But I think there are signs of the embers flickering back to life.' As if on cue, a log in the fire cracked and a spark flew on to the hearth.

The bishop smiled, and said, 'Not to be hurried, Douglas. In my experience, what emerges is a good deal more genuine than what was lost.'

Douglas took a sip of his tea and surprised himself with the directness of his question. 'Do you mean, you lost your faith once?'

She nodded and looking into the fireplace said, 'Mm. As you know, in my last job - as Archdeacon - I received such a battering. You know,' she said, looking back at Douglas. 'Nasty people firing emails and stuff at me. People who claimed to be followers of Christ.

167

Well, after a while it just got to me. I suppose it wasn't a faith crisis as such. Just a sense of, "What's the point?" She took another sip of tea and continued. 'It was depression, Douglas. I was off for two months. "Stress-related illness" they called it. I couldn't find any sign of God in those dark days. It was very bleak indeed.' She sighed and looked into the fire.

'I am so sorry,' said Douglas, taken aback by such a personal disclosure from his bishop.

'It's all right,' she said, smiling and looking back at Douglas. 'I was lost and then… I was found. And I was led on to a new track, and a much better one, I think. Maybe a similar pattern for you?'

'Yes, maybe,' said Douglas, as he took another sip of the fragrant tea.

'Now, Douglas, you did say something interesting about St.Philip's,' she said, marshalling a stray lock of hair behind her ear and returning to a more formal mode. 'Something about your successor needing to be robust because of some strong characters in the church.'

'Ah, yes. Forgive me if I was outspoken….'

'No, I don't think you were, Douglas. I… it would not be expedient of me to name names, but I think I know the kind of people you might be referring to.'

'Yes, well I will name one name: Gerald Bentley.' Douglas felt he had little to lose now.

'I think people rather misjudge poor Gerald,' said the bishop, raising an eyebrow. Douglas felt 'poor' was a most inaccurate epithet and was about to protest when the bishop continued. Furrowing her brow, she said, 'I know he can be unpleasant, but it's very difficult for him, with... you know... Angela and her difficulties. I do think he means well.'

'I'm not so sure,' said Douglas.

'Well, this will no longer be your problem, Douglas,' she said curtly.

Douglas wondered if he should do more to warn his bishop of Gerald's devious ways, but he felt tired and did not want to discuss this man any more than was necessary. So, in a rather weak reply, he said, 'No. Of course.'

'So, what are your plans now?' the bishop asked, draining her cup and placing it neatly on the ornate table beside her.

'To stay in Ireland for a few more weeks. I need to look into what's required for me to stay longer. I'm not sure. But I've been helped by a friend with a very generous gift.'

'Yes, you mentioned,' she said as she crossed her leg.

'So, we will see. Maybe back to parish ministry one day.' Douglas drained his cup.

'But not to Sheffield?'

'Er, no. It's not personal...'

'I understand Douglas, I honestly do. You have to make a clean break. But I do want you to know that you are a very good priest and you have led St.Philip's well. I know you had a very tough final couple of years, but don't let that disguise the fact that yours was an excellent ministry. You will be much missed in the parish and the diocese.'

Douglas had pretty much lost all track of the years of ministry before his personal tragedy. It seemed like it was another world blocked off by a great wall of death. But he was touched by the bishop's words and said, 'I'm very grateful, Pauline. And thank you for your kindness and understanding. I will now set about packing up the Vicarage and releasing it back to you very soon. I know the Parsonages Board will be keen to let it as soon as they can.'

Bishop Pauline smiled warmly. 'That they will,' she said. 'But seriously, Douglas, take as long as you need, and once the house is clear, just let me know. Will you be having a farewell event in the parish?'

'No, I don't think I am up for that. I will write a letter for the wardens to read out.'

'Yes, that's fine, Douglas. Well,' she said, glancing at her watch, 'I mustn't keep you. Would you permit me to say a blessing before you go? Do say, if you'd rather not. I don't want to presume.'

Douglas did feel a little put on the spot but agreed nonetheless. Instinctively he left his chair and knelt on the floor. And so, the bishop laid her hands on the head of her priest, and in the glow of the warming fire, she prayed her blessing: 'Douglas Romer - follower of Christ and priest of God. May the radiance of God's love now shine upon you, bringing light to your heart and soul. May He visit with His healing your place of wounding. I release you now from St.Philip's Church where you have served your Lord with great love and faithfulness. I call down the power of heaven to lead you on through the pathways of this world, that you may find fulfilment and peace in your life and ministry. May holy angels surround and protect you. In the name of the Father, and the Son and the Holy Spirit, Amen.'

She made a large sign of the cross over Douglas, and then, much to his surprise, she leant down and kissed him on the cheek. 'Go in the peace of Christ,

Douglas,' she said as she took his hand helping him to his feet.

As Douglas drove away from the bishop's house, he found himself marvelling at the sensitivity of spirit he had witnessed in his bishop, whom he had too often judged to be cold and impersonal. The sense of blessing he felt from her prayer settled deep in his soul. He would feel it for many days to come. And he would need it.

*

It was from a disturbed sleep that Douglas awoke the next morning. During the night he had awoken to the sound of Saoirse's voice and for a few moments, he thought he was back in the blessed days when she was a living, loving warm companion next to him in his bed. But reaching out he found her place in the bed empty, and he was revisited by the weary sense of desolation that had been his near-constant companion during the years or emptiness following her death.

Daylight was so long in coming at this time of the year, and he felt a yearning for Springtime light and life. Eventually, after his shower, and a breakfast of tea and toast, the daylight did begrudgingly make its appearance, though it was a grey dawn over Sheffield on this January day. Douglas was just about to do some packing up of his much-loved books when there was a loud knock at the door. It was a knock he recognised, so he opened the door and, sure enough, there was the neatly-dressed and slight figure of Mavis. Beside her,

171

with her hand tucked in the crook of her aunt's arm, was the taller figure of Alice.

'Good to see you both,' said Douglas, ushering them into the hallway. He checked outside in the driveway to see if anyone was observing this activity in the Vicarage. Satisfied that all was quiet, he shut the door, took their coats, and led his guests into the kitchen. It was the first time Alice had been into the house and she took an immediate interest in the pictures that hung on the walls of the kitchen. Both prints were chosen by Saoirse. Due to her poor eyesight, she went up close to them, and gently brushed her slender fingers over them. Mavis sat down at the table.

'Tea as usual for you, Mavis?' asked Douglas, as he put on the kettle. Mavis thanked him. 'And Alice - tea or coffee?'

'Oh, coffee for me please, Douglas,' she said, betraying her hint of a West Country accent.

'I can do a latte if you like?'

'That would make it very special,' said Alice, turning for a moment from the picture and smiling.

'It's a Japanese artist. Saoirse was fond of Japanese art,' commented Douglas as he set up the coffee maker.

Alice studied the print carefully, and then said, 'The artist... He or she suffered, didn't they? But look what they have done with their pain. Something so beautiful.'

'Oh, come and sit down, dear, and don't get too mysterious on us first thing on a Saturday morning,' said Mavis, patting a seat by the kitchen table. Alice smiled and obediently made her way to the table, taking care to feel for the seat before she sat down.

172

Douglas chuckled at Mavis' rebuke. He recalled from their visit to Dingle before Christmas that although Mavis was very fond of her niece, she did not have much time for what she called "her mystical side." There was a time when Douglas would have been none too fond of it either, considering it 'unsound'. But the glimpses he saw of it in Ireland, he rather took to. He had changed.

'How have you both been doing?' called Douglas over the sound of the boiling kettle and the milk frother.

'We've been managing fine, haven't we, Alice?' said Mavis, sweeping away some crumbs she spotted on the table.

'Have you found work, Alice?' asked Douglas.

'No, I'm still looking - well, with my one reasonably good eye!' She smiled.

'I never really liked to ask about your sight,' said Douglas as he came over to the table with two creamy lattes. 'But as you mention it, how much vision do you have, if you don't mind me asking?'

'That depends by what you mean by vision?' she said, smiling a teasing smile.

'Ur... say more,' said Douglas, bringing Mavis' tea to the table, and settling down beside his two friends.

'Well, I have two eyeballs in these sockets,' she said removing her glasses and touching an eye. 'This one on the right is done for, I'm afraid. But my left is not too bad. Just a slow deterioration which makes things look a bit hazy.'

'Well, a little more than a bit, dear,' said Mavis, feeling a need for Douglas to be fully aware of her condition.

'Aunt Mavis, I'm no blind Bartimaeus just yet,' she scolded, tapping her aunt on the hand. 'But Douglas, that's only one way of seeing, isn't it?'

'Er, yes... of course,' said, Douglas, thinking that Dorchadas would be very at home with that kind of comment.

'You never seen or read Shakespeare's Lear?' she asked, looking at Douglas with her ice-blue eyes, which looked to him to be in perfect working order.

'Yes, of course. Know it quite well.'

'Well, remember poor old Gloucester at the end, after they put his eyes out,'

'Oh, for pity's sakes, Alice...' protested Mavis.

Alice and Douglas both laughed.

'It's Shakespeare, Mavis. That sort of thing is normal in his plays.'

'Explains why I've never been to one,' said Mavis. She took a cautious sip of her hot tea.

'Well,' said Alice turning to Douglas. 'Remember old King Lear says to poor, blind Gloucester, "Your eyes are in a heavy case, your purse in a light. Yet you see how this world goes." And how does Gloucester reply, do you remember?'

Douglas frowned and looked at the ceiling for a moment, then said, 'You'll have to remind me, Alice.'

'He says, "I see it feelingly." So, that's how I do some of my seeing - *feelingly*. The word works, doesn't it?' She held her eyes on Douglas, and he smiled back at the thoughtful face in front of him. When he first met her on her trip to Ireland in the autumn, for some reason, he had never really looked at her. But now, he saw something in her face that drew him. It was an interesting face, which he guessed had

174

been around in this world a similar time to his. He saw both humour and sadness in the failing yet bright eyes. He liked the tangle of blond hair framing her face. He noticed distinct strands of grey and liked the fact that she had made no attempt to deny their existence through hair dye. This was a face he could rest in. A face he could trust.

'Yes,' he said as he slowly drew his coffee to his lips. 'The word works very well.'

'Now listen, Douglas,' said Mavis, not following the conversation's drift at all. She rose from her chair and said, 'I was all full of good intention to come and do the hoovering last week, but time got the better of me and I never made it. I'm so sorry, as I wanted to have it nice for you this weekend. So, I'm just going to run the hoover over the lounge and your study.' Before anyone could stop her, she had risen from the table, and, taking her mug of tea with her, she bustled out to the cupboard under the stairs.

Alice raised an eyebrow and, lowering her head, she said in a quiet voice to Douglas, 'Is she trying to set us up?'

Douglas was taken aback by her directness, but also felt a sense of relief. He smiled with a raised eyebrow and said, 'I rather think she is.'

Alice leaned back in her chair. 'Well, Douglas, there's no need to worry. I shan't be hurling myself at you. When we came over to Ireland in the autumn, I told you that I was divorced. I didn't honestly feel like saying too much then, but the fact is, it was a pretty messy divorce. Well, a pretty messy marriage if I'm honest, and I'm not ready... You know.' She sipped her latte and looked out of the window.

'Oh, I understand, Alice, of course.' The sound of the Dyson starting up momentarily distracted him, then he said, 'I am so sorry yours wasn't a happy marriage.'

Alice pulled off her glasses and slowly polished them on her burgundy scarf. 'It was OK at the beginning. I think I mentioned to you that I loved Astronomy. I got this wonderful job at the observatory in Marseilles. You know, research and teaching. I had turned thirty and I suppose was starting to think about settling, having a family and so on. And I met Georges.' She held her polished spectacles up to the light, peering at them as best she could. 'He was a handsome taxi driver and we fell deeply in love.' She smiled and put her spectacles back on. Douglas cupped his hands around his mug. He remembered such feelings all too well.

Alice drained the last of her latte. 'Could I have a spoon, please? I can never bear to leave the froth, can you?'

Douglas fetched a spoon and passed it to her. 'So, is he the guy you married?' he asked.

'Well, we lived together for a few years, then got married. My mum wasn't too impressed, but then she was never going to approve of anyone I was going to marry.' She spooned the last of the milky froth from the mug. 'And getting married turned out to be a mistake. He... he became an alcoholic. We'd have good years and bad years. The bad years usually involved his drinking. We couldn't have children and I think that got to him. And then he started to become more aggressive.' She placed the mug and spoon carefully in front of her.

Douglas frowned. He hardly knew Alice, but the thought of anyone lifting a hand to her appalled him.

'Oh, I'm so sorry,' he said, with his brow deeply furrowed.

'No, no...' said Alice, waving her hand. 'It was terrible, yes. It did get frightening and I picked up a few bruises. But, you know, the more he tried to hurt and humiliate me, the more something strong grew within me. I never hated him.' She breathed in and stared at her empty mug for a while, then looked up at Douglas and said, 'But I knew I had to leave him. I actually felt very sad the last time I saw him. But I knew he would never change. I tried for ten years and that was enough.' She looked up at Douglas. 'That was three years ago now.'

'So you returned to the UK?'

The sound of the vacuum faded as Mavis left her labours in the hall, and set to work on the living room. 'Yes, I came back home,' said Alice.

'Where is home?'

'Bideford, North Devon.' She smiled as she recollected her home town. 'Beautiful little town. A very happy place for me in childhood. I was especially close to my Dad - Mavis' brother.' She smiled her endearing smile again. 'He died.' The smile faded.

'Oh, I'm sorry. Recently?'

'Oh, no. Long, long ago when I was at Uni. Car accident.'

Douglas felt shocked at the thought of this tragic and violent bereavement. He was trying to think how best to respond when Alice continued, looking back out of the window. 'And I'm afraid I've never got on quite so well with Mum, so I decided to start life afresh here in Sheffield. I've not found work yet, but I've been involved with a charity that develops resources for the visually impaired. I've always loved my Aunt Mavis, so I lived in a flat near her for a couple of years and then she asked me to move in, and I did. It has worked well, actually.' She looked back at Douglas and shrugged her shoulders saying, 'So that's how I'm here in this kitchen on this January morning drinking coffee and telling you my life story.'

'Thank you, Alice,' said Douglas. He paused for a moment and said, 'May I just ask - you said something grew strong in you. What was that strength?'

'Faith,' said Alice. She looked at Douglas and, with a slight upturn of her mouth, added, 'Probably not your official Church of England kind of faith.'

Douglas smiled. 'Go on.'

Alice sighed. 'No-one ever really gets this, but I'll risk telling you. The more my eyesight failed, the more a different seeing developed in me.'

'Feelingly?' asked Douglas

She smiled. 'Yes, feelingly, Douglas. And that feeling included a sense of presence. I felt things.'

'Presence?'

'Yes… Presence of angels, for example,' she cast a quick, uncertain look at Douglas. She risked continuing. 'Sometimes presence, I think maybe of… those who have passed on. But don't get me wrong, not that spiritualism kind of thing.'

Douglas listened in fascination. She had expected Douglas to recoil, but he showed no sign of shock or disapproval, so she continued, 'And I felt the presence of Jesus. It grew stronger in the dark days in Marseilles. I had never had much to do with religion, but...' She shrugged her shoulders again. 'But He just seemed to be there and I liked His company. That's it,

178

really. I'm not religious as you can see. I don't go to church, but I... well, I *feel*. And I'm OK with that. It helps.'

Douglas was aware that Alice had shared something very personal and delicate, and he wanted to tread very carefully. 'I am also learning to move through this world a little more feelingly, Alice. I think I could learn a lot from you.'

Alice laughed and replied, 'I am not so sure. You're looking at a mixed-up kid here, Douglas!'

'You are speaking to one as well, Alice!'

Alice frowned, 'I'm sorry, Douglas, I've done all the talking. Tell me a bit more about how things are going for you.'

'Hm...' said Douglas and looked thoughtful. He then raised an eyebrow and asked, 'Another latte?'

'Why not? Thanks, Douglas.'

*

After Mavis and Alice left, Douglas spent the rest of the day packing and sorting. By the time he was boarding the midday flight back to Ireland on Sunday, he felt he had made good progress on clearing his house and storing his furniture. The Sheffield world was now definitely closing down. Ireland was proving a very good interim home for him, and he would remain in this one until a clear future opened for him. He felt in no hurry.

As the plane soared up into the thick blanket of cloud, Douglas reflected on his weekend. He recalled the unexpected kiss from his bishop. He laughed out loud as he thought of telling Frank about it. But a deeper part of himself felt like weeping at the thought of it. It was not the kiss of a lover, but, strangely, more of a child. Douglas felt she did feel genuinely sad at the thought of his leaving her diocese. And there was a curious sense that by his leaving her, she was left more vulnerable. The kiss almost felt like a cry of help. Feelingly - that's how he experienced it.

And then he thought of Alice. It was nice to be in the company of a woman of his age again. And she felt safe. Yes, Mavis would love to match-make and hustle them into a relationship. But Douglas felt far from ready for such a step. There was more healing for his soul before space could be created for another romance. But in the meantime, Alice felt like a new friend and one that he could trust. And he was intrigued by her reference to angels and the dead and Jesus. If Dorchadas was around when she next came out to Ireland, they would have to meet. He smiled as he thought of seeing his friend Dorchadas again.

The plane never managed to break free of the thick cloud and, as it made its descent towards a gloomy Cork, Douglas started to think of the coming few days ahead of him. There was the funeral coming up on Thursday. He felt an uncomfortable shard of fear nick his soul at the thought of meeting Niall again. And then there was this cryptic communication from Intelligence and the worry that someone of violence could conceivably be turning their attention to him. And what of his suspicion of Gerald? Thankfully Gerald had made no visit to the Vicarage over the weekend. The bishop seemed unaware of his insidious influence over her diocese. What was he up to? As the plane landed, Douglas was recalling the disturbing dream of Gerald armed with a Kalashnikov.

On making his way out of the airport, he noticed that the land of Ireland, that he had come to love, now felt less safe. When he entered his ancient Fiesta, he surprised himself by bowing his head and reciting a verse from his favourite Psalm 91: 'For he will command his angels concerning you to guard you in all your ways. On their hands, they will bear you up, so that you will not dash your foot against a stone.' The Fiesta was in a good mood and started without complaint, and Douglas drove back to Dingle to embark on another week of his life. It would be another week that he would never forget. A week, when he would need the help of angels more than ever.

On me the Son of God suffered a little time;
wherefore in glory now I tower up beneath the sky;
and I may bring healing unto every one of those
that have regard for me.

The Dream of the Rood

Those in authority were right to fear Jesus' power
since it was so much greater than their own,
but it was not manifested
in ways that they recognised.

Paula Gooder
Journey to the Empty Tomb

CHAPTER 15

He knew he shouldn't have, but he deserved it. He had worked very hard to secure this deal. It had not been without considerable danger. But it was done. So why shouldn't he enjoy the spoils just a little? Church in the morning had given him the idea. How ironic! The visiting preacher referred to Jesus not condemning the prostitute. So, no worries, then of great disapproval from the Almighty. It had all gone nicely to plan this evening. He left Angela slumped by *Countryfile,* with him saying the Archdeacon needed to meet with him urgently. She believed him (or was too soused to hear) and off he went to the usual hotel. And there was the girl, all ready and waiting. Very attractive, but not too conspicuous. Just a business colleague, of course. This was a good agency. Excellent girls, though they were inclined to use rather too much perfume for his liking. There was always the risk that Angela might wake up and catch the fragrance. But then she was usually dead to the world by this time of night. There were times when her fondness for the bottle came in very handy.

He crept into the house. No lights in the hall which he took as a good sign. He crept up the staircase carefully avoiding the creaky stair. He used the toilet, careful not to flush, entered his dressing room and put on his silk pyjamas, and then with great care crept into bed. Just as he thought he had negotiated everything so well, he heard her voice, slurred yet firm. 'How was the girl tonight, then?'

He was shaken but did not panic. This could be easily managed by a few white lies. 'What are you talking about, woman? I was seeing the Archdeacon, I told you. And he's male.'

She rolled over and removed her eye mask. He could just make out her face in the dark. The odour of gin was stale on her breath. 'There's really no point in trying to lie to me, Gerald. I know where you've been when you come back late like this. Don't make out there's some diocesan meeting or other. A meeting even with that Archdeacon wouldn't go on this late.'

'There was ...'

'Gerald - it's all right. I've come to accept it. I don't like it, and I want it to stop. But I'm never going to make you.'

Gerald sighed - he hated being caught out, so maybe it was best just to come clean and have the kind of marriage that has 'arrangements'. But he was too tired to discuss arrangements now, so he avoided further conversation on the matter and asked, as he yawned, 'You had a good day?'

'Can't remember much of it.'

'No, don't suppose you can.'

She then pulled herself up a little and turned on her sidelight. He screwed his eyes tight and said, 'Oh, for God's sake, I need to get to sleep.'

'Not yet, Gerald. We need to discuss the problem priest.'

Gerald opened his eyes and pulled himself up a little in the bed. He could smell the perfume strong on him, so he slid back again, hoping the duvet would cover the tell-tale fragrance.

'Mm - that's a nice one,' said Angela, sniffing the air. 'Can you bring some back for me next time. Now, listen. Today I have been working on a plan. It's a crude one, but I think it will work.'

'A plan?'

'Mm. He's in Ireland, isn't he? A wretched little town called Dingle. I spoke to that Mavis today. She was very nosy about our house, by the way. I'm definitely not having her round to clean. I told her so. Anyway, that's where he is. And I have looked on the map and it's in the south.'

'OK. So, what's the great plan?' asked Gerald, staring at the ceiling.

'We go there Gerald. We go there and you kill him.'

'I what?' Gerald did sit up this time.

Angela was gripping the duvet. Gerald saw the cold determination in the bloodshot yet determined eyes that were looking at him. 'Gerald, I have made it very clear. While he is alive, he is a threat to all of this.' She waved her hand around the room. 'I am *not* giving it up just because of some damn Vicar who's all upset because his Irish hussy of a wife got bumped off for being too nosy. I've made it quite plain. I'm not relaxed while I know he is alive. He will find out that you are the one behind her killing. I just know it.'

'How do you know it?'

'I've explained it a hundred times to you, Gerald, but you won't listen. I have no doubts that the moment he discovered that there's someone in the UK who was behind that girl's murder, he wanted revenge. That tidy, forgiving Christian faith of his collapsed long ago. He will be seeking you out, Gerald. I'm convinced of it. I can't rest in this house while he's alive.'

Angela had now got into her stride. She continued, 'I know you normally get others to do your dirty work.

Well, it's time you did it yourself. But I'm happy to be your accomplice. So, tomorrow I'm going to book flights. I'll find a hotel in Dingle and we'll have a nice few days away, only we won't tell a soul.'

'Oh yes,' said Gerald, smacking his hands on the surface of the duvet. 'And just how exactly do you imagine we are going to kill off our dear Vicar? Do we find him in a pub, take out a pistol and say, "Hello, Douglas. Nice to see you. Goodnight!" and shoot him dead, and hope everyone in the pub roars their approval?'

'Of course not,' said Angela, irritated at his sarcasm. She then continued in a calm voice. 'Gerald, you are the expert at this kind of thing. You think of something. There must be a way of doing this without getting caught.'

'For God's sakes, Angela,' said Gerald shuffling awkwardly in the bed. He sighed a nervous sigh and looked back at his wife. 'Besides, if we do manage to bump him off, then I have wasted a hundred thousand pounds on a gift to the Diocese!'

'Yes, well, as I said, I didn't think that was a brilliant plan. No. Killing is better.'

Gerald sighed a long sigh and returned his head to the pillow. He could see that she was not going to budge on this one. He knew how stubborn she could be when in this kind of mood. And the guilt from his evening's pleasure had weakened his resistance. Her plan was ridiculous but he knew there was no point trying to change her mind. So he turned his mind to practicalities.

His eyes darted from side to side as he turned over plans in his mind, then said, 'Look. We'll have to go under other names - I've got those handy passports. I'll get you the details and then you book the tickets. But book us on the ferry, not a plane. It's safer. Security is not as tight. And get a hire-car there. We don't want ours to be seen over there. I'll have a think about the means of his demise. He's pretty naïve, so it shouldn't be too hard to think of a way of bumping him off. But I'm not getting caught, Angela. I haven't worked this bloody hard to spend the rest of my days in some putrid Irish jail. Maybe you should do the deed as you're so keen to see him dead.'

Angela was delighted that he had conceded to her plan with the minimum of resistance. The timing turned out to be brilliant. She had caught him when he was guilty And the thought of doing this deed herself rather excited her. 'I'd be pleased to, Gerald,' she said, relaxing back on to her pillow. 'I can use one of those things, by the way. You taught me in Sri Lanka, remember?'

'Those were the days, darling,' he said, closing his eyes. He hardly ever called her 'darling' these days. Despite his unfaithfulness, she unexpectedly found herself feeling quite fond of him. She took him completely by surprise by kissing him. He chuckled and pulled the duvet up to his chin as his wife turned out the light.

He lay awake for some time. He had to concede that Angela was right - the vicar was always going to be a threat while alive. He did need to be eliminated. But, while it was relatively easy to bump off the Irish girl remotely in a far-off land, to do a similar task so personally, and so close to home, felt a good deal more uncomfortable, not to say risky. And besides, though he had no fondness for the man, he did not particularly wish him dead. But he knew his wife. He knew that when she was this determined, there was no changing her mind. And she was right, the man was a threat to their security. So the deed had to be done. He was confident he would think of a clever way of doing it. But now, it was time to sleep. He inhaled deeply and, filled with the fragrance of his earlier liaison, his mind turned back to memories of his comparatively less risky, and far more pleasurable, exploits earlier in the evening.

Angela was up unusually early the next morning and, before Gerald was awake, she had already researched ferry times, car-hire, and a hotel in Dingle. And she managed it all without touching a drop of alcohol. She was feeling much better. She was determined to deal with this problem, so that once again her world would be safe. And yet, and yet... Why was it that none of these plans managed to quell that disturbing homesickness that kept revisiting her soul? A longing, a yearning, as well as a worrying sense of guilt attempted to edge into her consciousness. Was she honestly planning to take a man's life? Such thoughts were dangerous and needed to be checked before they caused trouble. Such thoughts were a threat to her hard-earned security. Maybe she should just check the fridge.

CHAPTER 16

The scenic drive to Dingle in beautiful, late afternoon sunshine calmed the fears that had recently gnawed at Douglas' soul, and by the time he was opening the door of St.Raphael's he was feeling more settled.

'Is that you, Douglas?' came a voice from the parlour.

'Yes, Elsie, I'm back,' said Douglas shutting the door and placing his case on the hall floor.

Elsie appeared and Douglas noticed that her hair had now become as normal as he had ever seen it. It was still jet black with traces of the vivid green, but it was a good deal more ordered. 'So, what do you think?' she said, standing back and patting the back of her head.

'It looks really good, Elsie.'

'You're not just saying it?

'No,' reassured Douglas. 'I think it is the nicest I have seen it. I honestly do.'

'Well, thank you, son. Now listen,' she said, clasping her hands in front of her. 'Do you have any plans for this evening?'

'No, Elsie, I don't.'

'Well, now you do,' said Elsie, peering up at him through her spectacles that were catching the light of the hall lamp.

'I have?'

'Aye, that you do. My sister Kath wants us round for a meal.'

'That sounds nice.'

'Well, yes… Now, she's not the world's best cook, Douglas, if you get my meaning, but you should be able to get it down you without too much trouble.'

'I'm sure it will be fine. Will there be anyone else there?'

'Oh Aye. You, me, Kath, Peter and Kevin.'

'Sounds splendid, Elsie,' said Douglas, picking up his case. 'What time?'

'We should go up about 6.30. Will that suit you?'

'Yes, suits me fine,' said Douglas as he climbed the stairs.

'Oh, how was England?' she called up the stairs.

'Cold,' replied Douglas.

'Oh aye. You'll be glad to back here, then. Good to have you home, son.'

He spent a quiet afternoon in his room, unpacking and browsing through all the books he had managed to squeeze into his case. It felt good to have them here in his Irish home. He was so engrossed in one of them, that he quite lost track of the time and he was startled to hear Elsie calling up the stairs, 'We'll need to be going in five minutes, Douglas.'

Douglas had only ever been to Kath's coffee shop in the daytime, so he was quite surprised to enter the familiar premises to discover that what was normally the small coffee shop had been converted into a very welcoming dining room. The fire was lit and there were a couple of colourful candles flickering on the table that had been set for dinner. There was no sign of

191

Kath, but her presence was evidenced by several loud protestations coming from the kitchen. Through the fly curtain emerged not Kath, but a smartly-dressed and aproned Peter, who seemed to be acting as chef's assistant and wine waiter, for he was clutching two bottles of wine.

'Let me put these down and welcome you both,' he said, placing the bottles on the table. He greeted the two guests and said, 'Sit yourself by the fire, Elsie. It's a cold night.'

'It's a kind offer, Peter, but I'll be getting into that kitchen to see if my sister needs a hand.'

A look of concern crossed Peter's face as he watched her disappear through the fly curtain into the kitchen. Both men then heard a cry of 'Sweet Jesus, Joseph and Mary, what's been happening in here, Kath?' They looked at each other and smiled a knowing smile.

'Kath is not the tidiest of cooks, shall we say. Let's be sitting ourselves here, Douglas.'

Douglas sat by the welcome warmth of the fire as Peter asked, 'Red or white? Or would you like a glass of beer?'

'Got no beer!' came a cry from the kitchen.

'Red please, Peter,' said Douglas.

'Very diplomatic, Douglas,' said Peter smiling, and carefully filled a glass with a deep red Argentinian Malbec.'

'Same for me, Peter, please,' called Elsie from the kitchen.

'And me, love,' joined in Kath. 'At this rate, I'll be needing most of the bottle.' Peter poured out two glasses and took them through to the kitchen. Douglas breathed in the fragrance of peat which he had grown to love.

'It's been a bit of a testing time in the kitchen this afternoon, I would say,' said Peter.

'It's kind of Kath. I hope she's not too stressed.'

'Oh no. She clearly loves it, despite the aggravation it gives her.'

Peter was just about to sit in the chair on the other side of the fireplace, when Kath came through the fly curtain, and came straight over to Douglas and embraced him as a long-lost friend saying, 'So good to have you back in Ireland, Doug. It's never the same when you leave.'

'Well, I was only gone for a couple of days.'

'Two days too long, Douglas. Now listen, you must excuse me. If I don't get back into the kitchen, my sister will start wreaking havoc in there.' She started back to the kitchen calling back, 'You all right with the Irish stew, Doug?'

'Love it!' said Douglas as she disappeared back through the fly curtain.

'And Peter,' she called again. 'Put another briquette on that fire if it gets low, won't you?'

'I will, Kath. Don't you worry now,' he called, chuckling.

'Sláinte,' said Douglas raising his glass to Peter's. 'You stopping the night, Peter?'

'Well, no. Not here,' said Peter with a broad smile. 'That would provoke a bit of craic among the neighbours, don't you think? As it happens, Elsie has offered me a room so I'll be stopping at St.Raphael's this evening.'

He was just about to continue when the front door opened and Kevin entered, clutching some cans of Murphy's. 'Evening to you gentlemen,' he hailed as he put down the beer and came over to both men and gave them a warm greeting.

'How was the UK?' he asked Douglas as he bent towards the fire, rubbing his hands together.

'Oh, you know.'

'Aye, well it's good to have you back, Doug. It always is.' He briefly visited the kitchen to greet the ladies, only to be turfed straight out, so he took one of the cans of beer and came over and sat with Douglas and Peter. 'Can't drink the wine, I'm afraid, so I'll be sticking to this tonight.'

'Good plan,' said Peter.

It was not long before a flustered and red-faced Kath emerged from the kitchen with a large dish of Irish stew. Her sister followed behind with a couple of dishes of vegetables. 'Sit yourselves down gentlemen. Let's see what we can do with this. God knows what it will be like. It's fought me tooth and nail all afternoon, it surely has.' But it was not long before even Kath had to agree that the result of her strenuous labours in the kitchen was a delicious meal.'

'So, Doug, you got to meet the famous Bull,' said Kath, nudging Elsie.

'Oh now, Kath. For God's sakes let's leave that subject alone, can we,' said Elsie with a frown.

'To be fair,' said Kevin, scooping up some gravy with a spoon, 'the man had a lot about him. Fearfully knowledgeable about music, he was. You weren't far off the mark there, I'd say Aunty Else.'

'Well, I'll not be going down that road again, thanks all the same, Kev,' responded Elsie.

'But, if I may say so, Elsie,' said Peter, replenishing her empty glass, 'I think your hair, as you have it today, looks most charming.'

'Och, Peter, there's no need for flattery,' said Elsie, revealing both pleasure and coyness in the slight bend of her head. She took a large sip from her wine.

Kevin put down his spoon and placing his hand on his aunt's arm he said, 'What we'd all be saying here Aunty Else, is that you are a fine and beautiful woman. And, please God, one day you will meet a man worthy of you.'

'That's for sure,' said Kath, raising her glass, and in turn, all the table raised their glasses to Elsie. Douglas noticed how bright her eyes glistened behind her glasses. There was much that was beautiful in his landlady.

'This is a fine place to be. A fine place to be,' she said, looking around at the group. 'And Kath, the stew is exceptional.'

For a time the conversation turned to more mundane matters such as the weather and the latest shenanigans of the local politicians. The group did justice to Kath's Irish stew, Kevin even coming back for a third helping, much to Kath's delight. Kath and Kevin cleared the plates to the kitchen, and on return, they brought with them one of Kath's special chocolate Guinness cakes which was welcomed by a cheer from the table.

Douglas marvelled at the sense of warmth and safety he felt in the group, but his mood changed abruptly when Peter said, 'Douglas, I hope you don't mind my mentioning it, but I'm wondering how you are feeling about Saoirse's parents coming up to Dingle this week?'

Douglas put down the piece of cake that he was about to enjoy, and he inhaled deeply. 'If I'm honest, I'm pretty frightened about seeing them again, Peter.'

'We're all here for you, son, and if that man so much as says a word to you…' started Kath, thumping the table.

Douglas smiled as he imagined Kath striding down the church aisle with a rolling pin. 'Thanks, Kath. I know, I know. It's just…'

Kevin leaned forward and in a quieter voice said, 'We need to be careful here. I mean, the man Niall Flynn has form.' He pulled back a little. 'Don't get me wrong Doug, I'm not saying the man intends violence towards you.'

'I do wonder,' said Douglas with an unconvincing smile.

'I have found out a bit about him,' continued Kevin frowning, 'and he was senior in the army some years ago. He was in a cell that was… Well, let's say, notorious. I don't think the venom is out of him yet. And I believe he is still active. But, if grace can reach even my bitter soul, then there is hope for the man yet. Maybe this week will be his chance. What do you think?'

The mood of the room lightened, and Peter said, 'I much prefer to think of beckoning out the good, rather than protecting ourselves from the evil.'

'This man does speak a hell of a lot of sense, Quaker or no,' said Kath, beaming at her friend.

196

Peter noticed that Douglas seemed a little withdrawn from the banter that ensued, so he enquired, 'You're troubled, though Douglas, aren't you?'

Douglas took a sip of his wine and said 'He's not the only man I'm worried about.' He knew he should not have said it. He was sworn to secrecy, and yet in the last few days, a fear had crept under his skin. Some instinct in him kept alerting him to the fact that he was in danger. And it was not just from Niall.

'Och, there's plenty of men that worries me,' said Elsie, whose slurred speech betrayed her enjoyment of the wine.

'Time for coffee, I think,' said Kath rising from the table and grabbing the arm of her sister. When Kath and Elsie had departed, Douglas leaned forward and said, 'Please keep this completely confidential, but I trust you as two very dear friends.'

'Of course, Doug,' said Kevin, grasping his hand.

'I can't say too much. In fact, I don't really know too much. But... Saoirse was not killed in a random terrorist drive-by shooting in Egypt. I've had word from British Intelligence that she was murdered by a contract killer who was targeting her because she was on to an illegal arms-trader.'

'Oh, God Almighty,' said Kevin in a loud whisper. He leaned back in his chair. Memories of his old life returned vividly. 'You need to be careful, Doug.'

These were not the words Douglas needed to hear. He was longing for reassurance of his safety, not confirmation of his plight. 'W... why?' he asked, aware that for the first time in a long time, there were signs of his stammer returning.

'Because you've been told. Why the hell did someone tell you this?'

'They felt I might have witnessed some suspicious activity.'

'Well, did you? Do you have your suspicions?'

Douglas looked down. All he had to go on was a dream, and that was not enough evidence, so he just said, 'N... no.'

'You mean, "yes," but you'd rather not tell us,' said Peter, with his usual perceptiveness.

Douglas looked up at him and nodded.

Kath and Elsie returned with a tray of coffee, and as she placed the tray on the table Kath said, 'Good God, have we been visited by a ghost? What have you men been talking about? We can't leave you for a minute, can we?'

'Too right, Mam,' said Kevin, and laughed. 'We were talking about you, of course. All good, wasn't it lads?'

'Of course,' said Peter smiling, but inwardly he was feeling concerned for the Englishman.

As Douglas walked back with Elsie and Peter to St.Raphael's that night, his initial sense of guilt that the wine had loosened his tongue too much, was replaced by a great sense of relief at his having shared a burden with trusted friends. He felt light-headed with the wine as he lay down on his bed and entered a fitful sleep. He was awoken by another disturbing dream. In the dream, he was back in his Vicarage kitchen, and Mavis and Alice were there. The door then opened and in came Gerald Bentley. He said not a word but pointed to Alice. It was a dream of little action, but much weight. There was a great sense of dread in the room. Both the

198

dream and the dread kept visiting Douglas'
increasingly nervous soul in the days to come.

CHAPTER 17

When Douglas was getting dressed the next morning, he heard voices downstairs and when he descended to the dining room he found Dorchadas and Peter enjoying a cup of coffee and chatting to Elsie.

'Well, good morning to you Douglas,' Dorchadas said, beaming. 'Welcome back to the holy land of Eire. Hope you had a good trip back to England.'

'Yes,' said Douglas, sitting down at the table, 'and Peter will have told you that I was given an excellent meal last night on my return.'

Peter smiled and said, 'Aye, we enjoyed a great meal and good craic, we certainly did.'

Elsie got up and said, 'Can I be getting you some eggs, Dorchadas.'

'Well now, that would be grand, Elsie. Thank you,' replied Dorchadas.

'It's good to see you, Dorch,' said Douglas, grasping the arm of his friend.

The three enjoyed a good breakfast at the end of which, Dorchadas said, 'Now, listen, Douglas. It's a beautiful morning and it looks like the sun will be fair smiling upon us throughout the day. So, what say you, we go in that vehicle of yours, if it's in the mood for it, and drive a few miles north to the Gallarus Oratory? We keep saying we'll visit it one day.'

Douglas said, 'Yes, that would be great Dorch. I'd love that.'

'You not been there yet?' asked Dorch.

'No. In fact, I had never heard of it, until I read Seamus Heaney's poem on it.'

'Ah yes, your man Seamus. Talks about them coming up out of that wee chapel seeing the sea as a censer and the grass as a flame.'

'Yes,' said Douglas smiling, admiring his angel friend's love and knowledge of poetry.

'Will you be joining us, Peter?' asked Dorchadas. Peter replied that he needed to be getting back to Adare so, sadly, could not go with them.

Thus it was, on a chilly sunny morning, that Douglas and Dorchadas drove out of Dingle on to the lanes where the road signs were only in Gaelic and where the green fields either side of the lane rose to gentle, beckoning hills. After a while, Dorchadas directed them to a single-track lane and to a lay-by where they parked. They walked down a hedge-lined pathway with the simmering sea on their left and a frost-tipped hill on their right. After only a short walk they came to an area of green enclosed by a low stone wall. Set in the midst of this area stood the Gallarus Oratory, a beautifully constructed, dry-stone structure that appeared like the hull of an upturned boat. No-one else was present as Douglas and Dorchadas made their way to the building. It was one of the smallest chapels Douglas had ever seen. For a while they walked around the outside of the structure, admiring the dry-stone corbeling that succeeded in keeping the interior dry.

Even before entering the building, Douglas felt a sense of archaic holiness about it. He felt a need to keep touching and feeling the ancient stones of various colours and sizes. 'What do you know about this place, Dorch?' he asked.

'To be fair, Doug, I don't know much about its history. Maybe back to the seventh or eighth century, and if that's the case, it makes it one of the oldest church buildings still standing in the world. But that's not what's important for me. It's the power of the place. Such a tiny, insignificant building, and yet remarkable power, don't you think? I mean, can you imagine it alongside them great buildings in Dubai or Shanghai? Or your enormous bank buildings in London, for that matter? Humans love to build humungous, great buildings, and I think many of them are handsome, for sure. But too often they have been built to impress and to assert power. Everyone wants to have the highest building in the world. But the power of such things is usually only to do with money, status, politics - all that kind of stuff. And then you come here to this place which, set alongside your sky-tipping Shard in London say, would look no more than a wee pebble from the beach. And yet, Doug, this oratory was once a powerhouse - one of many that transformed the fortunes of the people. And the power's not gone, has it?'

'No, Dorch. I don't think it has,' said Douglas. He stepped towards the doorway and asked, 'Can we look inside?'

'Sure, go ahead.' Douglas entered first and Dorchadas followed stooping a long way, for the lintel was low. They entered the dark interior, lit only by the pale January light making its way into the chapel through the doorway and a small window set into the deep east end wall. Instinctively, they both remained silent for a good many minutes.

202

'We keep coming back to power, Dorch, don't we?' said Douglas, whispering out of respect for the sense of holiness he felt in the church.

'We do, son. We do.' They continued to stand in the church for a little longer in the quiet. Then Dorchadas turned to Douglas and said, 'Doug, you're afraid, aren't you? I've seen it in you. What is it you fear?'

'Yes, you're right,' said Douglas. 'I know it's silly, but I'm afraid of meeting Niall and Orla - well, especially Niall. I know he hates me and blames me for Saoirse's death. And then I've also been getting worried by this business with the British Intelligence and their trying to track down this arms-dealer behind the death of my Saoirse. I mean, don't get me wrong, I'm desperate for them to find out who's behind it all, but I can't see what I can do. And...'

'Go on.'

'Well, I just have this dread, that the person responsible, who is clearly a violent man... Well, once he knows that I know....'

'I get your meaning, Doug.' Both were silent again for a while, then Dorchadas said, 'Evil has turned even the kindest people to violence. And violence breeds violence. Oh, how I have seen it destroy the sweetest lives.' Dorchadas was about to continue when he checked himself and said to Douglas. 'Doug, where exactly are we?'

Douglas was about to say, 'In the Gallarus,' when he realised he was not. The door through which they had entered had disappeared, and the little window at the east end of the chapel had now become a long stone corridor.

'You tell me, Dorch,' said Douglas.

But Dorchadas was no wiser and only said, 'Let's find out.' As they took a few steps towards the corridor, they noticed oil lamps mounted on the walls, which shed enough light for them to see by. They took tentative steps over the paved floor, for there was a sense of danger in the air. Wherever this was, it did not feel like a welcoming place. They seemed to be in a windowless section of a fortress. The air felt warm and stale and smelt of damp stone. Dorchadas stopped for a moment and said in a whisper, 'Listen.'

They stopped, and for a moment Douglas could only hear the sound of his nervous breathing. But then he heard the unmistakable, rhythmic sound of music and human conversation coming from somewhere above them. To his ear, the style of music sounded Arabic. 'Let's explore a little further,' said Dorchadas in a low voice, and on they went along the low-arched corridor which was made of large straw-coloured stones. They turned a corner and saw a chamber ahead of them with more light, and Dorchadas stopped again. The sound of music and laughter was stronger, but there was also another sound. It was the sound of someone weeping. Dorchadas looked at Douglas and beckoned him on with a nod of his head.

As they entered the chamber, there was a staircase on their left, and sitting on that staircase with her head buried in her hands, was a young woman. She was slim and of medium height. The design of her dress suggested to Douglas that they had stepped into an ancient time. It also suggested that the intention of the dress was to draw the attention of male admirers. Her face was hidden by her long dark hair. Dorchadas made his way towards her. He looked back at Douglas. It was clear that he was still uncertain of both their whereabouts and the identity of this young woman.

When Dorchadas reached her, the woman looked up and cried with alarm. Dorchadas put up his hand and said, 'Please don't be afraid. We come as friends.'

Douglas could see from her reddened eyes and smudged makeup that the young woman had been weeping for some time. He was also disturbed to see blood on both her hands and her dress. Dorchadas knelt by her side and said, 'What is it, lass?'

'Who are you?' she asked looking at both men with great uncertainty and suspicion.

'We are visitors. But please regard us as friends,' said Dorchadas. Douglas moved closer and sat on the other side of the girl. 'What is it that stresses you, lass?' said Dorchadas. Neither men knew where they were, but if past experiences were anything to go by, Douglas assumed they had stepped into some biblical narrative.

'He wanted me to dance...' she began, her voice betraying a Middle Eastern accent.

'Who did?' asked Dorchadas, longing for a clue to her identity.

'My stepfather. You surely know who I mean?' She pulled part of her fulsome skirt up to her face to dry her eyes.

'No, lass. I'm sorry to say we don't. We are not from these parts.'

'You are not at the party, then? His birthday party?'

'No.' said Dorchadas.

She sighed, and her face started to crumple again. Both Dorchadas and Douglas were so eager to find out who she was and into which story they had stumbled, but they had to patiently wait while she gathered her emotions sufficiently to be able to speak. 'My

205

stepfather is Herod, and what you hear upstairs is his party.'

Dorchadas leaned back and Douglas observed a look of horror on his face.

'Oh, dear God. Tell me, lass. Is your name Salome?'

She nodded and sniffed. Dorchadas turned to Douglas. They both now knew where they were. Dorchadas shifted his position and asked, 'Could you tell us what happened, love. It might help you to talk about it.'

She sniffed again, sighed, and said, 'Thank you.' She looked at them both and said, 'You seem to be good men, so I will tell you.' She drew a deep breath then embarked on her story. 'I don't really like my stepfather, but I don't think he's a bad man. Anyway, it's his birthday today and he's having this big party. Well, one of the things I love doing is dancing and so I decided to do a special dance for him. My mother says I'm a very good dancer.' She smiled briefly through her tears, then continued. 'Well, I'd had a glass of wine, and I suppose felt quite... you know, free, and... I danced. And after a while, I realised everyone had stopped talking and they were watching me and I was enjoying myself. Eventually, the musicians stopped and I went over and bowed before my stepfather and it was clear he was very delighted. So, I thanked him and was just about to walk away, when he took my hand and said something extraordinary.' She then wiped her face again and looking at the two men said, 'Excuse me, what are your names?'

'My name is Dorchadas and this is my friend Douglas.'

She shook her head and frowned. 'I am sorry, I do not know those names. Which country are you from?'

'Oh, a long way away,' said Douglas. 'You may find it easier just to call us Dorch and Doug.'

'Dorch and Doug?' she said, her brow furrowing further.

'Never mind lass,' said Dorchadas, looking a little irritated with his friend. Please get on with the story. We are keen to hear. What extraordinary thing did the king say to you?'

'Ah yes,' she said as her face dropped. 'Well, he said that he liked the dance so much that he would give me whatever I wanted. Even up to half his kingdom, would you believe! So, I did as I always do, I went to check with my mother, as she knows what to do. So I asked her, "What do I choose?" I was hoping she might say something like "ten wonderful horses" or "a beautiful house with servants"!' For a moment the girl's face lit up and her natural beauty shone through. Then the same face darkened as she said, 'But my mother said none of those things. Instead, she said that I should ask for the head of John the Baptist.' She then covered her face with her hands again, and for a while, all she could say was, 'I am so sorry. So sorry.'

'It's all right, lass,' said Dorchadas. 'Take your time.'

She breathed in again and continued. 'I did not know who this Baptist was, but my mother insisted. She said he was a man who hated her, who hated Herod and hated God and he was threatening the whole kingdom. She said, if we did not kill him, then his followers would kill all of us in a few days. She said Herod needed an excuse to kill him, and I could provide that now. So what choice did I have? I went

207

back and said exactly what my mother told me. I said I wanted the head of the Baptist on a fine silver plate. Why she wanted it on a plate, I don't know.' She looked mournful for a moment and then looked at Dorchadas and said, 'Your name is "Pork"?'

'Dorchadas,' he corrected, frowning briefly at Douglas.

'Well, Dorchadas, you should have seen Herod's face. Oh, he was so distressed. It was clear that he did not want to kill John the Baptist, but he had given his word, you see. I could tell that he didn't think this man was as bad as my mother said he was. Anyway…' She struggled for a moment and buried her face in her damp hands. She then looked up and said, 'After a while, they brought it in. Everyone gasped. It was horrible. I had never seen such a thing before. And… worst of all, they gave it to me. I stood there holding this dreadful thing, not bearing to look at it. My mother was next to me, laughing and clapping. And then Herod just told me to take it away.' As she said this she waved her arm as she remembered how Herod tried to wave the sight of it away from him.

'So, I brought it down here,' she continued. 'And…'. She breathed in deeply again and said, 'When I put it down on a table over there,' she nodded in the direction of a small room ahead of them, 'I finally dared look at the head.'

Douglas recoiled from the ghoulish nature of the thought and looked down at the stone floor. Salome noticed and said, 'I am sorry… your name is "Doug"?'

'Yes,' said Douglas

'I am sorry, Doug. It is not a nice subject to talk about. But I did look at the face and it was not what I expected. I expected to see a look of horror, or fear. Or

perhaps hatred at his murderer. But no, it was not that.'
Here she looked at Dorchadas and said, 'It was,
Dorchadas, a look... how can I say?' She looked up
and then back at Dorchadas. 'It was a look of complete
adoration. Sometimes I have watched the people
worship God, and I see the same look on their faces. I
could tell with John, that when the sword came down
on him, he was not thinking about his death. He was
like a man looking over a wall and seeing something
beautiful. Or better, someone beautiful. I don't know,
maybe he saw an angel? Or maybe he could see the
face of the Almighty?' She looked away from
Dorchadas and pulled in her lips for a moment.

'And one more thing,' she said, now looking to
Douglas. 'I spoke to him. I... I bent down and cupped
his face, and I said, "John please, please forgive me." I
know that the face was the face of dead man, and yet
there was something in that face, Doug. There was
something in his look that told me that he had forgiven
me.' She turned back to Dorchadas and said, 'Did you
know him?'

'Yes, that we did, lass,' said Dorchadas. 'We met
him not long ago.'

'Was he a great man?' she asked, turning her head
to one side.

'He was a great man,' said Dorchadas in a quiet and
sad voice. 'He most certainly was.'

'He was not who my mother said he was?' she
asked, frowning?

'No, lass.'

'I am so sorry. Would you...' she said, hesitating
for a moment. 'As you were friends, would you want to
say goodbye to him?'

Douglas felt instinctively nervous about seeing something so macabre, but before he could say anything, Dorchadas said, 'We would be very pleased to.' He helped Salome to her feet and as he stood, he towered above her.

'So tall!' she said, looking up at him and offered a rare smile. 'Come.' She took his hand, and with her other hand, she took one of the torches hanging on the wall and walked them down the corridor to a small room that appeared to be some kind of storeroom. As they entered, her torch lit up the room. She walked over to a table where was placed the grim spectacle of the head of the man. Douglas was in no doubt that this was the head of the man they had met in that desert cave - the man who was then so full of strength and vitality. All three edged towards it, and Douglas found as he approached it that, rather than recoiling in horror, he was filled with a sense of profound reverence. As he arrived at the table, he instinctively knelt before it, and the other two also knelt.

'You are right, Salome,' said Douglas. 'This is a face of worship and wonder, not of fear.'

'Aye, that it is, son,' said Dorchadas, almost in a whisper.

Salome looked up to Dorchadas and said, 'Dorchadas, would you please say a blessing for this man?'

'That I will, love,' said Dorchadas. He released his hand from hers and reaching both his arms towards John he said in a strong and clear voice, 'John, beloved of God, prophet of the people, and forerunner of the Christ. We commend your dear soul to your God whom you served so faithfully. Be free of the ills and hurts of this world. Walk this day in the flowering fields of Paradise, and may the song of your heart be heard for all time to come, in this world and the next. Amen.'

'Amen,' said both Salome and Douglas. They were silent for some moments, and they all rose and left the chamber.

When they got to the staircase, Salome stopped and said, 'God sent you, I am sure, and I thank you. I now feel some peace.'

'I think, dear Salome,' said Dorchadas, 'that you were sent to us.' Her countenance lifted as she smiled. 'But I am so pleased we have been able to help your sweet soul. What will you do now, lass?'

'I shall live differently,' she said.

'Will you still dance?' asked Dorchadas.

She smiled and nodded saying, 'God made me to dance. But now my dancing will be to lift the people's spirits. Never again will I dance to darken the world.' And with that, she lifted both her hands to the skies so that her sleeves fell to her shoulders. She then began to dance with the most exquisite and ethereal dance moves that Douglas had ever seen in a dancer. He drew up his hands to his mouth as he watched her with delight and amazement. She stopped as quickly as she had started, then waved at her new friends, and ran up the staircase.

'Thank you,' called both Dorchadas and Douglas and waved until she was out of sight.

Douglas felt giddy and leaned against the wall. As he did so, the light from the oil lamps was replaced by a brighter light. It was daylight - the daylight filtering through the small window of the Gallarus Oratory. Dorchadas was standing next to him, with his head

211

stooped under the arching roof. 'We're back, Dorch,' said Douglas.

'Aye, we are,' said Dorchadas. His eyes were closed and he was exhaling slowly. He then turned to Douglas and said, 'Shall we go?'

'Yes,' said Douglas, and both of them made their way back out of the chapel. They stood still for a few moments by the entrance to the ancient church and breathed in the fresh Atlantic air.

'The sea as a censer and the grass as a flame,' said Dorchadas, and put his arm around Douglas's shoulder.

"Hm…' said Douglas. 'But I don't suppose old Seamus saw what we've just seen.'

'Well, he saw a few things in his time, that he did. But no, I don't suppose he saw that. Now let's go and get ourselves a warm coffee.' And with that, the two made their way back down the track to the car and in pale sunshine, they drove in search of a coffee shop.

*

They had to return to Dingle to find an open café, but soon enough they were enjoying the warmth of a hot cup of coffee around their hands.

'It's hard to believe what we've just seen, Dorch,' said Douglas holding his steaming cup to his mouth and savouring the fragrance.

'I wasn't expecting that meeting, Doug,' said Dorchadas, who was playing with the milk on top of his cappuccino with his spoon. 'What a fine man he was. Remember him in that cave?'

'Of course. How could I forget?'

'Such vulnerability in the man, don't you think, Doug?'

'Certainly. But also, such strength.'

'Aye - I've often seen the two go together. With his strength, he challenged the powers - the whole religious and political establishment of his time. Made no bones about it, did he? Not surprising he ended up in a dungeon in that fortress of Herod's.'

'Sounds like it was Herod's wife who was the driver of his death in the end.'

'Aye, but if it had not been her, it would have sooner or later been one of the others. John knew he was never going to get out of that place.'

'So, did he lose or did he win, Dorch?' asked Douglas.

Dorchadas smiled and took a long sip of his coffee. 'What do you think, Douglas?'

'I asked you first. I want the angel's line on this.'

Dorchadas laughed. 'Do you know, we angels never had "lines" on anything. You see - your man Antonio. He was right - Jesus had authority over evil, sickness, and all the things that make life tough for his humans. Over that stuff, he was very controlling. But do you notice that over people he wasn't? He told them about what he believed and invited them into that belief. He told stories; he asked questions. He liked people thinking for themselves. And when you think for yourself, you are starting to win. John was a great thinker for himself - clearly right up to the end. That was the face of a winner we looked on, Doug, not a loser.

'You see the Herods of this world,' continued Dorchadas after supping his coffee again, 'they and the other religious leaders, they were always trying to control the people with their heavy-handed policing, and their ridiculous religious rules they imposed on the people. But that was not the way of Jesus - not as I saw it at any rate. I mean, you don't control people by washing their stinking feet, do you now? No, He was very different.' He paused for a few moments and then asked, 'Why do religious leaders always want to use their religion to control people, Doug? Were you like that as a Vicar?'

Douglas finally took a sip from the cup that had been hovering before his lips for a while and put the cup back on its saucer. 'Yes, Dorch. I think I was. I felt I was the one who had to get them to believe the right things and behave in the right ways. At least, that's the way I was until I met Saoirse.'

'That was not her style, I imagine?'

Douglas smiled a warm smile. 'I went into the school from time to time - you know, to take assembly or a Governors' meeting or whatever. On one occasion, Saoirse was teaching a group of children, as the class teacher had gone home sick. It was the top group of the school, so the kids were around ten or eleven years old, and getting to that stage where they would try it on a bit with the teacher. I stood outside the classroom and I listened. I could hear Saoirse attempting to teach them, but I could tell the class was getting a bit restless. I then heard Saoirse slam down her book and I thought she was going to read the riot act. But she took them away from their desks and she and all of them sat on the floor together, and she said, "I want to talk about what makes us afraid." And she started telling them about what made her afraid. She then asked them, and one by one most of the kids in that class talked about what made them afraid - spiders, nightmares, tv programmes, angry parents, and so on. And then she asked what they did with their fears, and, do you know, those kids came up with some cracking ideas. I must have stood by that door for most of the class. It was clear, she was genuinely learning from them – as was I. I could swear, Dorch, that by the end of that class, every child respected Saoirse, because she showed that she was convinced that *they* had knowledge and wisdom, not just her as the teacher.'

Dorchadas was leaning forward, resting his chin on his clasped hands. 'That's good teaching, Doug.' Both men were quiet for a while, then Dorchadas asked, 'And what about your fears, Doug? What are you going to do about them?'

Douglas shrugged his shoulders a little and said, 'I don't know, Dorch. I mean, I'm not exactly challenging a huge religious and political institution like John did.'

'But you fear you have enemies, Douglas.'

'I do. Am I imagining it, Dorch?'

'Douglas, someone, somewhere arranged the death of your dear wife. Someone very violent has come near your life. I'd say you have good reason to be cautious, at the very least.' Dorchadas paused for a moment looking down at his coffee cup. He then looked up at Douglas and asked, 'If you don't mind me asking, Doug, do you have any clue as to who was behind her murder?'

Douglas shifted in his chair for a moment and looked around to see if any other customer was close to them, and assured he could not be overheard, he leaned forward and said, 'I do, Dorch. I have my suspicions about a man who was in my congregation. He's a very wealthy man and much involved in the life of our diocese. I suspect that he is involved in arms dealing. But Dorch, I have absolutely no evidence for this. To be honest, I've only got a couple of dreams to go on and a hunch. Hardly a basis for challenging the man or going to the police about him.'

Dorchadas looked hard at his friend for a time and then said, 'I've noticed how dreams and hunches are very underrated in your world, Doug. Do you know, the only way some of our messenger angels can get their messages through to humans is through their dreams when they are asleep. Their defences are down, you see. So I would trust your dreams, Doug. But I agree, there is not much you can do about it. Just be on your guard.'

'Well, I'm safe here. He's back in the UK and when he does travel, it is usually to Africa or the Middle East. I'm certain he would never make his way to Ireland.'

'Then, there's no need to be afraid, son,' said Dorchadas, draining the last of his coffee.

'Not of him. But of course, there's still Niall!'

'Oh aye. We'll deal with one enemy at a time, shall we? But seriously, Doug. I'm around this week, and I'll be coming to the memorial mass, so let's make sure we sit together.'

Douglas felt reassured by this offer. Yet he still felt a gnawing anxiety. He could not dislodge that hunch. He could not ignore the dream. Douglas would soon be one who would share the conviction of the angels, that dreams and hunches are to be much respected.

CHAPTER 18

On the following day, the clouds hung low and heavy over the peninsula, and the town of Dingle was shrouded in a foggy melancholy. Elsie did not join Douglas at breakfast as Tuesday was clean sheets day and she always set about this piece of laundry work as one who would approach a major and challenging expedition. Douglas had learned that it was best to keep well out of the way. And it was always important to place his sheets and towels outside his bedroom in good time. As he ate his breakfast he heard Elsie upstairs putting new sheets on his bed. Despite offering to do it himself many times, she stubbornly insisted on doing this landlady duty herself.

When it was finally safe to return to his room, Douglas felt this was most definitely not a morning for going out, so he decided to spend the time reading some of the books he had brought back with him from England. As he sat down, however, he spotted his journal and realised he had not written in it for a few days. So, he opened it and did some catching up.

Journal   14 January

Quite a bit has happened since I last wrote. Two interesting emails on Thursday. Bishop wanted to see me - more about this soon. Then a cryptic email from Intelligence. Seemed to be from the guy I met in Killarney. First time he's made contact since then. No news to report. Not sure if they are making any headway on this at all. Just how motivated are they to find the guy who hired her killer? I suspect this is a fairly minor case to them. But the email also told me to 'be on your guard.' Well, that was enough to put the frighteners on me. Does that mean the said killer has his sights on me?? I can't help feeling I'm getting paranoid about this. But he had no qualms about killing my Saoirse and if he knows I know something... And I had another dream about Gerald. He was trying to kill Alice this time. Dorch says I should trust my dreams, but I think my subconscious is just locking on to Gerald because he was always so unpleasant to me in the parish. He never liked me and Saoirse, but unpleasant though he is I can't see him as a murderer. But if not him, then who???

And talking of Alice, I was back in the UK over the weekend and she and Mavis came round. So nice to see them. When Mavis went out to do some house cleaning, Alice asked me if I thought Mavis was trying to set us up! Loved her honesty and it really cleared any sense of awkwardness. She made clear she was not ready for a relationship. Told me quite a lot about her broken marriage. Poor thing, she's been through a lot. And she has some eye problem and is partially sighted which must add to her burdens. I can't deny, there is something very beautiful in her and I enjoy being with her. But Saoirse is still too big in my heart, and there's no room for anyone else at the moment.

And I went to see bishop Pauline. Such a surprising meeting. Thought I'd meet the formal bishop, but I got the wonderfully kind and pastoral one. She even kissed me!! Frank will never believe that! But actually, it was very sweet and I got the impression that she was genuinely sorry to see me leave her diocese. But I do feel relieved, and I can't thank God enough for Frank and Daisy's wonderful gift of a year's salary. And yes, I do mean that - I thank <u>God</u>. Little by little He is creeping back into my life. He seems very different from how He used to be. Or, I suppose I should say, how I used to see Him. I am discovering a much kinder God - more mysterious, and more surprising. Very unpredictable. Impossible to second guess. Not a God I can control. And it seems, not a God who wants to control me. I think it is a God who wants simply to be a friend. Well, a friend and a Lord, but the kind of Lord who washes feet - even the feet of a clapped-out vicar. Had an interesting chat with Dorchadas about the gender of God. I've decided it honestly isn't that important. But Dorch made the interesting point that if we are allergic to either 'him' or 'her', it probably suggests there's a wound somewhere within us.

And yet one more "meeting". In many ways, the most disturbing yet. Only a few days ago, Dorch and I had a wonderful meeting with John the Baptist - on the day he baptised Jesus (listen to me, writing about this kind of thing as if it's the most normal thing in the world!!). Yesterday Dorch and I went up to the Gallarus Oratory. Wow, what a special place. But it became even more special because while we were in it, it "became" the Fortress where Herod lived, and who should we meet but Salome, the dancing daughter. And not only her but, gruesome though it sounds, the head of poor John the Baptist. So awful seeing the severed head of someone who I had been with only a few days ago. And yet both Dorch and I had to agree, it wasn't a terrible sight, because the look on John's face was so beautiful. He seemed to be in a rapture. He had caught sight of something in his final moments - it must have been a vision of heaven, or of God, maybe. All the grim powers of the state and the religion killed him, and yet there was something triumphant in him. You felt he was the victor. And Salome turned out to be a sweet girl. Bit distracted at first because her dress was pretty revealing. Not surprised Herod was so impressed! But once she started speaking, I stopped being distracted because her story was so sad. And yet, this experience with John changed her life. Before she left us she danced, and it was exquisite - it felt like her spirit had taken flight. She was like a human bird flying free in that dark fortress hallway where we found ourselves. Made me long to be able to dance like that. To be so light on your feet in this world would be an awesome gift.

As I write I keep thinking of Psalm 55:
> My heart is in anguish within me,
>> the terrors of death have fallen upon me.
> Fear and trembling come upon me,
>> and horror overwhelms me.
> And I say, 'O that I had wings like a dove!
>> I would fly away and be at rest;
> truly, I would flee far away;
>> I would lodge in the wilderness;
> I would hurry to find a shelter for myself
>> from the raging wind and tempest.'

Dorch asked me about my fears and I was honest about my fear of Niall and also of Saoirse's killer. As I spoke to him, I realised that if my hunch about Gerald is right, I needn't be too bothered as he's never going to come over to Ireland. And he won't know I'm here in Dingle anyway. So if it is him, I just have to trust that the Intelligence guys will be on to him soon. I'll give them another couple of weeks, and if nothing happens, I will speak to them about Gerald. But Niall and Orla definitely are going to be here for Aunt Ruby's memorial on Thursday and I can't avoid them. Will they have forgiven me?? Saoirse always said her father's bitterness was so deep-rooted she could never see him accepting me. So sad. I'm not looking forward to Thursday. "I would hurry to find a shelter for myself".

*

Douglas put down his pen, left his desk, and lay down on his bed. He remembered a conversation he had had with Saoirse not long after they were married. They had just been to Oxford to see Douglas' parents and they stopped off at Stratford on the way back. It was a lovely summer's day and they hired a rowing boat and spent two happy hours on the river. He smiled as he remembered her reclining in the boat, wearing a pretty cream-coloured summer dress. She pulled on a straw sunhat over her dark hair and told him how she had enjoyed the overnight stay with his parents. Thankfully his father had been sober and his mother was not too nervy. In fact, they had behaved pretty well, he reckoned. Then the conversation turned to Saoirse's parents. Douglas had only seen them once - briefly at the wedding. Saoirse had always been reluctant to say much more about them.

'I don't say much about them, Dougie, because I'm not proud of them,' she said, letting her hand drop over the side of the boat into the cool waters of the flowing river.

Douglas said nothing and held the oars steady, letting the boat drift for a while. He knew she would say more if she wanted to. A swan glided by, occasionally dipping its regal head beneath the otherwise calm surface. The only sounds were of the water lapping against the boat, and the reeds and grasses of the riverbank whispering in the light breeze. Saoirse leant back in the boat, took off her sunglasses, and let the sun warm her face for a while. Douglas noticed the intriguing frown. After a few moments, Saoirse said, 'I was determined my da would not spoil our wedding. I wanted it to be the perfect day. But I did not want him walking me down the aisle, because I knew I would feel his anger burning in his chest. It was my

222

wedding and I wanted it my way. It angered him that I asked my Mammy. I loved her company as she walked me down the aisle. She did a grand job that day, didn't she?'

'I don't know,' said Douglas with a smile. 'It wasn't her I was looking at.'

She smiled back and teasingly sent a splash of water in his direction. 'She was grand that day,' she continued, putting back her sunglasses. 'But I could see my da was so filled with anger.' Douglas started gently rowing again. Saoirse sat more upright in the boat. 'You know, he was a really good daddy when I was a wee girl. He was real fun and would play with us and that. But when I got into my teens, he felt this desperate need to instruct me about true Irish culture.' She mimed inverted commas around the word "true". 'Everything he taught me was about how we should hate the British and hate the Protestants. I mean, not all the time of course, but usually after he'd had a couple of beers or whiskies.' She paused and looked into the water. 'And, I'll admit, I was not the easiest of teenagers…'

'Really?' interjected Douglas with an eyebrow raised and a downturned smile.

'Reverend Romer, do you want more than a splash of water sent your way?' Douglas simply beamed back and started rowing again. 'Well, I was no worse than most teenagers, I'll have you know,' she continued. 'But the thing is, I really could not accept his worldview. I kept thinking, "Well, surely not all Brits are evil oppressors? And not all Proddies are out to destroy the Catholic church". I tried to put up counter-arguments but he would not tolerate any different view. So every time I tried to offer a reasonable alternative to his views, he would just get angry. And I mean *really* angry, Doug.' Douglas noticed the change in her countenance.

223

'How angry, Saoirse?' asked Douglas, pausing his rowing for a moment.

Saoirse looked out across the water for a while. 'He could be violent, Doug. He could be violent with both me and my mammy.'

Douglas looked very pained and instinctively wanted to move closer to her, but he needed to keep hold of his oars. 'Did he... did he ever...?' he ventured, unable to bring himself to use any word that might suggest someone could harm his beloved wife.

'Yes, Dougie. Both me and my mammy. And to be honest with you, the only thing that kept me in Ireland, was worry for her. As I got older, I learned how to avoid his fist. But Mammy wasn't always so nimble. I did my best to protect her and would have stayed in that home simply for that reason. But I was also mixing with the wrong sorts and they introduced me to the drugs. Mammy knew that, and she could see I had to get out of the home. In the end, she insisted. Her instinct was right, and I'm pleased to say, once I was out of the house, it seems the main source of his aggravation had gone. Mammy said he never touched her after I left. For that, I'm truly grateful. Should have gone sooner, I suppose - in retrospect.'

'I'm so sorry, my love,' said Douglas, still holding the oars above the water and aching to come near to comfort her.

She smiled back at him. 'Would you have been my knight in shining armour, Reverend Romer, and come dashing to my aid?'

'Of course,' he said. She then sat up and, with some awkwardness that almost resulted in a capsized boat, she made her way over to Douglas and clasped him tightly. 'I'm no longer afraid, my Dougie,' she whispered in his ear, and silently the boat slid into the reeds and rushes and

224

there they rested for a long time in a healing silence, welcoming the peace, and the summer warmth

It was with that memory in his mind and heart that Douglas slipped into sleep, and only woke when there was a knock at the door about an hour later.

'Douglas, son, are you in there?' It was Elsie.

Douglas sprang off the bed, feeling somehow guilty for sleeping in the day time, and opened the door for Elsie.

'Och, Douglas, were you having a wee nap? Well, I don't blame you on a day like today which, in my humble opinion, is fit for nothing other than sleeping. However, I've got Father Pat downstairs who asked if he might have a quick word with you.'

'Of course, said, Douglas and followed Elsie down the stairs.

'Do use the parlour if you wish, gentlemen,' said Elsie. 'Make yourselves comfortable and I'll fetch you a nice hot cup of coffee.'

'I don't want to put you to any trouble, Elsie,' said Pat protesting.

'Oh, to be sure, it will be no trouble at all,' said Elsie and returned to the kitchen.

'I won't keep you a moment, that I won't,' said Father Pat as they made their way into the parlour. They sat in the two chairs that were in Douglas' estimation the least uncomfortable in the room. 'Now Douglas,' continued Pat adjusting his glasses, 'I thought you'd find it helpful to know that Niall and Orla are coming into town tomorrow, a day ahead of the memorial.'

'I see,' said Douglas making an immediate mental note to keep well out of the centre of town if that was the case.

'Now, the thing is,' said Pat shifting his position in the chair, 'I'm not sure what you will think of this… but it

225

seems to me... I mean, I know bygones and so forth...
Well...'.

Pat was clearly struggling and Douglas was beginning
to guess what he might be suggesting. He asked, 'Pat, are
you about to suggest that I should meet with them
tomorrow?'

'Aye, that I am, Douglas,' said Pat and pulled off his
glasses and started wiping them hard on the edge of his
black suit jacket. 'I mean, I know he's not the easiest of
men. But I was thinking, Douglas, that it might be... well,
less awkward shall we say, to meet them... not in the
service.' He put his freshly cleaned glasses back on and
looked hard at Douglas. 'What do you think?'

'They know I'm here, I take it,' said Douglas.

'Aye, that they do. I told them when they phoned.'

'And how did they sound?'

'Well, it was Orla that I spoke to and she... well... She
was surprised because she thought you'd still be living in
England. But, no... She was quite all right about it. And
er... yes, she seemed quite all right about it.'

'Father Pat, you are not making me hugely confident
about any meeting with these two, whether it be tomorrow
or in church on Thursday,' said Douglas.

Pat sighed and leaned back in the armchair which
protested with a loud creaking sound. 'I'm sorry, Douglas,
I'm useless at this sort of conversation. Dear God, I
wonder why I'm a priest of the church, sometimes. Honest,
I do. I'm not one for conflict, Douglas. Do you know what
I mean?' He brushed his hand through his hair and for a
moment looked at the ceiling. He threw Douglas one of his
rapid smiles and then said, 'I mean, the bishop sent me on
one of those highly-polished training affairs - do you know
what I mean? "Conflict resolution" was the title, I believe.

226

Well, I'm sorry to say, it did nothing for me other than make me even more anxious about conflict.' He looked back at Douglas through his heavy-framed glasses, with his hair wilder than ever.

Douglas could not help but feel some compassion for the man, and it was that compassion which finally overrode his anxiety and he found himself saying, 'I know what you mean, Pat. It's not exactly been my strength either. I never wanted to be at odds with Niall and Orla and I'm sorry…'

At that moment the door was kicked open, and in walked Elsie with two cups of coffee and a plate of digestive biscuits. As she put the coffee and biscuits down on a side table, she said, 'Now, I know I'm desperately nosy, but I did hear part of the conversation was about the Flynn's visit for the memorial service.' She passed a cup to Pat and then one to Douglas. 'Did I hear they were arriving tomorrow, Father Pat?'

'You have good ears, Elsie,' said Pat smiling. 'Thank you for the coffee.'

'We're just a bit concerned, Father, for Douglas, that's all,' she said, placing a hand on Douglas' shoulder. 'We hear that this Niall Flynn is none too fond of our lad here.'

'Well, Elsie,' said Pat, 'that does sadly seem to be the case. But this may be a great opportunity for some healing.' Pat took a sip of his coffee and continued, 'And I thought I'd ask Douglas round tomorrow afternoon for a nice cup of tea, and they could have a bit of a chat.' He looked back at Douglas, his face betraying his uncertainty about his plan.

Douglas sipped his coffee and said, 'Pat, if you think it's a good idea, I'm willing to go with it. I don't have high hopes, I must confess. But, why not?' He took another couple of nervous sips from his cup.

'Well, Father, you make sure that the meeting *does* go well,' said Elsie. 'Now, if you'll excuse me, I've got the laundry to be getting on with.'

Both Pat and Douglas smiled as she left. 'Heart of gold,' said Pat.

'Indeed,' said Douglas.

'So - three o clock tomorrow?' said the priest, raising his eyebrows over the dark rim of his glasses

'That's fine,' said Douglas, feeling very unsure about whether it would be fine or not.

Pat put down his mostly undrunk cup and stood up. 'Well, that was a grand cup of coffee, but I need to be on my way now. I'm glad I caught you, Douglas. I'll be seeing you tomorrow, then.'

Douglas saw Pat out of the front door and returned to his room to fetch his coat and scarf. He made a brief sortie out into the damp street to fetch a sandwich and then spent the rest of the afternoon back in his room reading more of the books he had brought with him from England. He did not feel in the mood for eating out in the evening, so he got himself a takeaway curry. He spent the evening watching comedies on YouTube, but not one of them managed to dislodge a sense of anxiety he felt at the thought of seeing Saoirse's parents the following day.

CHAPTER 19

Douglas did not sleep well that night and in the morning declined his usual egg and bacon, much to Elsie's surprise and dismay. Outside the cold fog had thinned to a drab mist that moodily drifted down the street on a light sea breeze. After what Elsie regarded as a very inadequate breakfast, Douglas strolled around Dingle in the morning hoping to find Dorchadas, but there was no sign of him. For a time, he took refuge from the cold in the coffee shop where he had met Antonio, but it would take more than a good coffee to settle his soul today. He was trying to form a picture in his mind of his former parents-in-law whom he had only seen at his wedding. Even then, it was only a brief meeting. Thankfully, there was so much fun and laughter at the wedding, that the disapproval of the Flynns of their daughter's choice of a husband did not dampen the occasion.

As he held the hot cup in his hand, Douglas did call to mind one memory of that wedding day that he had not thought about for a long time. He remembered Orla coming over to him soon after the cutting of the wedding cake. Niall was not with her. She took Douglas' hand, squeezed it, and simply said, 'I hope you will both be very happy.' It was then that he noticed how similar her eyes were to her daughter's. He recognised that away from Niall, Orla would have been more warmly disposed towards him.

As he sipped his latte he wondered how Orla felt about not attending their daughter's funeral. They had asked for the funeral to take place in Cork, but Douglas declined. Niall had stubbornly refused to attend, declaring it was not a proper service as it was neither Catholic nor Irish. So, as far as the Flynns were concerned, their daughter had never had a proper funeral service. No doubt they were still hoping one day to return her ashes to Irish soil and to see the job done properly. For a few moments, Douglas felt compassion for Orla, who surely would have found some comfort in that service, had she been allowed to attend. She would have heard all the wonderful things that were said about her daughter both in the service and at the wake afterwards. But Orla was under her husband's spell, and who knows what it would take to free her.

The time passed slowly but eventually, 3 pm arrived, and as the church clock struck the hour, Douglas rang the doorbell of the Presbytery. Underneath his large overcoat, he was, unusually for him, wearing a tie, hoping in some way it would convey respect to his parents-in-law. Father Pat, came to the door, looking his usual dishevelled self, with a large amount of his black shirt tails escaping from his navy Aran knit jumper. 'Do come in, Douglas,' he said, beckoning Douglas to the lounge. The room, lit by only by the gloomy daylight from the window, felt cold, and Douglas was reluctant to yield his coat to Pat.

'They should be here at any moment,' said Pat, taking the coat. 'It's a bit chilly in here, isn't it? I'll fetch the heater.' He returned after a few moments with the single bar heater from his office. Douglas sat down, and for a few moments, they discussed the weather until the doorbell sounded. Pat was back up on his feet and made his way to the front door. Douglas listened to the greetings and after a few moments, Niall and Orla Flynn, the parents of his dear and deceased wife, entered the room.

Douglas rose to his feet and studied the couple who entered the room. Niall was of medium height and stocky in stature. His face looked hardened, and there was evidence that his nose had been broken at least once. His dark eyes, peering out from beneath bristling eyebrows, surveyed the room. What little hair he had was close-cropped. His red complexion betrayed high blood pressure. The impression he gave was undoubtedly severe, and yet Douglas sensed that somewhere in that face there also resided traces of kindness. He imagined that if he ever saw the face smile, it would be transformed. Niall was not wearing a tie, which made Douglas feel overdressed.

Orla was perhaps an inch taller than her husband. She was neatly dressed and wore a scarf around her neck in various shades of green. Douglas thought how much Saoirse would have liked it. As at that brief meeting at the wedding, he saw again Saoirse's eyes in hers. Her shoulder-length hair was mostly grey, yet still with hints of the mahogany brown that was also Saoirse's hair colour. Her blue-green eyes conveyed sadness. Her nervous smile conveyed signs of warmth and tenderness.

'Hello, Orla. Hello, Niall. Good to see you both,' said Douglas after Pat had made a floundering introduction.

Orla nodded and, with another brief smile said, 'Hello Douglas. Good to see you too.' Niall simply nodded and looked at the floor. He offered no smile.

'I'll bring the tea in,' said Pat, and Douglas felt alarmed at being left in the room on his own with the Flynns.

No-one knew what to say, but eventually, Orla said to Douglas 'Did you ever get to meet my sister, Ruby?'

'No,' said Douglas. 'I very much regret I never did. She sounds like she was a wonderful woman.' Another faint smile from Orla that abruptly ended with the sound of Niall's voice.

'What brings you to Dingle?' asked Niall in a tone that suggested accusation rather than enquiry.

231

At that moment, Pat reappeared holding a tray with teapot, milk and three mugs. 'You must excuse me. We've run out of the biscuits would you believe. And it's not even Lent,' he quipped. But only he laughed.

'Niall was just asking what brought me to Dingle,' said Douglas, as they all sat down. As Pat poured the tea, Douglas explained how he had come over on spec to visit Ruby, only to discover she had died. But he liked the town and was stopping for a time. Pat responded by saying how much he also liked the town and was proud to be a priest in the community. An awkward conversation proceeded regarding the various merits of the town of Dingle.

'We didn't expect you to be here,' said Niall ominously, now looking directly at Douglas. Douglas did not know how to respond so he just supped his tea. 'You attending the memorial?' said Niall, probing further, his eyes fixed on the Englishman.

'Yes, I would like to. Saoirse was very fond of her aunt,' said Douglas.

'Was she?' said Niall. 'You wouldn't think so. She never visited her. She never visited any of us.' Douglas remembered that Saoirse wanted to visit, but was reluctant to return to Ireland because of her father's hostility.

'It was always her intention, but sadly…' Douglas was annoyed with himself for inadvertently referring to Saoirse's death. And yet, now that he had, he decided to take advantage of the mention. He decided it was time for courage, so he continued, 'It's sad to be remembering both Ruby and Saoirse's passing.'

He felt his words tumbling into the room like lumps of granite. Niall inhaled deeply and said nothing. Orla took several sips of her tea. Pat coughed and said, 'Aye, there's been much sadness in recent years for you all.'

Douglas felt a rising sense of desire for some kind of resolution. He did not want to remain in this deadlock of silence with Niall and Orla. He surprised himself by saying, 'How have you both been since we lost Saoirse?'

Niall put down his mug on the side table. He leant forward to the edge of the chair and clasped his hands in front of him. He stared at the floor. Orla fidgeted in her seat and said, 'It's a hard road...'

She did not finish as Niall looked up at Douglas with frightening coldness and said, 'Our daughter should still be with us. She should *not* be dead. She *would* not be dead if she had stayed here where she belonged.' His face reddened and he prodded his finger at Douglas and said, 'You took her from us. You took her from the land where she belonged. You took her from her true religion. She died in mortal sin. She sinned against the Holy Ghost and now she is lost. And you did this, Romer, and I can't forgive you.'

He was about to say more, but Pat halted the tirade by saying, 'Niall, please no more. You have said enough. I have already explained that it is the view of the Church that your daughter did *not* die in mortal sin...'

'For God's sake, Father,' cried Niall, now rising from his chair. 'Don't you be starting to defend this man here. You know my view and I've made it plain. Come on Orla. I think we have been here long enough.' Orla was sniffing hard, fumbling in her handbag for a tissue. She obediently rose. Pat and Douglas both rose to their feet.

Douglas felt his knee shaking so hard it could hardly support his weight. He hated being the recipient of such venom. 'I am so s...sorry,' he stammered, but his apology was to no avail.

Niall came right up to him, and Douglas stepped back. Niall prodded his sturdy finger into Douglas' chest. 'I can't bloody stop you from being at the service tomorrow. I am going to be there to honour Orla's sister. But I don't want you there. You'd be defiling a sacred event. There is no reason for you to be there. You never knew the woman. So you stay away, do you understand? Stay away!'

Pat was trying to take Niall's arm, which he shrugged off with some force. Douglas felt Niall was precariously close to a violent outburst, so to calm things he said, 'I understand, N… Niall. I understand.'

'Come on, Niall. Let's not be keeping the gentlemen,' said Orla, as Niall slowly backed away from Douglas yet still glaring at him. She turned her frightened eyes to Pat. 'Thank you, Father, for the tea.' She said nothing to Douglas, but for a brief moment looked at him, and once again Douglas saw the shy kindness in the glimmer of a smile.

'Much obliged, Father,' said Niall tersely. 'We'll meet you in the church later, as arranged, to go over the service.'

'Aye, that would be grand,' said the priest, relieved that for the moment, the anger had subsided. He took them to the door and Douglas fell back in his seat, his knees still shaking. Pat returned after seeing the Flynns out. He turned on the light saying, 'Oh, it's dark so soon,' and then left the room. Douglas hardly noticed as he sat still, staring at the threadbare carpet. Pat returned with a green bottle and two tumblers. 'I know it's early, Douglas, but I think we need some help,' he said. He poured a generous supply of Irish whiskey into each glass.

Douglas found it welcome and warming as he downed half the supply in one gulp. Pat also took a generous swig and said, 'He's a hard man, Douglas. He surely is. I am so sorry, son. It was a terrible mistake to try and get you together before the service. Do forgive me, will you please?'

Douglas looked up at the vulnerable eyes of the priest and said, 'Of course. But there's nothing to forgive, Pat. It was a good idea. Honestly. It just didn't work, that's all.'

'I see a lot of bad stuff, Douglas, as I'm sure you do in your ministry. I know that people can behave badly when they are hurting. God knows, I do. But that man...' He sighed and drank from his glass. 'Well, what can I say, Douglas?'

'Not a lot. It was my fault. I shouldn't have raised the subject of Saoirse's death. I just thought two years on he might have... you know, softened. Come to terms with it. But he seems as vitriolic as ever. And vitriolic towards *me*.' He paused and took more of the welcome fiery liquid. He then looked up at Pat with such vulnerability that Pat felt great compassion for the Englishman. 'If only he knew how *much* I loved his daughter. If only he knew how happy she was in the years we were together. If only he had seen her laugh like I saw her laugh. If only he had witnessed her brilliant teaching of the children. My, how proud he would have been of her. If only he knew how she was starting to explore faith again.' He shook his head and some of the bitter pains of grief that had been buried in recent weeks started to break through the surface again. 'If only he had seen her, as I saw her, Pat...If only he knew what a sweet, wonderful, generous, kind daughter she was...' The emotion finally broke through the surface and Douglas, still clutching his tumbler, bowed his head, trying his best to hide the signs of strain and sorrow that were overwhelming him.

Pat put down his glass and went and knelt beside Douglas. 'I'm so sorry...' said Douglas, as he pulled out a tissue from his pocket. 'I've been doing my best to manage this bloody awful grief. To have to manage that anger as well is more than I'm ready for right now.'

Pat leaned back, and pulling off his glasses, he wiped his eyes on his sleeve.

'I think it's best I don't go tomorrow, Pat,' said Douglas after a few moments when he felt more composed. Pat stayed by his side rubbing Douglas' arm and thinking hard.

He then rose and went back to his seat. He finished his glass and said, 'Don't commit yourself either way, Douglas. Remember the service is for Ruby, not for Niall. And it was Ruby who brought you to Dingle, and I think you feel that was a good gift of hers?'

Douglas sighed and looked at Pat with his still red eyes, 'It was truly a most wonderful gift, Pat, and I shall be forever grateful to her for that.'

'Well, then,' said Pat, and drained his glass. At that moment they heard the front door open and shut and, after the sound of feet being brushed on the mat, the lounge door opened and in walked Dorchadas.

'Well, there you are now, Douglas,' said Dorchadas with his warm smile. 'I've been looking for you everywhere.' He then looked at the empty glasses and said, 'Well, I should have known you'd be at the Presbytery, drinking with the Priest!' All the men laughed. With the arrival of Dorchadas, all the tension of the previous meeting dissipated. Dorchadas sat his tall frame in one of the chairs. He could see the signs of grief in Douglas' eyes but was careful not to draw attention to such vulnerability. In a cheerful voice, he asked, 'So where are you eating this evening, Doug?'

'Oh, not decided yet. But it would be great to meet up with you, Dorch, if you're around.'

'Well, you are welcome to eat here,' interjected Pat. 'Mrs. McGarrigle has prepared a dinner for Dorch and I and, honest to God, there's enough to feed half the town, there surely is.'

'Aye, that housekeeper of yours is certainly generous,' said Dorchadas with a chuckle.

'That's decided, then,' said Pat. 'Will 7 pm do for you, Doug?'

'Yes,' said Douglas, then hesitated. 'As long as you will have finished with the Flynns by then?'

'Oh, aye. I'll be back here well before seven.'

'Fine. I'll leave you now and will be back here for a Mrs. McGarrigle's special,' said Douglas, feeling very relieved that he would not be alone during the evening. The encounter with Niall Flynn had done little to settle his nerves. But an evening with two good friends would help.

He stepped out of the Presbytery into the evening gloom and walked back up to St.Raphael's. As he waited to cross the road, a large SUV with dazzling headlights drove past him. He watched it drive slowly up the road. It caught his attention because he had not seen many SUVs as smart as this one in Dingle. Had he seen the occupants of the vehicle, he would probably have packed his bags and got out of town as soon as he could. For behind the wheel of the rented SUV was the lean figure of Gerald Bentley OBE. Beside him in the passenger seat, with her head bent over a sheet that detailed directions to a local hotel, was his wife, Angela.

CHAPTER 20

As Douglas had got involved in a conversation with Elsie before leaving, he was a little late arriving at the Presbytery. However, when he got there, he was warmly welcomed by Pat and Dorchadas. Mrs. McGarrigle had gone home, but she had left a table set in the dining room, a fire lit, and a dinner in the oven.

'Thought this might be useful,' said Douglas, passing Pat a bottle of Rioja. 'Ah, thank you, Douglas,' said Pat, unscrewing the top and placing it on the table. 'That will go very nicely with Mrs. McGarrigle's dinner. She tells me she has prepared a pot of coddle pork with cider. I hope that will be to your liking, Douglas?'

'Sure, it will. He eats anything,' came a voice from the staircase. Dorchadas came into the room chuckling. 'We sure eat well, here, Doug,' he said, giving Douglas a welcoming hug. He could see his friend needed support this evening. Douglas had never been a great one for hugs, but somehow a bearhug from Dorchadas was different. It always strengthened him.

Father Pat, wearing a brightly coloured pair of oven gloves, brought a large casserole into the dining room and placed it carefully on the table. 'There we are, gentleman,' he said, removing the lid, and, once the clouds of steam dispersed, Douglas saw in the pot an inviting mix of chops, bacon, potatoes and other vegetables. Pat threw the oven gloves to one side, and taking his seat, he drew his hands together and said, 'For these and all thy mercies given, we bless and praise thy name O Lord.' He made the sign of the cross, as did Dorchadas, and he served his friends.

'How did the meeting in the church go?' asked Douglas as he gratefully received a well-loaded plate from Pat.

'Mm, well now,' said Pat, carefully loading a plate for Dorchadas. 'On the positive side, I think we have a good service for Ruby. We shall celebrate her seventieth, even though she never lived to see it, God rest her soul. And I think it's a good memorial we have planned.' He passed the plate to Dorchadas.

Dorchadas carefully received the plate and said, 'And what about the negative side, Pat?'

Pat spooned the food on to his plate, then looked up and said, 'Douglas, do you mind serving the wine, please? That's mighty generous of you to bring it.'

Dorchadas, knowing Pat's tendency to avoid difficult subjects, ventured again. 'On the negative side, Pat?'

Pat was just about to load his fork, but paused and looked at Douglas. 'Douglas, my friend, I'm sorry. I was hoping Niall might have... well, you know. But he's much the same.'

'That's all right, Pat. He's just angry. But I don't think he is violent, so I'm not too worried.'

'No, no. Quite,' said Pat and set to work on his pork chop.

Dorchadas said, 'Doug, we're all going to be there tomorrow, and I agree with you, son. The man's packed full of anger and bitterness as I understand it, but I don't see as he's going to turn violent on you. Certainly not in church. But it all makes you sad, doesn't it?'

'Yes, it does,' said Pat, who sounded weary of the multitude of sadnesses that he had encountered in his ministry.

'I mean,' said Dorchadas, 'it's not really you, Doug, that he is angry with.'

'Well, you could have fooled me, Dorch. You should have seen him today,' said Douglas taking a sip of his wine.

'I know, I know, Doug,' said Dorchadas. 'Pat did tell me about it. But I mean, his anger is really against the British and the Protestants and it's all to do with past hurts. It's historic, that stuff, Doug, but it's very much alive in him. That's the problem when you can't forgive. All that stuff remains very much alive and kicking inside of you. And you, Doug, just happen to be the unlucky representative of all that.'

'And the irony is,' added Douglas, 'I'm not at all proud of that part of British Protestant history. But he has never given me a chance to talk to him. To let him know where I stand on it all.'

'It's about power, too, I think,' chimed in Pat. 'For some men, to let go of their anger and their hatred feels like letting go of the very thing that is giving them a reason to be. Take that away from them, and what are they left with? You have taken away the cause that's given their life meaning in this world.'

'We keep coming back to that kind of thing, Doug, don't we?' said Dorchadas spearing a carrot with his fork and glancing at Douglas. 'We went up to the Gallarus on Monday, Pat.'

'That's such a grand place, isn't it?' said Pat. 'I mean, if we are thinking about power, Dorchadas, then think of the people who built that darling place. They had the perfect view of power, don't you think? You know, it was a multitude of those tiny chapels inhabited by simple lives that changed the world. Not palaces, castles and cathedrals. Blessed are the poor in spirit. In fact, cheers to the poor in spirit.' With that, Pat raised his glass, as did his two friends.

240

'We got to chatting about John the Baptist while we were there,' said Dorchadas, careful to give a version of the story that Pat could accept. Dorchadas had not introduced the priest to 'travelling'. Not yet.

'Well now, there's a man,' said Pat. 'I mean there he was, not in the city, but the desert. Not in a palace but in a cave. Not in fine robes but in rags held together by a cord around his waist. And what does he do? He challenges the whole infernal religious establishment!' All three laughed.

'But he paid for it,' said Douglas.

'I don't think he saw it that way,' said Pat. 'I know, Herod removed his head. Or Herodias, should I say. But I think John knew that God was allowing that, don't you? John had done his work. He had paved the way. His heart was already half-way stepped into heaven.'

Douglas paused eating and remembered the expression he had seen on the face of the beheaded John. He looked up at Dorchadas who winked at him. 'It's just,' continued Douglas, 'when you look around at our world, the powerful do seem to win so much. When it comes down to it, don't you think it is the banks, the big institutions, the wealthy, the loud, the proud, and the bullies who are the ones who really shape what happens in our world. I mean, I don't understand much about politics, but I can't help noticing that most disputes between nations are resolved with guns. And the bigger your guns and the more you have of them, the more you are likely to win. The builders of the little chapel at the Gallarus would not hold out long against a Kalashnikov, let alone against a battle tank.'

All three were well aware that Douglas had strayed into this line of thought because of his own story of loss perpetrated by the use of a gun. Pat put down his cutlery, and for a moment looked hard at his near-empty plate. He then looked up at Douglas and said, 'That's what they thought on that first Good Friday, don't you think? The whole might of the ecclesiastical and political powers conspired to kill our Lord. He could have called down Elijah's fire from heaven and burned them all up there and then, and cried "Good riddance!" But no. He gave us another way. It's the way I prefer, Douglas. For me, it is the way that changes the world. It's the way that brings the best out in humans, not the worst. It's a way that disarms all the powers and principalities of this world by the sure audacity of it. For me, Douglas, it is the way that gives us hope.'

Douglas couldn't argue, but inside he was struggling with the concept of this surrender to the powers. He was feeling tired, so he decided to change the subject. 'So tomorrow, the service is at 11 am?'

'Yes, it is to be sure, Douglas,' said Pat whose plate was now empty. 'And there is a bit of a gathering in the hotel afterwards.

'Do you think there'll be many there?' asked Dorchadas.

'Oh, aye, I think there'll be a fair few. Can I tempt you with some more?' said Pat looking at both Dorchadas and Douglas. Both men accepted a topping up of their plates, as did Pat.

The rest of the evening was spent discussing less weighty matters and after a generous helping of Mrs. McGarrigle's apple tart, Douglas started to feel very tired. So, with a 'Gentleman, if you'll excuse me, I think I'll not be late to bed tonight,' Douglas left the Presbytery.

It was a clear but very cold night, and a frost was already forming, causing the pavement to sparkle under the streetlights. The presbytery had been cold, so to warm himself up he took a brisk walk around the town. As he rounded a corner, he saw the same SUV that he had

242

noticed earlier. It was parked outside a hotel. He wondered if the car belonged to some wealthy friend of Ruby's who was coming to pay their respects at the service tomorrow. But he decided this was unlikely. From what he heard of Ruby, she kept less pretentious company.

Once back at St.Raphael's, he made his way to his room and decided to make one brief entry in his journal before the end of the day.

Journal   15 January

Met Saoirse's parents at Father Pat's today. It was Pat's idea. He thought it would be better to meet them before the service tomorrow. Turned out to be not such a great idea. I hardly recognised them when they walked in, though I did see a strong resemblance of Orla to Saoirse. I thought she was quite sweet actually. Made me feel rather sad. I think she could have been a nice mother-in-law. But Niall was altogether different. There's no question he hates me. I don't think I have ever been so hated in my life. But it was as bad as I feared. He hated me for marrying his daughter. He hated me for taking her to England. He hated me for burying her in England. All that stuff. Chatted to Dorch and Pat later about it at supper at the Presbytery (Pat's housekeeper is a brilliant cook, by the way). Dorch says it's not me he hates, but it is what I represent. I suppose he is right, but it feels pretty personal to me. Niall told me not to come to the memorial service tomorrow, but Pat and Dorch think I should go. They don't think he'll cause trouble, and I'm pretty sure they're right, so I shall go and just keep well clear of him.

We had a bit of a theological discussion at supper. I didn't really feel up to it. Funny, in the old days I'd have leaped at the chance of a chat like this. I suppose it was really about who wins in the world: the rich and powerful, or the poor and meek. I appreciated Pat's pious choice of the poor in spirit. But in reality, I'm not sure it works. It was a gun that killed my Saoirse, and that gun has had more power over her life and my life than anything else.

Still find I'm feeling nervous, though. Not altogether sure why. Mary, in that beautiful meeting in the Garden, said I would need courage. That somehow feels ominous. But maybe all this is just my usual paranoia. Saoirse used to tease me about that! I loved her teasing. I loved her. I still love her. Where are you tonight my Saoirse? Come and calm my fears, like you used to. Please reach through that thin veil while I sleep tonight.

Triumphant was the Son upon that journey,
mighty with speed of fortune,
when with a multitude, a host of spirits,
He, ruling alone, Almighty,
came unto the kingdom of God,
to the joy of angels and all holy souls,
who dwelt in heaven in glory then,
when their Lord, the mighty God,
came where was
His home-land.

The Dream of the Rood

Jesus' power was at its greatest
when his opponents believed him defeated.
Hanging on the cross was the supreme moment
when Jesus was revealed to be
King, Revolutionary and Messiah.

Paula Gooder
Journey to the Empty Tomb

CHAPTER 21

He had not slept well. He knew that Irish hotels would not suit him. This one was well below standard. The evening meal was very ordinary. There was no decent wine on the menu, and the cheap stuff they served was undrinkable. The bedroom was too small and it was cold. The shower was feeble. Hopefully, he would only have to suffer this for one night's stay.

Angela was still fast asleep. The bar did at least provide her with her required supply of gin and tonics, and she seemed to be still sleeping them off. He got up and inched back the curtain. 'Oh, God,' he murmured as he looked out on the street below. Though it was still an hour before sunrise, the world outside was surprisingly bright and this was because there had been a light covering of snow in the night. He drew the curtain back and went to the toilet. He pressed the flush button and the ensuing roar of water was enough to awaken the dead, let alone Angela, who groaned out, 'What time is it?'

'Just after seven.'

'Might as well put the kettle on, then. God, I've got a bad head,' she said as she turned on the sidelight.

'Not surprised. You did put a few away last night.'

'Pot calling the kettle black,' said Angela as she hauled herself out of the bed and made her way to the bathroom. 'You sunk a few whiskies. I saw you.' Gerald obediently turned on the kettle and it steamed into life. He crawled back into bed and turned on his sidelight.

Angela returned having taken some paracetamol and made them each a mug of tea.

Gerald took a sip and grimaced and said, 'Is there a hotel anywhere in the world that provides milk that isn't revolting?'

Angela started drinking hers without complaint. She turned to Gerald and said, 'Right Mr.Ingleby, we need to sharpen up this plan.'

He briefly chuckled. 'They worked, didn't they?'

'The passports?' she said, turning up the corner of her mouth. 'I don't know how you do it, Gerald. You actually have contacts that can provide you with forged passports and driving licence.'

'It's not that difficult. Just expensive. I had them done last year when I thought we'd need them for that job in Nigeria that never came off. Anyway,' he said turning to his wife, 'I rather like you as Gertrude Ingleby.' He chuckled again.

'Yes, well that would not have been my choice of name… Percival!' They both laughed. She quickly drank her cup of tea and decided to have another, so she made her way over to the tea tray and turned on the kettle. 'We did some good enquiries last night,' she said. 'And we have established that our turbulent priest *is* here in this foul little town. God knows why he chose to live here. Anyway, that's beside the point.'

Gerald put his undrunk mug down on the bedside table and said, 'Angela, is this really such a great idea?'

Angela turned and looked hard at him. 'Gerald, we have not come to this godforsaken country to have a holiday. We have come to do a piece of work. We have come to secure our future. I am not going to surrender all that we have worked so bloody hard for. I don't want you going soft on me now.' The kettle boiled and she refilled her cup.

Gerald winced as he watched her pouring the milk from its plastic container. 'All right, so now we are here, what exactly is the grand plan, then?'

'Well, your choice of weapon has made it here safely,' she said tapping the wardrobe.

'The lethal injection. Yes, thank God nobody at customs stopped us. That would have taken some explaining. Not likely though at the port.'

'Oh, I'm sure they let all kinds of things in here,' said Angela waving her hand. 'It's always been a violent land. Anyway,' she said taking another sip from her mug, 'I'm happy to do the deed.' She climbed back into bed and sipped at her fresh mug of tea.

'So,' said Gerald, 'we heard last night that he will be at this big funeral taking place this morning.'

'Memorial mass, darling, to be precise. And what could be better? There's going to be quite a crowd so we were told.'

'And you are going to sidle up to him, syringe in hand, and say "Cup of tea, Vicar?" and then plunge the syringe in and wave him goodnight?'

'Gerald, we've got to be serious about this.'

'We certainly bloody have. That's why I want to know how this is going to work. I keep asking you, and you won't give me a clear plan.'

Angela sipped more tea and continued, 'You must keep well out of the way. He'd easily recognise you, whereas he hardly knows me and may not even recognise me. But to be safe, I will make sure I keep behind him. So, my plan is, we go to the service and sit at the back - at least, well away from wherever he is sitting. Then when everyone is filing out of church, I'll get behind him. In the crush, I can easily do it.'

249

'He will feel it, for God's sake.'

'Maybe. They told you it was a very fine needle. But even if he does feel something, the last thing he'll expect it to be is a hypodermic needle.'

'Ok,' said Gerald, nodding his head thoughtfully.

'It takes about ten minutes for it to take effect,' said Angela who had researched this particular method of despatch very carefully. 'Then it really will be "Goodnight, Vicar and God bless you." At first, they will all think it is a heart attack. Everyone knows he's been through a lot and they will put it down to stress.'

Gerald nodded and said, 'Yes, we will need them working with that assumption for several hours to give us time to get back up to Dublin and on the boat.'

'Indeed. And if and when the police suspect murder, they will never think of Gerald and Angela Bentley, because there has been no sign of them entering or leaving the country.'

'They may wonder about Mr. and Mrs. Ingleby from Margate, I suppose.'

'They may indeed, Percy,' said Angela chuckling.

'Oh, by the way,' said Gerald as he got out of bed and made his way to the window. 'It's been snowing, would you believe.'

'Oh, typical,' said Angela. 'I will be glad to get back to civilisation this evening.' She downed the rest of her tea.

'Yes, indeed,' said Gerald. 'I'll be very glad to get this business behind us. I've got an important meeting tomorrow. You'll be pleased to know that I'm making some headway up that greasy pole.' He turned and looked at her. His expression of malevolence was also tinged with humour. 'You never know, one day it might be Dame Angela Bentley.'

250

She smiled. 'Don't you mean Dame Gertrude Ingleby?' They laughed. It was a rare moment of their both laughing simultaneously. But for Angela, the laugh was followed by a sudden thought that came like a sharp jab in her side. Hearing her own voice use another name for herself, provoked a profound and disturbing question. If she dared put words to it, it would have been something like, 'And who are you, Angela?' Who was she becoming these days? Was she really a murderer? And if she was, was she honestly a competent murderer? If she really thought about it, the plan seemed so naïve. She had no experience of bumping people off. Could she honestly think she would get away with this? But to give heed to such questions at this crucial time would be disastrous. What was she thinking of, entertaining such things?

She rose from the bed and made straight for the shower to rinse away all the disturbing thoughts and questions. She had a job to do and she would not be thwarted.

CHAPTER 22

'I thought it never snowed in Ireland,' said Douglas to Elsie as she brought in his eggs and mushrooms.

'Och, the saints preserve us,' said Elsie as she put the plate before Douglas and took a look out of the window. 'Will you look at that? The street is fair covered, isn't it now? That is an unusual sight, Doug, I would say. But it's been as cold as purgatory these last few days, don't you think?'

'Well, I thought purgatory was hot,' said Douglas smiling.

'If that's the case, then we could do with a bit of its heat here today, sure we could.' Elsie left him for a moment, then returned with her coffee and sat at his table.

'So, are you coming to the memorial, Elsie?' asked Douglas.

'Oh, aye, that I am, Douglas. Not that I knew Ruby well, but I'd like to pay my respects, and Father Pat has asked me to help at the door. Kath and Kevin will be there, of course. I expect Dorchadas will look in too.'

'Yes, he told me he would be there.'

'We love funerals and memorials here in Dingle. Nothing like a bit of death to cheer us up, I say,' she said with a laugh.

Douglas felt she looked much more relaxed since the experience with Bull and he said, 'Elsie, you are looking beautiful this morning.'

'Och, get away with you, Douglas Romer. I'll not be having your flattery at this time of the day.'

They both laughed, then Douglas added, 'But since that meeting with Bull, I see you as more… More yourself. I mean, your hairstyle is perfect now.'

'I know, I know, son,' she said, patting her hair. 'I do feel much more myself, I have to say. And that's thanks to you, Douglas.'

'To me?' said Douglas. He paused eating his breakfast and looked at her.

'Well, you and Kevin. That wee chat with the both of you did me a power of good, it most surely did.' She took a sip of her coffee and then said, 'I don't know why, son. But I never really felt comfortable in my own skin, if you get my meaning. God knows why, because I've had myself a happy life. It was sad of course losing my husband those years back, but, all in all, the good Lord has blessed me and I have much to be thankful for. But…' She shrugged her shoulders and looked down at her coffee for a moment, then looked back at Douglas and said, 'To tell the truth, I've seen you become more yourself, son. And that's given me the confidence…. You know. To be more me. And, to be honest, I'm even daring to believe that the Almighty might not be quite as disapproving of me as I used to think.'

Douglas was frowning with concentration as he listened. He put down his fork and said, 'If me becoming more me has helped you to become more you, Elsie, then I do indeed thank God.'

Elsie started to feel strong feeling rising, and with a memorial service coming, she did not want to invite additional emotion into her day, so she said, 'Now Douglas, I don't want those eggs and mushrooms going cold on you. Will you eat them up, please. You'll need their help today.'

'They're delicious, Elsie,' said Douglas and he dutifully finished his breakfast.

'Now them roads will be slippy today, Douglas, so you be careful, won't you?'

'Yes, I will,' said Douglas. 'Is it far to the hotel where we are going afterwards?'

'Oh, about ten miles, I'd say.'

'Ok, I'll drive to the church then, so I can go straight on after the service. Do you think it will snow more today?'

'Not sure, Douglas. But it may stay below freezing. It can do this.' She was interrupted by the front door opening, and in came a heavily coated Kath grasping an unlit vape.

'Morning to you both,' she said. 'What a god-awful day it surely is.'

'Aye, that it is,' said her sister. 'Will you be stopping for a coffee, Kath?'

'No, Else. I'm just dropping by to say to you, Douglas, that Kevin and I will be here at 10.30 so that we can all go down to the service together. We don't want you being on your own today, son. Would you mind, Douglas if we go in your car? It would be a bit of a squeeze in the front of my truck. Then we can go straight on to the hotel together afterwards. We know where it is.'

'Of course,' said Douglas. He was very touched by the protective gesture, and he thanked Kath who was soon bustling back out on to the snowy street.

'I'm helping to give out the hymnbooks,' said Elsie, 'so I'll be gone a bit before you. And, to be honest, I don't particularly want to go up to the hotel afterwards. But Kath and Kevin will see you right, son.'

'I'm sure they will, Elsie,' said Douglas. He finished his mug of coffee and returned to his room. Some of the anxiety of the previous evening had dissipated and he had enjoyed a relatively good night's sleep. He checked the forecast for Dingle and it looked like there could be another sprinkling of snow, but nothing too threatening. He sat and read in his room, but as the time for the service grew closer, that nagging sense of danger returned to him. He kept sighing and needing to make regular visits to the toilet. He went out and checked his car, and wonderfully it started at the first attempt. It looked like it would be in a good mood today.

Punctually at ten-thirty, he heard the sound of the front door opening and then the voices of Kevin and Kath in the hallway. He put on his coat and scarf over his suit and went down to greet them. They stepped out into the cold street and piled into the car for the short journey to the church.

Thus began a day that Douglas would never forget.

*

Even though they arrived twenty minutes before the start of the service, quite a few people were already there, and most were in the vestibule, gathered in small groups of animated conversation. Father Pat had made sure that the heating was on overnight, and Douglas was grateful for the warmth. Elsie was handing out hymnbooks and service sheets, and Douglas was pleased to see the tall figure of Dorchadas chatting to an elderly man who was animated by the subject of their discussion. Father Pat appeared in the doorway and in a loud voice encouraged those present to make their way into the church.

'Can we sit somewhere in the middle, nicely hidden?' said Douglas to Kevin.

'Good plan,' said Kevin and led him and his mother to a suitable pew.

After a few moments, Dorchadas came through from the vestibule and came up to their row and asked, 'You all right if I take my seat with you three?' They all nodded with smiles. Dorchadas settled next to Kath and engaged in a whispered conversation with her. Kath had one of her coughing fits and spent some time rummaging in her handbag for her throat sweets, which she eventually found. The organist was playing some music and Douglas recognised some of the tunes from his evenings listening to music groups in the pub. He had a look at the service sheet he had been given, and on the front was a picture of Ruby. It was the first time that he had seen a photo of her. There was a clear likeness to Orla. He saw signs of the sweet nature of which Pat had spoken.

Little by little the church filled up with friends of Ruby, and then Douglas recognised the somewhat hunched and stocky figure of Niall walking up the aisle alongside Father Pat. He was still wearing his coat and was grasping a handful of service sheets. He had a brief conversation with Pat, and there was much pointing to the lectern. He then went over to the organist and spoke to her. After a few moments, Orla came down the aisle, with another woman whom Douglas assumed had been a close friend of Ruby. The two ladies and Niall seated themselves in the front row. Douglas felt relieved that they appeared not to have seen him. He bowed his head as low as possible, as the Flynns were inclined to turn around in their front row to survey the growing congregation behind them. Were they looking out for him? Douglas determined to keep low throughout the service. What Douglas did not notice was a couple entering the church only a minute or so before the start of the service. It is possible that had he seen them, he may not have recognised the lady. But he certainly would have recognised the distinctive and lean figure of Gerald Bentley. And that figure had spotted Douglas.

At eleven o'clock, the organist stopped playing and Father Pat came to the lectern and tapped the microphone, the harsh noise of which brought an abrupt end to all conversations. There was then a high-pitched hum, and Pat looked anxiously to the back of the church where somebody fiddled with a control which mercifully brought an end to the ever-increasing and shrill noise.

The priest surveyed the sizeable congregation and began, 'Well it is brutally cold outside today, but I am pleased to say it is beautifully warm in this lovely church. I can also feel the great warmth of the love everyone here had for Ruby Kennedy. Today she would have been seventy years old. Very sadly she passed away from us the Christmas before last into the hands of God. Some of us gathered here just after that Christmas for her funeral and then at the cemetery for the burial. But it is good to see so many more have been able to come for this memorial today.

'And so in the name of the Father and the Son and the Holy Ghost,' he said, crossing himself and everyone in the church instinctively raised their right hands to their foreheads and made the same sign over themselves. Then after a prayer, he announced the first hymn. It was the kind of hymn that a few years ago Douglas would have steadfastly refused to sing. It was a hymn to Mary. He was not familiar with the tune, but as everyone stood around him singing, he followed the words carefully.

Ave Maria! maiden mild!

Listen to a maiden's prayer!
Thou canst hear though from the wild;
Thou canst save amid despair.
Safe may we sleep beneath thy care,
Though banish'd, outcast and reviled –
Maiden! hear a maiden's prayer;
Mother, hear a suppliant child!
Ave Maria!

Something about the words touched Douglas. He thought of the mother of Jesus, exalted in the Catholic church in ways he never fully understood nor liked. And yet here in this service, where the wound of death would surely have hurt every soul in the church at one time or another, the thought of this maiden of God watching over the world with a mother's love, felt tender and comforting.

When the hymn finished, Pat came back to the microphone and asked Orla to say a few words. She made her way to the lectern and at first, stood too far back from the microphone so that no-one could hear her. Pat gently urged her to get closer and she started again.

'My sister Ruby was the sweetest, kindest sister anyone in this world could ever ask for,' she said and, as she spoke, the emotion within her threatened to strangle her words. However, she managed to contain her grief for the rest of her brief eulogy, in which she commended to the congregation the sister she had clearly loved with great affection. Douglas could not help but notice that one of the qualities she cited in her sister was a strong ability to forgive. This was surely a quality she did not witness in her husband.

When she finished she returned to her pew, and Douglas noticed the telling gap between her and Niall. Pat then came back and led in some responses that were followed by another hymn. He then invited Niall to come forward and read a Scripture from Paul's epistle to the Corinthians. He had by now removed his heavy coat and Douglas could see he was wearing a rather ill-fitting dark suit. As he made his way up to the lectern, Douglas heard Kevin whisper, 'Oh, dear Lord, no.'

'What is it?' whispered Douglas to Kevin as Niall began the reading.

'The man has a gun, Doug,' whispered Kevin, covering his mouth.

'What?' whispered Douglas, loud enough for Kath and Dorchadas to turn their heads. 'How can you possibly see he has a gun?'

Kevin composed himself and whispered, 'Doug. I know the shape of a revolver in a man's suit pocket. I've seen it too often. Just take it from me. Now, maybe he always carries that thing, but we know the man's feelings about you, and I know what he is capable of. I don't want to alarm you, but I suggest we all leave this church quickly after the end of the service.'

Douglas felt a spasm of fear shoot through his body. He looked aghast at Kevin for a moment and then sat back in his pew and looked up at the high ceiling, taking in a deep breath. At the front of the church, Niall had come to the end of his reading, and as he moved away from the lectern, he looked down the length of the building. As Douglas brought his eyes down from the ceiling, he saw the figure of Niall Flynn at the front of the church, who was gazing straight at him with his cold, unforgiving eyes. There was no question - Niall knew the Englishman that he so hated was in the building.

Douglas bowed his head again and whispered to Kevin. 'But he's not going to use that thing in broad daylight, surely? And not in church?'

'No, no. But the man will be clever. He'll know how to cover over his tracks. He'll have contacts here. You're safe in the church, but it's outside where we need to be careful. I need you to trust me now, Doug, and do what I say. You'll be fine, honest.' Kevin turned to his mother and Dorchadas and whispered something to them. They both looked at Douglas with concern. Kath buttoned up her coat in readiness for a rapid departure from the church.

By now, Pat was preaching a homily, but Douglas heard none of it. He was just desperate to get away from any proximity to a demented man who appeared to have violent intent towards him. Pat's preaching seemed to go on forever, but eventually, it came to an end. He then celebrated the mass and many came forward to receive their communion. Douglas and the others remained in their pew. They wished to remain as unseen as possible.

After the final hymn, Father Pat came up to the lectern. In his deep and resonant voice, he announced, 'Would you please stand.' All in the church dutifully rose from their seats and Pat then said, 'I'm told that one of Ruby's favourite prayers was the Breastplate prayer of the blessed Saint Patrick. I think this would be a very fitting prayer to end with today.' It was clear that Pat knew the prayer by heart and he lifted his head and his arm as he prayed. Despite his fear, or maybe because of it, Douglas grasped hold of the words being recited by the priest.

I arise today
Through the strength of heaven:
Light of sun,
Radiance of moon,
Splendour of fire,
Speed of lightning,
Swiftness of wind,

Depth of sea,
Stability of earth,
Firmness of rock.
I arise today
Through God's strength to pilot me:
God's might to uphold me,
God's wisdom to guide me,
God's eye to look before me,
God's ear to hear me,
God's word to speak for me,
God's hand to guard me,
God's way to lie before me,
God's shield to protect me,
God's host to save me
From snares of devils,
From temptations of vices,
From everyone who shall wish me ill,
Afar and anear,
Alone and in multitude.
I arise today.'

Douglas felt the power of the words thudding into his soul. His senses felt awakened and energised by the images of sun and fire, lightning and wind. He felt a strong sense of shielding around him. He felt a new and solid sense of protection. The fear that had developed such a strong hold on him released its grip, and Douglas felt he could start to breathe freely again. And to his amazement, he felt something in his guts - something that felt remarkably like courage. Whatever malice Niall wanted to send his way, Douglas would resist and stand his ground.

'We leave now,' said Kevin nudging Douglas.

'Agreed,' said Douglas.

As Father Pat was proclaiming God's blessing over his congregation, he spied a group of four people from the middle of the church shuffling to the aisle. Apart from Pat, no-one else particularly noticed this premature departure until, in her haste, Kath managed to catch her foot on the edge of the pew kneeler and stumbled headlong into the aisle in a noisy and ungainly fashion. As she fell to the floor, she rebuked herself, crying, 'Oh, for the love of God, you clumsy arse!' forgetting that not only was she in church but also that her task was to leave the building discreetly. Pat was momentarily distracted by the commotion, but once he saw Kath back on her feet, he continued his blessing. In the front row, Niall was hastily putting on his coat and saying something to Orla.

Despite Kath's stumble, Kevin still managed to get his group to the back of the church before any others, and they made a speedy exit. 'Will you come with us, Dorch?' said Douglas as they walked fast down the pavement. Dorchadas nodded and when they reached the car, he clambered into the front, using his full strength to wrench open the door. Kath and Kevin made their way into the back seats. Douglas turned the ignition and was dismayed to hear the unwelcome sound of a sluggish and reluctant engine. 'Dorch, we need angel power!' cried Douglas to Dorchadas, who was attaching his seat belt.

'Doug - just give it a moment,' came Kevin's calm voice from the back. 'Just wait… OK, now try again.'

Douglas did and was highly relieved to hear the welcome sound of revving.

By now others were starting to come out of the church. One of the first was Niall, who was hastily making his way to his car. Others in the church assumed his haste was due to his need to get to the hotel ahead of others to make preparations. But what was less clear was why an English couple were also so eager to make a swift getaway from the church. The couple speeded to a smart SUV parked near to the church.

'Where am I going, Kev?' called Douglas as he drove down the street.

'Right at the bottom, Doug, then straight ahead and out of town.'

'So, what the hell's going on?' said Kath reaching for her vape and attempting to ignite it, much to the dismay of the other passengers.

'Mam, I really didn't like the look of Niall,' said Kevin. 'The man may want to be violent to our Douglas here, so I just want to get Doug away from trouble.' Douglas drove fast along the town streets and was soon on to the open road. Kevin was looking out of the back window. 'Now, Doug, do you see in your mirror that green Toyota behind us?'

Douglas looked in his wing mirror and, sure enough, he saw the Toyota, and he could also make out the distinctive figure of Niall at the wheel.

'Don't let him pass you, Doug,' said Kevin. For a few moments, Douglas was almost paralysed by the thought of Saoirse being in exactly the same predicament on a road near Cairo airport. Now it was possible that it was Douglas' turn to be the victim of a drive-by shooting. Was this his destiny? To die in the same way as Saoirse? He muttered to himself, 'God's shield to protect me; God's host to save me; from snares of devils...' He glanced again in the rear-view mirror, and to his surprise, he saw a large SUV overtaking the Toyota.

Dorchadas was also looking at the wing mirror, watching the manoeuvre, and said, 'What's that Charley think he's doing, overtaking like that on these roads?' The

SUV was a good deal more powerful than the Toyota and it successfully passed it. It was now the vehicle immediately behind Douglas' car.

'Well, whoever they are, they've done us a favour, putting themselves between us and Niall,' said Kevin, still looking back and checking. 'But keep your foot on the pedal, Doug.' The incline of the road was now getting steeper as they drove into the hills.

'Dear God, do we have to go this fast?' called Kath, grasping her son's arm tightly. Douglas was concentrating hard on the winding road but then checked his mirror again. A shaft of bright sunlight shone on the SUV that was now dangerously close behind him, and for a few moments, it highlighted the driver, who was leaning forward and gripping tightly the steering wheel. To his utter horror, Douglas saw that the driver was none other than Gerald Bentley. Moreover, Gerald was now attempting to overtake Douglas' car.

'Oh my… Oh no, it's him…' said Douglas, starting to move his car into the middle of the road to block the SUV.

'Douglas, take care!' called Dorchadas as they approached a sharp bend. Douglas had been so transfixed by what he saw in the mirror, that he had not seen the sharpness of the approaching bend. Neither did he notice the icy surface of that part of the road that lay in the shade of the hill.

Afterwards, those in the car had varied recollections about what happened next: Douglas remembered the sickening feeling of losing control of the vehicle, and the unremitting pressure of the steering wheel hard against his ribs; Kath remembered the violent thud of a large car shunting them from the side, and catching sight of a woman in the passenger seat of that car, her face contorted in terror; Kevin also remembered the sickening blow of the

SUV into the side of the car and then, through his window, witnessing the green Toyota spinning on the road towards them, before it delivered another blow to their car.

Only Dorchadas remained conscious throughout the car's brief rolling journey down the grassy incline. He heard the sound of steel against stone as the car broke through the low wall at the side of the road. He felt the sharp tug of the safety belt on his waist and shoulders as the world span around him. He watched the windscreen burst into a thousand pieces, and he felt the ensuing rush of cold air on his face. He heard voices belonging to those he loved screaming unearthly screams. When the rolling stopped, he smelt the distinctive scent of freshly torn peat, and he felt the taste of mortal blood on his tongue. He felt the thud of another vehicle coming to rest next to theirs, a final violent blow before the stillness. He heard the tic tic tic of a cooling engine, and then the quiet. He watched the approaching of the dark. He was ready.

He knew this was the time. They had arrived. All of them, destined to be here at this place and at this time.

CHAPTER 23

'Where are we?' was a question most of them asked. They were standing side by side on some rough and stony ground. It was gloomy - the gloom of brooding and heavy clouds that hung in the sky above them. It was no longer cold. There was a light and a warm breeze, bringing the smell of burning wood from a nearby fire. Douglas looked at the group with whom he was standing. Kath was on his left and Kevin stood next to her. Yes, they were in the car with him. The car? He remembered being in a car. A few paces beyond Kevin he saw someone else he recognised. It was Niall Flynn. Douglas instinctively flinched. He remembered fearing him, but he could not remember why. There was nothing about him now that looked threatening. All of them were dazed and stared blankly ahead of them.

'Doug', said a familiar voice to his right. He turned, and there was Dorchadas. My, was he pleased to see him.

'Dorch!' he said, as he reached out to grasp his arm. 'What's going on?'

'Doug, we're travelling again,' Dorchadas said in a quiet voice.

Douglas looked ahead of him, and all he could see through the gloom was the smoky outline of a hill. He looked up at Dorchadas and asked, 'This is not Gethsemane, is it?'

'No, son. Not Gethsemane.' Kath and Kevin, once they heard the reassuring voice of Dorchadas, gathered close to him.

'For God's sake, it's good to see you, Dorch. But just where are we?' pleaded Kath.

Dorchadas stood before his three friends and hesitated for a few moments, then looking over their shoulders, said 'If you want to know where we all are, you need to turn around.' Up until then, all of them had been staring at the distant hill ahead of them. They all carried a sense of foreboding about the place, and none of them wanted to turn round, for they sensed there was danger behind them. But they trusted Dorchadas, so together and with caution, they turned.

Douglas grasped Dorchadas' arm tight as he beheld the scene. Kath and Kevin grasped tightly hold of each other. Niall took several steps forward. He pulled a quivering hand up to his open mouth.

'So this is where you go when you die,' said Kath.

'No, Kath,' said Dorchadas. 'You are not dead, love.' She looked up at him, frowning. 'We've all been called here. This is for life, not death.'

Kath turned away from him and looked ahead saying, 'But Dorch, look at that.' She held out her arm and pointed ahead. 'Is that not...?'

'It is, Ma,' said Kevin in a voice cracking with emotion, and he fell to his knees.

Niall took an unsteady step forward. His face was contorted as he said, 'Oh, God. Oh, dear God.'

As Douglas looked ahead, he saw a scene that he had so often pictured in his mind but never imagined he would actually see. In the far distance, he could see what looked like a huge and ancient city wall. In front of that was gathered a large crowd of people with soldiers in Roman dress preventing them from taking any steps forward. He could hear from the crowd the sounds of their voices, some of which were raised loudly. He could also hear the sounds of anguished wailing. Then, some distance in front of this

267

crowd were gathered just a few people and several more soldiers. And in front of this group rose from the ground the distinct and grim shapes of three large, rough-hewn wooden crosses. The hideous sight of thin arms trailing from the cross beams told him that the dying remains of human lives were attached to each one. Douglas was in no doubt that they all had been brought to the place named in the Scriptures as Golgotha - the place of the skull.

'We have to go to them,' said Dorchadas.

But before anyone could move, a harsh voice from behind them said, 'Just what the hell is going on?' The group all turned around, and none of them except Douglas recognised the couple walking towards them through the gloom.

Douglas knew the voice, and he recognised the lean figure walking towards him. It was the figure of Gerald Bentley. Again, he remembered a fear, but could not work out the cause of his fear. Walking just behind him was a woman. She looked familiar. Smartly dressed. Yes, he remembered. He had only met her a couple of times, but this, surely, was Angela Bentley.

'Is that you, Romer?' said Gerald as he and Angela approached the group. 'Do you mind telling me what exactly is going on here. Who are all these people? And what's all that ahead of us?' He waved his hand dismissively in front of him.

'Gerald...' said Douglas.

'Are you behind all this nonsense?' Gerald snapped, pointing his finger at Douglas.

'Gerald. For pity's sake!' called Angela, and tugged hard at his arm.

'Douglas, who exactly is this?' asked Kath to Douglas.

'A friend from England,' said Douglas, not quite sure how to introduce him to the group. 'Friends plural, I should say,' he continued. 'Gerald and Angela.'

At that moment, Niall took a few steps forward. Douglas was taken aback by the look of sheer horror on his face. He was shaking as he said to Gerald, 'For the sake of God, stop your whining, man. Don't you see? We're in purgatory, I swear to God we are.' he then fell to the ground sobbing like a child and calling out, 'Forgive me, Lord. Have mercy, please!'

'Oh, for Christ's sake!' snapped Gerald, and again Angela attempted to scold him.

'No, son,' said Dorchadas going over to the kneeling Niall. 'You needn't fear that…'

Niall looked up at him and snapped, 'Just who are you? How can you be so sure?' He sobbed again, and then pointing ahead of them with a shaking hand he said, 'Look at that. Look where we've been brought. It's our sins and wickedness that have brought us here. O, God…'

Dorchadas tried to console him as the others looked on unsure what to do. Gerald was the only one to show no sympathy for him and stood with his arms folded with eyes raised to the sky.

Douglas then noticed that one of the soldiers started walking towards them. 'Dorch, look,' he said, pointing to the soldier. 'Is it…?'

'Aye, that it is,' said Dorchadas, and he went forward to greet the soldier. As he approached closer, Douglas recognised that it was Antonio, whom they had met recently in the café. Only this time he was dressed, not in modern Italian military uniform, but the uniform of an ancient Roman centurion.

'Tony,' said Dorchadas, with affection and relief.

269

'Dorchadas and Douglas,' said the soldier. His face was wet with tears. He came over and greeted his friends.

'Dorchadas, and all of you' he said. 'I've come to tell you that what you see is… I believe it is called "the deep memory."'

'Yes, that it is, Tony. And Douglas and I are familiar with that,' said Dorchadas.

'This is the place of the greatest sadness,' said Antonio. 'It is also the place of the greatest glory. You must prepare your eyes to see both.' He then looked towards the others in the group and said, 'Now these are your friends, no?' He went over and grasped their hands. Niall rose unsteadily to his feet.

When Antonio came to Gerald, he was about to greet him, when Gerald said, 'For Christ's sake. I don't know who you think you are dressed up like that, or what kind of circus we've somehow landed up in, but could you kindly show us the way out of this god-forsaken place.'

'Come,' said Antonio, ignoring Gerald's request. 'Please follow.' Thunder rumbled in the heavy skies above them. Dorchadas and Douglas walked beside him and the others followed. As they drew near to the crosses, Antonio stopped and looked at Dorchadas and said, 'Dorchadas, my friend. You have done your work and this is where you must leave us.'

'Oh, no,' said Douglas, and grasped tight hold of his friend's arm. 'Tony, we need him here, we really do. Please, don't send him away. We can't do this without him, you must understand that.'

Dorchadas placed his hand on Douglas' and said, 'Doug, I need you now to trust Tony, as you trusted Mary in the garden. I have done my work…'

'No, Dorch...' said Douglas, still clinging hold of his friend.

'It is not farewell, Doug. You will be seeing me again before long, I promise you. But this is not the place for argument. Go with Tony now.' With great reluctance, Douglas released his grip. Dorchadas leaned forward and enfolded his friend in his long arms for some moments, before stepping back and turning away. The rest of the group looked on in some confusion as they watched Dorchadas leave them and walk towards the crowd of onlookers.

Douglas turned to Kath and Kevin and said, 'Don't worry. He's all right. We are in Tony's hands now.'

'Thank you, Douglas,' said Tony. 'Now, if you please, will you come with me.' With that, Tony led the group towards the blood-stained ground where the three stark, wooden crosses rose to an ever-darkening, ominous sky.

*

Four weeks after the accident, after the last one of them had been discharged from hospital, they all met at the Presbytery. It was the first time that they had gathered as a group since that fateful day of the memorial mass. They had visited one another during their time in hospital and had heard snippets of each other's stories, but Father Pat suggested having a day together where they could hear a full account from one another. He also persuaded Orla to be with them, even though she initially protested that, as she wasn't part of the group that was involved in the accident, she should not be there. Mrs. McGarrigle had

271

prepared a sumptuous buffet lunch, after which they settled in the lounge to hear the stories. Pat had lit the fire and the room felt welcoming. Though being the last day of February, the air outside was still chilly. Nonetheless, the sun that shone through the window that afternoon had some warmth about it, and there was a feel of Spring in the light that filtered into Pat's spacious lounge.

'So, it's grand you can all be here,' said Pat, throwing one of his rapid and endearing smiles into the room. 'And so good to see you all recovering so well. Now, I thought you could just take it in turns to tell us your story of what you experienced.' He paused for a moment, then added, 'And of course, what we say here stays among ourselves. There will be few beyond this room who would understand the things you have witnessed together.' Pat smiled briefly again and, grasping his coffee mug with both his large hands and looking around the room at the assembled group, he asked, 'So, who would like to go first?'

'Och, let me,' said Kath, who ignited her vape with difficulty due to her arm still being in plaster. But once it was successfully alight, Kath was ready to relate her experience on that day.

And so, the stories of Golgotha began.

CHAPTER 24

Kathleen's story

Kath was sitting on the only chair in the room that could be regarded as comfortable. It was next to the fire and she was enjoying its warmth. Her left arm was in plaster. She had removed the sling which lay on the table next to her. She shifted her ample frame as she prepared to speak. After taking several inhalations from her vape that sent plumes of wild cherry and cinnamon into the room, she put it down on the table and said, 'Well, first of all, let me apologise for my tumbling out of that pew, like I did. I can be as clumsy as a half-pissed bear at times, I can. Didn't exactly help us when we were all trying to make a speedy exit from the church.'

There was a chortle of laughter at the memory of that moment, that now seemed such a long time ago.

'Aye, well. Moving on. I remember feeling mighty agitated at the thought of Niall Flynn armed and angry, and I was glad to get out of the church. But I don't remember anything about the car chase, which, by all accounts is a very good thing.' Several in the room smiled and looked at Douglas. 'So, the first thing I can remember after that was arriving at that dreary place.' She glanced at her vape then thought better of it. She cleared her chest for a few moments and continued. 'At first, I was just dumbfounded, I surely was. I had no idea I'd been in a car accident. I suppose, I thought I was in a dream - stepped out of my normal life as it were. And yet it didn't have that dreamy kind of quality about it, did it?' Douglas nodded as he listened, eager to hear every detail of Kath's account. 'No,

I was wide awake but had not the first idea about where I was. I was so glad my Kevin was with me. And it was mighty good to see Dorch and Doug there as well. I was a bit unnerved to see you there, Mr. Flynn!' The rest of the room laughed and looked at Niall. Orla smiled and nudged him with her elbow. 'And I hadn't a clue who the English couple were!' Angela offered a shy smile.

'Well, as you know, it was a mighty grim place, sure it was. And then Dorch got us to turn round and we saw that appalling scene ahead of us. I'd seen enough crucifixes in my early days to know what they were. Well, once I'd seen that I began to believe that we were all dead and had landed straight in purgatory. "So, the church was right after all," I thought to myself. "You should have gone to church, Kathleen Griffin. You sure to God should have. Your sins have finally found you out, lass." But then Dorch, bless him, quickly assured me I was not dead. My God, I was a relieved woman, I surely was.

'My Kevin was at my side. Fell to his knees, poor boy.' She looked pained and glanced towards Kevin. 'Then I was aware of this snobby English gent - sorry, Angela, no disrespect.'

'Quite all right, Kathleen,' assured Angela.

'But he was being a pr...' She stopped herself and, glancing at Pat, said, 'Oh, pardon, me, Father. I am trying to improve my language, honest to God I am, but not always succeeding. But I think you all felt much as I did.' All in the room nodded, including Angela. 'And there was that Italian gent dressed as a Roman soldier. Wasn't sure what to make of him at first, but once I saw he was a good friend of Dorch's - and yours, Doug - I took to him. But he upset me when he told Dorchadas to get packing. Oh, I was awful sad when I saw Dorchadas walk away from us, I surely was.'

274

'Aye we all were, Mammy,' said Kevin, who was sitting on a creaking upright chair near the door.

'Don't suppose there's been any word of him?' she asked.

'No, none,' said Pat. 'You know Dorch. He comes and he goes.'

'He did promise he would be back,' said Douglas.

'Oh aye. That's good to hear. So where was I?' she said, lifting her eyes to the ceiling for a moment. 'Ah, well, that Italian fella. He took me by the hand, so he did, and he said something like "You're up next, lass." Only he said it in his Italian accent. Well, to be fair, I wasn't quite sure what he meant. I mean, my first thought was that it was my turn to get up on one them crosses. So, for a moment I was a wee bit timid.' There were more chuckles in the room. But then Kath's demeanour dimmed. 'It was sure dreary and dark there, wasn't it?' The others murmured agreement.

'So, he walked me to the front of them hideous crosses, and honest to God I could not bear to look up. I mean who wants to see some poor boys hanging from nails. I told him straight that no decent person would want to gawk at such things.' She shook her head and reached for her cup of tea. 'Now, I don't know if this happened to the rest of you, but he introduced me to someone there. A very nice lady and apparently she was the Mary Magdalene of the bible.' Douglas nodded knowingly. 'Well, wasn't she supposed to be a slapper, Father Pat?' asked Kath to the parish priest.

Pat, who had been looking at her intently, raised his eyebrows and replied, 'There's no real evidence for that, Kath. But she'd had a hard time in life, that she had.'

'Ah well, I didn't raise the subject with her, you'll be pleased to know,' said Kath. 'But as I say, I thought she was a very nice lady, regardless of what she'd been up to earlier in her life. But poor soul, she was in quite a state, because one thing was perfectly clear, was that she loved that man fastened to the cross next to us. Now, this is where it gets a bit complicated for a simple mind like mine, so I'll need you to put me right on this, Douglas, if I've got it all befuddled. There we were in that terrible place, and sure to God it was real enough to me. No question. But it was also a thing called "deep memory" - I think most of us were told that were we not?' She looked around the room and people nodded. 'Yes, well, I can see from your looks that you were no wiser than me about that. Never mind, the point is this. In the actual thing, Mary was perfectly beside herself in an agony of grief, sure she was, poor soul. But in this deep memory whatsit, she was able to step to one side of it all, if you get my meaning.'

Kath drained her mug. 'Is there a drop more in that pot, there, Father?' she said raising her mug towards Pat. 'Got a dreadful throat on me today, so I have.' The priest duly came across and topped her mug up with tea, milk and sugar while Kath cleared he throat for a while, and then continued her story.

'This Mary got talking to me, and my, she seemed to know my life, she surely did. Well, my first thought was, "How come you's been nosing around my life like that? Who's been talking?" I did have my suspicions about you, Douglas,' she said pointing a finger at Douglas, who smiled at her. 'But I soon got off my high horse, and listened to the girl. Well, she then told me a bit about herself, and though she gave no details, it was clear she had been badly hurt, poor lass. And then she said it was this fella here, on this cross, that healed her sorry wounds. To be sure, it all sounded very nice and I was pleased for her, but to be honest, I was feeling mighty uncomfortable. I mean, a poor soul was dying right next to me. Not easy

276

having a conversation with that going on. Not the most convivial of places,' she said, pleased with herself for using what she regarded as a rather grand word.

She sighed and took another sip of her tea and then continued. 'Well, this Mary - she was very persuasive, and she said that the one thing I had to do was to look up at that cross. Now, you know me. As stubborn as a constipated mule, I am. I was determined *not* to look at such a hideous sight. It seemed mighty disrespectful apart from anything else. But in the end, she won the fight, and I did dare to look up.' She put her cup on the side table and sighed again. 'Oh, it was dreadful to see the blood on that wood. The feet were pretty much at the level of my eyes, and I could see they were such good, strong feet. I then looked up, and I saw that the poor boy was without a stitch of clothes on him. Oh, I felt so shocked and saddened by that. I mean, how humiliating for the lad. I turned away out of respect for a few moments, but then found I was drawn to look up at His face.'

Here Kath paused and her spongy cheeks reddened. 'I don't know…' She waved her hand for a moment. 'I've tried to find words for this, but honest to God, they can't be found. I just know what I saw, and I'll never be able to put it into plain English. Not even in Irish. All I know is that I saw a man who had been terribly, terribly hurt, and yet was more forgiving than you could ever imagine. I saw a man who was most certainly close to death, and yet more alive than anything I've ever seen. And I saw a man who had been more battered and beaten than any man should be in this life, and yet He was a man who looked like the champion of the world. Now how do you explain all of that? Honest to God, I don't know.'

Kath paused and stroked her plastered arm. 'You see, you folks don't know my life story. God knows, it's not the

277

worst story by any means. But the fact is, for most of my adult life, I have not got on well with the church, and, if the truth be told, I've not got on well with God either. You know all this, Father,' she said looking up at Pat. 'We had lots of great conversations in hospital, you and I. I owe my recovery to you, Father, I surely do,' she said with her eyes filling with water.

'Come now, Kath. It was your courage and determination that aided your recovery. And as I keep saying, Kath, please call me "Pat". None of this 'Father' business. Not unless it really helps you.'

'I know, I know. It's just habit, I suppose... Pat.' She smiled through her tears. 'But... where was I now?'

'You, the church and God, Kath,' said Douglas.

'So I was, Doug. So I was. Thank you. Well, I loved my church when I was a wee lass, and me and God got on well, until there was, well... a hell of a mess in my personal life. And that's when all the faith and church stuff came to a sudden halt. Well, this Mary Magdalene - she seemed to know about all of this, and I thought she'd be shocked about it all. But no, none of it. She told me how she'd not been that fond of God herself, and how religious people had treated her so badly. Then she met the man now hanging on that wood above us. She told me how she spent a couple of years as part of His church, so to speak - not sure that's what she called it, but you know what I mean. But she said how she'd walk the lanes with Him and she'd ask Him questions. She'd try and catch Him out, she said, but He never minded. She said she couldn't believe that someone as nice as Him could be God. Aye, she told me all of this and quite a bit more. We must have been there for a while. And she said how in time she came to believe He was - well, you know - the real thing: Himself - God.

'So I says to her, "But lass, if He's God, what's He doing up there, for goodness sake?" And this Mary looked at me and said, "What do *you* think He is doing up there, Kathleen?" She got me to look up at that dear, wounded face again. Well, you all have your own story about this, but in those moments, I felt I was the only person there at the foot of that cross. He was looking down at me... Well, there was only one word for it.' Here Kath started swallowing as the emotion started to get the better of her. She reached out for her tea with her good arm and took a sip before she continued. 'There's only one word for it, and that word is "Love". I know, I know,' she said, struggling to find a way of expressing herself. 'The word is used millions of times to mean all sorts of things, is it not? But when I looked at that face up there, I can tell you, I saw love like I have never seen it before, and doubt will ever see it again.' She sighed for a few moments. 'It was then, as I looked up at the cross that it happened.' There was more clearing of the throat, and more tea and a long pause.

'Take your time, love,' said Pat.

'Aye, thanks, Pat. You know what's coming next, but let me try and get it out so as people here get my meaning.' She looked around at the room as all eyes watched her. She was stroking her bandaged arm again. 'When I looked up at Him, at first he was just looking straight out ahead of Him. It was like that love was just spreading out over the whole world before Him. I mean, there were people there shouting all kinds of abuse at Him. And I could see He wasn't ignoring them. He was looking straight at them. And He was... well, just loving them. There's no other word for it. But then...' Another sigh and a pause and more stroking of her arm. 'But then, He looked down at me.' She bit her lip and nodded for a time. 'That's all I can say.... He looked down at me....' She looked at Douglas. 'Doug, darling. You know all that poison that was inside of

279

me. Remember your man Cecil Oakenham and all that stuff?' She smiled a brief smile, recalling their visit to him a few months back. 'Well, in those moments, when them dear eyes looked on mine, I felt all the poison flood out of my soul, honest to God I did. Those hideous powers of the church. You understand my meaning, Father Pat?' she said, not wanting to offend the priest.

'Of course, I do, Kath,' said Pat.

'Well, all the dark powers that I had experienced from the church when I was young... I mean, in the light of those dear eyes, they seemed so... well... puny. The power I saw in those dying yet living eyes was the power that not only changes the world but changes stubborn old eejits like Kathleen Griffin.'

The room was silent for quite some time, as the early Spring sun re-emerged from behind a cloud, sending a shaft of light on the group. 'Thank you, Kath,' said Pat.

'Oh, I'm not quite done,' said Kath. 'That Mary - she did one more thing for me, and this was remarkable. You may remember, Doug, that when we first met, I told you how, when I was a wee girl, I used to love that window depicting the lovely Brigid of Kildare. Do you remember that, son?'

'Yes, I do, Kath,' said Douglas. 'I remember how the old priest- the one you liked - used to tell you stories about her.'

'You remember it well, Doug, bless you,' said Kath. 'Well, what does Mary do? She takes my hand, and we walk to the crowd, and there, at the front of a little group of people, is a young woman. And Mary says - honest to God, this is no lie - she says, "Kathleen, meet your friend, Brigid"! Can you believe that now, Pat?' she said, chuckling.

'I'll believe anything these days,' said Pat.

'Well, I know - it's all far-fetched. But I can tell you, that was a special moment for me.'

'What did you talk about, Ma?' asked Kevin.

'Oh, this and that, Kev. It's… It's more private, that bit. But it was special. It was very special. So,' she said, taking a deep breath and patting her knee with her good hand, 'that's just about all there is to my story. So now, this poor old priest here, serving us tea and doing us all good today, is lumbered with me as one of his flock.' She wheezed a laugh.

'Not if you become a Quaker, Mother,' said Kevin, smiling.

'Kevin. I respect Peter and his faith. You know I do. But do you really think your mother is cut out for all that sitting around in a quiet room with my mouth tight shut?'

They all laughed. Pat said, 'Kathleen, I can assure you, you are so welcome in our church.'

'You may come to regret that welcome, Father!' said Kevin and there was more laughter.

After a short time of questions to Kath and conversation, Pat said, 'Shall we have another story, and then I'll get us another cup of tea and a piece of that cake that Mrs. McGarrigle has made us. Would anyone like to go next?' he asked.

'I think maybe I would like to,' said the cultivated English voice of Angela Bentley. She was sitting on the other side of the fire from Kath and had been listening to her story intently. 'None of you know me very well, but you have all been so kind, and I'd like to fill you in on what happened to me. To me and to Gerald, of course.'

'That would be grand, Angela. Please go ahead,' invited the priest, who stepped away from his chair for a moment and put another log on to the fire. The group settled back into their seats. They were certainly eager to hear Angela's story and they listened with anticipation.

CHAPTER 25

Angela's story

Angela was sitting in an upright chair, which was the most comfortable for her injured back. 'It was so good getting to know some of you during those long days when I was stretched out on that hospital bed,' she started. 'Thank you again for coming along and sitting with me. Especially as you were all injured too. You'll know bits of this, but let me try and put it together into one coherent account if I can.

'My story does not start well.' She looked down and fiddled with her hands for a moment. 'I've already spent a long time with Douglas, and he has been most forgiving.' She glanced at Douglas. '*Incredibly* forgiving. I think you all know why Gerald and I came to Ireland. I feel so deeply ashamed now when I think of it, and there is absolutely no excuse. All I can say is that my mind had become deranged, I was racked with bitterness and fear. And I was... I *am* an alcoholic.'

She sighed. 'Gerald and I had been married thirty-eight years. That's a miracle in itself.' She attempted a smile. 'I think in the early days we were very much in love actually,' she said, looking out of the large window that opened up on to a garden bathed in afternoon sunlight. 'I don't know what went wrong, but money was an issue from the early days of our marriage. As far as my parents were concerned, I had married 'beneath' me. I had come from a wealthy family - educated at Roedean and all that. That school would set you back forty grand a year in fees now.'

'So that's why my mammy didn't send me there, then,' said Kath, and several in the room laughed.

Angela smiled at Kath and continued, 'Gerald was not from a wealthy background - didn't have my posh accent, did he, Douglas?' She looked over to Douglas who shook his head. 'The first thing my parents wanted to know was how much he was worth and, I'm sorry to say, I was always a bit ashamed of him in front of them. So I put pressure on him to earn. And...' she sighed a deep sigh. 'Well, he didn't do badly in his work in the bank, but I didn't think it was nearly enough, and I'm afraid I told him so. But he would have craved more money even without my wealth. And when he couldn't get enough from his job, he looked for other ways to make money. That's how he got into this wretched arms trade business. Well, I say "wretched", but at the time I thought it made very good sense. I'm sorry to say, I had no qualms about it at all. I thought that if people were so keen to fight their jolly wars, why shouldn't Gerald sell them the guns. My only concern was that he wouldn't get caught.' She looked at each member of the group, checking for signs of shock and rejection. But seeing everyone was still with her, she continued.

'I terribly regret it all now, of course. But at the time I thought it was wonderful. Off Gerald would go on some trip and would come back with huge amounts of money. And in time, we were able to buy that massive house. Hooray! At last, we were earning enough to impress my parents, and living in a house that they would finally approve of. Only, by then they were not alive to see any of it. Anyway, we moved into that house, and then almost immediately it hit me - none of this was making me happy. I was living in this glorious big house with the kind of money that would make even my parents' eyes water. But I wasn't happy. Neither was Gerald. He had developed a taste for big wealth by now. Whatever he earned was never enough for him. He seemed to have the perfect skills and character to do this arms work, and he was always on the lookout for the next deal.'

Angela looked around the room and guessed the thoughts in the minds of some. 'I'm sorry, I appreciate that for some of you, lack of money may have been a real issue for you, and it's not easy to hear this. But I just want to give this to you straight.'

'You're right, Angela,' said Niall, 'Poverty's been a terrible blight in our family. But you carry on, lass. I want to hear your tale.'

'Thanks, Niall,' said Angela, as she shifted her position in the chair to ease her painful frame. 'So yes, I had all the money anyone could want in this life, but it was poisoning me and it was poisoning Gerald. His lust for money developed into other lusts. He went off me, for a start. He was having affairs all over the place, which made me feel pretty bad about myself. And I... I started my affair - with the bottle.'

'No shame in that, love,' said Kath. I've known that demon in my time.'

'Me too,' said Niall.

'Many of us have known it tugging at us, sure we have,' said Pat, staring at the floor.

'Yes, thank you,' said Angela offering a hint of a smile. 'Well, as I said, Gerald adored the wealth. But it was not things like the big house that gave him pleasure. No. He loved the sense of power it gave him. He became horribly skilful at using money to manipulate people. He did it with people in his banking world. He did it with people at his lodge. He did it with your church, Douglas, as you know. And for some reason, he loved playing power games with

285

the bishop and the diocese. To be honest, I think taking on the diocese made him feel like he had taken on God and was now controlling Him.'

Douglas looked sad and nodded.

But that wasn't the worst thing.' She looked down and played with the hem of her silk scarf for a few moments. Her dyed auburn hair fell over her eyes.

'Take your time, love,' said Pat.

Her eyes filled as she said, 'He became hardened to… Well, frankly, disposing of people who got in his way.' She swallowed and continued to look down at her lap. 'If you had met him you would never imagine he was capable of that.' Her voice dropped as she said, 'Then there was that terrible thing in Cairo.' She paused, working hard to control her quivering lip. 'I supported Gerald in the plan. Again, I've had a long chat with Douglas about this, and he has been unbelievably forgiving.' Her face crumpled, and in a broken voice, she looked at Douglas across the room and whispered, 'I'm so sorry, Douglas…'.

This part of the story was far from easy for Douglas, but with genuine conviction, he was able to say, 'Angela - that's in the past.'

'Thank you, Douglas,' said Angela in a whisper. She pulled out a tissue and blew her nose. Clearing her throat, and raising her head she resumed her story. 'Well, you all know about that dreadful business. So, when Gerald got wind of the arrest of the hitman he had hired, I was seriously alarmed. It seemed obvious to me that very soon the trail would lead back to Gerald. I could see it all too clearly: he would be sent to jail, we would be headline news in the Mail and the Sun, and I would lose everything - my house, my wealth, and whatever reputation I might have had. Gerald kept trying to reassure me that the British Intelligence would never be able to - or even want to -

track him, but my nagging worry was that Douglas would find out. The terrible thing is, once you have taken one life, it is never so hard taking the next one.'

'Aye, sadly that is true,' said Kevin nodding. Niall looked at the floor and said nothing. Orla, next to him on the sofa, brushed some imaginary crumbs from her skirt.

Angela shuffled in her seat. Her back pain was feeling sharp. She looked at Pat and said, 'Thanks, Pat for your word about confidentiality. This bit I'm about to tell... it's... well...'

'You're alright here, love,' said Pat. Others in the room nodded.

Angela inhaled deeply, then said, 'I told you that Gerald got hardened to killing people. Well, it wasn't just him. It had somehow got into my system as well. Getting rid of people who got in your way just seemed...' She shrugged her shoulders and, gripping her tissue, said, 'Well... the most practical way of solving a problem.' She heaved another long sigh and then continued, 'Alcohol does a great job of muting your conscience. I... I don't know. I'd become so lost. So lost. When I think now of who I had become, I feel so shaken. So very ashamed.'

She played with her tissue for a few moments, attempting to straighten and fold it, then continued. 'Well, it was my bright idea - to come over here, to track down Douglas and do away with him. Gerald had no qualms about getting rid of poor Douglas, but he wasn't convinced my plan was a great one. Which, of course, it wasn't. You don't think up brilliant plans when your brain is soaked in gin. Anyway, I had this not such a bright idea of poisoning him. A lethal injection.' She closed her eyes for a moment and inhaled before continuing. 'Gerald knew how to obtain all these ghastly things and somehow managed to get the necessary equipment very quickly. So, we came over on

287

the boat. Gerald - typical Gerald - already had false passports for both of us, so we arrived in Dublin as Mr. and Mrs. Ingleby. Hm.' She shrugged a brief laugh.

'There was a kid at my school called Ingleby,' said Kath, clearing her throat as she spoke. 'Not a nice girl at all. Never washed her hair. I swear you could smell her coming a hundred yards off. Most unpleasant, it was.'

'Ah, yes…' said Angela, glancing at Kath and somewhat thrown off her track for a moment. 'Well, Inglebys we were as we arrived in Ireland. Oddly enough, when the Garda questioned me in hospital, he didn't seem that upset about the false passports.'

'Won't be the first time he's come across that,' said Niall.

'Hm,' said Angela. 'Well, I was relieved, I must say. Anyway, moving to that fateful Thursday - is it only four weeks ago? It seems like a lifetime.' All in the room nodded. 'Well, as soon as we heard about the church service, this seemed like the ideal opportunity for putting my brilliant plan into action. Off we went to church, with me armed with a hypodermic full of poison in my handbag.' She shook her head. 'So hard to believe now. Anyway, as soon as Gerald spotted Douglas in the church, he turned to me and said, "You've done the right thing, Angela. That man definitely needs to be eliminated". He was fidgety throughout the service. Then, at the end of the service, when he saw Douglas making his escape from the church, he grabbed my hand and rushed us out to the car, and off we sped. "Forget Plan A", he said. "We'll shunt the …" well, I won't give you his actual language, but words to the effect of "We'll shunt him off the road." I was terrified. I hadn't even had a chance to have a couple of G and T's to steady my nerves. I remember clinging to my seat belt as we swerved our way up that hill. I think it was

288

just before the collision that I noticed that Gerald had forgotten to put his on. I remember telling him, but he just swore at me.'

For a moment Angela looked sad.

'Can I get you a glass of water, Angela?' asked Pat.

'Thank you, Pat. That would be most helpful,' she replied. Pat got up and after a few minutes returned with a jug of water and some glasses.

'I don't remember anything about the accident. Apparently, the car rolled over a couple of times. But it was a colossal car - typical Gerald - and, as you know, though I injured my spine, it's not serious, probably thanks to the size of the car. But I was knocked out. The next thing I was aware of was standing in that bleak and dreary place with all of you, not knowing where we were or what was happening.'

Pat passed her a glass of water. 'Thank you so much, Pat' she said, taking the glass and sipping from it. 'I was terrified in that place. When we were told to turn around and I saw those ghastly crosses, I assumed that was it for me. I felt I had been found out. There could only be one direction this could go in for me, and it was downwards. For the first time in my life, I became terrified of hell. If you remember, I hardly said anything as we walked towards those crosses. I just felt so scared. Gerald, of course... Gerald was being Gerald, I'm afraid. I don't know. You'd have thought...'

She paused for a few minutes, then said. 'As we got near the crosses, do you know what the worst thing was for me?' Everyone in the group shook their heads. 'I looked at Douglas, and for the first time, I saw him as a kind, wounded, grieving, generous man. I saw the way he walked alongside that tall gentleman who was with us. The one you called "Dorch."'

289

'Dorchadas is the full name, in case you are wondering,' said Kevin.

'Ah yes,' continued Angela. 'Dorchadas. Well, I never got to meet him. But it was Douglas that I was looking at. I remember thinking to myself, "Were you honestly wanting to take this poor man's life?"' She shook her head, and then looked at Douglas. 'I had allowed an awful evil to get into me, Douglas.' She was frowning and brought the tissue to her nose again.

She looked down at the floor for a moment as she gathered her thoughts and then looked back up and said, 'I don't know how, but somehow I found myself at the foot of the centre cross. Now, I'm sorry to say, I have never had much to do with religion. Gerald always did that sort of thing. I couldn't see the point of God. I never liked all those stuffy hymns, hard pews and being preached at.' She waved her hand in the air, and then looked at Pat and said, 'Oh, sorry, Father Pat.'

'I feel much the same at times, love. Do continue,' said Pat.

Angela turned up the corner of her mouth a little in response, then continued, 'I just stood there for quite a while. Like Kath, I honestly did not want to look up at what was hanging above me. But I guessed it was the body of Jesus. But then a woman came up and stood next to me. She told me she was grieving for this man hanging on the middle cross. And she also told me she was the mother of a couple of chaps, one called John and the other James. I'm sorry, but I don't read the bible, so I haven't a clue who they were. But she drew me a short way away from the cross, and both of us sat down on that dusty ground. There were a few other groups near us, all crying and sniffing.'

Angela attempted to cross her legs but then thought better of it due to the pain it caused in her back. She continued, 'Straight away I liked this lady. She was red-eyed and full of sorrow. I told her how sorry I was for her grief, but, to be honest, I didn't really know what to say. Then she told me how her boys had got to know this Jesus. And it sounds they did well with Him. She said how she had very high ambitions for them, and she imagined that one day Jesus would be a mighty king, and her two boys would be - I can't remember how she put it - something like princes alongside Him. They would be the most important and powerful people after Him. But she then said they had come to realise that they had all completely misunderstood what this kingdom of Jesus was all about. It wasn't about this kind of power at all. And then that sweet lady grasped my shoulder and, pointing up at the cross, she said, "Look. Now we can all see what kind of a king He is."' For a moment Angela raised her arm to an imaginary cross as she recalled the scene.

She then lowered her arm and moved awkwardly on her seat again, wincing at the pain in her back. 'And so I did look at the cross. There we were, sitting on that cold earth, looking at a young man cruelly nailed to a piece of wood and left to die. And this was, so she told me, the son of God. I foolishly said to her, "Well, that is not much of a king and not much of a God, to be in that state." I glanced back at her and I found her looking so intently at me that I felt very uncomfortable. But after a little while of this gazing at me, she said, "Take another look, Angela." So I did. And I then started to see something. Yes, there was something kingly about this figure on the cross. I can't explain why, but I was beginning to see it. He owned absolutely nothing - no wealth at all. Pinned to that wood He was completely helpless and powerless. And yet, I could sense that something was happening that was more powerful than anything I had witnessed before. I got to my feet and knew I had to get closer. When I got to the cross,

291

my eyes were at the same level as the feet, just as you said, Kath.'

She shook her head for a few moments, looking into the fire that was next to her. She then looked up and said, 'They were ordinary, regular feet, but... For reasons I don't fully know, I simply leaned forward and kissed them.' She shook her head, still wondering at her actions. She then looked around the room and said, 'And do you know, something huge changed inside of me. Right down here.' She tapped her abdomen. 'I felt such strength in those feet. I mean, it doesn't make sense, does it? They were the feet of a dying man. He couldn't move. He had no power even to breathe, let alone rule the world, nor be a god to any of us. And yet, and yet...'

She sat nodding for a while. 'I don't think I'm ever going to explain it,' she said. 'All I know is that in those moments, something at the core of me profoundly changed. It was like an old Angela died, and a new one woke up. A bit like a butterfly breaking out of a dead cocoon. I knew, for example, that my longing for wealth had gone. I knew it. I felt it. All that money just looked so pathetic. So superficial. So beside the point, somehow. And - and frankly, this really is miraculous - I also knew that I would never touch a drop of alcohol again.' She tapped her throat as she said, 'I felt some power break down here in my throat, in that place where I used to feel the longing for drink. I just knew that the desperate longing had gone. I felt a freedom. I felt I had come to my senses after a long time of being far away from them. A good and kind bit of me, that had been crushed by my fears and ambitions, was finally allowed out. I suppose you could say, I finally dared to be myself. I was no longer afraid. It was wonderful.' She smiled and looked at Pat and said, 'If that's not power, Father Pat, I don't know what is.'

'Aye, lass,' said Pat, and not for the first time, Angela grew great strength from the kindness in his face. She looked around at all the eyes fixed on her and added, 'So that's me really. I honestly can't explain what happened there, but I know I will never be the same. I may not have the beauty of a butterfly, but I honestly do feel like a new creature. I feel I now have wings. I don't know what people will think when I go home. They won't recognise me, they really won't. Not sure how I'll explain it all.' She smiled and put away her tissue in her sleeve.

The room was quiet for a few moments, when Orla, who had been quiet all afternoon, asked, 'Angela, do you think you could say something about…' She paused for a few moments, then continued. 'Could you tell us about Gerald, please.'

'Ah yes,' said Angela, taking a deep breath. This was part of the story that as yet she had told no-one. But now she felt ready to relate it.

She shifted in her seat and took a sip of water. 'Well, those of you who were there saw how he was behaving. I can't disagree with your very apt assessment of him, Kath. In my time with the mother of James and John, and then with those wonderful feet, I had lost track of him. It was so dark, wasn't it? So I went to look for him and soon found him. He was standing a little way away from the crosses. He had his back to them and had his hands in his pockets. I went over to him and was longing to tell him about my beautiful experience. But before I had a chance to speak, he said, "Oh, there you are. Where the hell have you been?" His words sounded so loud and harsh. He then said, "You'll never guess what's happened to me". He then proceeded to tell me that the soldier - I think he was called Antonio, is that right?'

'Yes, that's it,' said Douglas.

'Well, Antonio had taken him to one side and told him he had something very painful to show him, but it would be followed by something very wonderful. I can still hear Gerald's harsh voice. "Do you know what he did, Angela? He took me to a valley and it was a valley that was full of hordes of people, and they were all looking up at me. Men, women and children - all gaping at me. It was grotesque!" As soon as he said it, I realised to my horror what he was being shown. I just knew. He didn't get it, though. Antonio had to tell him who they were.' She paused for a few moments and then slowly shaking her head, she said, 'He was being shown every life that had been killed by the weapons he had sold over his years of illegal trading. And, I am sorry and very ashamed to say, but he told me there were thousands of them. For me, that would have been enough to break my heart.' She drew out a fresh tissue from her sleeve and blew her nose hard, then reached out for her glass of water.

'I thought he might feel the same as me, but I very much regret that he had a terrible Gerald moment. He utterly refused to believe it. He was red-faced with fury and said Antonio was deceiving him - trying to emotionally blackmail him. He had no right to show him this and so on and so on. I'm afraid you can probably imagine it, Douglas.'

Douglas frowned with sadness and nodded his head.

'I stood there,' continued Angela, clasping her glass. 'And he just went on and on about the injustice of it, and how we had to get away from this dreadful place. I finally stopped him and said, "But Gerald. Antonio said that was the terrible thing. But he also said he would show you a wonderful thing. So, what was the wonderful thing?" He looked at me, and the expression on his face was so hard and cold.' Angela was now speaking in a very quiet voice.

'He said, "I never got round to asking that..." well, several choice adjectives, "...soldier about that."' All I could see in his face was terrible anger. And then...' She paused and looked down at the floor for several moments. 'He seemed to somehow get paler. And then he suddenly jolted backwards. He stood for a few moments looking dazed, and then...' She looked up at Orla who was sitting opposite her. 'He sort of evaporated before my eyes. I tried to look for him, but there was no sign of him. Then I noticed that the lovely lady - the mother of those two boys - was by my side again, and she simply said, "He has made his choice, Angela". That's what she said, "He has made his choice". And I agreed with her. He was given a chance, and he refused to take it.' She paused for a few moments and looked down at her lap and said in a whisper, 'I knew what it meant.'

The room was silent for a while until Pat said, 'I'm so sorry, Angela. You poor soul.'

Angela nodded and looked up at Pat with her watery eyes. 'During my first week in hospital, someone from A&E came and told me about him when they had brought him in. He'd been thrown through the front window of the car but was still alive when they found him. They said he made it to the hospital but he was very badly injured. They also said that they tried to resuscitate him with the defibrillator. I think that was the moment when I saw him jolt backwards.' Orla got up and came over to Angela, and knelt beside her and Angela sobbed on her shoulder.

'Best let it all out, love,' said Kath. 'No point in holding that kind of grief all locked up inside. Your tears are safe here.' Everyone in the room nodded.

After a while, Angela raised her head from Orla's shoulder. She smiled through her tears. 'Oh, dear, what a sight I must be!' Orla kissed her and returned to her seat.

Angela inhaled deeply, blew her nose, and said. 'Of course, I shall miss him terribly, but I accept what has happened. I will be lonely. But whatever years I have ahead of me, I am determined to live them well now. I have to accept that I encouraged Gerald in that ghastly trade. I must take some responsibility, and I now feel a strong need to somehow make amends.' She inhaled deeply and looked up at the ceiling for a moment. 'So, I have been researching charities that are to do with saving lives in Africa. I have asked God that he won't take me until I have saved as many lives as Gerald took through his weapons.' She paused for a few moments. 'And yes, I seem to be on reasonably good terms with God now. Quite a surprise!' She smiled a kind, watery smile to all in the room. 'Thank you so much for listening. You have been most kind.'

'Well, I think Kath and Angela have certainly earned a cup of tea,' said Pat. I'll go and make us a fresh brew.'

'That would be grand, Pat,' said Niall. 'And would anyone mind, if I were to tell my story next?'

All in the room agreed. So, after a break and fortified by tea and slices of Mrs. McGarrigle's cake, they settled down to listen to Niall's story.

CHAPTER 26

Niall's story

The scar on Niall's cheek was healing well, but his right hand was still heavily bandaged. He put down his mug of tea carefully with his left hand and commenced his story. 'Before I start on my story, could I just ask you something, please, Angela?'

'Of course,' said Angela.

'Well, you said you had a syringe packed with poison in your handbag. What did the gardai say about that, if you don't mind my asking?'

'Well, that's an interesting question,' replied Angela. 'There was no sign of it in my handbag. And there was no mention of it by the police - sorry, the gardai. It seems it was never found. I just assumed it must have somehow got lost in the accident.'

'I did wonder,' said Niall. 'The same thing happened to me. As I think most of you know by now, I had a revolver in my pocket. So when I came round in the hospital, the first thing I thought was "Have they found the gun?" When Orla got my suit home, there was no gun in the pocket and I assumed the gardai must have taken it. But they never spoke of it, and they sure would have done if they'd found it.'

'Well, maybe Dorchadas was not the only angel there that day,' suggested Pat.

'That's what I'm thinking,' said Niall. 'And I'm truly grateful.'

He then shuffled on the sofa, looked briefly to Orla who was sitting close to him on his left. She took his hand for a moment as he commenced his story. 'So, like Angela here, the start of my story is not a pretty one. I think you all know that Orla and I are the parents of the sweet girl that was once the wife of Douglas, may she rest in peace.'

'And rise in glory,' said Pat instinctively.

'Aye, indeed,' said Niall. 'Now Orla here was a wonderful mother to our Saoirse…'

'Oh, I'm none too sure of that, Niall,' protested Orla.

'Orla, love,' he said, turning to her. 'I'm going to say my piece, and you will just have to accept the honours accorded you as I tell my tale. Because, honest to God, you have been my salvation.' Orla blinked several times and smiled. 'So, where do I begin?' Niall asked, looking at the ceiling and scratching his unshaven chin. 'I won't bore you with my whole life history, sure I won't.'

'Thanks be to God!' said Orla, to the amusement of the others.

'Let's just say,' said Niall, 'that I have always carried in my heart a deep passion for my country. My beloved Eire. But, as I see it now, that passion was a mix of love and hate: love for my country, but a heavy hatred for all those who tried to do us harm. I see it differently now, I surely do. But for most of my life, I have carried a deep and bitter animosity towards - and Douglas and Angela, excuse me for this please, - towards the English. And alongside that, I hated the Protestants. To me, an English Proddy was the devil incarnate. Well, I can tell you, when our Saoirse chose to marry an English Proddy minister it lit a fuse in me, sure to God it did.'

He turned to Orla who had taken hold of his uninjured hand. 'Sad to say, the poison in me seeped into Orla too.'

298

He looked at her and added, 'But it was never as bad in you, love.' Orla nodded.

'It was Orla who persuaded me to come to the wedding,' continued Niall. 'It was my first visit to England. I hated every minute of it, I can tell you. I just felt that my daughter must surely hate her parents with a venom to do the very thing that would hurt them the most. I couldn't work out why she should treat us this way. Early on in life, we got on great, we did. She was such a sweet girlie when she was a youngster. We had great times together, didn't we, love?'

'Aye, we did, Niall,' said Orla with a hint of a smile.

'But listen, I see it all differently now,' continued Niall, releasing his hand from Orla's and leaning forward. 'I see now why she needed to get free of us. Well, of me, I should say. I realise now that I *so* misunderstood her. And I regret to say, I realise just how much I must have hurt her.' He bowed his head, and with his left hand, he reached up and pressed his eyes that were threatening to release yet more water. The recent weeks had seen a flow of water from his eyes that he did not believe possible.

'Excuse me,' he muttered to the group.

'We all understand, Niall,' said Angela.

Niall breathed in deeply and continued. 'Well, as I say, I shan't bore you with all the details. But you can imagine how the death of my daughter hit me. I don't know how Orla has managed to live with me these last two years.' He looked at her and said, 'You're a saint, Orla. Honest to God you are.'

'Niall, just get on with the story, else we'll be here until midnight,' said his wife.

He smiled and continued. 'Douglas and I have had long chats in recent days, so he knows all this. And I agree,

299

Angela. This man here is one of the most forgiving men you will ever get to meet on this earth. God knows how you do it, son. But you are a walking miracle, you surely are.'

Douglas felt unworthy of such an accolade, but he also had to marvel at the radical shift that had taken place in his heart. He said nothing but smiled at Niall as he continued. 'So we came here to Ruby's memorial. The service was Orla's idea and I thought it a good one. Ruby was a fine lass and we wanted to honour her. The funeral had all been so rushed last Christmas and lots of people couldn't get to it. It felt right to have this memorial. So, we come over to Dingle to get set up for the service, and what do we hear from Father Pat, but that your man, Douglas is also in town. Well, honest to God, when I heard that, I only had one thing in mind. Kevin will understand. Some of us have learned only one way to deal with our hatred. It's not difficult for us to see ourselves as judge, jury and executioner, all in one.'

He was sitting forward on the sofa now and was holding his wounded hand with his good one. 'Orla tried to persuade me against it, but the rage had too tight a grip on me.'

'I thought I'd lose you, sure to God I did,' said Orla, shaking her bowed head. 'I pictured you being in prison for the rest of your days, and I'd have then lost both my daughter and husband.'

'I know, I know, lass,' said Niall. Then, resuming his story he said, 'I wasn't sure quite when I'd do it, but before the day was out I was determined to see a bullet lodged in the head of the Englishman who had come to represent everything I hated. Only things didn't go quite to plan, did they?'

'Oh, no,' said Kevin, smiling.

Niall returned the smile, but it quickly faded. 'When I saw Douglas escaping the church, I knew I had to go after him quickly. And that's where we come to the car chase. He drove fast through the town, and it was clear that he knew I was on to him. I could see there were others in the car with him, but by this stage, I didn't care if they were killed too. I assumed they were also English Proddies. As we drove wildly up those lanes, I decided I would either take my chance of taking a shot at him, or I would ram him off the road when we got to the hill. But then this oversized SUV overtakes and gets in the way. I am so mad at this stage, I decide to try and shoot his tyres, only I never get a chance to work that plan. Suddenly there are cars spinning in front of me, and the next thing I know is that I am in something like a tumble dryer with metal and glass flying all over the shop. Then an almighty crack to my head and the next thing I know is that I am standing in that eerie grey place.'

Niall reached out for his tea but discovered the mug was already finished. Pat was too captured by the story to think to offer him a refill, so Niall continued without refreshment. 'Well, like Kath here, my first thought was that I was in purgatory. I mean, why not? I was not proud of the way I'd lived, and I remember thinking, "Niall, son. You are now going to get what you deserve." I fell to my knees. And do you know, for the first time in my life I felt real fear. In all my days - shall we say - of living my violent life, I had been in many perilous situations, but I never felt the fear. Well, I did now, I can tell you. You see, ever since the brothers taught us about it in school, I carried in my soul a dread of purgatory and eternal damnation. I suppose I always knew that's where I'd be heading. I knew God wouldn't take to the likes of me.'

He paused for a few moments. Kevin, sitting opposite him, said. 'I remember I felt just that way at one time in my life. Sure to God, it's not a good feeling.'

'Aye,' said Niall, looking at Kevin. 'Well, anyway, there I was on my knees. Apart from Douglas, I had no idea who any of you were. Just assumed you were other candidates for hell, I guess. Once that guy dressed as a Roman soldier led us towards them crosses, I knew my fate was certainly sealed. I mean, to be taken to the Holy Cross had to be bad news for the likes of me. This was surely the place where all my sins would be exposed. I just assumed that it would all begin with me being hung up on that wood. "This is how your purgatory begins, Flynn," I said to myself. And do you know, I felt I deserved it, honest to God I did. I just felt so bad about myself and my life. I felt sick at heart.'

Niall was sitting even further towards the edge of the sofa. Orla reached out her hand and for a few moments gently rubbed his back. Niall looked up at the group, and all eyes were fixed on the anguished face. 'Well, your man, the Roman soldier. He leads me right up to the middle cross and I fall, kneeling in the soil. There's blood coming down the wood. I've seen blood many times, I'm sorry to say.' He sighed a long sigh. 'I've seen it on my friends. And, I regret to say, I've seen it on my victims, of which, I'm awful sorry to say, there have been several. Well, when I see this blood dripping to the ground, I felt the grief of every friend I've lost. And... I also felt the guilt of every drop of blood I've shed. Both grief and guilt pressed so heavy on me, they did. So heavy on me. I thought they'd crush me.'

Niall was looking at the floor and slowly shaking his head. He sighed a long sigh, then continued, 'The soldier - Antonio, I believe his name was - well, he kneels in the soil beside me. He takes off his helmet, and his head is damp with sweat, even though it's cold in that dark place. He looks mighty sad, kneeling there next to me. Then he puts a hand on my shoulder and says something that surely took me aback. He says, "I have done this."' Niall raised his eyebrows and looked around the room and repeated, 'Truly, he says: "I have done this."

'Well, I stop my sobbing, and look at the man straight in the eye and say, "You mean, you put this lad up there?" and he says without any hesitation, "I did". Well, I nearly get up and thump the living daylights out of him there and then. Because one thing was perfectly clear to me, and that was that this lad, hanging by nails to the wood above me, had done no wrong whatsoever. But then the soldier says, "I carried out the orders of my government. They all wanted Him dead - the government and the religion." He tells me how this Jesus of Nazareth had come to free the people from all the powers that oppressed them, and, do you know, for a few moments I felt my heart lifted.' Niall touched his heart at this point and looked up.

A log in the grate flared up and Niall studied it for a few moments, then continued. 'As Tony is telling me about this lad on the cross, I realise that He was a man after my own heart. He hated the suffering of the people caused by states and religions and all the rest of it. And for a time, kneeling in that dust and blood, Tony and I talk together about this. And then Tony says, "Do you know, He could have destroyed all us Roman soldiers and all the religious leaders if He had wanted to. But instead, He chose this." And as he says that, he points up at the cross.' Niall pointed up and lifted his eyes.

'And I lift my eyes to the body hanging there above me. It was scarcely moving now, but the head turned slowly and looked down on me.' At this Niall lowered his eyes and his shoulders heaved for a time.

'We are in no hurry, son,' said Pat.

'I'm sorry… He says some words,' whispered Niall. He then looked up and said, 'This man, pinned to that dreadful cross, in terrible agony, hardly able to open his bruised and swollen eyes, and with his blood streaming down to the earth beneath Him, opens his mouth and says, "Father, forgive them." Just that - three simple words: Father; forgive; them. He was forgiving the very people who had hammered Him to that wood. He was forgiving all those who conspired to put Him there. But the bit that…' Niall had to pause again, needing to control the powerful emotion. Orla said something to him that no one else heard. Niall bit on to his bottom lip for a few moments, and then looked up and said, 'He then looks me in the eye, and… He forgives me. I'd not said a word to the man, but I could tell that He knew all about my life. Don't ask me how I knew, but it was clear from the look in His eye, that He knew everything. Every terrible and wicked thing I've done, and every murderous and hateful thought I've held locked in my cold heart. All my dreadful deeds and acts of cruel violence. He knew it all. And yet, and yet, and yet… He forgives me. And that's when I realise that I am not going to get the purgatory I deserve. It was like… well, like He was taking it for me.'

Niall was quiet for a few moments, lost in thoughts. Then he said, 'So I am kneeling there on that cold earth, trembling like a reed in the breeze. And I get this strange sensation on the inside of me. It's so hard to explain to you, but I feel something like an ancient and solid wall of ice shattering deep inside me.' He looked out across the room and a brighter mood lifted his countenance. 'I knew that in those few words that He uttered, a power had been released, greater than all the bombs, bullets and weaponry of this world. This was a power to change the heart. So I am kneeling there in the dust, with the shadows of death covering us all, and yet in my heart, I feel this burning life that is stronger than any life I had ever known.

'I look at Tony, who's still kneeling there at the side of me, and he's got his eyebrows raised and he's nodding at me. He says no words, but I know what he's asking. I know he's asking, "So, son. How about it? Can you now forgive those who've hurt you and yours?" And I never thought I'd ever hear myself say this, but straightaway I say, "Yes. Yes, I can forgive them." You see, something so massive had shattered within me. That ice wall - destroyed!' Niall shook his head in wonder. 'And as God is my witness, there's me, the most unforgiving of men, kneeling there in that dirt, dust and blood, reaching out in my soul to all who had done harm to me, my family and my countrymen, and I am forgiving each and every one of them. Somehow that demented, obsessive craving for vengeance had been ripped out of my heart. Instead, the sweet warm waters of forgiveness were running free and wild. Just flushing out the bitterness, it was. It was something I never, never imagined would happen. I felt thick poison had drained from my soul in those moments, sure to God I did. It poured out of my heart, like the red blood on the wood falling to the earth below.'

He leaned back in his chair and breathed in through his nose a long breath. 'When I was ready, Tony helps me to my feet and leads me away. I thought that was the end of it, but it wasn't.' Niall paused for several moments. He then turned to Douglas, who was sitting on the chair next to the sofa. He reached out his wounded right hand to Douglas who took it gently in his left. 'Douglas, I've not told you this yet. But, son... I was then allowed to see her.'

Douglas looked on the face of the man who, until recent weeks, had seemed to him to be the epitome of hatred. And yet now it was a face that despite being weathered by many years of hatred, now looked full of gentleness. But it was a face that was also reporting something to do with his Saoirse, and Douglas felt the familiar disturbance of grief.

'I did not see her clearly, Douglas,' said Niall, drawing his bandaged hand back to the sofa. 'But I saw my daughter as through a swirling mist. I reached out my arms to her, and do you know what she did, Douglas? She stood there and made the sign of the cross over me, like the priest when he gives the blessing after mass. She not only forgave me, Douglas, but she blessed me. And once again, I fell to my knees. But not in shame this time, but in such gratitude.' He looked at Douglas. 'I don't know what you'll make of this, son. God knows the girl should not forgive me for what I put her through. But in that sacred moment, I can honestly say she did.' He looked around the room to all the group and said. 'I walked into that place as a man condemned, deserving of every punishment God could hurl at me. But I walked out as a man free of every wretched chain that has bound me in my sorry life. I'll never be the same. And that's the truth of it. That's my story, folks. Thanks for listening to me.'

Orla wrapped her arm around her husband. 'That's a mighty wonderful story, Niall,' said Kath, who was mopping her eyes with a handkerchief that she had pulled from her cardigan. 'Honest to God, it's a precious story. Thank you.' She heaved herself awkwardly out of her chair and looking at Pat said, 'If you'll excuse me, Pat, I'll need to deal with all that tea you've been giving us,' and she made her way to the door. Niall looked towards Douglas and said quietly, 'Douglas, I hadn't the guts to tell you that final piece earlier. I hope, son...'

Douglas did feel a conflict of feelings within him, but the sight of Niall looking so vulnerable reminded Douglas of the many conversations he had had with Niall in hospital, where he had become convinced of the radical change of heart in this once violent man. He looked at Niall and said reassuringly, 'Niall, I'm OK. If I'd heard all that before the accident, I'm not sure what I'd think. But now… It's a tender and beautiful story. And I know, without question, that she has forgiven you. And if she has, then of course I have.'

'Aye, son. I do know that,' said Niall and he pursed his lips and nodded.

'It's a remarkable story, Niall,' said Kevin. 'I've also known too much of that world you were in once.' He looked across to Pat who was talking to Angela and said, 'Excuse me, Father Pat. Could I have my turn to tell my tale when my mother's back with us?

'Surely, Kevin,' said Pat. Kevin leaned forward in his chair and clasped his hands and prepared to tell the group his story of a healing of his soul that he never imagined would happen this side of Paradise.

CHAPTER 27

Kevin's story

Kevin was sitting near the door, and when Kath came back into the room, she placed her large hand on his shoulder and said, 'You're a good son, Kevin. You know that, don't you.' He nodded and placed his hand over hers before she returned to her seat.

'Well,' started Kevin looking towards the sofa, 'As with Niall here, I too nursed a bitter hatred in my heart. Now, one or two of you know this, but as a younger man I served in the IRA.' He fidgeted for a moment in his seat and looked at the floor in front of him. 'And, the truth is…' He paused and played with his hands for a moment as if he were washing them. 'The truth is that I took some lives during my time in the Army. Mostly with the rifle. One with a bomb. That's why I was inside for a few years.' He sighed and paused for a while.

Pat, who was sitting next to him, leaned over and grasped his shoulder for a few moments, and said, 'Keep going, son. We're with you.'

'Aye,' said Kevin, looking up at the priest. 'I'm not proud of it, but it happened and I'm not going to deny it. I need to tell you this because it becomes relevant to my story. But first, going back to that Thursday. I was in the church with the rest of you. Dorchadas, Mam, me and Douglas were sat in the middle of the church. And then I saw Niall get up and I recognised the shape of the lump in his jacket pocket.'

'Aye, that was clumsy of me,' said Niall.

'They'd have had words with you about that, Niall,' said Kevin. 'So, I knew then that Douglas had a sure reason to be disturbed. And I knew we needed to get him out of there. So we made a quick escape, with no thanks to my mother…'

'I'll thank you for omitting that part of the story, if you please, Kevin,' called Kath.

'I'm not here to shame you, mother,' said Kevin smiling at Kath. 'Anyhow, we get into that terrifying car drive. No disrespect, Douglas, but I don't think I'd get you to be the driver if ever we have to make another fast getaway.'

Douglas chortled, and Kevin continued. 'I don't remember much about the tumble we took down the hill, but I do certainly remember suddenly finding myself in a place that definitely was not an Irish hillside. Well, when Dorchadas got us to turn round and I could see them crosses, I knew exactly where we were. I know, Douglas, we were told about the deep memory thing, but it was real enough, was it not?'

Douglas nodded. Kevin shuffled, and the ancient kitchen chair on which he was sitting, creaked loudly. 'I just fell to my knees, because what else could you do when you see what we saw? I noticed we were joined by an English couple. I had no idea at the time who Angela and Gerald were, but I could see your man Gerald was full of rage.' Angela looked into her lap for a few moments.

'Now, the thing I need to tell you all about is this. Douglas knows this, so forgive me repeating myself, Doug. But when I first met Dorch, some years ago now, he took me to meet someone. You know, one of his style of meetings. So, I got to meet one of the men who hung on the cross next to Christ.'

'You mean, you'd been to Golgotha before?' asked Orla.

'No, Orla. That wasn't where I met him. I believe the place I met him was in Paradise.'

'You've been to Paradise?' gasped Orla. 'My, how beautiful.'

'Aye. That it certainly was, even though I wasn't allowed to see it in its full beauty,' said Kevin. 'Well, in that meeting, the man from the cross helped me more than I can say. And in that Paradise place, he looked mighty wonderful. But back to our meeting at Golgotha. Well, the place we landed in certainly was no Paradise. And when I saw them crosses, I knew my friend would be on one of them. So, naturally, the first thing I did, was to go up to his cross. I recognised him straight away, even though the poor lad was so disfigured. Most other people were making a fuss about the cross of Christ, but I wanted to see a man who felt like a dearest friend to me. And I just stood there looking up at the kid, and, honest to God, he looked close to death, he did. His wretched body was…. Well, you know. His battered eyes were closed, and I began to wonder if he was already dead. I went up close to his cross and touched his feet. In fact, I wiped his feet, trying to clean them. I couldn't think what else to do. I just wanted to love the fella.'

Kevin uncrossed his legs and folded his hands around his knees for a time. 'I then looked up and he had opened his eyes. He was only just alive. I was about to speak to him when there was a sharp prod to my backside. I looked round, and there was a Roman soldier with his spear pointing at me. It wasn't your man, Tony. It was a younger fella. Well, he was full of cussing and swearing, and he spoke to me about my friend on the cross there. And he ranted about how the guy had killed innocent men and

310

women and how he deserved to die. He delivered a mouthful of abuse about the lad. I was sure glad when he left us.'

Kevin unclasped his hands and leaned back on his creaking seat. 'I looked up at my friend again, and he was looking down at me. And he just had enough strength to speak, and he said, "What the soldier said - it's all true." And the lad looked so sore and tired, he did. But then he added a few more words. He looked across to the body next to him - the body of Christ. And he said, "But Him. All is well. All is Peace." And with that, the man closed his eyes. I don't think he had long to go in this world.'

Kevin paused for a few moments. 'How was it, seeing your friend like that?' asked Angela, leaning forward in her chair to see past the figure of Pat.

'Well, I didn't feel sad, because I knew the man would soon be on his way to Paradise. But do you know what I felt more than anything?'

'What?' said Angela, captivated by this story.

'Envy, Angela. I was envious of him,' said Kevin, looking at her, and then looking back at the floor. 'You see, I knew God had forgiven me, but I could not forgive myself for some of the things I'd done. I'd taken life, I'm ashamed to say. And there was one life I'd taken - that of a young woman. I didn't target her, but she was killed in an explosion that I caused. I saw pictures of her in the press, and it was clear that she was such a sweet young lass with all her life ahead of her. It was the first time that I felt a great burden of guilt. I have been haunted by it ever since it happened. And, well, I just couldn't forgive myself for that, and I was certain neither she nor her family could ever forgive me. I mean, why in heaven's name should they?'

The room was quiet as the group listened to this sombre report. 'There was something about that fella on the cross,'

311

said Kevin, looking up. 'I could tell he was completely at peace as he left this world. Don't ask me how, but I knew that his soul was totally at peace. That's why I was envious of him.

'Well, then two more things happened.' He inhaled deeply and said, 'First, I looked over to the cross of Christ. I mean, you have to pinch yourself, don't you? But deep memory or no, I was there and He was there, hanging from them brutal nails and looking down on me. Can't have been easy looking down on the likes of me, when He was in that state. Anyhow, there was... I don't know what words you give it, but the words that came to me were "almighty kindness." Aye. Almighty Kindness. A kindness that overcomes all the cruelty of this world.' He looked around the room with his glistening eyes. 'I'm just a simple man, sure to God I am, so I don't know how you speak of these things. But something shifted in me in those moments.'

Kevin paused and seemed lost in his thoughts for a few moments. Niall then said, 'You said two things happened, Kevin. What was the second thing?'

'Oh, aye,' said Kevin, roused from his thoughts. 'Well, I was just staring at the man, and He was staring at me. And then He looked beyond me. He was beckoning me to look over my shoulder, which I did.'

Kevin paused and looked down and his shoulders started to shake. By now, the group was used to the depth of emotion these memories evoked, and all waited with patience. Pat leaned over and gripped Kevin's shoulder with his strong hand. Kevin breathed in deeply. 'Thanks, Pat,' he said, putting his hand over the priest's. He then wiped his eyes with the back of his hand and said, 'I turned around, you see, and... and standing there behind me was a young woman. I knew exactly who she was. It was terrible.

312

I saw her so clearly - her fair hair, her bright blue eyes, the honey complexion of her cheeks. She was a beautiful girl. I fell to the ground - I knew this was the dear life I had snatched from this world. I can't describe to you how terrible I felt in those moments. Honest to God, I wanted to die there and then.'

He felt in his pocket and pulled out a handkerchief and blew his nose. Kath was also blowing her nose. 'I'm sorry. I didn't mean to get this emotional on you all,' he said shaking his head.

'You're all right, Kev,' said Pat.

'Well, I'll just keep it brief. I was there kneeling in that dirt and blood, and the girl came over to me. I can tell you, I only wanted one thing. I wanted her to pull out a gun and shoot me then and there. That would be justice. But I didn't get my wish.' He shook his head from side to side and looked down at his hands that were clenched in his lap. 'She lent down and said words that were *so* precious. They... they were just *so* precious. That's all I can say.' He was quiet for quite a while.

'You need to mention the other thing that happened after that, son,' said Kath, leaning forward in her chair. 'Not everyone has heard that.'

'Aye, Mam, I'll tell them,' said Kevin. He was frowning and smiling. 'The young woman then drew me back up to my feet and led me over to the cross of Christ. She reached out and she put her hand on the trickle of blood that was running down the wood. Now, I know this sounds pretty gruesome, but you have to remember that for a terrible time in my life, I lived in the world of blood, like your man Niall here was saying. I saw a great deal of it. This was not new for me. Well, she covered her sweet hands with the stuff, and it looked horribly familiar. But then she came over to me and placed her hands on my

313

head. As I say, it may sound gruesome to you, but when that blood touched my head...' He nodded his head and looked out through the window. 'I knew then, I had been given the power to forgive myself. The girl took her hands away from my head, and for the first time, I looked at her straight in the eye. Her face was full of wonder and delight. She was so... So very alive. And she said, "There is life; there is death. There is light; there is dark. There is love; there is hate. Which do you choose?" And I looked at her, and I said without a moment of doubt, "I choose life. I choose light. I choose love." And that's when I woke up in the hospital bed. The nurse told me I was saying "I choose life" out loud!' He smiled at the memory.

For a time, the room was still with a respectful silence. Then Niall said, 'That's some story, Kev.'

'It surely is,' said Pat.

'Well done, son,' said Kath, and blew her nose loudly on her handkerchief.

'It's a wonderful story,' said Douglas.

'Thanks a million, Kevin,' said Pat. 'Now look, we all need a breather I think, and it's getting dark, so let's put some lights on so we can actually see each other. Angela, could you stoke up that fire to keep us warm. Now, it won't surprise you all that Mrs. McGarrigle has prepared some sandwiches for us, and I got in a few cans of the Murphy's just to help us along, and a bottle of your favourite Elderflower, Angela. So let me go fetch it all, and then it will be time for Douglas to tell us his tale.'

Although Douglas was feeling tired and the injury to his lungs was aching, yet he was glad of the chance to relate his story.

CHAPTER 28

Douglas' story

Though Mrs. McGarrigle had provided a generous lunch and tea, several in the group did justice to the ample supply of sandwiches that she had also prepared. Cans of Murphy's Irish Stout were snapped open and the room became full of animated conversation. Though Pat tried to press the final sandwiches on his guests, he did not succeed and so removed the plate of remains to the kitchen, returning with a new supply of Murphy's, elderflower and water. He drew the curtains, stoked the fire, and then called for quiet. Looking across the room at Douglas, he said, 'So Douglas. It's your turn. Let's be hearing your story now if you will.'

'Remember the lad's a preacher, so don't give him too much rope, Father,' said Kath, and laughed herself into a wheezing cough. When she recovered, she looked across the room to Douglas and said, 'Seriously, Doug, you take as long as you need, son. Don't listen to an eejit like me.' She lifted her can of Murphy's and said, 'And it looks like the Presbytery is well supplied, so we'll be just fine.'

'Sláinte,' said Douglas, smiling and lifting his can. He placed it on the floor beside him, leaned back in his chair, and commenced his story. 'Do you know, I don't remember that Thursday very clearly. Though I do remember your little moment in the church, Kath.'

'Oh, God, don't you start, Douglas,' said Kath.

Douglas started to laugh, then checked himself. Laughter was still sore for him, though his lung was nothing like as painful as it had been during the early days

315

in hospital. He breathed in as far as he could and continued. 'I don't remember much about the car chase. But I do remember being seized by a terrible fear. It was like I was being pressed down by a hideous darkness. I have no memory of the accident, but the time at Golgotha is still crystal clear in my mind. I knew straight away that we were 'travelling' as Dorchadas calls it. I remember looking around at the group of us who found ourselves in that place. I felt very reassured by the presence of Dorch, Kath and Kevin. But then I saw Niall and the fear returned. I remember gripping Dorch's arm tight. He reassured me that no harm could come to me in that place. But I still felt fear. And I felt the presence of evil. There's no other word for it.'

'Aye, I picked up a sense of that as well,' said Kevin, who was making a valiant attempt at closing the ill-fitting door to keep out the draught.

'At first, I wondered if Dorchadas and I had returned to Gethsemane,' continued Douglas. 'I've told some of you about that experience. But Dorch put me right as he turned us round to face those crosses. Once I saw those, there was no doubting where we were. I remember Dorchadas urging us to walk towards them and none of us wanted to. I remember the sound of wailing from that group of people nearby. It was terrible, wasn't it?

'Sure to God, it was,' said Niall.

Douglas looked across to Angela. 'And I remember so clearly hearing Gerald's voice. I couldn't believe it. I saw you with him, Angela. I'd only met you once or twice before that.'

Angela nodded and said, 'Oh, yes, I kept myself well clear of church and Vicars in those days.'

Douglas gave her a downturned smile and continued, 'Well, I assumed it was you. I remember you looking so

316

lost and shocked. But Gerald... He... well.' Douglas looked at Angela and shrugged his shoulders.

'Yes,' said Angela with a long sigh.

'Well, after a sort of conversation with Gerald, I looked back at those terrible crosses. Then, to my surprise, I heard another voice I recognised. It belonged to Antonio, the Roman Centurion. Or "Tony" as Dorch called him.'

'It looked like you had met him before, Doug,' said Kevin.

'Yes. Well, in a sense I had. It was at another of Dorch's meetings. He...' Douglas frowned and looked around the room. 'I know this is really weird for some of you, but Dorch arranged for this guy to turn up and meet us at a café in town. He wasn't in his Roman uniform but in modern-day Italian army uniform. So, yea - I had met him. And I liked him. So it was quite a comfort to find him there at Golgotha, actually.'

'He seemed like a good man, that he did,' said Kevin.

Douglas nodded. 'As you know, he led us nearer to those crosses. Everything in me wanted to resist, but Dorch was being pretty persuasive with that strong arm of his. If you remember Antonio said something like "This is the place of the greatest sadness and the greatest power."'

'Aye, that's a bit I do remember, Doug,' said Kath leaning forward in her chair. 'A curious paradox and enigma, I thought to myself.'

A murmur of admiration went around the room. 'Well, I did go to school, you know,' she retorted. 'Even if it was a few years back.' She smiled and said, 'Sorry, Doug, son. Do go on.'

Douglas breathed in and momentarily winced before he continued. 'And then there was such a sad moment for me. Tony said to Dorch that Dorch had done his work, bringing us to this place, and now it was time for him to leave. I grabbed hold of him and pleaded with Tony to let him stay.'

'I think several of us felt that way, son,' said Kath. 'We've grown to love the fella, we surely have. And sure to God we needed him with us in that place.'

'I agree, Kath. I certainly needed him,' said Douglas, and his eyes fell to the ground for a few moments. 'But I also knew he had to leave us.'

'And I did hear him say that it was not farewell,' reassured Kevin.

'Yes, and I believe him,' said Douglas lifting his head back up.

'We've got used to him coming and going,' said Kath, reaching for her vape and igniting it, filling her end of the room with wisps of blue smoke.

Douglas smiled briefly at Kath and continued, 'Well, I was in Tony's hands after that, and he led me to the middle cross. It seems we all had our special moments in that place, but I must admit at that point I lost touch with you all. It seemed to be just me and Tony there. I told him that I couldn't bear to look at the body impaled on that wood. I could see the blood in front of me right enough. It's not that I'm squeamish, it's just...' He shook his head for a while and then looked at Pat. 'You know Pat, we religious professionals - we think we know so much.' Pat frowned a frown of concern and understanding. 'But being there, Pat...'

'It must have been something, son,' said Pat.

Douglas noticed the reverence in his voice. 'It was, Pat. I mean, being there... But to be honest, I really did not know what to do or say. Of course, I fell to my knees. Tony also did, and he turned to me and said something like, "Douglas, this is the best that Roman power can throw at him. But look at him, Douglas. Look at him - he has surrendered everything. But he has not surrendered to the Emperor. He has not surrendered to Herod. He has not even surrendered to death. He has surrendered to love, Douglas." I remember him clasping my arm, and saying, "Look, Douglas. Look!" And he was pointing up.'

Douglas shifted in his seat for a few moments, then continued, 'So I did start to look up. It was so dark by then, and I remember the sound of thunder from the heavy black clouds that glowered over us. I was so frightened - I mean which of us wants to look into the face of someone who is dying an agonising death? And I felt somehow responsible as well. And, don't forget, I had given up on faith last year, so was hardly in a fit state to meet with God. I felt such a weight of guilt and fear, it is a wonder my eyes ever made their way up that poor broken body to the face that hung just below that awful crossbeam.'

Douglas took time to compose himself. All in the room had no difficulty understanding the waves of emotion this scene evoked. 'There are no words... How do I possibly describe what I saw? All words feel useless. But, most of you were there, so you know...'

'Aye, we do indeed,' said Kevin.

Douglas acknowledged Kevin and continued, 'I did eventually look at the face which was looking down directly at me. Those dark, wounded eyes, peering into mine.' In this company of friends, Douglas felt no need to hide the tears that were dampening his cheeks. He looked across to Kath and said, 'My experience was like yours, Kath. I was staring at Love - absolute, glorious, terrible love. There is no other word for it. You're right, Kath. The word is used millions of times, but I felt I was looking at the source of all the rivers of love that flow through this world. This was like the beginning of it. This is where all the love leads back to eventually. You'd think such love would be a dazzling light, so bright that you'd have to look away. But that wasn't my experience. It was not a light to shock or dazzle. Nor one to highlight all the wrongs in your life. No, it was a light that healed your wrongs, and beckoned you into all that is good and fine in this world.'

Douglas paused for a few moments. He was looking at an old landscape picture hanging above the fireplace, but it was not the landscape he was studying, but a scene from a sacred memory that he knew would never be dislodged from his soul. 'And there was another quality,' he said, still looking towards the picture. 'You see, what I noticed about this love was the extraordinary power in it. Not military. Not religious. Not political. Not economic. I could see what Tony was getting at. The face that I was studying so intently - and was so intently studying me - was the face not of a victim. Quite the opposite. It was the face of a victor. But a victor who was suffering so deeply. I can't honestly explain it,' he said, his eyes falling from the picture to the faces in the room. 'I shall never understand it, but I know I saw it.'

The room was quiet for a time. All who had been there with Douglas understood very clearly.

'But there was another thing,' said Douglas, breaking the silence that had fallen on the room. 'I mentioned that I felt a dreadful sense of the presence of evil in that place. The air felt thick with it.' Several in the room nodded.

'Were you all there when He gave that great cry?' Douglas asked.

'No-one could miss that cry,' said Niall.

'Well, I was still near the cross, and I was astonished that a man so near death could make such a sound. It nearly deafened me. But I noticed that during that cry, the

320

evil left. I was in no doubt. Whatever that evil was, it had dispersed. It had fought Him with everything it had, and it had lost. Did anyone else feel that?'

'Oh, aye, I surely did,' said Kath. 'And I felt that someone, finally, at last, had dealt with all the crap that has troubled and bound the poor, weary souls of this world.'

'And did you notice that the sky started to clear at that point?' said Niall.

All in the room nodded again. And again, there was silence for a time. Not an awkward silence, but a hallowed silence.

'Thank you, Douglas,' said Pat, gently leaning towards Douglas.

'Oh, Pat, if you don't mind there was just one last thing.'

'Of course, son,' said Pat and settled back in his chair.

'Most of you here know just how much I struggled with the loss of my wife,' said Douglas. 'I never knew the pains of grief could be so sharp. Nor that they could go on so long.' Douglas noticed Orla squeeze Niall's hand. He inhaled carefully to avoid the pain in his lung. 'Well, after His great cry from the cross, I could tell He had died. There was no question. The last time I had seen life leave a body, was when I was with my Saoirse in hospital. Seeing the lifeless body hanging there brought back sharp, sharp memories of that day in the hospital. I felt that awful, aching, sobbing grief rising up in my soul once again. I felt that I too was going to let out a great cry. But before it got near the surface, I was aware of someone standing behind me, and they rested their hand on my shoulder.' Douglas tapped his right shoulder. 'I looked at it and I knew, without any doubt that it was hers.'

'Oh, Douglas, you've not told us this,' said Orla, leaning towards him so she could catch every precious word of this story.

'No, Orla. I'm sorry, I wasn't ready until now.'

'Of course, son,' said Niall.

'Naturally,' continued Douglas, 'when I saw it was Saoirse's hand on my shoulder I wanted to turn around and see her, but I distinctly heard her voice saying, "Douglas, stay facing this cross, and stand up. Don't turn around." It took all my strength not to turn and see her, but I did as she said and I struggled to my feet. I put my hand over hers as I did so, and it felt so strong and warm. I felt such strength from her presence just behind me. Then she said, 'Look upon the body of your Friend. It is he who now bears your griefs and carries your sorrows."' Douglas looked at Orla and Niall. 'I never did turn and see her,' he said. 'I didn't need to. In those moments I felt something like a great, heavy overcoat slip from my shoulders and fall away. I had been carrying the weight of it for over two years. Don't ask me how this works, but I knew that I was free and at last I could stand up straight. Even though the body in front of me was lifeless, yet I knew that in His dying, He had gathered my grief into Himself, and I was free.'

Douglas looked up at the faces that were all fixed on him. 'It doesn't mean I'm not going to miss her - of course, I will for the rest of my life. But I am free of that awful, heavy, suffocating grief. And for that, I am so thankful.' He looked at Niall and Orla, a little uncertain how this would sit with them.

'We feel much the same, son,' said Niall, nodding his head.

Orla added, 'And Douglas, if I may. What did she do or say after that?'

Douglas looked down at the floor for a while, then lifted his head and said, 'She said something to me, Orla.' He smiled the warmest smile. 'She said something to me.'

'Of course, Douglas,' said Orla, and clasped her hands in front of her.

Douglas was frowning as he peered at the coffee table that was set in the middle of the room. 'And there was another miracle,' he said. 'I told you how I felt this great fear building up in me that reached a peak that Thursday. In particular, I was afraid of Niall for obvious reasons. But I was also afraid of Gerald.' He looked over to Angela. 'I knew, Angela. I knew he was the one behind Saoirse's death. I guessed about his arms dealings.'

'How did you find out, Douglas?' said Angela, frowning with curiosity.

'A dream, Angela. A dream.' Angela continued to look puzzled. 'But it was not just Gerald I feared. I feared myself. I feared that if ever I was alone with him, and I had access to a weapon, then I would gladly murder him. So, you see, murder was in my heart too. Once I suspected Gerald was behind Saoirse's death, I wanted to see him hurt in every possible way. I wanted vengeance. I wanted justice.' Several in the group saw a hardness in Douglas' expression that they had not seen before. He was thumping his fist on his knee. 'I was determined that I was never, ever going to forgive him.'

Douglas unclenched his fist and looked up and the darkness fell from his countenance. 'But her words changed all of that. Her words and that cross…' He looked across the room and gazed for a few moments at the burning wood in the fire. He shook his head and then looked around the room. 'I can't tell you how such things change in a heart, but some huge weight of bitterness left my soul in those moments. And that's why in those days in hospital, we could have those chats, Angela.' He looked at her and smiled. Turning to Niall he said, 'And Niall - that's how we could have those conversations. And I could see in the way you were talking with Angela, you were also forgiving Gerald for being behind Saoirse's death.'

'Aye,' said Niall quietly. 'Once I had heard that Gerald was behind the killing, I felt the fury rising up in me. It was in the early days in hospital. I was pleased Gerald was dead, but only sorry I couldn't have killed him myself. Forgive me, Angela, but I know you understand.'

Angela nodded and Niall continued, 'But every time the fury rose up in me, I felt myself transported back to that place. It was like each time I went back there, I took a piece of my hatred and anger and dumped it in that blood-stained earth - a great pile of it.' He shook his head and then looked up at Douglas. 'And eventually, it was all gone. He had taken it all. I don't know how, but He had taken every poisonous drop of it, and I was free.'

'Same for me,' said Douglas. 'And you both said I had been very forgiving,' he continued looking at Angela and Niall, 'But in the end, it was given to me.'

'Aye, son. But you still chose to receive it,' said Orla looking at Douglas.

'And you, Orla,' said Angela. 'You are the real saint here. You forgave Gerald, and yet you didn't get the help that we got. You had no vision.'

Orla shook her head. 'No, I had no vision - if I'm honest, I am a bit envious of you all. But I saw what happened in my Niall. I knew the path of bitterness and hatred all too well. It was a path I had trodden with Niall for many years. But when I visited him in hospital and saw that he had truly chosen a different path - well, it gave me a liking for the pathway of forgiveness, it surely did.' She

324

turned to Niall. 'You helped me, sweetheart. My change of heart - it's your doing.'

Niall smiled and squeezed her hand.

Douglas looked over to her and said, 'Orla - I said this to you when you visited me in hospital, I know. But I want to say it here as well. Saoirse may have departed this life, but as far as I'm concerned you are still my mother-in-law. And you, Niall - my father-in-law. And I'm proud to be part of your family.'

Niall nodded his head as Orla said, 'Aye son. And we are proud to have you as part of our family. That we surely are.'

'I never thought I'd hear myself saying this,' said Niall, chuckling, 'But I'm delighted to have an English Proddy in my family.'

Douglas acknowledged his parents-in-law, and then looked over to Pat and said, 'Well, that's me and my story. Thank you all for listening.'

'It's a grand story, it surely is, Doug,' said Pat rising to his feet. 'There is just one more thing we need to do before the evening is out,' and he left the room.

Everyone in that room had shared their story of that time after the fearful accident, where somehow or other they arrived in a place of deep memory - a place that turned out to be a place of deep healing for all of them. As Pat returned to the room with a bottle of whiskey and tumblers, he said 'I hope you don't mind if I share with you a few thoughts before you go. And Angela, I'll fetch you your elderflower juice.'

'Pat, I'm awash with elderflower juice,' said Angela. But a cup of coffee wouldn't go amiss.'

'Of course,' said Pat, and it was not long before he returned with a cafetiere of coffee and a mug and settled back into his seat. It was now his turn to share his reflections on all that he had heard regarding the extraordinary events recounted by his friends.

CHAPTER 29

'I hope you don't mind, it's Paddy's,' said Pat pouring a generous helping of the whiskey into each tumbler.

'It will serve us well, Pat, that it will,' said Kevin as he received his glass from Pat.

After serving all his guests including the coffee for Angela, Pat settled his tall frame into his chair. Douglas had grown to love the way this priest was quite comfortable with his dishevelled appearance. He had removed his clerical collar early on in the meeting. His Aran sweater had lost its shape, and the many stray strands of wool were testimony to its age. His grey trousers could have done with someone turning down the turn-ups, to cover the large expanse of white, hairless shin between the trouser leg and the loose elastic of a thin black sock. Although his countenance was that of a depressive, Douglas loved his endearing habit of scattering a shower of brief, beaming smiles into the room apropos of nothing in particular. As everyone settled down, he dealt a generous supply of the smiles to the group before embarking on his reflections.

'This is an afternoon I will never forget,' he said in his rich, baritone voice. 'I feel so unworthy to hear such sacred stories, and I truly thank you for entrusting me with them. I do want you to know that I will treasure and guard each of your stories for the rest of my days, I truly will.'

'Bless you, Pat,' said Kevin reaching out and grasping his shoulder.

'It's the priest who should be doing the blessing, son,' said Kath with a wheeze.

327

'Oh, dear God. You're right, mother. Apologies Pat,' said Kevin.

Pat threw one of his infectious smiles to Kevin and then said, 'I'm in as much need of blessing as the rest of you. And truly I have been blessed today. I've listened to each story. And Orla,' he said, glancing towards the sofa where she was sitting close to Niall. 'Neither you nor I were present in that Golgotha experience, but don't you feel our friends, through the telling of their stories, have taken us to that very place today?'

'Oh, aye, Father, that they have. They surely have,' said Orla.

'So,' said Pat, removing his glasses and starting to wipe them with the hem of his jumper, 'I just have a couple of reflections to offer you, if you don't mind me sharing them with you. I know it's getting late.'

'Fire away, Pat. The night is yet young,' said Kath raising her glass. 'And this Paddy's is none too bad. None too bad at all.'

'Well, there's a drop more in the bottle when you are ready,' said Pat. He carried on working on his glasses as he continued. 'I think of the lives you were all leading before you went to this sacred place. Take you, Kath, for example,' he said, returning his glasses which appeared not much cleaner. 'Look at you, lass. You've always been a wonderful soul, but not that long ago you were a troubled soul. And you certainly did not have much time for God, as far as I remember.'

'You're not wrong there, Pat,' said Kath taking another sip from her glass.

'And a work of grace got going in you in the autumn. And at Golgotha, you discovered His love. Well, you might say, you discovered Love full stop. And what a

328

healing has taken place in your soul. And look at you - a sworn atheist not so long ago, and now a believer!'

'Aye, but hardly a Saint Theresa just yet, Pat,' said Kath, downing her glass. 'So don't get too excited.' Pat responded by passing her the bottle for her to refill her glass.

'And Angela,' said Pat, turning to the English lady sitting next to him. 'I feel so sorry for your loss.' He reached out and held her hand for a few moments before releasing them. 'I never got to meet your husband. I'm so sorry. Honest to God, we all are. But you - I'm so impressed by you. I didn't know you before all of this, but from what you tell me, my, there has been a change in your heart, lass. That meeting with the mother of those two boys - what a thing! And, as you kissed those feet, you found out what true power is in this world. And then the cure to your mind and your body, that it no longer craves the alcohol. My, that is a power indeed. You are a walking miracle, Angela, you truly are!'

'Thanks, Pat,' said Angela, who clasped her hands, and nodded in gratitude.

'Then Niall, my friend,' he said looking over to the sofa. 'Well, well, son. I mean, I remember our meeting at the graveside of dear Ruby a year back.'

'Oh, Pat, don't shame me, please,' said Niall, shaking his head and looking at the floor.

'Oh, dear God, no. I wouldn't want to shame you at all,' said Pat. 'But I recall it simply to remark what a change has taken place in your soul.' Niall looked up at the priest. 'I mean you could have lived out the rest of your days in bitterness of soul, could you not?'

'Aye, indeed. That I could, Pat. That I could,' said Niall, nodding his head.

329

Pat removed his glasses again. Apparently, they needed another wipe, and this time he pulled his black shirt tail clear from his jumper and set to work on the lenses. 'I've known so many men like you, Niall. The hurt goes back so many generations, and soul after soul has been poisoned with bitterness. So much blood has been spilled in this land because of unforgiveness. But people can't forgive until something tugs at their soul and begs them to change. And that is what you were given, Niall.'

'Aye, that I was,' said Niall quietly.

'You were forgiven, and you forgave,' said Pat, now holding his glasses up to the light and checking for smears, of which there were many. 'And then, Niall - to be blessed by your own daughter. Oh my. Thank you for sharing that precious moment with us all.' Pat placed his glasses back in their rightful place and threw another smile into the room.

'And then, Kevin,' he continued, turning to his left so he could take a good look at Kevin. 'You know, so many travel through this weary world and never get to forgive themselves, sure they don't. And it's such a sorrow, it is. I've seen so many parishioners coming to the church with their hunched shoulders and guilty looks. Sunday by Sunday I proclaim God's forgiveness to them, yet they make their way to the altar rail still carrying their burdens. And I see the worry in their faces, their souls flinching, not for fear of God, but for fear of the words of condemnation from their own hearts. But Kevin, I know how much you hated what you did in your early years. You've lived with regret for a long time. But you look different now, son.' Pat reached out his long arm and grasped Kevin's forearm. 'You were in the Maze a few years. But you've been in a jail of your own making for much longer. The jail of not being able to forgive yourself. Well, the touch of Calvary

330

is evident in you now, son. You've finally forgiven yourself and you can walk free.'

'Aye, Father, that I can. That I can,' said Kevin, looking briefly at Pat and then turning his eyes back to the floor. Kath sniffed loudly and then reached over, and with the poker, prodded at a burning log in the grate.

'And last but not least,' said Pat turning his attention to Douglas. 'Our fella from England who came to us last autumn.' Pat smiled as he looked on Douglas and said, 'Perhaps we might say now, the fella who was *sent* to us from England.'

'Aye, I agree with that, Pat,' said Kath, still prodding at the fire.

'Here, here', said Kevin, raising his glass.

'I've not done much for you all,' protested Douglas, which in turn was met with protests from the group.

'The thing is Douglas, many of us felt your grief. You were ripped to shreds by the thing, sure you were. What is grief, if it is not love? You would not grieve if you did not love. And you were a man who loved greatly.'

'That is true, Father,' said Orla in a quiet and kindly voice.

'And because you loved greatly, you suffered greatly,' continued Pat. 'Last autumn we nearly lost you in the sea. And in the winter, we nearly lost you on the hills. Will you kindly take care of yourself now, son?'

All in the room laughed. 'But seriously, Douglas,' continued Pat, moving rapidly from smile to frown, 'you came as a sorrowing, grieving, lost soul, sure you did. But you came as an *honest* lost soul, and that's what we loved. You'd given up pretending, and you dropped that fine professional religious mask of yours, and almost from the off, you showed us something of your true self. But you were lost, son. There's no doubt about that.'

'I was, Pat. I was,' said Douglas, looking sad.

'But you had your moment with Dorchadas in that garden, and then another a few weeks back on the mount of Golgotha. And there all your fine theology fell away in the face of great Love. There you met the one who carries your grief and your sorrow. And there you were healed of your fears. And there you discovered a power that even conquered evil itself. It was quite a thing to behold, Douglas, was it not?'

'Yes, it certainly was,' said Douglas nodding.

'And that touch, Douglas. That touch on the shoulder and the word in your ear. Not the ending of your grief, Douglas, I know. But I think the end of the weight of it. You will miss her for the rest of your days, you know that. But the grief will no longer overpower you. The man on that cross is carrying the weight of it now.'

Douglas looked up at the good-hearted priest and said, 'Pat, I truly believe that now. Like Kevin, I have been released from an inner prison. I feel I can walk free now.'

'And Douglas, we mustn't forget. You stand among us as a man who has achieved something remarkable. You have chosen the path of forgiveness. We honour you for that son, we truly do.'

'Aye, we do,' said Niall.

'Yes, we certainly do,' said Angela.

Pat leaned back in his chair, and after one of his warm yet fleeting smiles, he said. 'I've listened to all these remarkable stories and it seems to me they all have one thing in common. Each one of you - I include you, Orla, in this incidentally, even though you weren't at Golgotha. Each one of you, through going through what you have gone through, have in a sense come home. You've come home to being the person God always intended you to be. And I like what I see!'

There were nods and words of agreement. Then Pat added, 'And one more thing, then I must let you all get to your beds. As you were saying earlier, Douglas, we religious professionals have preached God knows how many sermons over the years on the Cross of Christ. We have all had our views of what it's all about. Think of all the stuff on the theory of atonement, Douglas. Oh my, I've read some pretty heavy tomes on the subject, I can tell you. And to be honest, I was never much the wiser. But after my visits to you all in hospital, and after hearing your stories today, I have a whole new view of that precious life hanging from the cruel wooden beam at Golgotha. And do you know what, I found there was something so human about it.'

'Human, Pat?' asked Angela, looking puzzled.

'By that, Angela, I mean this. The man hanging from that wood seemed to understand our humanity so well. He knew your stories. He knew what drags us down in this world. And in this world, we look to all kinds of powers to try and lift ourselves up. But there He was, the Prince of Peace, as the dear Book calls him, just looking down at our struggles and doing something there that has transformed our lives. No, I'm not going to preach to you about it or try and explain it.' He looked around the room, his dark eyebrows twitching above the rim of his glasses. 'But now I've seen the power of it in normal human lives. That's what moves me, what stirs my heart.' He reached over for his glass and cupped it in his hands for a while, then said, 'It's not just for Good Friday, is it? It's not just for a quick mention at the mass on Sunday. This is for each and every day, isn't it?' There were nods around the room, some of them sleepy nods.

Pat was looking up somewhere above the curtain rail for a while, then said, 'I thought of a poem earlier. Douglas and Angela, you may not know one of our much-loved poets and heroes. His name is Joseph Plunkett.' There was a murmur of approval and appreciation from the Irish people in the room. 'You know him?' he asked, looking at both Angela and Douglas.

'No, sorry,' they both answered.

'Ah, well now, we have to go back about a hundred years in our history. Joseph was a bright lad, he surely was.'

'That he was,' said Niall nodding.

'From a wealthy family as it happens Angela,' said Pat, turning to the lady on his right. 'In his teens, he spent some time in North Africa and learned Arabic, and even wrote some poems in the language.'

'Now did you get that at your Rowbean school?' interrupted Kath, turning to Angela and winking.

'No, I didn't study Arabic,' replied Angela with a smile.

'And neither did I,' said Pat, realising he needed to give a summarised version of Plunkett's life if everyone was to get to bed on time. 'Well, the fact is, this young man was passionate for his country and he was one of those who were part of the growing Republican movement during the first of the World Wars. Did a bit of arms dealing himself, as it happens, Angela.'

Angela raised her eyebrows as Pat continued. 'Well, some say he was a mastermind behind the Easter Rising of 1916. Though he was not long out of hospital, he still managed to be one of those at the Post Office on

O'Connell Street in Dublin. Well, I'm sure you know the gist of the story that followed. Sad to say, Joseph was arrested and he was sentenced to death.'

'Aye, and a few hours before his death, he was married to his sweetheart,' added Kevin.

'A lass by the name of Grace Gifford,' said Kath. 'A fine woman, she was.'

'Well, I don't mention all of this just to stir up old wounds,' said Pat, worried at quite where such reminiscing may take some in the group. 'This is a very sad moment in our history, and a very bad moment in the story between our two nations.' He looked at Angela and Douglas. 'But the point I wish to make before I send all of you to sleep by my history lesson, is that despite all of this, Joseph had a sweet spirit and wrote some delightful poetry. So often, in the heart of human strife and troubles, you find a poet who shows us a way out.' Douglas, who had been feeling distinctly drowsy, listened with new alertness.

'And there's one poem, where he shows he had a deep appreciation of the cross of Christ and how the cross is so intimately tied up with our beautiful world. I am convinced that as that young man went to the site of his execution, he would have had a profound awareness of the Saviour and Friend who also died an unjust and cruel death at a similar age.'

'Do you remember some lines of the poem, Pat?' asked Orla. 'I'd love to hear them again.'

'Yes, I do, as it happens, Orla. I learned it by heart at school. I think I can remember it, and here it is.' Pat emptied his tumbler and removed his glasses again. Leaning back in his chair, with his shirt tails escaping his jumper, and trouser legs climbing even higher towards his knees, he shut tightly his eyes and recited the poem:

335

I see His blood upon the rose
And in the stars the glory of His eyes,
His body gleams amid eternal snows,
His tears fall from the skies.

I see His face in every flower;
The thunder and singing of the birds
Are but His voice - and carven by His power
Rocks are his written words.

All pathways by His feet are worn,
His strong heart stirs the ever-beating sea,
His crown of thorns is twined with every thorn,
His cross is every tree.

The whole group listened intently to Pat's lilting voice.
When he finished, no one spoke and all that could be heard
in that Presbytery lounge was the sound of a ticking clock
and the soft sounds of the glowing timber burning in the
grate.

When Douglas returned to his home that night, he
looked up the poem, and, reading it several times, he
inhaled it into his mind and down into his heart. It
occupied his last thoughts as he lay his head on the crisp,
clean pillowcase, and the words of that young poet
travelled with him into his sleep and shaped the contours
of his dreams in the darkness of that quiet Irish night.

CHAPTER 30

<u>Journal   14 February (Valentine's)</u>

It's been a long while since I have written in this. I didn't have this journal with me when I was in hospital, and since I have been back here at St.Raphael's I have felt very tired. But I'm recovering pretty well and each day my chest feels a bit easier. I see that the last time I wrote it was the day before the BIG DAY. I don't find it comfortable thinking back to that memorial mass for Saoirse's Aunt Ruby. I remember a sense of desperation and needing to get out of the church. I remember for the first time in my life feeling really scared that I was going to be killed. Then that car chase. Thought I was also going to be killed in a drive-by shooting. Strange sense of comfort to leave this world in the same way as she did. But then the crash. Don't remember too much about it, thank goodness. Then ending up at Golgotha. Yes, Golgotha - the sight of the crucifixion. Only a few months ago if I'd read my accounts in this journal about going to Gethsemane and Golgotha, I'd have thought I'd completely lost it. But as it happens, all of this stuff has helped me to completely find it.

It wasn't just me and Dorch this time. Several others were there - Dorch, Kev, Kath, Niall, Angela and Gerald. Yesterday we had a brilliant day at the Presbytery where Pat gathered all of us to talk together about what had happened. I'd heard bits of all these stories when I was in hospital, but it was special hearing it from each of us yesterday. Each person's experience was different - so moving. It's incredible to see what happened to Niall. That man literally wanted to kill me. So it wasn't paranoia - he really was out to get me! But before that meeting at the cross, all his hatred and bitterness flowed out of him. What a difference in the man. It's hard to believe.

Then, of course, there is Gerald. So my dream was right. Gerald really was a violent man - involved in the arms race. Got a note from the Intelligence officer when I was in hospital and they confirmed Gerald was the man who had ordered the shooting of Saoirse. Doubt if they'd have found him without the accident and everything. I didn't see Gerald at Ruby's service. Only saw him in the Golgotha vision and I couldn't work out why he was there at first. Sadly, he was his usual self. And I discovered that he and Angela had come over to Ireland to kill me. So, two people after my blood! Still can't quite get my head around that. But, sad to say, Gerald died in the accident. Didn't have his seat belt on. I don't know how these things work, but I wonder if he would have survived if he'd been more reasonable at Golgotha? Only God knows. But it was so sad - he had the chance to change, as Niall and Angela did. But he refused. Couldn't let go of his power. Poor Angela. Really felt for her. Never really knew her before this. She says she used to drink heavily, so the rumours about her were true. She hasn't touched a drop since the accident. But she had a massive change of heart. Both she and Niall, two of my adversaries, were completely transformed in that place. She's actually a very sweet lady. She's got a wonderful plan to try and remedy all the harm Gerald did by his arms dealing. I'm sure God must be so pleased by that.

So (and I don't know how this works) I was there, at the foot of the Cross. My eyes were the level of His feet. I looked up at His ensanguined face. I tried to tell the group yesterday about it, but not sure I explained myself very well. Not sure I can explain it now. How do you find words? But, and it sounds a bit corny as I put it this way, but I saw <u>Love</u>. I saw the Love that conquers everything. I saw the Love that is stronger than any military or political or religious power. Those powers all looked puny by comparison. And I heard His great cry. It was so loud! And I had such a strong sense of evil shifting when I heard that cry. My fears just dissolved at that point, and something of the great Love that I had seen in His face - I felt it in me.

Then there was such a sweet moment. She was there. I only saw her hand - on my shoulder. She was standing behind me. It was just like old times, except she was somehow 'newer'. Not quite sure how to put it. She said things. Such beautiful things. Such things that only she could say. And only she in Paradise could say. I'm not going to record them here - it would somehow spoil them to see them written down. But I'll never forget them. When she was alive she was not a believer. And yet, in that little conversation we had, it was clear she had been a believer, but in a way that only Christ could understand. I always felt so close to her spiritually and I now know why. We just did not have the words in those days. Now she has the words that I struggle to find.

So here I am in early Spring still here in Ireland. I am changed, transformed. Still missing my beloved. It's Valentine's Day today. In the last two years, these were terrible days for me. I locked myself in the Vicarage and spent the whole day inebriated and in tears. But I'm no longer the total wreck I was. 'He has borne my griefs and carried my sorrows' so the Scripture says. I am beginning to understand what that means. Today on this Valentine's Day, I can celebrate the love I once knew so deeply and wonderfully. And I know that the love we share in this mortal world is only part of it.

Now I've got to work out what to do with the rest of my life. I really need Dorch's help with this. I wonder where he is? Does he go off to another age? At least I have a photo of him on my wall! Nice to see him here in Dingle all those years ago. But I could do with him back here now. I know he'll turn up again soon - he promised. Well, I can hear Elsie calling - time for breakfast.

*

In the days following the Presbytery meeting, Douglas felt happier and more peaceful than he had done for a long time. Niall and Orla stayed in Dingle for a couple more weeks. Pat came round to St.Raphael's one day and had a cup of coffee with Douglas in the parlour which, on this particular day, was bathed in Spring sunshine.

'Douglas, I have a favour to ask of you,' said the priest, and Douglas could see anxiety on the man's face.

'Yes?' said Douglas, curious to know more.

'Well, I've been talking with the Flynns, and they have been speaking about their daughter.' Pat shuffled in his seat and threw Douglas one of his quick smiles.

'What is it, Pat? I don't think I'm going to mind, whatever it is.'

'Thank you, Douglas,' said Pat. 'It's just that they and I don't want to go pulling at any raw nerves in you, son. But you remember that when Niall was in his angry place, he felt upset about Saoirse having a.. you know…a Protestant funeral. Well, as you know, Douglas, they have got over all of that stuff now.' Pat paused and did his usual trick of removing his glasses and cleaning them on his jumper.

'Pat, I think I know what you are going to ask,' said Douglas. 'Let me put you out of your misery. Are Niall and Orla wanting some kind of Catholic service for Saoirse?'

'Well, Douglas, how did you know that?' said Pat exhaling loudly and replacing his glasses to his face.

'It's what I would have wanted if I had been them,' said Douglas. 'I was thinking about suggesting it. Why not a memorial mass as you did for Ruby?'

Pat looked delighted and, returning his spectacles said, 'Well, that's what I had in mind, Douglas. I thought we could put together a wee service that would comfort her parents.'

'It would comfort me, too. Let's get to work on it soon,' said Douglas.

Thus it was, on a bright March day, that Pat, with his black robes swirling around him in the sea breeze, led a group of people down a narrow path to the seashore. Niall and Orla agreed with Douglas that Saoirse would not have wanted a service in a church building. They let Douglas choose the location, and he knew just the spot: a stretch of beach overlooking the Blasket Islands. A small group was gathered for the service. Kath and Elsie were there, as were Kevin and Angela, and a couple of friends of the Flynns who had come down from Cork.

Pat set up a somewhat rickety table in the sand and set upon it a white embroidered cloth held down by large seashore pebbles. He placed on it a small pottery plate that held the communion wafers, and a matching chalice into which he poured some wine. There to the sound of the crashing Atlantic waves, he celebrated the memorial mass, with Kath doing her best to hold the missal open for him at the right page. Douglas read the twenty-third psalm. Elsie read some prayers, including a couple in Gaelic. Pat celebrated the mass and each took their communion. Then Pat walked to the edge of the sea, and with the salty water

341

lapping over his unpolished shoes, he raised his hands high to heaven, and in his powerful and rich voice, he commended the soul of Saoirse Romer to the love and care of her creator.

At the end of mass, the group looked up to the skies and delighted in a flock of gulls that swooped and danced over them, playing on the sea breeze. Douglas stepped forward and laid a stone on the shingle and said some words about Saoirse. Orla followed, placing her tear-dampened stone beside it and she also said some words. One by one the others did the same. The little cairn remained on that beach for many weeks and the locals reported that the gulls returned to the very spot at the same time of day as the service, and would circle, swoop, sing and dance above it, until the day when a high Spring tide enfolded the stones and drew them back to the ocean.

The following day, Niall and Orla packed up, checked out of their hotel, and met with Pat and Douglas at the Presbytery. After many fond farewells, they drove away from Dingle, taking a route past the very place of the accident, and the place that became the gateway of grace that had so dramatically changed Niall's life.

A few days later it was Angela's turn to leave. The SUV was a wreck, and she had hired a much more modest car in its place. Gerald's cremation had already taken place in Cork, but she decided she would like a memorial back in Sheffield. Douglas returned for the service as Angela had asked him to do the tribute, which proved no easy task. Together with Angela, they trawled through the complex story of Gerald's life which had become so devious and darkened, especially in his later years. Angela made it clear that she did not want Douglas to sugar-coat Gerald's life as she wanted people to recognise that Gerald had made his choices in life, many of which had caused great harm to others. They had contacted Bishop Pauline to see if she wished to send any message, and they received a brief, carefully-worded message which was read out at the service.

During this time, at Douglas's suggestion, Angela invited Mavis round for tea. Much to her surprise, she found Mavis quite different from the lady she imagined her to be. In fact, she invited her to become her cleaner. As time went on, Mavis was round there every day and became much more than a cleaner, but a cook, friend and confidant.

While he was in Sheffield, Douglas also did more tidying and packing of the Vicarage and finally got it emptied, with his furniture stowed safely away in storage. He also saw Mavis and Alice every day and they all decided that Mavis and Alice should soon make a return visit to Dingle.

When Douglas returned to Ireland, he continued to stay at St.Raphael's, which was now starting to receive tourists. Soon after his return to Dingle, he received another FaceTime call from Frank who told Douglas that he and Daisy were booked on a flight to Cork in the early summer and wanted to do a tour of Ireland but could Douglas book them in to St.Raphael's. Their dates would mean they would overlap with the visit that Mavis and Alice were planning, but Douglas could see no problem with that, and there were enough rooms at St.Raphael's for them all, and Elsie was more than happy to book them all in.

*

Towards the end of March on a blustery, sunny Spring day, Douglas was walking by the sea again and he saw a youngster on the shore holding an apple in one hand and throwing stones into the water with the other. As he got closer, he realised the youngster was Grace, the girl he had met a couple of times before.

'Hello, Grace,' he called as he got closer to her.

She turned around from the sea to face the Englishman walking towards her. 'Hello there, Douglas. How are you doing?' she enquired, dropping a stone, and raising her hand to her forehead to shield her eyes from the glare of the sun that had temporarily emerged from behind a cloud. 'You got time for a chat?' she asked.

'Yes, I have,' said Douglas and they made their way to a nearby bench that overlooked the seashore. They chatted for a time generally about life in the town, and then Douglas asked with a smile, 'So, you still a bored teenager, Grace?'

She chewed some apple for a moment and then said, 'Well that depends.'

'On?'

'On you.'

'On me?' asked Douglas, turning down his mouth and frowning.

'Oh, aye,' said Grace, nibbling at the core of the apple.

'You've lost me, Grace.'

Grace turned to look at Douglas. She threw the apple core away and then cleared her long, ash brown hair from her face. 'I know, we've talked a couple of times about life being a dump and that. But you see, I like to help people.' The breeze caught her hair again, and she impatiently pulled it behind her. She fetched a grip from her pocket and bundled her hair into a ponytail.

'So, is it me you are going to help, Grace?' enquired Douglas.

'Perhaps,' she said shrugging her shoulders and looking out to sea. 'I'm not bored when I'm helping people. Do you know what I mean?' She looked back at Douglas.

'Just how will you help me, Grace?' asked Douglas. He felt amused at the thought of this stroppy teenager trying to be helpful in some way. He imagined her mother urging her to help with the dishes. What errand, he wondered, could she be offering that would somehow assist Douglas in his life here in Dingle.

She did not reply to Douglas' question, but instead asked, 'How do you feel about death?'

He was rather taken aback by the question, but replied, 'Well, Grace, I have lost some people who have been very dear to me. A few years back I lost my wife which was very, very sad. And once or twice I think I have been close to death myself. So, I suppose I know quite a bit about it. How about you?'

She was looking intently at Douglas with her mahogany eyes. 'So few people understand it,' she said. 'If only you knew the half of it, Douglas.'

'I'm sorry? I'm not with you, Grace.'

'No, but you have caught a glimpse, you have. But you'll need more than a glimpse.' She looked back out to sea.

Douglas felt a mix of irritation and puzzlement. At one moment Grace was a stroppy teenager, and then the next, she was a mystic. 'So what do you think about death then, Grace?' he asked.

'I'll tell you about it one day,' she said, still gazing out over the waters. She then turned back to look at Douglas and said, 'I didn't want to come back, but I was called, you see. It's why I'm restless – you'd call it "stroppy", wouldn't you?' She smiled a winsome smile.

'I would, Grace,' said Douglas also smiling.

Her smile then turned to a frown as she said, 'Your friend, Kathleen.'

'Kathleen of the coffee shop?'

'That's the one,' said Grace. She looked at Douglas, turning her head to one side. 'You know she's dying, don't you?'

Douglas drew back. 'No, Grace, you've got that wrong. Kath's not dying. You're thinking of someone else.'

'I'm not, Douglas,' said Grace with conviction. Douglas felt unnerved by her confidence. 'Kathleen Griffin. She's got the cancer.'

'How do you know this?' snapped Douglas, not willing in the least to hear such unwelcome news. He felt the girl was starting to play games with him.

'I know things, Douglas. I told you that before. But you'll be all right. Dorchadas is back soon. And… well, you two will be busy.'

Douglas looked at her firmly in the eye and asked, 'Grace, who exactly are you?'

She slipped off the bench and stood up saying, 'As I told you. I'm Jerry's daughter. It's not a big deal. Anyhow, I must be going. It's good you are staying around. Kath will need you. You'll be a great help to her. See you soon. Bye now.' And with that, Grace walked back along the path that led into town.

Douglas stared at her for a while, his brow furrowed with curiosity and concern. 'Kath?' he said out loud. He sat still on the seat, looking out to the restless sea in front of him. Just who exactly was this Grace who turned up mysteriously from time to time and now was bringing such a distressing message? Was she now on her way to meet up with a little gang of friends, to laugh together about how she was fooling a gullible Englishman? Or was she someone who really did 'know' things? She seemed to know Dorchadas. How did she know he would be back soon?

'But suppose she is right?' said Douglas out loud again. He thought of Kath, a woman he had grown to love greatly in recent months. He recalled meeting her for the first time in her café, sitting at the table with himself and Dorchadas, relating her sad, painful tale of her broken heart and injured soul. He smiled as he thought of the time he had taken her to see Cecil Oakenham, and she had caused such a stir in that care home. He could see her clearly, in that armchair by the fire in the Presbytery telling the group of her experience at Golgotha. He thought of Peter, the man she rediscovered later in life, and how it was looking likely they would settle together. This was Kath, the woman who was discovering new life. Surely, she could not be facing death? Then he thought of that cough about which she was always so dismissive. But it had been getting worse of late, he couldn't deny it. Could it be a sinister cough? Sadly, it was not improbable. She had been a heavy smoker.

Douglas rose slowly from the bench. A heavy cloud was now overshadowing the town, releasing a fine drizzle that felt cold on his face. He sauntered back towards the town. The more he thought about it, the more he felt Grace might be right. Although he hated to acknowledge it, he realised that the future, which had just started to look so good and secure, might turn out to include another pathway through the valley of the shadow of death. He had known too much of this valley in recent years, and he could feel a strong instinct rising in him to get out of town quickly and get well clear of another death story. But he soon put all thoughts of escape out of his mind. Kath had become a dear friend, and he could not leave her if she was seriously ill. And she and Kevin had helped him so much.

For most of his days in Dingle, Douglas had needed others. Those others had become a new family for him. Maybe now, as he was feeling so much stronger in himself, it was time for him to give something back to them. And besides, he couldn't just hive off away from here, because other friends from England and the USA would soon be coming to visit him. And there was Dorchadas. He very much wanted to see him again. No, he was here for the time being, no matter whether the future held life or death. The Golgotha experience was releasing new energy and life in him, and he wanted to use this for others.

He pulled up the collar of his coat as he turned to face the heaving surface of the grey sea. As the spray turned to rain, he closed his eyes. He stood there for some time, enjoying the feeling of the rain on his face. The water felt like holy water – baptismal water even. The ancient ritual of dying and rising. The ritual of the Baptist in the waters of life. The dove in the clouds and the voice from heaven. The triumphant smile on the face of the murdered prophet. The face of the Victor under the glowering, dark sky. The sound of heavenly thunder. The breaking of the powers. The revelation of the greatest power. The touch of the hand on the shoulder. The healing of tender, human souls.

As he opened his eyes that were blurred with the water of the heavens, he discovered one word lay in the profoundly calm hollow of his heart. It was the word, destiny. He felt an acute sense of being in the right place at the right time. He was meant to be here. The people, the town and the land had all been a healing to him. But now his destiny was shifting. Surprising though the thought felt to him, he had a strong sense that this mysterious God, whom he was discovering in such a new way, needed Douglas Romer for some purpose. Douglas sensed that such purposes might lead him into further unexplored caverns of his soul. Such a thought felt daunting. But any other route looked pale and lifeless by comparison.

*

As the rain fell softly upon the town of Dingle, young Grace, the daughter of Jerry, leaned on a sturdy wooden five-bar gate. The field before her stretched down to the beach path where she had just met with Douglas. She watched him get up and make his way thoughtfully along the path back into town.

'Well, he has found his way home, now,' she said.

'Aye,' said Dorchadas. 'Aye, that he does, lass. That he does, for sure.' As the figure of the English priest disappeared behind some buildings, Dorchadas added, 'God's peace go with you, dear friend.'

Grace stepped back from the gate and asked, 'So you going to go and tell him you're back, then?'

'Not just yet, lass,' said Dorchadas. 'We've plenty of time.'

'Och, I'll be seeing you, then,' said the girl and walked away briskly down the hill.

Dorchadas leaned on the gate and gazed on the face of the wild, restless and beautiful ocean that stretched ahead of him to a misty horizon. How he loved this world. As he inhaled the damp and briny air, he recalled words from a poem that never failed to touch his angel heart. He knew it was a poem loved by his English friend. He recited much of the poem in the quiet of his heart, until one line, a timeless question, broke the surface of the silence, and he said out loud, 'Are they not all the seas of God?'

After a long time, almost in a whisper, almost as a prayer, he added 'O farther, farther, farther sail.'

NOTES

The quote from St.Paul on page 3 is Colossians 2.15 and is from the New Living Translation

The Quotations from the *Dream of the Rood* are from the translation by Charles W. Kennedy, In Parentheses Publications Old English Series Cambridge, Ontario 2000. It is reckoned that this poem was written sometime around the eighth century AD. In this writing, the wooden cross that held Christ tells its story. It does not concern itself with complex theology but rather celebrates a remarkable mystery: that the one surrendering himself to this hideous and cruel death is not a victim of political and religious powers, but is rather a triumphant victor. The power of evil is conquered by apparent powerlessness.

The Quotations from Paula Gooder's *Journey to the Empty Tomb* (Canterbury Press, Norwich 2014) can all be found on p.130 of her book. Reproduced with kind permission of the author.

The Bible stories referred to in this book can be found in:
John the Baptist and the baptism of Jesus   Luke 4.1-32
The healing of the Centurion's servant: Luke 7.1-10
Salome and John   :   Matthew 14.1-12
The crucifixion at Golgotha: Mark 15 25-41

All the non-biblical characters in this story are fictional.

The Fairest of Dreams is part 2 of a trilogy of stories centring around the character of Douglas Romer. Part 1 of the Trilogy is *The Face of the Deep,* Amazon 2019.

My thanks to Jonny Baker for the commendation. Jonny is Director of Mission Education at Church Mission Society that is based in Oxford, UK. He describes himself as an advocate for pioneers, lover of all things creative, and an explorer of faith in

relation to contemporary culture. His blog can be found at
jonnybaker.blogs.com

Further details of my work and contact information can be found
at michaelmitton.co.uk

APPENDIX

Summary of *The Face of the Deep,* Book 1 of the Dorchadas trilogy

The story opens with the Revd Douglas Romer, Vicar of a once thriving church in Sheffield, suffering an emotional and spiritual breakdown, following the sudden and violent death of his young Irish wife after only two years of marriage. He seeks solace in his wife's homeland hoping to meet her aunty Ruby, only to discover that she had died some months previously. However, he remains in her home town of Dingle and stays at a Guest House run by Elsie O'Connell. He meets a character called Dorchadas who claims to be a retired angel, now to be found in human form. Later in the book, Dorchadas explains that he stepped down from being an angel because he felt he had terribly failed his Lord. He was the angel deputed to support him in the Garden of Gethsemane, but when he saw Jesus in such a deep agony of spirit, he could not bear it and ran away.

In ways that Douglas finds impossible to explain, Dorchadas introduces him to various characters from the bible who open Douglas to new insights of God, life and faith. During his days in Dingle, he also meets some of the residents, notably Kath, Elsie's sister, and the owner of a café in the town. On his first visit to her café, she tells him the story of an affair she had as a teenager with a young priest called Peter. When it was discovered, she was painfully rejected by her family, her community and the church. Later in the story, she takes Douglas with her to meet the elderly senior priest who had been particularly vitriolic towards her. He is unrepentant for the cruel manner of his treatment of her at that time, but the experience of this meeting liberates and heals something in Kath.

As the story progresses, we discover that Douglas' wife, Saoirse was killed in a drive-by shooting by a terrorist while she was visiting Cairo for an Egyptian friend's hen party. Kath has a son called Kevin, and, to his horror, Douglas discovers that Kevin once served with the IRA. Although Kevin tells Douglas about his remarkable conversion in prison, Douglas cannot cope with meeting someone who once killed innocent lives through acts of terror. So Douglas returns to Sheffield where he meets up with his good friend, Mavis, the one person in his church whom he feels understands him. The day after he arrives back in Sheffield, he meets with the churchwardens and Gerald Bentley, an influential member of both the congregation and diocese. At this meeting, Gerald demands Douglas' resignation. Douglas also meets with his bishop, and finds her understanding and compassionate, granting him a three-month break. He receives an email from Dorchadas. This contact with Dorchadas reminds him that, despite the problem with meeting Kevin, he was missing Dingle and the new friends he was making.

Douglas decides to return to Dingle. He comes to accept the fact that his faith has now all but collapsed, but is heartened by the fact that his new friends love and accept him nonetheless. Kevin asks to see him again to explain himself, fully aware that the first meeting had been a bit of a disaster. They agree to meet in the church, just as a storm is brewing. Kevin tells him more of the story. Douglas feels increasingly uneasy and is especially disturbed when Kevin says that God has forgiven him. Douglas is filled with indignation as he considers a God who can forgive someone so easily for murdering an innocent victim. He is horrified at the thought of God forgiving the murderer of his beloved Saoirse. As the storm builds, he gets a message from Dorchadas to meet him on the seashore. He heads down to the beach where he finds Dorchadas, who wants Douglas to experience the glory of the wind and the waves in a storm. As the storm rages, Douglas erupts in anger to Dorchadas, telling him about his meeting with Kevin, and his horror at the idea of God allowing the murder of Saoirse and freely forgiving the murderer. All his grief and anger erupt, and he finally has had enough. He makes a mad dash into the sea, and Dorchadas leaps in to save him. As they both go under the waves, they find themselves miraculously transported to a Garden, which turns out to be the 'deep memory' of the Garden of Gethsemane on the night Jesus visited it for prayer on the eve of his crucifixion. This is the one place Dorchadas has dreaded revisiting.

354

As they sit in this Garden, they are joined by Mary Magdalene. She takes Dorchadas over to the figure of Christ who is prostrated on the grass and highly distressed. Douglas watches Dorchadas lie down next to him. Through this experience and his conversation with Mary, Douglas feels the beginnings of a healing of his heart. He does not receive answers to his questions about suffering and the unjust death of his wife, but he does feel his earthly questions have been profoundly heard in heaven. He wakes up in hospital where Kath and Kevin are caring for him. Dorchadas has temporarily disappeared from Dingle, but Douglas is assured that he survived the episode in the sea.

Douglas feels significantly brighter in the days that follow. Then one day, he is summoned to a mysterious meeting in Killarney, where a man from British Intelligence tells him they have received information that Saoirse was killed, not by a terrorist intent on killing Western tourists, but rather by a hired assassin who was specifically targeting Saoirse. Douglas is told that Saoirse gained information about someone in Sheffield who was involved in illegal arms trading and that someone had arranged to have her killed as she had gained too much information.

Printed in Great Britain
by Amazon

54176824R00210